A Night So Dark and Full of Stars

NIKKY LEE

First published by Deadset Press in 2024.

© Deadset Press 2024

All rights reserved.

Cover design Copyright © Nikky Lee.

Edited by Austin P. Sheehan.

isbn: 978-1-7636966-0-0

To my family, you are my lights and stars.

Acknowledgement of Country:

In the spirit of reconciliation, Deadset Press acknowledges the Traditional Custodians of country throughout Australia and their connections to land, sea and community. We pay our respect to their Elders past and present and extend that respect to all Aboriginal and Torres Strait Islander peoples today.

CONTENTS:

TRIDENT'S SONG

Sign: Aquarius
Element: Air
Symbol: The water bearer
Dates: January 20 to February 18

The Muses say a voice is the song of the soul. If that's true, then my soul is rotten.

I dart across the rocks, dodging swirling water as it rushes in from the sea. Kelp pops underfoot, like Aunt Ligea's cackle when she saw the ship round the headland of our island in the midday sun.

"Go see to it," she'd instructed, stabbing a gnarled finger in the direction of the cliffs, before hobbling off to join her sister in the kitchen. "Get the hearth going!" she called to Menesmy.

Down on the sand, the chiming of pots and cutlery still rings in my ears. I reach the end of the beach and clamber up over the limestone headland. Pebbles and spiky grass stab at my feet, and I hop, curse, and press on, ignoring the drop of the cliff and the crash of the sea below.

Ahead, the mast of my quarry rounds the peninsula. I scurry after it, chasing it like a fox after a rabbit, wind pushing at my back, urging me on. A few more steps and they'll be in my reach. My voice is not that of my aunties', but with the wind to carry it, it will be enough.

I come over the rise and the cliffs give way to Mercies Bay, all tumbled rock and white sand. A ship is dropping anchor. Doubled over, I take two full breaths, let my heart slow, lungs ease. Then I straighten, throw my head back, and sing.

My screech echoes down from the clifftops. On the ship's deck, men jump, like mice startling at the kee of a hawk. Someone shouts, a few try to cover their ears, but already the crew are laxing still, eyes glazing as they listen. Their faces turn up to my cliff.

Come. I silently entreat. *A feast awaits.*

Slowly, one by one, they move. A shuffle, bumping shamble, like a herd of sleepwalkers. Their hands find the pulleys and ropes that drop their skiffs into the water and then the oars to row them ashore.

I meet them on the beach, still humming under my breath—if you could call my rasping notes a hum. *"If a snake could sing, it'd sound like you,"* Aunt Ligea had once said.

No matter, it does the job. I march our fare off the beach, humming them down the goat tracks to our cave and into the pens. Only when Aunt Menesmy swings the bars shut and I let my song die, do they blink, owl-like in the dim, and take stock of the damp rock walls and the cell door.

All too late.

Like the others before them, they fling themselves at the bars, cries erupting off the stone, ringing in my ears.

"Hush," Menesmy sings, her voice rising above them, sharp and honed as a knife. "Hush my lovelies." The barbs of power in her notes silence them, and they sway, like chickens settling into their coop, oblivious to the fate awaiting them on the other side of the door.

I scuttle into the kitchen before the power of her song dies and they start clucking again.

Aunt Ligea looks up from the stone slab that serves as her carving stable, iron blade in her hand. "Get the pit started, Fídi," she snaps, thrusting her knife at the flint box by the hearth. When I hesitate, her eyes sharpen on me, as if wondering whether to carve out my innards along with our catch.

The hunger is in her. Best not to argue while she's like this. I swallow my question, scoop up the flint box and climb the stairs. Up and out onto the headland, to the fire pit among the limestone and salt-blasted olive trees. Two twisted trees, old as my aunts, hunch over the coals, the log of a spit slung between them. Story goes, according to Menesmy, that she and Ligea each sang one up from a seed.

I've only seen them work power over men. Sometimes, when they're hungry and not seen sight of a ship in months, they try to work their magic on me; a faint vibrato that curls off their words, and every now and then a sentence that slides into near melody. A test, checking yet again if their tone-deaf niece might not have enough human in her worth eating.

Yet I remain impervious as ever. My mother's blood, what little I have, runs in me; too weak to wield the same power as they, but strong enough to resist it. So I stay. A snake, Fídi, who sulks at the edge of their cave, song like a serpent's hiss.

The flames are hot and high when a squeal ricochets up from the cave below. My hairs prickle, they do every time. The sound is quickly silenced; a flash of Ligea's knives probably. I hurry, throwing more logs onto the pit, and fan the flames, sending them skyward so that when they calm, my aunts will have hot coals to work with.

Menesmy and Ligea come to the fire, hunched over like their two olive trees. The sailor's body weighs them down; hollowed and naked, and marinated in salt and sage. My aunts are not the young sirens they once were. Once, Ligea tells, they were as hawks—strong and straight-backed, chests proud. A force of nature.

Now they are vultures. Picking the bones of their island dry.

They would escape if they could, but our bloodline is bound to this earth by a witch. Cursed never to leave until we know love. That was how my mother escaped. And also how she died, so my aunts tell me.

"Love is death," Menesmy said years ago, eyes hungry on the horizon as if waiting for something more than men to come to our shores; Charon's wooden boat, perhaps, come to whisk her heart away to the underworld. "You must never love, Fídi." The advice as close to kindness as my aunts ever came. I'd nodded, thinking of the years she'd been trapped here. The years more that lay here for me. Because who would ever love a snake?

Aunt Ligea turns the spit; the meat bubbles and hisses, dropping fat into the coals. Menesmy hovers at her shoulder, flecks of red in the hem of her apron. Smoke hazes the air, thick and musky, and Ligea and Menesmy stare into the fire and grin at one another. The scent descends the stair and the voices of the soon-to-be-dead rise from the cave:

"Monsters." "Release us." The wind tosses their words to the waves beating the cliffs below.

Ligea huffs and jabs a finger at me, nail long as an eagle's talon. "Go feed them."

It's no accident my aunts have forgotten to throw them their scraps. This is how it goes. Every time, they find some excuse to send me away before I can share in the spoils. But this time, I hesitate. This time I had been the one who met our fare on the shore and sang them into their pens. Had I not earned my place with them? Ligea jabs the air again, glaring. "Go on. Get!"

Apparently not. Snakes, it seems, do not dine with hawks.

With one last look at the spit and the twisted trees, I leave.

#

The oars are heavy as I pull them through the water, an uncomfortable burn simmering between my shoulder blades and along my arms. The little rowboat lurches forward in the chop again. Ahead, the sailor's empty ship looms, creaking and swaying with the sea.

"Fetch their stores, before it all goes to seed," Aunt Ligea had snapped by way of a morning greeting when I'd entered the kitchen for breakfast. Again, I'd hesitated, eyes landing on her bloated belly, round as a nesting hen's, and felt the empty pinch of my own stomach.

"What are you waiting for? Go on," Ligea had shooed a hand at me. "And be quick about it." But my attention lingered on the dried fruits Menesmy was preparing beside her sister, desperately hoping for eye contact, a bone, some measure of affection. Idiot that I was. Ligea's fingers had curled around my shoulder, biting deep. "Don't make me raise my voice," she'd cooed in my ear.

I'd nodded and made a quick retreat.

"Lazy snake," Ligea had muttered as I rounded the stair, before reciting her favourite barb, the one she uses when she knows I'm still in earshot. "Tell me again, why can't we eat her?"

"Hush, Ligea," this from Mesnemy. "We do not eat our own."

3

I pull the oars again, anger lending me strength. One day, I'd find a way off this cursed land. It's an old oath, a mantra I repeat under my breath when Ligea's taunting or Menesmy's disinterest gets the better of my temper. Like today. One day, I swear, I'll leave.

My rowboat comes to a rest against the ship with a gentle thud. She's low in the water, her hold full. No wonder Ligea lusts after it. I stow the oars and rise from the seat, but too fast and set the rowboat pitching. My heart pounces into my ribs, and I grapple for a hold, knuckles white on the boat's rim.

Never go in the water. Menesmy's warning rings in my head. *We are of the air. Poseidon and his ilk don't take kindly to trespassers. Enter the sea and Poseidon will snare you, pull you into the deep where you will rot. Trapped forever, never to see the sky again.* My aunt's face looms out of my memory, black eyes boring into mine. *Do you want that, Fidi?*

No, I'd squeaked.

The rocking eases. I release my breath and curse my carelessness. When I stand again, it's more of a crouch, stance wide, knees bent as I fetch my rope and grapple. After a few attempts, it catches on the rail and I clamber up. The deck is quiet, nothing but the faint hum of the wind in the rigging.

I throw open the hold and examine the cargo. Rows of amphorae pots are stacked inside, lashed together with rope and with straw stuffed between them to stop them breaking. Painted figurines on their sides shift in the light, in time with the buck and sway of the ship. I grab the first, sniff the seal once. Grain. The same for the next. The third sloshes when I haul it free—a bitter, sweet scent. Wine. I put it to one side. My aunts will never come out here to check the hold themselves. They dare not cross the water. And a single crock of wine won't be missed.

Deeper in the hold, something clunks; one full pot falling onto another. I start, head snapping up, and I squint into the dim hold. Nothing moves. My eyes narrow. Someone is here. I know it in my gut. The same way I know when my song snares a human. I dig my nails into the seal of the first amphora, pull the lid and spill the contents out. Then I grab the handles and raise the empty crock above my head, ready to strike.

"Come out," I say, then curse myself for a fool. "Show yourself." I push my will into the words. They wheeze out in a rasp.

No movement. No sense of a mind ensnaring.

I frown, shuffle forward, empty crock raised.

A shadow flits to my right. I round on it, catch a glimpse of eyes and a mouth open in a silent scream. It trips, gangly limbs sprawling into a row of pots, sending them tumbling. I yelp and swing my crock down, cracking it over its head with a tinkle of breaking terracotta. The limbs flop, eyes roll back into its head.

Silence fills the hold.

Swallowing my thumping heart, I lower the shattered crock and peer at my prey. Human. Out cold. I mutter a word of thanks to the *Anemoi*—gods of the winds—and move closer, then cock my head, suddenly unsure of my initial assessment. Where the men I snared from this ship were broad and thick-necked from working the oars, this one is smaller, knees knobbled as a newborn goat's, and thin. Bare skin stretches tight over ribs like hide over a drum. So thin not even aunt Ligea would eat him.

But you could. The thought freezes me on the spot. Could I? My aunts assumed I'd rounded up all the sailors, they didn't know I'd missed one. And what they didn't know...

My hollow stomach emits a growl. *Do it,* my hunger wills. Fill the emptiness. Feast. Taste a man's flesh, just once. Ligea and Menesmy will never know.

I fumble for a shard of broken crock. The piece my fingers wrap around is long and jagged and digs into my skin. I nudge the human with a toe. A groan. Not deep like the voices in our pen, but high and scratchy. Like mine. My gut clenches. I teeter, makeshift knife raised above my head. *Do it.*

But then his eyes open, deep brown and dazed, and suddenly I'm the one sprawled on the ground as a memory of Ligea towers over me, her fists bunched.

"Idiot snake," she'd barked. *"Give it here."*

In my hands, I cupped a songbird, feathers still downy from the nest. One of its wings was bent. I'd found it like that under the olive trees, beak slightly ajar and eyes glazed from the fall.

"Give it," Ligea had spat. Reluctantly, I had. And in less than a heartbeat, her talons curled around the bird's neck and snapped it dead. She handed the body back to me. *"We have enough vermin in our den. Get rid of it."*

In the ship's hold, my resolve wavers. My stomach gurgles, but my arms won't move.

And the boy stares at me, hair crusted into salty whorls, cheeks as pinched as my stomach. Hungry, just like me. Something flashes behind his eyes. Fear. *Just like mine.*

It's like watching a reflection.

My resolution breaks. I can't. I put the shard-knife down, arms trembling as if I'd hefted an axe twice my size. "Can you stand?" I ask.

He stares at me, blank-faced. For a moment, I wonder if he doesn't speak Mycenaean. I scrounge together my limited Doric and ask again. Same response. Could be he's from further east, Anatolia perhaps, though that doesn't help me. My aunts have never seen, let alone wooed, an Anatolian ship—not in my lifetime at least. I revert back to Mycenaean, turning my words slow, pushing power into them again, transcending language.

"Tell me your name."

But the words run off him like water. He blinks at me. I purse my lips. I might be a candle to my aunts bonfire, but I have power enough to know when it's working. Or should be working. And yet it doesn't. Nothing is going to plan today.

"Caleus." The word comes too loud for the quiet hold. "I am Caleus."

So, he does speak Mycenaean. But it's nasally, accented in a way I can't place. He pushes himself onto his elbows and taps a hand to his bare chest. "Caleus."

I scowl. "I heard you the first time." I pick up an unbroken amphora from its row. It's heavy, full of more wine, and I lug it over to the step ladder. "Make yourself useful and help me carry these."

He doesn't move. Just peers at me, a furrow working across his dark brow. "Caleus," I say, slowly, looking him dead in the eye. He straightens, nods, almost enthusiastic.

I point to the rows of amphorae. "Carry... the... pots." I wince as the words leave me. It's same tone Ligea uses when I don't do a chore quick enough or to her liking. Ridiculing. Stripping all sense of worth away as she might the skin off a goat.

But Caleus brightens. Face lighting up, understanding. Is he simple? I'd seen men like that before in my aunt's caves. They'd not lasted long. Their crewmates had pushed them to the front of the pen, offering them up first. For some reason, the sight of it had always set my blood boiling.

For his part, Caleus nods to himself again and scoops up a pot. He carries it up the ladder, crosses the deck in long confident strides, holding the pot with ease, as if he'd been doing it all his life. Perhaps he has. Though, if he is one of the crew, he is a far cry from the men penned up in my aunt's cave. Feet and chest bare, and nothing but a wrapped linen skirt around his waist. And thin as a sapling. Though how he'd come to be so, with all that food and grain around him in the hold, was beyond me. Perhaps he hadn't dared eat it, even with the crew gone. The same way I didn't dare to steal a sliver of meat from my aunt's fire pit. I'd always sensed that somehow they'd know, find out, and then I'd be in for a reckoning that would make Hades shudder.

Caleus thumps the pot down beside the ship rail and peers over the side at the rowboat, head tilting as he considers the best way down. He moves along the rail, finds a loose rope and gathers it, weighing it in rough hands before tying it around the neck of the amphorae. With a clatter of terracotta on wood, he lowers the pot over the side of the ship.

I blink. Not a simpleton then. So, how did he escape my song?

Caleus steps one foot onto the railing, as if about to leap off into the sea. Panic seizes my chest. Is he trying to kill himself? Menesmy's warning fills my ears. *Posideon will pull you into the deep where you will rot.* Cold rushes up my arms, twists in my belly. I wouldn't wish that fate on anyone.

"Wait!" I fling the word at him, my power turning my voice hoarse. But my song slides off him. He doesn't pause. Doesn't so much as twitch at my rasp. And with a flash of sun-tanned skin and linen skirt, he's over. Jumped. And water droplets splash over the deck from below.

Gods be.

I run to the side, heart in my mouth, and there he is, unharmed and streaking through the water like a porpoise.

In two strokes, he's at my boat, water splattering the planks as he pulls himself in. Horror seizes me. He's going to steal my skiff; leave me trapped on this dead ship.

Power swells in my throat, and I grip the rail, nails digging into the wood. "Don't you dare."

He doesn't listen. Doesn't even deem to hear. *How? Why* doesn't it work?

"Caelus," I say, panic rising as he shifts around in the boat below. No response. "Caelus!"

He reaches for his amphora, twists the knot free about its neck, and releases the rope. He flings it loose, looking to me once more with a grin, motioning me to haul the rope back up.

Then it hits me. "You're deaf."

Caelus frowns, cups a hand over his eyes and squints at me. When I make no sound, no movement, he flicks the rope and motions again, miming me pulling it up hand over hand and wind it around the pot I'm carrying. Something in the jerk and sway of the gestures suggests impatience, as if he's saying, *hurry up, can't you see I'm waiting?*

Deaf. My power won't work on him. I swallow. Nothing to stop him doing what the men in the cave often threaten, once they realise begging doesn't work. And now it was too late, I'd let him live. I glance down. But not all humans in the pen had been violent. Some had been kind, an intuition in them had sensed that while not in the cage with them, I was as trapped as they.

My hands find rope, winds it around the pot, and lowers it over the side. Below, Caleus unties it and stashes it next to the first. I run and fetch another pot, then another, and another, lowing each in turn. After the tenth, Caelus throws up a palm. *Stop.* Then he waves at me. A beckoning to come down.

I hesitate, the thought of crossing over the sea with a virtual stranger twisting in my stomach. One push and I'd be dead. Caught in Poseidon's grip. The hairs rise on my arms. *Where you will rot...* I swallow.

Caleus raises an eyebrow, folds his arms and makes a show of tapping his foot. *Well?*

My eyes rove over him. Skin and bones and human. But different.

Like me.

Gods curse it, if this decision gets me killed... I clamber down, chafing my palms as I go. Caleus moves over on the skiff's wooden bench and takes up an oar. Squashing my misgivings, I do the same on the other side.

The row to shore is uneventful, though Caleus tires quickly. It's not long before he's wheezing beside me, but he refuses to let me take his oar, as if determined to earn his passage. A scrape of wood on sand and pebble and we hit the beach, I crouch on the bench preparing to leap over the water to the safety of the shore and pull the boat in by its rope. But before I can motion at Caleus to stay put, he's in the water again, up to his knees, hauling the nose of the boat higher up the beach.

Then the prow wedges, unable to go further, and he staggers away, sprawling onto the dry sand above the tideline, chest rising and falling. I open my mouth, words already forming in my head to call him back, only to stop, remembering he won't hear. Not that he's looking my way at all. His eyes are shut; fingers curled into the sand as if in some strange prayer. Perhaps he thought he'd die on that ship. While he might have had food a plenty in those amphorae, I hadn't found any that contained fresh water.

I dig my grappling rope into the sand and go over to him. And stare.

He's fast asleep.

#

I hide him in one of the sea caves at the furthest end of the bay. My aunts rarely venture far from our cave, not unless there's a quarry to catch. And with the sailors in the pens, eight at my last count, they would not leave. My aunts like their comforts; Menesmy her woven chair beside the hearth and Ligea her long couch draped in animal furs.

At first, I tried to bring Caleus food from my aunts' table. But when Ligea caught me saving my scraps, she fed the bowl to the sailors below.

"If you don't want them, they will," she said. "Zeus knows they need a bit of fattening before the pit."

Menesmy had watched it all without comment, as always, her gnarled fingers working her loom with a mind of their own.

So I returned to the ship, taking Caleus with me, and each day we shuttle another boatload of amphorae onto the beach. One load going onto the little hand-drawn cart that I pull back over the cliffs to my aunts. The other I left in the cave.

"Don't worry," I tell Caleus when we unload the last of it a week after our first meeting. He frowns at the stacks of amphorae pushed up against the cave's limestone wall. "They're not coming back. You can eat from them."

I make sure to look at him when I speak. I'd discovered that so long as I face him, he can see the words on my lips. His frown deepens, hands laxing to his sides. His gaze lingers on my face, eyes catching mine before they dart, once, back to the ship anchored in the bay, expressive in a way I've never seen. I understand his meaning at once.

How can you be sure?

I shrug, keen to avoid the topic. "Trust me, they won't."

He scowls. Eyebrows flattening to a line. *Liar.*

I sigh. "Just eat."

Those dark eyes stay on me a heartbeat longer, until he huffs and moves off to rekindle his fire of driftwood and bracken. He cooks a portion of the grain, turning it into a burnt slop that sticks to the pot he'd taken from the ship on our last trip over. When it's done, he scoops it into two bowls, also from the ship, and offers me one.

I shake my head, eyeing his knobbly limbs. "I've already eaten." I had. Back at my aunts'. "You need it more than me."

I stand to leave. Stay too long and my aunts will grow suspicious. Well, Ligea will. I doubt Menesmy would care. Caleus starts up from the fire, rising with me. He taps his chest. "Caleus," he says, the only thing I've ever heard him say, then mimes two people walking with his fingers. I shake my head.

"No, you stay here."

His eyebrows flicker. *But—*

"It's not safe."

One eyebrow arches, disbelieving.

"It's not." Gods, if he follows me back, Ligea would snap his neck. And mine. Cold prickles in my gut. Somehow, the idea feels wrong. I swallow, clench my fists. "Stay here." As always, my voice rebounds off him. He blinks, but something must sink in. His ridiculing eyebrow settles, and he looks earnest into my face. *You're serious?*

"Yes. I'm serious." *By the gods I wish I weren't.* "There are..." I hesitate, "others here."

He pinches the end of a lock of my hair and holds it up between us, questioning. It's curled, like a snake, and mottled green; so unlike the fine threads my aunts flaunt. Where their heads are white and grey like feathered down, mine is the colour of kelp. I pull my hair free. "Not like me. Bad people. They'll hurt you if they see you."

Caleus's eyes study me a long moment, weighing my words. At last he nods.

When I leave, the knot in my belly doesn't fade.

#

Three months later, Ligea leans across the table and sniffs. "You smell like human," she says, and my heart thuds into my throat. "Human and—" her thin nose twitches, as if she has an itch, and it's all I can do not to flinch, "*salt.*"

I force my voice steady, hoping she can't hear the strain of my guts knotting like a sailor's rope. "I just took the scraps down." True. I always make an excuse to go to the pens after visiting Caleus's cave. There's only three of them left now. Soon, I'll have to come up with another excuse.

Ligea prowls around the table, nails scratching on stone. "You've been sneaking off a lot lately." Her head snaps close, breath tickling down my neck and she sniffs again. "Back to that ship is it?" Her hand unfurls, palm up. "Give it here."

I hang my head and dig one hand into a pocket, pulling out the driftwood charm Caleus had pushed into my hands a few days earlier. He'd not let me leave without it, eyes earnest when I tried to hand it back.

His lips had worked, shaping two words several times until he put his voice behind them. "Keep safe."

Like a bit of driftwood could protect me from my aunt's wrath. I should have thrown it away. But its weight in my pocket had been comforting as I climbed back up the cliffs to face another day with my aunts. A pebble of hope made just for me.

Ligea snatches the charm up. Turns it over. The symbol of Poseidon flashes into view, the triple trident scored into the wood in careful cuts from Caleus's knife. (I'd swiped the blade from my aunts' table weeks ago after watching him try to whittle a carving with a piece of limestone. Luckily for me, Menesmy assumed she'd misplaced it and made another.)

Ligea shrieks and drops the charm. It bounces across the table. Strange. Menesmy, in an unusual fit of responsiveness, shoots up from her loom spitting curses, saliva frothing on her lips as if she'd just sipped poison. With a flick of her loom needle, she swats the charm into the fire and rounds on me.

"You dare to bring the sea into our home?" Her voice is low, melodious, power pulsing through every syllable. I blink, bewildered. I've grown used to Ligea's scolding, but this is something new. This is a Menesmy I've not seen before. Why so much fuss over a silly trinket? Posideon can't reach us here. *Or can he?* Gooseflesh shivers up my arms. Menesmy hums another note and her song pushes against my skin, into my ears. For the first time since I can remember, my muscles twitch at its sound. I fight for composure and force the panic down. *Lie, Fídi, lie like your life depends on it.*

Perhaps it does.

"I found it on the ship, I thought it harmless…" I stop, hearing the tremolo in my words, some unconscious power working to preserve itself. I swallow, waiting for my aunties to notice.

Only they don't. My power slides off them like it does with Caleus. Weak. Wheezy. *Useless.* I might as well not have a voice at all. A new thought occurs to me, one that turns my bowels to water. Is my power fading? My mother's influence slowly wearing off? Is that what they smell? Am I becoming more human?

Ligea pushes in front of her sister and shoves a honed nail into my face.

"You'll send that ship away," she says. "Sink it, set it a-sail. Get rid of it. Tomorrow."

My heart sinks. I'd had plans for that ship. I had Caelus hidden on the beach, and he knew how to sail. All I needed was a few months to stockpile enough food away from my aunt's notice. Then we'd take that ship and travel it far away from this wretched island. And if Goddess Tyche and her luck were with us, I'd do it all without ever touching the water.

Ligea leans in, so close her crooked nose almost touches my cheek. "Do it, or..."

She leaves the threat unsaid. But there's no missing her hunger. And with a lurch, I recall it's been a month since their last feast. I swallow. Human and salt. *At last, their snake is seasoned and ready.* The thought turns my blood cold. Was that what they'd been waiting for all along? My flesh to turn human? The sweetest meat of all. I try to calm my racing thoughts. They can't, won't. Not yet. There are still three sailors below. Easy pickings.

As if reading my thought, Ligea's finger swings away, pointing to the stairs. "Go prepare the pit."

I go, and it feels like I'm building my own pyre.

#

We watch the ship round the peninsula, bobbing in the waves. The wind catches its half-strung sail and rolls and pitches. I've half a mind it will sail past the horizon, but Caleus is convinced it will smash itself to pieces on the cliffs.

Turns out, he's right. A gust of wind whips the ship's prow towards the sheer limestone and the current does the rest. Splintering groans echo up the beach as the waves break its body on the rocks.

"You're not as bothered about it as I thought you'd be," I tell Caleus when we're back in his cave, warming up a pot of gruel at his fire. "That was your way home." He studies my face as I talk, slowing his stirring of the grain until he wipes his hands, picks up a cold piece of charcoal from the edge of fire and moves to the wall.

Too big to sail alone. He scrawls in a large, untidy hand; a fresh line on our wall of conversations. *Changes nothing.*

"Oh." The thought had never occurred to me. And suddenly I feel stupid for not realising it sooner. Why else would a ship that size have so many crew? I stare up at the dozens upon dozens of sentences, each one dancing in the fire light. I'd taught him the letters to give him something to pass the time, but I'd never expected him to take to them so well.

Caleus taps the wall, pointing to a fresh line squeezed in between a conversation we'd had about where he'd come from (Knossos it turns out) and how he'd come to be on the ship in the first place (not knowing what to do with him, his parents had sold him to the captain as a deckhand when he was seven).

We need something smaller.

"But where would we find something like that?"

He flashes me one of his grins, picks up a flaming stick from the fire, and motions for me to follow. He leads me deeper into the cave and I can't help but glance at the dwindling store of amphorae as we pass. Two pots remain. And I'm sure one of them is wine. If he rations that last amphora, he has about a week of food left. Then what? If he starts hunting on the island, he risks running into my aunts. One fresh track left behind is all it would take for them to find him.

At the thought of preparing the pit for a spit carrying Caleus, my chest turns suddenly tight. So tight it's hard to breathe. I pull my thoughts away, put a hand to the wall to steady myself. *Breathe.* They won't find him. So long as he stays on the beach. Close to the sea where my aunts fear to tread.

A cough from Caleus snaps my head up. He sweeps out his torch, shining light over the back of the cave. Gods be.

Somehow, when I wasn't looking, he'd gone and built himself a raft.

Driftwood and the remains of two rowboats are lashed together with the ropes from the ship and amphorae. Caleus points out a swathe of ship's sail he's used to create his own smaller version using an oar lashed near the raft's centre. He steps onto the deck and jumps. The raft bounces, but no ropes snap and the wood doesn't bow under his weight—not that he has much. Hands on hips, he puffs out his chest. *See, it's sturdy.*

I stare. "You can't be serious."

Caleus folds his arms, juts his chin.

He is.

I run my gaze over it again, shake my head. "It'll never work." If the wind and current could smash a ship twenty times the size of this to splinters, it'd have no trouble with Caleus' creation, sturdy or not.

He stamps his foot, grabbing my attention again. *It will!*

I sigh and turn back to the fire.

Caleus follows and as soon as we're back within the halo of the flames, he's writing on the wall. *It's not finished yet.*

"Clearly, there are still holes in the bottom."

He rolls his eyes at me, spins on the wall again. *It's supposed to have holes. The water needs to drain.* His stick of charcoal pauses, and then, slower, he scratches. *Don't you want to leave?*

I sit up, I had never said anything about leaving the island to Caleus. But, somehow, he knew. When had that happened? I cast my thoughts back. Had he always known? Picked up the cues I'd never said aloud?

My gaze drifts to the back of the cave. He was better at reading me than I'd given him credit for. "I can't."

A tightening of the jaw. Angry tapping on the wall. *Why not?*

I flounder, trying to find a way to explain. "I can't... swim."

I will teach you.

"No, you don't understand. I *can't.* For me the sea is..." I search for the right words, mouth dry at the thought of setting sail on that death trap. "Dangerous." I fix my eyes on his, then enunciate the next two syllables. "Lethal."

Caleus's fist tightens around the charcoal. With a 'plick', it snaps. Then, without warning, he spins and stomps out of the cave.

"Caleus," I call after his retreating back, curse when he doesn't hear, and run after him.

I catch him up on the beach. He's ankle deep in the water and stoops to the waves, bowl in hand. When had he grabbed that? He scoops the bowl through the water, then paces up to me at the tideline.

"Caleus," I begin, hoping to explain. Curse it, he's not looking at my face. I grab his shoulder, try to get him to meet my eyes.

He pours the bowl over my head, dousing my hair and face in seawater.

I shriek. So loud, I see the gooseflesh ripple up his arms. He stumbles back, wide eyed, mouth open in that silent scream again. I claw at my hair, expecting pain to bloom across my scalp and run fire down the path the salt had taken. I blink. There's no pain. No fire.

I check myself. I'm fine. Everything is fine. But how can that be? The sea is our enemy. It killed my mother; it should harm me too.

But it hasn't.

I shake my head. I'm mistaken. Must be. I haven't been exposed enough. As soon as I think it, I have to test it. I stagger to the water's edge, hesitate a heartbeat, then step in.

It... tingles? I stare at my toes through the white foam. I'd always imagined the sea to be deathly cold, cold like the Stix. But here, it's warm. I push in deeper, up to my knees. The water swirls around my calves, a gentle push-pull against my skirts. Somewhere inside me, that pinched emptiness I'd always thought was hunger, eases. It feels right.

But how could that be? The sea is dangerous. *It will pull you into the deep.* That's what my aunts always said. Over and over. All my life I'd felt their fear when they'd spoken of the ocean, how they've avoided going near it if they could help it. I'd never thought to question.

A choke from the beach snaps me back to myself. Caleus sits, hunched over and rocking at the tideline. Oh no. I splash out of the water and go to him.

"I'm sorry," I say, but he waves me off, shoulders shaking.

He presses a finger to the sand. It's trembling. *I heard you,* he writes, pauses, digs his index in again. *I felt it.*

And without warning, his arms are around me, hugging me close.

Not sobbing, I realise.

Laughing.

#

That night, I dream of the sea. Wild visions of waves crashing against the cliffs, gurgling in rockpools, and the strange silence of an ocean floor. I hang below the waterline, weightless, sand eddying in circles below my toes. It's quiet, the wind and rage of the world above muted.

13

Is this how Caleus experiences the world? The thought drifts through my dreamscape. My mind latches onto it, imagining a waking world underwater. Envying its silence, the freedom of not hearing my aunts send men down to Hades; the comfort of knowing that nothing they sing will ever steal my mind. The thoughts pull me from the dream, and I rise, buoyant, as my mind starts its turning again.

Last night, Caleus shook my arms, half-crying, half laughing. For the first time in his life, he'd experienced sound. To him, my hoarse, wretched shriek had been beautiful. Snatched his breath away, he'd described in shaking letters. I'd wanted to correct him, tell him that what I have is a curse. A voice too weak for siren-kind and too powerful for human. A voice that doesn't belong.

A pot bangs above my head, and Ligea's words dig into me like splinters. "Get up, lazy Fídi. The hearth needs starting."

I open my eyes to the rough walls of my aunt's cave and the cold coals of the hearth. When I don't move quick enough, Ligea cracks her spoon against the pot again. I wince, shielding my ears. Funny, here I am, lying here desperate not to hear, while down on the beach in another cave lies a boy who's desperate to hear more.

"Serves you right for running off so late," Ligea sneers, then stops, spying my skirts drying over the hearth grate. Her eyes narrow. "Why are your skirts wet?"

I scramble up, snatching my clothes. The hems are still damp but I pull them on. "I went to the spring," I lie. "It was dark, I slipped. Put a foot in."

Would you sing for me tomorrow? Caleus had asked on the beach. *Sing with all your strength so I can hear?* A bad idea, I knew. If my aunts heard, they might get curious. Yet, I'd nodded.

Ligea's leans in. Sniffs, and wrinkles her nose. "Furies should have pushed you all the way. You reek," her index jabs at the stairs. "Go bathe. At once. I'll not have my kitchen smelling like the pens."

My legs stiffen and I fight not to suck in a breath. I'd not visited the pens last night. I'd wandered back in a daze, mind churning, legs still tingling from the push-pull of the surf. I'd forgotten to take the scraps to the two sailors still down there.

I recall the press of Caleus's hug, how his warmth had spread from him to me and the tears of joy soaking into my shoulder. No one had ever held me like that. Ice crawls across my skin. Ligea could smell him. *Idiot, Fídi.* If Ligea went down the pens, saw their scrap bucket still there, she'd catch me in my lie.

"I'll go at once," I croak, and scurry away, heading for the stair.

"Fídi, where are you going?" Menesmy asks from her loom.

I teeter on the step. "To feed them," I say. "Before I bathe."

A long silence, and my gut twists tighter and tighter, until at last, Menesmy nods. Once. "Hurry up then."

I take the stairs in threes, leaping down and down again to the door. Inside, the floor is sticky, and the copper scent hits the back of my throat before I change to breathe through my mouth. I grab the bucket, full of scraps, fruit cores and old bread mostly, and tip it through the bars. The two remaining sailors huddle in the corner of the pen, eyes sunken, cheeks gaunt. I feel their eyes track me to the trough of scraps against the far wall. It lies directly under a small hole in the ceiling that runs from the kitchen. Whether my aunts chiselled the shaft themselves or found it there and built the kitchen and pens around it I've never been able to tell.

I dig the bucket into the trough, scooping out an extra helping, and pause as Menesmy's voice murmurs down the shaft. "Where do you think she's going?"

Ligea snorts. "Unlike you to take an interest."

A faint tick-tick echoes down the hole: Menesmy's nails and needle working the loom. Then: "You don't smell it?"

"Of course I do! Everyday her stink grows stronger." I imagine Ligea's wrinkling her beak of a nose. "It's that wretched sea in her veins."

I stiffen at the edge of the trough. *Sea in my veins?* The bucket slips from my grasp and strikes the ground with a crack.

A pause from above. "So, can we eat her now?" Ligea asks, and I hear the crooked smile spreading her lips, revealing chiselled teeth. My mouth goes dry. They know I'm listening. I snatch the bucket, throw its slop through the bars and turn for the stair. Anger and fear vie for control. Sea in my veins. They knew. They'd always known. And there was only one way that could be. If the siren in me came from my mother, then the sea—

I burst into the kitchen, huffing from my ascent. Clear my throat. Ask the question I'd never dared to before. "Who was he?"

Menesmy's fingers slow on the loom, but she keeps working. Needle darting in and out between the threads. Ligea adjusts herself on her couch. "He's dead that's all you need know," she says.

"I'm not leaving. You'll have to deal with my stink until you tell me."

"A sailor."

"A man with the sea in his heart," Menesmy says, so quiet I almost miss it.

Ligea grunts from her couch. "And his crotch. Swept your mother up and away with his charms he did. Then poisoned her. All to hatch a wretched snake." She spits the last word, eyes boring into me, accusing.

"Ligea," Menesmy warns from her loom. Too late. Because, suddenly, it all falls into place. All their anger. Ligea's hate. Menesmy's distance.

My mother didn't die at sea. She died for me. *Because* of me.

Menesmy's words come back to me. *Love is death.* Because love had created me, and it'd killed their sister. And looking at Ligea now, all that bitterness seething behind her gaze, perhaps Menesmy also meant death of a different kind.

And here I stand with the lineage of air and sea inside. Two worlds at odds. My tongue is thick in my mouth and it's all I can do to stop the gorge rising in my throat. "What did you do to him?" I ask, knowing and dreading the answer.

Ligea cackles. "We ate him of course!"

"Ligea!" Menesmy chides.

Ligea rounds on her sister, teeth clacking. "Why not tell her? Tell her how we cooked his meat until it fell off the bone. How we cracked him open and drank the marrow of our enemy. Tell her how it made us *strong*." Power licks her words, resonates in my head. "Strong enough that we could sing in a ship from *beyond* the horizon."

"Hush, Ligea." Menesmy squawks. She's risen from her loom. Beady eyes staring her sister down from across the table. "Say no more."

I stare at them, their lies unravelling like a loose thread on Menesmy's loom. "A witch never cursed you to stay," I say aloud. Eating a sailor of Poseidon's line—even if he was several times removed—would have angered the sea to no end. "Your own folly trapped you here."

Menesmy's long ago advice returns to me again. *Love is death, Fídi. You must never love.*

Why *that* lie?

Unless it was to keep me here. To stop me seeking more.

My chest constricts, like a hand has closed about my ribs and begun to squeeze. I take in their stooped shoulders, thinning white hair. Whatever power they'd gained, it was long faded. Age, time, maybe both to blame. That was why they kept me.

Power. They didn't just want to eat me. They wanted to crack me open and drink Poseidon's blood. And all this time they'd waited, circled, biding their time for the sea to take hold.

Now it had. And its power was growing; swelling into a fruit they'd pluck once it was ripe.

All this I realise in a heartbeat. And so do they.

I back up, feeling behind me for the start of the stair. "You monst—"

Ligea moves first. She lunges, long talons spreading wide, only to snatch at air as I twist away. I round the stair, make to flee.

"*Stay where you are.*" Menesmy's song rocks through me. My legs turn heavy, as if I'm wading through mud. I hum under my breath, my husky notes unpicking Menesmey's spell. It sloughs away and I lurch up another step.

Then Ligea cracks the hearth's poker to the side of my head. The world tilts, dims, and crumples away.

#

I wake in the pens. The two sailors huddle in the furthest corner, like quail cornered by a fox in a coop.

Moving hurts. Breathing hurts. Even blinking. I'm not sure how long I lie there. A day, perhaps two, until my throbbing head subsides enough to attempt to rise. The moment I do, my stomach heaves and I retch onto the stone floor.

Not much comes up. Water, stomach acid, a trickle of blood from a wound reopened where I'd bitten my tongue. I shiver, curl into a ball and let the tide in my head take me back to darkness.

#

The second time I wake, my head is clearer. It still throbs, but when I move to put a hand to it, my vision doesn't spin. The blow from the poker has left a welt on one side of my head; fiery length starting at the top of my cheek and stretching a thumb span past my left ear. My fingers prob the swollen flesh. No wetness, just crusted blood that leaves little red flakes on my hand as I rove it over the wound. Healing then, but I'll probably have headaches for weeks.

A temperature-drop is the only sign that day has given way to night. I hug myself and eye the sailors. They're a miserable pair. Eyes distant, as if Charon has already claimed their souls and left these husks behind. Not one word passes between them.

By now, Caleus will wonder where I've gone. Probably worry too. My gut turns over. Enough to leave the safety of the beach? The thought pushes me to my feet and over to the cell door. Its hinges are rusted; it's been years since my aunts did any work on it. But when I shake it, the door holds.

Hades damn them. I spit on the floor, anger bubbling in my throat, threatening to overflow. I rest my head on the bars, wishing I could contort my body and slide through like my namesake. Breathe. Think. Think Fídi.

My traitorous mind stays blank.

Feet scuff on the stairs outside the pen. I turn my ear, two scuffs. Two sets of feet. Ligea *and* Menesmy. Together. Why? Menesmy's song resonates from the stairwell, notes high, cutting as a winter wind. My legs tremble, and without thinking it, one foot steps towards the door. *No, you don't.* I stamp and stuff my fingers in my ears before the song can claw more control away. Across the pen, the sailors shift, the first flicker of life I've seen in hours. They shake their heads, sway like sheep on a ship, and shuffle up to the bars.

My aunts sweep into view. Ligea grins at the sight of me, shameless as a child; wicked as a harpy. Menesmy looks bored.

I set my jaw and glare, and dig my fingers deeper.

"Stop resisting, little Fídi." Ligea coos. Her voice laps against Menesmy's, low and sultry, giving it a weight neither one has alone. My head spins. I shut my eyes, take a breath, open my mouth to sing my serpent song—then stop.

This was it. Risky. And only one chance. I swallow. If I don't succeed, I'll never leave this pen. Never see the sky. Never touch the sea again.

Never sing for Caleus.

I relax my hands, let them fall from my ears. *Trust your blood, Fídi. You are part siren too.*

Ligea and Menesmy's songs swirl into my head, snarling my thoughts like tangled rigging. Ligea's vibrato laughs in my ears. Menesmy approaches the door, draws out the key, undoes the lock. The bars swing open.

I stay the urge to lunge for the gap. Instead I'm meek, pathetic weak Fídi, whose power can't match that of her aunts'. Beside me, the sailors shuffle up to the door, file through. I struggle through my surprise. Both of them? Are they planning a multi-course feast? My breath catches.

I'm their sea-cursed dessert.

I suck in air, forcing my face still as my head swims in my aunts' song.

Please let this work.

I part my lips and hum. My voice is so faint, Ligea and Menesmy don't hear it. I concentrate on my own song. My snake's rasp and no one else's. Mine. Me. My head clears, my notes growing stronger in my mind, even as I keep my voice barely above a whisper. Ligea and Menesmy's melody pull my legs forward. Out I shuffle, behind the sailors. *Not yet.*

Ligea pulls out her knife.

I raise my voice, my song joining with my aunts' as I'd never dared do before. My rasp drives into my aunts' melody, sinks into it like fangs, chokes the harmony. The sailors blink. One twitches. The last hold on my muscles releases. A frown creases Menesmy's face.

The first sailor out of the pen, hair grey as a gull, gasps. I hiss one more note under my breath, pushing my will into the song. Not Ligea's, not Menesmy's, mine—my wish.

Fight. Live. Go free.

His face flushes, eyes ignite. He roars, drops his head, and barrels into Menesmy like a bull. She goes down with a screech. The second sailor wavers, head cocking to listen a little more. I turn my song on him. He stiffens, fist bunching as he rounds on Ligea. She dodges, skitters back from the stairwell.

"You!" she snarls at me. "This is your doing." Her talons reach for me, but I turn my voice louder, and cast off the last off the dregs of her power. I spin for the stairs. Flee. Get to Caleus and his raft. And pray to Poseidon it really is seaworthy.

"Come back, snake!" Ligea shrieks after me.

I block my ears and run.

#

He's stretched out beside the coals of a cold fire, sand sticking to his face.

Legs burning from running along the beach, I collapse at his side, grab both his shoulders and shake. "Caleus!"

His head wobbles once, snaps up. Dark eyes glint as he blinks. Recognition. A flash of a smile, then his forehead quivers. *Why are you here?*

"We've got to go." I hiss. He squints, rubs his eyes and throws a log on the fire.

"No!" I kick sand over the light.

Another frown. *What are you—*

I place my hand on his cheek and turn his head so he can see my face, nose to nose with his in the dim. "Danger." I tell him. "*They're* coming."

He sucks in a breath, jaw tightening, fingers stiffening around mine. Then he's on his feet and pulling me towards the raft. We scurry around its bulk. He tests the ropes; I pile the last two amphorae onto the deck, hearing the slosh of wine in one. Caleus returns and lashes them to the planks, only to stop and sniff. He clucks his tongue, pulls the rope free of the cask of wine and rolls it off. *Not that one.* He breaks its cork seal and red sloshes over the terracotta lip like blood.

Empty, he thrusts it into my hands.

Water, he scrawls on the sand. *Cannot sail without it.*

Dread seeps into my stomach. The spring. It's not far from here. But it lies along a well-trod path, one my aunts will be scouring. I want to yell at him to forget the water and let us go. But Caleus knows the sea better than me. And I've seen what happens when creatures don't drink. They dry out, like fish scales in the sun. Then they die. If Caleus says we need it, we need it. I swallow and nod, leaving him to see to getting the raft onto the water.

It's a short trip along the worn goat track. I've walked it a thousand times, but I see my aunts in every shadow. Every ancient olive on the twisting path spurs my heart into my ribs, and each time I think, *this is it, this time it's them.*

They don't find me. When I reach the spring, I slump down at the shore and sink the amphora in. Its weight pulls on my grip as water glugs over the lip. My hands shake, palms clammy. *Calm down, Fídi.*

A screech stabs through the air. So high and loud it rattles my bones, sets my head throbbing. I sway, catching myself on the bank so as not to fall in the spring.

The beach. It came from the beach. A strange fear surges inside me, submerging me in its tide. Cold frosts my gut, turns my breath short. Caleus.

I drop my amphora and sprint. Gods, please, no.

Down the track, past the twisted olives. Limestone cuts my feet; I barely feel it. A sob catches in my chest, I growl and force it down. *Tears won't help you, Fídi.* Onto the beach, across the sand, legs burning.

The cave is still when I reach it. Nothing moves. I slink inside, not daring to call out. A dim brightness shines from the fire: a single fresh log part burned through. *Damn it, Caleus, I said no light.* A shape lies on the other side of the flames. My knees turn weak, but I force my legs to cross the distance. One step, two.

The shape grows sharper, more distinct. Hope and horror douse me so fast I can't do anything but stare, unable to comprehend.

It's Menesmy.

She's dead.

A shaft of terracotta sticks from her throat. Blood flows thick from the wound, mixing with the wine in the sand. I shuffle closer, unable to stop my fingers from running over her silver hair, still as soft as down, even in death. Her eyes are open, mouth agape, confused shock etched forever on her face. Slowly, my mind puts it together.

My aunts had come looking for me, just as I'd known they would. Crossing the headland, their keen eyes would have spied the flicker of Caleus's fire from the clifftops. They'd found him here. Tried to work their magic over him. Only to realise too late that it didn't work.

And Menesmy had paid for that folly.

I can imagine Caleus' terror. It would have been as if the night had its claws into him. My stomach flutters as I study the sand: Menesmy's blood, no one else's. And unlike Menesmy, Ligea is quick on her feet. Which means—

"Oh Fídi," her song echoes from the headland. My muscles stiffen and a cool flush of strength rushing down my limbs. "Come Fídi, see what I have found."

#

She's perched on the edge of the cliff, heedless of the fall. Caleus hangs black and blue in her grip, head lolling. The sight throws me into a memory of Ligea throwing my doll into the fire. I'd clawed it out of the hearth, blistering my hands to save it. The toy had been irrevocably damaged, fire snarled burns all over it and stained in charcoal. If anything, I'd loved it more. It had been flawed, like me.

"Let him go," I say.

Ligea's juts her chin, drags Caleus a step closer to the edge. "So this *is* what you were hiding."

I lurch forward. "No, don't!" the words slip out before I can think.

Ligea cackles. As if laughing with her, the sky rumbles in the distance. She clucks her tongue. "Love is death, or didn't you listen to dear Menesmy? It can crush your heart, little Fídi. Let me demonstrate."

Her fingers clamp around Caleus's throat. He twitches, gasps, and begins to gag. And before I can move, she swings him out over the edge of the cliff.

Caleus's eyes bulge at the drop. He grapples with Ligea's fingers, lashes out a kick. Then he looked to me, expression pleading, mouth shaping the word. *Fídi.*

The sea roars in my ears.

She releases him.

He plummets.

"No!" I'm running, charging, for what I don't know until I am a step from the cliff edge, and feel the sea calling below. I streak past Ligea, gather my strength, and leap.

"Idiot Fídi!" Ligea screeches. Her hands snatch after me: her precious little sea snake. She misses. And the ocean rises to meet me.

#

For a heartbeat, I dream again; hanging suspended in water, sand swirling under my toes. An urgency tickles my lungs, twinges at my collarbone. Air. Need air. I cough, a bubble breaks for the surface. Then I'm not dreaming.

I'm drowning.

Panic blinds me. I thrash, grab at the water like I'm climbing a tree, only to find no purchase. I sink lower.

Skin tingles.

Lungs burn.

Until I can't hold it in—or out?—anymore.

Open my mouth, suck the water in. Wait for it to choke my lungs; pray it will be quick.

But I don't choke. Instead, my lungs lighten, head clears as the blissful... air? water? rushes in. Whatever it is, I'm breathing it.

I run my hands along my throat, down my chest, marvelling. My fingers brush against ridges under my collarbone. I follow their shape: the skin is puckered like scars, and only when I feel them release a rush of water over my fingertips does it dawn on me.

Gills. *Poseidon be.*

A figure floats into peripheral vision; face down above me. I blink and my vision sharpens in the gloom. Salt crusted hair swirls around a narrow face. Eyes shut, expressive brow lax. Caleus.

I dig at the water, scooping it like I might scoop sand. My body twists and I squirm through it like a worm. Gods damn it, I'm going nowhere. The sea might be in my veins, but I struggle like a hawk underwater. Caleus is dying and I can't reach him. I bite down a savage cry. *Swim you sea-blooded snake. How hard can it be?*

An itch tingles over my hands, up my toes. I glance down. My toes are longer than I remember. Long and webbed—like a frog. I hold my hands up. My fingers too. Webbing grows between each digit.

Another dig at water again and my fingers fan open, pushing the water past. I ripple forward. *That's it.* I fix my sights on Caleus; kick my feet. I shoot forward, so fast I almost barrel into him. I grab his shoulders and pull him upwards. Something is happening to my legs, but I don't look. All I can think is, *don't be dead. Please don't be dead.*

Our heads break the surface.

Air gags my throat. I cough, gills spilling the water in my lung out. The next breath feels too light, lacking substance. But I draw in another, then another. I shake Caleus, slap his cheeks.

No response. Panic rises again. Heat burns at the corner of my eyes. Don't let this be how it ends. I shake him again, thump his chest. He coughs up water, but doesn't wake. My vision blurs. Ridiculous, why can't I see? It's just water isn't it?

"Wake up!" I scream and I throw my power behind the words. "Wake up Caleus!" The sea jumps, great concentric circles rippling away from me. Waves as tall as I am slam into the limestone cliff.

What in the gods—

A cackle echoes from above. "That's all you got?" Ligea stands on the ledge, beady eyes staring me down, laughing as I struggle. "Disappointing." She spits. "You can't save him. You can't even save yourself."

She lifts her hand and the clouds split. Light blinds, strikes the beach. The sound of it sends splinters through my ears. I shriek, diving my head below the water. The world above muffles. I release a breath, tighten my grip on Caleus.

You can't save him. I shove Ligea's taunts away. I must get him to shore. He can't stay out here like this. But Ligea is waiting. I grind my teeth. I can't hope to match her voice, but I can dampen it again—just as I did in the pens. *But first, let's see if this snake can sing underwater.*

I breathe in the sea, open my mouth, and sing.

The notes that come out are not mine—or not as I've known them. Gone is the rasping, wheezing voice. What comes is a melody that resonates within the water, as if the sea itself is singing. My power pulses through the blue, rising into white-peaked waves. I revel in it—was this inside me all along? Was this what my aunts wanted to devour?

Rage swells inside me. *How dare they.*

I unleash my rage, pounding the waves into the cliff. All their lies—*crash*—years of loneliness—*crash*—and, my chest squeezed, fear. *Crash.* So much fear. Fear that Caleus is beyond my help, that he will die, and it will be my fault. My last wave engulfs the rocks, sending spray high into the air.

The sea subsides and I float, power spent, fighting to keep Caleus's head above water.

Above, Ligea laughs, spits over the edge. "Is that all? Even with the sea you can't reach m—"

A crack sounds deep in the cliff. Pebbles bounce down to the sea, plop into the water. Fresh horror floods my limbs. It's coming down, the rock giving way. I throw an arm around Caleus and dive, kicking hard.

My legs move as one. Scales flash in the corner of my eye. Away. Get clear. We surge through the water with a speed I've never known—even on land. And for a heartbeat, I imagine this is what it is like to fly like a hawk. A hawk of the sea.

Behind, the cliff crumbles. A shrill, soprano scream sounds before its lost in the roar.

For a long minute, I bob on the surface, staring at the cliff and the smattering of new rock in the sea. Caleus's cave is gone. Menesmy gone. Ligea gone.

A groan in my arms.

"Caleus!" I shake him again. He coughs, eyes flutter open. Slowly, one hand touches his ear, then my mouth, and he smiles. *I heard you.*

I pull him close and laugh through my tears.

#

He steps onto the raft; I into the water. One last look back to the limestone cliffs and the twisted olives on the headland. Given time, I might come to miss this place. My mind returns to my aunts' cave, for the horror I'd been party to—and had aided. I shiver. I've not been back there. There's been no sighting of the last two sailors from the pens, though I've seen signs of their passing. Tracks from the spring, a trickle of smoke from a campfire on the next headland. I wish them luck, but have no desire to meet them again.

The sea pulls at my waist. Already the changes are starting. I hold my fingers up, watch the webbing spread.

A brush on my arm. Caleus leans from the raft, eyebrows questioning. *Are you ready?*

I nod. I'm not sure what lies ahead for us, but it's time to put this island at our backs. Caleus releases the raft's sail. It flops limp on the mast—trust him to pick a day without a breath of wind.

I sigh. "Need a tow?"

Caleus grins, taps his voice box, then mimes the music coming from my mouth. Suddenly, I'm sure our lack of wind is no mistake.

Sing me your song, sea daughter.

SEAMARE

Sign: Pisces
Element: Water
Symbol: Fish
Dates: February 19 to March 20

12:00am, February 18, 1961.

A flash of scales and he was falling, spiraling, spinning down. Down, down, into oblivion.

Captain Sanders woke to the scream of metal on rock and a smarting pain as his body thudded to the floor.

What in the—

A siren welled up from the deck, its crescendo drowning the shouts of his men. Sanders pulled himself up and groped in the dark, feeling along the wall for the switch. Found it. Yellow light flared from the lamp above, revealing his sorry state of a cabin. All four walls and floor were off-kilter, charts and papers scattered, his only photo of Maggie face down in a shattered picture frame.

The sight jarred in his head, and for a heartbeat he saw double. Or thought he did. He rubbed his eyes and the room snapped sharp again.

Sanders brushed off the glass, scooped out the photo and placed it into his breast pocket, and then reached for his shoes.

"What happened?" he demanded on entering the helm. "Did we hit something?" The moment he said it, he blinked, frowned, suddenly sure he'd said something like that before, long ago. Perhaps in a dream once.

The First Mate, Marin, beckoned Sanders over to the wheel. The man's face was pale, freckles livid on his cheeks and a sheen of sweat coated his forehead. "We're ... run aground."

Aground? Sanders gawked, wondering if he'd heard right. He cleared his throat and managed to garble out, "Impossible, we're in open seas."

"I thought so too." Lines of worry wrinkled Marin's brow; an oddly familiar expression, but Sanders couldn't think when he'd seen it before. Marin rubbed a peephole into the fogged-up port window and pointed. "We should have clear sea for miles, but there's no arguing with *that*."

Behind the glass, the floodlights from *The Oneiros'* helm flickered. For a heartbeat, her bow illuminated—thirty square feet of sloping deck and tangled rope. Fishing nets hopelessly matted. Below, jagged rocks crunched into the hull. Beyond, the cliffs of a headland lay. Land. Impossibly, undeniably, land. Then it was gone. Lost as the lights failed again and darkness flooded in.

"Shit." Sanders scrabbled to the forward window, rubbed another peephole. Too dark to make out how bad the damage was, but something in the way the ship flopped on the hidden reef said the keel was broken. Not good.

"Our radio's out too," Marin reported.

Sanders swore again. "Where the hell are we?"

"Not sure. Last reading said we were 217 miles off the Fox Islands. There shouldn't be anything here." Marin glanced at the instruments in the dash, then outside at the crippled vessel.

A flash lit up the headland in the windows again, the sloping cavern of the cliff was a shade darker in the black and scarcely sixty feet off the port side. Sanders gut turned cold. It was a miracle they hadn't sailed headfirst into it.

Marin cleared his throat. "We're taking in a lot of water."

As if it'd heard him, the ship groaned: a deep, reverberating shudder that Sanders felt in his bones. Another spark of light. Water sluiced over the bulwarks, washing the deck in spray. Fishing buoys spun away in the swirl. The siren still blared.

Seas curse it. "Evacuate the crew. And find out where we Goddamn are."

Marin nodded, clamped a hand around the ship's PA and ushered the command. Men scampered across the deck, scurvy rats in orange overalls as they wrestled the lifeboats free from their holds.

Sanders watched them go. The summer night was unusually warm, hot and sticky, but at least his crew wouldn't die of cold. *Get them to shore, sort it out at daybreak.* Their cargo would survive a bit of flooding—as long as the hold wasn't breached. *A right pain if it was, after all that trouble catching her.*

He patted his shirt pocket, feeling the stiff photo paper flex under his touch. One last voyage. For Maggie. He glanced through the fogged glass at the hold, hatch still latched tight below on *The Oneiros'* deck. His last catch. With it, they'd finally have enough. Enough for Maggie's surgery. Enough to prove he wasn't an old sailor who'd traded his marbles for salt crystals. Enough for the white picket cottage he and Maggie had dreamed about for thirty years.

All he had to do was bring it—*her*—home.

Wind buffeted *The Oneiros,* bringing the stench of rotted fish with it. And something else. Sanders cocked his head. "You hear that?"

Marin frowned. "You mean the singing?"

Sanders waved him off. "No, not that. She's been doing that since yesterday." He paused again, ears straining.

In the midst of pulling the emergency flares out from under the skipper's seat, Marin stopped and frowned. "Whistling?" He looked at the roof. "From above?"

They crowded against the portside window. Saunders wiped the condensation away with his sleeve. Another hot, sticky gust of wind buffeted the ship, teetering her like a broken seesaw on the reef. A prickle ran over Sanders; an echo of cold on his skin. He shuddered and felt for Maggie's photo again. *I'm coming home,* he promised.

He peered out through his peephole, waiting for the next flash of *The Oneiros'* floodlights. Then he saw it. Rocks above. Yellow rocks. Rocks with splinted wood and metal caught in them.

Sharp rocks honed to points; the wind howling between them.

Dear God. Sanders looked down. The reef lay below them, a matching jagged set. Not rocks.

Teeth.

The Oneiros groaned again, listing further onto her starboard edge. The helm tilted, pitching onto its side. Debris slid across the floor: a packet of smokes—Marin's probably; a navigation chart; a coffee cup. Sanders grappled for a hold, found it around the wheel and held himself steady. Marin slid with the rest of his possessions, thumping to a stop against the starboard porthole, his boots leaving imprints in the fogged glass.

Sanders squinted through the forward window. The impossible land lay ahead, wide and cavernous. Gullet open. His men, just pin pricks of light on the water now, rowed towards it, paddles chopping at the water in their panic.

Turn back. He wanted to scream. *Go back. It's not—*

Too late. Already too late.

The jaws came down, the cavern closing upon the ship, ripping through metal and wire. Sanders closed his eyes, listening to the crunch of steel bones breaking. *The Oneiros'* lights went out. Water rushed in. Somewhere, Marin screamed.

And the singing stopped.

Sanders grip slipped on the wheel. The sea sucked him out, dragged him down. His body bounced off the rocks. Something shiny and sylph-like flashed in the dark water. Free.

Angry.

A cold hand coiled around his foot, fingers digging into flesh like teeth as she dragged him deeper. The black and white photo slipped from his pocket, fluttering in the gloom. *Maggie. Oh Maggie, I'm sorry.*

A face loomed close in the dim. Hairless, grey skin and orbs for eyes. Sanders screamed, bubbled and thrashed. She held him there, snared in her grip, as she had once been in his net. Sanders lungs burned; his head swam. She came close, displaying rows upon rows of teeth.

This is it.

He braced himself and waited for the end. Above, in his peripheral vision, bright scales flashed in the dark, darting through the murk. *Another one.* And there, a second glint of scales. A third. *A school of them.*

Together the mermaids circled.

Round and round. Mesmerising. Yes, he'd felt this before—this sinking. This cold pressing on his skin. But it was too late. All of it too late. He was caught. Trapped in this cycle of scale and fin.

Saunders sank. His eyes slid shut. The last air in his lungs emptied.

Falling, spiraling, spinning down. Down, down, into oblivion—

12.00am February 18, 1962.

—And he woke to the scream of metal on rock and a smarting pain as his body thudded to the floor.

Up on the deck of the Oneiros, a siren wailed..

RAM'S REVENGE

Sign: Aries
Element: Fire
Symbol: Ram
Dates: March 21 to April 19

I never meant to kill Sir Woolston.

I mean, the ram was a prick and an arse, but I didn't really mean him dead. At least, not dead under a truck. Dad kept him in the front paddock, where he couldn't ram the rest of the flock. And every day Sir Woolston would chase me through the grass, wicked horns bent low, aimed at my backside as I sprinted to the bus stop. Every day since middle school; since Dad sat me down three years ago and said:

"Emma, you'll need to take the bus from now on, okay?"

Mum had just passed and between taking care of Nan and keeping the farm afloat, he couldn't spare the hour-long drive to school anymore. I'd given him a mute nod, privately relieved. That hour had been Mum's and mine. Doing the drive with Dad wouldn't have been the same. So, at the age of thirteen, I packed my bag of books, a soggy sandwich, and ran for the door.

For as long as I can remember, I've always been late. Time passes differently for me; one moment I have thirty minutes until the bus comes, the next I spot it trundling up the road from the kitchen window. Like I did that first morning. Taking a shortcut across Sir Woolston's paddock seemed harmless enough that first time. What could one old ram past his prime do anyway?

I arrived at school with my butt bruised purple and ram-shaped teeth marks all down one forearm.

So began Sir Woolston's and my long-standing vendetta.

People say sheep are stupid. I tell them they haven't met Sir Woolston. I mean, that ram was as devious as he was vicious. Sometimes, he'd let me get within cooee of the paddock's front gate—right where the bus would stop—before springing out from behind the old gum to run me down. He'd herd me into potholes so I'd trip until I had every hidden drop and rise in that entire field memorised better than the alphabet.

The day he died began like any other. I was running late, as always. A glint of bus through the gums lining the road and I surged to my feet, snatching my bag up, pecking a kiss on Nan asleep in her recliner, and bolting through the door, fly screen snapping shut at my heels.

He was waiting for me, that prig of a sheep, as always. His beady little eyes trained on my approach. *Spiteful bastard,* I thought, pulling the straps of my backpack tight as I hurried to the rusty barbed wire fence. I gingerly pushed my homemade step up against one post. I'd made it one weekend, not long after that first scuffle with Sir Woolston; it had served me well in the three years since. Step secured, I climbed up it and onto the top of the post. It wobbled under me, as always, and I balanced on it, poised like a diver about to take the plunge.

Sir Woolston let out a low rumbling bleat and backed up two steps. Then he lowered his head.

"Come at me," I snarled. Down the road, the bus rumbled closer. A hundred meters away, max. Miss it and it'd be an hour before another came, and more to the point, I'd be sentenced to scratching gum off the underside of school desks. Mr Lombard had made me that promise last week.

I sucked in a breath, tensed my muscles, and sprang. My feet hit the grass and I bolted, arms pumping. *Go. Go, go, go.* Behind, Sir Woolston bellowed and launched towards me. I jumped Pythagoras' pothole, sidestepped Gauss' hidden log (yes, I named all the obstacles after mathematicians, for all the hell they'd put me through). With a "ha" I cleared Leibniz's rock, almost invisible in the long grass. Sir Woolston closed in. That was always the way of it. Four legs are quicker than two. His hooves thundered at my back, so close I could hear him snorting through his nose. My only chance came down to timing.

I glanced over my shoulder. And there he was, right behind me. Angry little eyes burning holes into the butt of my jeans. He lowered his head and sprang. I threw myself sideways, a 90-degree change of direction. Sir Woolston shot past, a horn nearly catching my shirt. "Thought you had me, didn't you?" I gasped, clutching a stitch in my side.

Sir Woolston slowed and turned, malleable lips twitching to show his flat teeth. *Just piss off,* I willed at him. Not to be. The stubborn bastard came on again. I turned and ran, bag bouncing on my back. Ahead, the bus pulled up to my stop—

—My foot squelched into a pile of sheep shit. Only, it had rained last night, so instead of the usual dry pellets, this was a sodden, soggy mass. My foot skidded out from under me. My world teetered. Arms windmilled.

Wham!

I hit the ground. Pain shot across my backside, up my back. Sir Woolston was on me in a heartbeat, fierce little teeth sinking into my arm as I tried to batter him away.

"Get off you prick!" I staggered to my feet.

Wham!

Fresh pain radiated down my left quadriceps. My leg went dead, nearly buckling under my weight. Bloody corked my thigh, he did. Fucking ram. I slipped my bag off one shoulder, covered in mud and shit, and swung it at Sir Woolston's head. Eight kilos of book and soggy sandwich collected him with a satisfying thunk. *Take that, bastard.* He swayed, black eyes momentarily dazed. Or perhaps surprised. I didn't stick around to find out which it was. I skedaddled, hightailing it for the bus. Through the doors, the driver checked his watch.

Don't you leave. Don't you dare fucking leave. I lengthened my stride. Somewhere behind, Sir Woolston let out another of those rumbling bleats. Stubborn git. I reached the gate, stuck one toe then another between the wooden slats and climbed.

Wham!

Sir Woolston barrelled into the gate. There was a crack of splintering wood and the gate buckled under me. My grip slipped, and I pitched headfirst over the railing, felt something—an exposed nail or bit of splintered wood perhaps—catch my jeans. With an awful, slow ripping sound my descent slowed and plonked me, headfirst, onto the road.

I scrambled up, saw the tear. It began just above my knee and went all the way to the ankle. A dribble of blood stained the edge. I ran a finger along the rip; the edges were already fraying. A fist closed inside my throat.

They weren't just any old jeans. These were mum's jeans. A bit baggy, sure, and *technically* I wasn't supposed to wear them at school, with them not meeting the school's fluid understanding of uniform and all, but I hadn't cared. They smelled like her. Eucalyptus and lemon. Even after all my washing them.

My vision grew hot. Then red. "Bloody ram!" I screamed. My foot lashed out, striking the gate. The wood was harder than I'd expected, and pain shot through my toes.

Sir Woolston just stared. Black eyes unblinking. Rage boiled inside me. I wanted to wrap my hands around that bloody ram's throat and squeeze; get Dad's shotgun from the ute and fire it between his Goddamn eyeballs.

"Piece of shit! Go die already!" I kicked again, this time connecting with one of the rusty hinges. There was a ping of metal snapping. The gate gave under my sneaker. With a creak, then a groan, the whole thing toppled over.

I was too angry to care. I glared at the ram through the broken gate, thinking murder until a blast from the bus horn made me jump. Sir Woolston skittered back. *Yea, you better run.*

"Are you getting on or not?" The bus driver shouted. "I've not got all day."

I didn't recognise him. A newbie then. Probably the first time he'd seen my daily rush across the paddock. I nodded, gathered my bag and stalked to my seat.

As the bus pulled away, I glanced out the dust-covered window. Sir Woolston had picked his way out through the wreckage of the gate and was standing on the road, watching my bus retreat into the distance.

"I hope you get hit by a car," I raged under my breath, inspecting the rip in my jeans again.

As it turned out, fate did one better. That afternoon, I later learned, Sir Woolston met his end under the wheel of a thirty-tonne cattle truck.

#

It was dusk when I returned home and made my long, slow walk up our winding drive. Gravel slid and ground under my shoes, the staples I'd used to hold the tear shut in my—*mum's*—jeans chafed a rash into my leg. When the road eventually rounded alongside Sir Woolston's paddock, I made to glare at the beastly ram inside, only to find it empty.

Weird. But not unheard of. Dad must have moved him into another paddock, what with the gate broke and all. A flicker of guilt rose in me at that. I could have texted him, but I'd been so angry that the thought hadn't occurred to me.

I clomped up the steps of our two-storey farmhouse, along our paint-peeled veranda, and stopped, hand hovering over the knob of the flyscreen as I heard the voices in the living room. Strange voices.

"We could start the listing at 1.5, but I can't promise you'll get that," a husky baritone was saying, as if it had spent its life on the end of a cigarette.

"There isn't any way to bump it up?" Dad's voice. My stomach clenched. His words had that distinct waver he got when he was nervous, or anxious—or sad. I'd heard it down the end of the phone line and I'd never forget it. *Emma, it's Mum.*

"I can paint the house—" Dad said.

A sigh. "It needs more than a fresh lick of paint, Reece. Your barn's infested with termites, the fences are rusting, gates are broken, your tractor doesn't look like it's been used in years."

They were right about the tractor, whomever it was. About all of it, come to think of it.

"The state things are in here," it continued. "You'll be lucky to get any offers over one mil."

Understanding dawned. My jaw dropped. *He wouldn't!* I yanked the screen open, shoved open the door—unlocked as always—and stormed in.

"You can't sell the farm!" It came out louder than intended and so close to hysteria I winced. Damn voice, betraying me at a time like this. I swallowed, took a breath, and turned on Dad perched on the arm of the couch. "You can't really be thinking—?"

"Ah, Emma, you're home early." Dad looked guilty, like the time I'd got him with a hand inside my spare change jar.

Beside him, a man with greying hair and equally grey suit stood up. "Let's call it a day." He shuffled the pile of papers and real estate brochures together. I recognised the logo for one of the nursing homes in the city on one of them.

"We're not selling," I told him.

Dad stood up, wringing his hands. "Emma—"

"No!" I said. I didn't want to hear it. Excuses. That's all it would be.

"It's Nan, Emma," he went on, ignoring me. "She's getting worse." His gaze flicked to Nan asleep in her recliner, eyes roaming under her eyelids. "She called me Michael this morning." Dad's brother, dead some ten years now. Cancer. I don't remember him well.

"She was just confused," I said.

The real estate agent gave a little cough, picked up his briefcase and with a nod to Dad, slid out the door. I don't think Dad even noticed. Instead, he rubbed his face, as if trying to scrub off the guilt. He sighed.

"She's been confused for a while now. Haven't you noticed?"

I stood seething before the couch and my father slumped further into it. I didn't answer. Truth was, I had noticed. Nan had always been a bit eccentric, to my mind. She used to make all her own clothes—and many of mine as a kid—crocheting sweaters and blankets in the brightest, most clashing colours she could find. For as long as I could remember, she'd never worn a matching pair of socks.

But recently, the sharp wit under those short, grey curls, had grown blunt. She slept more. Forgot what pills she'd taken at breakfast. Put yogurt in her tea instead of milk. There was a time when I opened the freezer and found her dentures in it. My chest squeezed at the memory, like I was being smothered in a too-tight hug. Of course I'd noticed Nan slipping away. Of course I *knew*. But neither one of us had said it. Saying it out loud made it real. I swallowed. This day was really going to the dumps.

"I worry about leaving her on her own for so long," Dad went on. "She needs a carer."

"Then I will come home early from school. Stay with her on weekends." I said, desperate.

Dad shook his head. He reached out, took my hands in his and gave them a squeeze. "Emma, it's not enough. And I can't ask you to do that." He looked past me, to Nan, and his expression softened to the point where I wondered if he might cry. With a swallow he returned to me. "With the sale of the farm we could put her in a care home, somewhere nice. And we could get an apartment close by."

I pulled my hands free. "An *apartment?*" The thought of being crammed into a 50 square metre shoebox made my insides curl.

Dad was quiet a moment, then his gaze drifted to Nan again. "It probably won't be for long."

My chest tightened. This was Nan we were talking about. Her marbles might have a few pebbles and bits of twine in the bag, but it wasn't like she'd sent them scattering across the floor. She was still there. Albeit intermittently.

Dad stood and ran his fingers through his hair. "I wish there was another way, Em. I really do. But I can't see it."

I stared up at him, the lump from this morning clogging my throat again. "But what about Mum?" My mind flittered along the track we'd worn up the hill out back, stopping at the old Karri tree there, the one Mum used to read under in the summer, and the tombstone next to it.

Dad wouldn't meet my eyes, but I saw the water in his, and suddenly I was struck at how tired he looked. Like he'd spent sleepless nights making this decision. So I knew his answer long before he spoke. "I'm sorry."

Something inside my chest cracked, probably a rib as he cut out my heart and strangled it. Heat crept up my throat, behind my nose. I clenched my jaw to stop my chin wobbling and strode for the door, banging it shut behind me.

Across the veranda. *Breathe.* Down the steps—skip the middle one that creaks. *Walk. Breathe and walk.* Crunch along the driveway.

And that's when I saw him on the back of Dad's ute. The tarp he'd used to keep the flies off had blown loose, revealing a lolling blue tongue, bloody wool and a broken horn. One dry, elongated pupil stared out at me, accusing. Sir Woolston. Dead as fucking dead.

\#

Dad loved Sir Woolston. God knew why, the ram was as much of a prick to him as it was to me. Sir Woolston had been a gift from Mum's dad when they'd married and he'd handed over the reins of the farm to them.

We buried Sir Woolston in his paddock. Out under the big gum. Well, Dad did. I watched from the veranda, dazed and adrift, not sure what to feel. Banjo, our ginger tom, rubbed his face against my shoulder, tail curling under my chin as I slouched on the top step. The farm, Dad was selling the farm. The thought spin-cycled through my head. Round and round.

A clunk of a shovel dropped on the gravel drive signalled Dad's return. He slumped down next to me, peeling off his gardening gloves. Bits of wool and blood stuck to them. His cheeks were flushed and sweat clung to the collar of his shirt. "He had a good run, Sir Woolston did. I'm sad to see him go."

I wasn't. And I wouldn't have minded if Sir Woolston's run had been a good deal shorter, but saying that would only upset Dad, so I nodded. A silence stalked over us. I let it settle and dig in its claws, and Dad shifted, uncomfortable, until at last, he turned to me. I kept my gaze on the paddock, though out of the corner of my eye, there was that wrinkle in his brow when he knew he'd done wrong.

"I'm sorry, Emma. I should have told you sooner. But it's the only way."

No, it's the easy way, I thought, and very nearly said. But I didn't. Words are like barbed wire. You want to pick through them carefully or else the barbs sink in. And if you're not careful about it, the wounds will go bad and fester. Mum had taught me that. I picked at the tear in my jeans and, because Banjo was nudging, scratched under the tom's chin.

"What about the animals?" I heard myself say.

Dad shifted again. "Well if the new owners want to keep them, we'll include them in the sale."

"And if they don't?"

"We'll find homes for some, sell off the others."

"And if we can't sell them?"

There was the slightest pause from him, then, "they'll go to the abattoir."

My lips pressed tight. It wasn't like we hadn't sent animals before. Old sheep mostly. Except for Sir fucking Woolston, but he'd been special, like I said before. No, it was the thought of carting our flock of fifty prime and healthy merinos off to slaughter that sat ill in my stomach. And what about our four-year-old sheepdog, Billy, and Banjo? My guts squirmed at the thought of them locked away in a shelter, alone and severed from everything familiar.

I'm not one for praying. I learned long ago at Mum's bedside that it was a waste of time, but that didn't stop me from closing my eyes and fervently hoping what I imagined wouldn't come to pass.

An arm curled around my shoulders. Dad. I blinked, coming back to myself. It was dark, and Banjo was curled up on my lap. When had that happened? Dad pulled me close. To his credit, he didn't make promises or try to give me false hope. He might not have started out as a farmer, but Mum had taught him well. He knew the realities of farm life, just as I did.

"Let's make dinner," he said, instead. A call of agreement issued from the lounge, like the warble of an old magpie. He grimaced. "Preferably before Nan gets the grumps."

#

That night I dreamed. It was twilight again and I stood among a flock of sheep, heavy wool coats pressing in on every side, my own wool coat thick and hot on my back. A dog barked at our heels and as one we jolted, stumbling forward. A panicked bleat rippled through the flock. *Going. We are going.*

Where? I wanted to ask.

Another bark, and we lurched on again, our hooves sinking into grass and mud first, then clattering up a metal ramp. A truck. The non-sheep part of my brain recognised it for what it was. Metal and death it smelt like. Death, metal and misery.

I locked my legs, but my hooves slid on hay and muck and the flock carried me on and in, packing together tight, and tighter again. My forehoof slipped and I fell to my knees, releasing a panicked bleat. *Stop,* I thought at them, *stop.* But they came on, dozens of them. Feet struck my side, knocked my head. Woolly bodies packing so tight that they couldn't move, and still more came. Tighter and suffocating, until at last it eased.

Under us, an engine hacked to life. Its rumble a roar to our ears.

Between the slats of the truck and knobbly sheep legs, the farm receded. The grass of the paddock pulled away, fences and trees zooming into the distance. Past the barn and shearing shed we went, past the hen house. I watched it all go, until with a wrench, the farmhouse flashed past in a blur of blue weatherboard and tin roof. Away. Away from everything I knew and loved. I opened my mouth, perhaps to scream, maybe to cry, and a long, low bleat came out—

I woke in a tangled mess, sweat soaking my pyjamas, and knew a moment of dislocation. Who was I? Where was I? When? For a heartbeat my head swam before my gaze landed on the desk in the far corner, a school bag slouched over the back of the chair, the patterned rug on the floor and a chest of drawers beside an open window. My room. I breathed out and flopped back to my pillows. Then vaulted back up again as a long, low bleat drifted in on the wind.

Not part of the dream.

Cold drenched my limbs, rising the hairs on my neck. I scrambled out of bed and ran to the window, pushed the curtain aside.

Sir Woolston was standing in the paddock. *Standing.* Right under the gum Dad had buried him by, clear as day. One look and I knew it was him. I could recognise the curl of those horns anywhere.

But that wasn't what sent fear clenching through my stomach.

It was that he was looking at me.

I staggered from the window. The ram was dead. I'd seen it, watched Dad bury its mutilated corpse—all twisted limbs and oil marks mixed with bloody wool. Sir Woolston hadn't deserved that end, I'll admit. Not like that. But the ram had definitely died. It wasn't like he'd come off second best with a scooter. He'd been crushed under an eighteen-wheeler cattle truck. It was amazing there had been anything left of him to bury.

I peered back out the window, sure I was imagining him; some subconscious guilt making me see things. A scream sputtered and died in my throat as my airways cinched shut.

Sir Woolston was still there, still looking. But he'd moved. He stood at the edge of our veranda, a faint glow haloing his body. My legs went weak and I gripped the windowsill. I could see *through* him. Right through his middle to the weeds and mottled paving stone under him.

Oh yes, he was dead all right. No thanks to me. But the stubborn git wasn't done. Not yet.

The ram let out another low bleat. A moan almost. Fuck.

I slammed my window shut, drew the curtains and dove for the bed, pulling the covers high over my head. *This can't be happening.* Of all creatures with unfinished business, of course it had to be Sir bloody Woolston who'd come back to haunt me. He was too stubborn to just go quietly. I ground my teeth, fresh rage working a heat up in my belly. Wasn't it enough that he'd tormented me every day while he was alive? And now in death too? My hand clenched into fists. How dare he.

I threw my blankets off, threw open my door and marched downstairs, not sure what I would do until I spied Dad's shotgun by the door. I snatched it up. Too light though—no ammo. I rooted around in the kitchen drawers until I found a round, shoved the shell into the chamber and pumped the slide. That ram would pay for crossing me. I whirled on the door. I would Ghostbusters it out of existence.

"Emma?"

A husky, warble fell over me, freezing me still with my hand on the door. I turned. Nan stood in the hallway, cane in one hand with her other holding on to the doorframe. Her white nighty hung off her like a sack.

"It's all right, Nan. Go back to bed."

Nan snorted and hobbled over, unusually spry for her eighty-eight years. She eyed the gun in my hands, then to my surprise, nodded. "Good," she said. "About time someone did something about that racket."

Her gaze travelled to the lounge-room window and out to the paddock. I stared at her. "You hear it too?"

"How can I not? He's been doing it all bloody night." She shooed a hand to the door. "Go on, silence the fucker. He's dead already, time he got the message."

I gawped. I mean, Nan had always had a mouth on her, but this was something new.

"Would do it myself," Nan went on, "but—" she gestured at her cane. "Do us a favour, eh? So we can all get some shuteye?"

I swallowed. We'd talk about this later, I promised myself, and headed for the door. Nan shuffled after me.

A twist of the knob and I was out on the veranda. Nan stayed there as I padded down the steps and across the damp grass to the edge of the paddock, heart in my mouth, finger on the trigger.

I scanned beyond the fence, waiting for a ghostly set of horns to come charging at me—maybe even *through* me for all I knew. And I'd probably shit myself if he did. I swallowed and took a few steps closer, palms clammy around the shotgun.

Then I lowered it, relief rushing out of me in a long breath.

Sir Woolston was gone.

The veranda lights flicked on, snapping shadows back into the recesses of the deck.

"Emma, what the hell are you doing?" Dad's voice roared from the front door, so loud I yelped and nearly pulled the trigger. I spun, my heart throwing itself into my ribs as if it was trying to break down a door.

It looked bad. I knew it did. "Dad, I—"

He strode forward, fury flushing over his face, and ripped the gun from my hands. In two practiced motions, he had the shell out of the chamber and in his palm. He glared at it, then shoved it before my nose. "You could have killed someone with this."

Well, that had been the idea. More or less. Perceptive, Dad was, in his way. "There was a..." my voice and confidence plummeted under his glare. "...noise," I said, switching the word 'ghost' out at the last moment. "Nan heard it too."

"And you thought to investigate with a *gun*?" Dad struggled for composure, deep breaths, clenched jaw. Not good, he was really mad. "With *Nan*? What if she'd wandered off, Em? Or fallen down the steps? Or grabbed for the gun?" He ran a hand through his bed hair. "Christ. You got to think about these things, Emma. *Think*."

I balked, indignant. "She came on her own. Fully lucid, I'll add. It's not like I bloody kidnapped her." I searched for my cane-totting grandmother to back me up and spotted her at the far end of the veranda having a heated argument with a flowerpot. My insides sank. "Nan?" I asked, going over to her.

"No, I won't fucking tell them. Tell them yourself—well, that's not *my* problem, now is it?" she hissed at the weed-stricken perennials.

I put a hand on Nan's shoulder, gentle-like. She jumped, coming back to herself, and swayed on her cane. "Emma? Oh good, did you shut up that goat yet?"

"It was a ram, Nan," I said, fighting down disappointment. For a moment, just a moment, I'd thought I'd glimpsed the old Nan back in the driver's seat. But no, the disease was at the wheel instead.

My strange and adoring grandmother was losing her mind.

Maybe we both were.

"But did you get rid of it?" Nan insisted as I guided her back into the house and to her room. Dad flashed me a look as we passed, one of those 'I'm not done with you yet' looks that make my insides curdle. "Is it gone? Can I finally get some sleep?"

Truth be told, I wasn't certain on either count. "Yes," I lied as I put her to bed and pulled up the blankets. "Night Nan."

"Night Anna."

Hearing Mum's name leaving her lips nearly broke my heart again.

#

Sir Woolston came again the following night. I was restless. After finishing my chores, I'd been marched back to my room to "reflect" for the rest of the day (Dad's idea of punishment, seeing as it was a Saturday). Didn't matter that I was sixteen and not six anymore. Not that I minded much, any excuse to avoid Dad's gaze was a welcome one. A master of the old Guilt Trip was Dad. Just thinking about his last words the night before made me squirm.

"I'm disappointed in you, Emma."

Like I said, I was restless that next night. The full moon was out, if you take stock of that sort of thing. I know I do. Animals go weird on a full moon. Ask any farmer. So perhaps that was why I twisted and tangled in my pyjamas half the night until I heard it again: a long, low bleat.

My eyes popped open. He was back. That was the first thing through my head. Back to finish what was started. I crept to my window, heart banging on my ribs like a judge's gavel. Guilty. Guilty. Guilty.

I chinked the curtain.

Nothing. No glowy woollen ram in the paddock, nothing off the veranda.

Another bleat. Loud and close. He was at the door. My stomach barrelled into my spine as if it might cut its losses and make a run for it.

When no one answered, Sir Woolston snorted and moved. I stood rooted by the window, listening to the *thunk-thunk* of the ram's feet travel the length of the veranda. A windowpane rattled. He was trying to get in. Must be. I imagined Sir Woolston's head pressing against the lounge-room window, angry little eyes peering in. A high-pitched squeaking rose from below: that would be his ghostly horns leaving a laceration across the glass. My belly shrivelled. He was looking for me.

A bleat sounded under my window. My heart shot into my throat, lodging somewhere near my larynx. I wheezed in a breath. Could he get up to the second storey? I slammed my window shut, flicked the latch, and backed away. Better not to find out.

Under my feet in the room below, I heard Nan stir: a creak of bed springs as she got up and her cane clacking on the wooden floor. Muttering, before she bellowed:

"Shut up, you flaming sheep. Fuck off! You hear me? Skat!"

Something cracked against her window. Loud. Too loud for Sir Woolston. Her cane, probably. Then the tinkle of glass breaking.

Strength drained from my legs. *Oh no. No, no, no.* Cold swept through the floorboards. Below, Nan cried out. I made to scream but the urge for silence seized me, its hands smothering my mouth and commanding me to not even breathe.

Sir Woolston stood before me. In my room. On my rug. Wisps of grey curling off his wool. He was bigger than I remembered, horns sharper, eyes darker. I scrambled backwards, tripped over my own feet and landed on my arse.

Warmth ran down my leg. Oh shit.

Sir Woolston lowered his head, black eyes fixed on mine.

"No," I begged.

He charged.

I screamed. Or I thought I did. Though I don't remember any sound.

He hit me dead on, right in the middle of my chest; horns to sternum. Horns *into* sternum. I boggled as Sir Woolston's ghost dove into me. Pain seared through my ribs; emptied my lungs. I flew across the room, slamming my head on the foot of the bed.

One last hit, was it? I thought, dimly. Wanted to have the last bloody say? I struggled to my feet, nursing my head. Sir Woolston was gone. "Fucking ram," I muttered, and rubbed my sternum. It smarted something chronic. Probably bruised the bone, if such a thing was possible. I winced and cursed again. Then my fingers ran over something hard. A knot of scar tissue between my breasts, shaped in a rough 'V'.

What the—

A bleat boomed in my head, as if I'd shoved my head into the flute of a church bell. Light exploded across my vision. The world tilted.

And I knew no more.

#

I woke to dark and a throbbing in my fingers, like I'd been digging through grit. Cold caked my knees, turned my toes numb. Above the tops of the gum trees, stars shone, a full moon high overhead. Midnight going on morning, to my mind. And my heart lurched. When had I come outside? Cold pushed against my fingers and I looked down. My hands were clawing at the earth, nails cracked and fingers bloody as they tore chunks of soil and rock free.

What the— I made to stand, but my legs wouldn't respond. My hands continued to dig. I tried to pull them away and a growling bleat reverberated in my head, rattled my teeth. Horror shivered through my gut, very nearly released my bowels, again.

Sir Woolston.

The ram's ghost was still inside me. It had to be. But what was he doing?

I watched one hand shovel out a fist full of freshly turned soil and deposit it in a pile beside the hole. *Freshly turned soil,* the thought returned, just as my fingers brushed something soft in the earth. Oh sweet shit—

My fingers dusted the dirt off Sir Woolston's corpse. The pungent scent of decaying flesh wafted over me. Ripe to the bone. Dad had only buried it the night before, yet it stank like it'd been the ground a week. The smell gagged in my throat, caught in my nose and I wanted to turn away and puke. But my body wouldn't obey. My hands dug around the woollen limbs, tracing up along the broken spine, dug some more until my fingers touched horn.

The centre of my sternum tingled, and I sensed an eagerness there; a presence leaning my body in, desperate to get my hands around it. I fought the feeling, gritted my teeth and tried to pull myself away. In a flash, my hands clenched around the exposed horn, knuckles white and bloody, and wouldn't budge.

Move, I commanded my legs. *MOVE*. Bit by bit, my knees unlocked, muscles twitched, pulled and lengthened as I stood—still hunched over as Sir Woolston refused to relinquish the grip on his own deceased head.

"Let go!" I grunted. I leaned backwards, fighting the weight of the corpse. Anymore and I'd pull the corpse from the ground like a blood-soaked daisy. My fingers tightened until they burned, and a furious 'baaa' rang in my ears. Bloody prick of a ram. I thrashed, an odd sight it would have been had anyone come upon me, a girl in the dead of night, filthy with grave dirt, and bucking her body as if possessed. Which I was, to my mind.

I was mid-thrash when the neck of the corpse snapped. A pop ran through my arms, as if I'd been bending a stick in two until it gave. One moment resistance, the next none. There was a wet, sucking sound and I pitched backwards, a severed, half-rotted ram's head in my lap.

I screamed—Sir Woolston allowed me that—and tried to fling the thing off, but my hands remained glued to the horn. It dangled in my grip, eye sockets empty from where the critters had gorged; the second horn still snapped mid curl. His nose was gone, a black cavity in its place, as if his face had fallen in on itself—which, I considered, as my heart eased back down my throat, had probably been the case. But to decompose this fast... I pushed the thought aside as the bile rose in my stomach.

"Now what?" I demanded into the night. If Sir Woolston thought I was taking this rotting skull back inside the house he had another thing coming.

The ram's presence shifted inside me. A cold chill creeping along my bones as he moved away from my hands and down to my legs. Control returned to my fingers and I dropped the head in a heartbeat. It landed with a splat in the grass, rolled sideways once and was still.

Wham! Rage flooded my senses; bellowed in my ears until my head spun. The place where Sir Woolston had hit my sternum smarted. I rocked on the spot, blinking hard to clear my vision, and felt the accursed ram gathering strength—or energy or *something*—to attack again. Bastard was not letting this go.

"All right! All right!" I threw my hands up in surrender—I'm not sure why I did, with him being inside me, but it felt right. I picked up the sheep's head again.

Sir Woolston settled inside me, as much as a cranky old ram can settle. A whisper of cold clenched my fingers tight around a curling horn, as if to say 'keep hold of that', before its presence descended down my legs to force one step, then the next.

"Where are we going?"

A belligerent bleat, short and clipped. Shut up. Righteo then.

We crossed the paddock and for a horrible moment I thought Sir Woolston was headed for the farmhouse, only to veer off course at the last minute and head up the hill. We crossed dewy grass, hay and dead leaves sticking to my bare feet. Up and over fences, across fields, under shadowed gums. I lost track of time. We walked for what felt like hours. I sought out the moon, thinking to find it low in the sky and dawn not far off, only to see it still at its peak.

Time was at a standstill.

A bleat and a burning tingle across my chest roused me out of a stupor. I blinked awake. We stood on the edge of a lush field, too lush for our neck of the woods. A bonfire blazed in the middle of a field and around it hunched figures danced, knock-kneed and stamping. Cold prickled down my legs as Sir Woolston set us moving again. We drew closer, and the chimes of bells seeped into the night, oddly muted, as if I were listening through a closed door. The fire's heat licked over me as we came close, stinging my cold cheeks. And there, at the edge of the gathering, we stopped. The cold in my feet oozed away as Sir Woolston released my legs.

We were here. Wherever here was.

The figures were smaller than me, the tallest barely came up to my chest. But as though to make up for it, their shadows stretched absurdly long in the wake of the fire, two, perhaps even three times bigger than my own (I checked). Their limbs were thin, too. Spindly.

"Where are we?" I demanded. "Who are they?"

Silence for my troubles.

One of the figures detached from the frolicking and approached us, coming closer and closer again, until I could make out its features.

I gawked. A bird might have built a nest in my mouth it was open that long.

They were sheep. Well, not sheep *per se*, not as I knew them with their woolly four-legged bodies and long faces. This was a sheep-*person*. What I'd taken for a hunched back was a cape of unwoven wool around her shoulders. I say her, but I had no way of knowing, her chest was flat, and a woven wool frock covered everything else. The face was long like a sheep's and she had the ears poking through the tight coils of her white hair. A sheep bell tinkled around her neck. The rest of her features appeared human, in a stretched and angular sort of way.

She stopped before us, gold-yellow eyes studying me, and the weight of that gaze bore into me—old and ancient. I shifted, suddenly aware that I was still gripping Sir Woolston's rotting head. I swallowed and imagined how I'd meet my end at the hands of a flock of fairy sheep. What would it be? A lynching? Stoning? A roasting over the fire? Did fairy sheep even eat meat?

Then, to my surprise, she beckoned.

A tingle of anticipation rippled through my chest, then a soft bleat in my ears, almost ... gentle? Encouraging? I scowled. What was he playing at?

The fairy-sheep girl turned and strode back towards the fire. Five steps in, she stopped and turned to check if I was following.

A faint flush of cold ran across my shoulders, as if Sir Woolston had put a hand to my back and nudged. Then a stronger chill rushed down my legs and into my feet as he prepared to take control again.

"All right, I'm going!" I snapped, exasperated and adjusted my hold on his head and strode into the gathering.

If bleats could purr, Sir Woolston's did then.

#

"Emma." Warm hands tapped my face. "Emma, wake up."

My eyes opened to blue sky, a smattering of cloud, and Dad's face leaning over mine. Relief flooded his features.

"Thank God," he breathed. His hands fluttered over me. "Can you sit up?"

He helped me sit and I squinted through the morning. I was in the middle of a paddock, under an old familiar gum. Downhill I spotted a familiar broken gate. Sir Woolston's paddock. I rubbed my head. It felt heavy; tight behind my temples, like I had a migraine coming on. My eyes stung.

"What happened?"

"I don't know. When I saw you lying here through the kitchen window, I thought…" Dad's voice choked off into a sob; he rubbed his eyes. "God, Em, I thought it was bad. Real bad." My gut knotted, guilt and grief clutching my chest. I knew what he meant. An aneurysm, like Mum. He'd been the one who'd found her, unconscious in one of the back paddocks. Nothing the doctors could do. Her brain was gone. Watching him— *letting* him—turn off her life support was the hardest thing I'd ever done. And he'd thought it was happening all over again. I hugged him, hard.

"I'm okay," I lied and mumbled the only excuse I could think of. "I must have sleepwalked."

We broke apart, a muddy imprint of me left on his shirt. I plucked my filthy pyjama top, sniffed and nearly gagged. It smelled like shit. Literally shit. And probably a hundred other things I didn't want to think about. What had happened last night? Everything was clear—well, clear*ish*—until I stepped up to the fairy sheep's fire. Then nothing but flashes. The fire roaring high. Dancing. Woollen fairies swaying and stamping. My shadow ballooning and stretching across the ground.

I glanced over at Sir Woolston's grave, hoping Dad hadn't yet seen what I'd done to it, and stopped. It was whole. The overturned soil was neatly packed down under the old gum. No sign of my midnight grave robbery. No ram entrails exposed for the crows. Nothing but a quiet mound.

My stomach dropped, a tremble working up from my knees and into my hands. I clenched the hem of my top to stop their shake. Had I imagined it? Had *any* of it been real? I felt giddy. Was I losing it? Cold sweat prickled over my body.

"I need to go have a bath," I heard myself say. I pushed past Dad and stumbled for the fence and the way out of the wretched paddock.

Dad hurried after me. "Are you *sure* you're okay?" he asked.

"I'm fine." I pulled apart two lines of barbed wire and slipped through. The rusted barbs grabbed at my pyjamas, scratching through fabric to skin underneath, then I was clear and marching for the house. My skin felt clammy. My vision tunnelled.

"Em!" Dad called after me, and I heard him swear as the barb wire fence caught him where he tried to squeeze through after me. "Do you want to talk about it?"

It's nothing, you know. Just me losing my mind. No biggie. On second thought, no. Dad had enough on his plate as it was. Nan was enough work already. I all but ran up the steps and through the front door.

"Emma, is that you?" Nan called from the lounge as I blew through. I didn't answer, instead I strode down the hall, into the bathroom, shut the door and turned the shower on as hot as I could stand it. Then I curled into a ball under its stream, clothes and all, and shivered.

#

It took nearly an hour before the chills subsided. At last, when the heat returned to my fingers, I turned off the shower, peeled free my sodden night garments and towelled myself dry. The tension around my temples hadn't eased, but at least the smell had. Mostly. When I moved, I still caught a faint whiff of smoke. I rolled on extra deodorant for good measure and paused at the sight of my nails.

They were ragged and torn, and despite my soaking, flecks of muck were still trapped deep under each fingernail. Like I really had spent half the night digging. My stomach did a little twist, a flush of adrenaline spiking my veins. Maybe I hadn't imagined it. Hope seeded in that little well of doubt.

I crushed it. Who was I kidding? Possession? Fairy sheep? *Come on, Emma, just listen to yourself.*

Towel wrapped around me, I dug around for a comb to tear out the grass burrs stuck in my hair. "Get a grip," I told myself. I wiped away a streak of condensation from the fogged-up mirror—and nearly screamed.

A ram's skull looked back at me.

My heart cracked into my ribs, and I leapt away. In the mirror, the skull did the same. It wore a blue towel wrapped around its human body. Slow dawning sank in. Swallowing, I took a shaky step forward. So did the skull, bobbing closer on a sunburnt neck and a familiar set of shoulders—one bore a fresh scratch from a barbed wire fence.

Me. It was me.

I lifted one hand and pressed it to my cheek. Smooth skin met my touch, but in the mirror, my fingers met skull.

Explains the headache, part of my brain muttered. I pushed the thought away and studied my reflection. The skull rested on my head like a morbid carnival mask, covering half my face. My human chin jutted out under its nasal cavity; my eyes stared through two hollows. One horn curled down from my temple, almost touching the nape of my neck, before sweeping up again to a tip level with my cheek. The other was snapped mid coil.

My belly knotted. This was Sir Woolston's skull.

It was not the rancid thing I'd dug up last night. No rotting flesh or peeling skin. It was smooth, clean bone, near white but for a blackening of soot around the eye sockets and nose cavity. *As if flames had burned away the last of the flesh.*

I scrunched my forehead. In the mirror, the eyes behind the skull wrinkled. This was connected to whatever I'd done, or rather what Sir Woolston had done. Assuming I wasn't batshit mad, of course. Which was likely. But there had to be a logic to it.

So, what the hell had happened last night? What wasn't I remembering?

I sank onto the rim of the bath and closed my eyes. Retrace your steps, that was what Mum had always said whenever I'd lost something. Never thought I'd have to use her advice to track down my own memory. I pictured the last thing I recalled: teetering at the edge of the gathering as the sheep girl with the weight of a millennia in her gaze beckoned me in.

My feet crunched over the grass, the long and unkempt stalks had tickled my aching calves. She'd drawn me to the fire, motioning me to throw something in. A bleat sounded in my ears. Excited, eager. The sensation built, travelling from my chest and down my arm. Sir Woolston nudged my hand, his presence brushing cold around my fingers gripping his head.

I'd frowned. "Why?"

The fairy girl rested a light hand on my arm, guiding it to the flames. "To make right." *Then with a long look that make my skin shiver, "You owe him that."*

Guilt clenched its gnarly fingers into my gut. "But I didn't mean to…" I began.

The fairy's fingers clenched around my forearm. Her eyes turned hard as faceted amber. "Do it."

Sitting on the bathtub, I ran my fingers down my forearm, bumping over the beginnings of a bruise under the skin. Bastard fairy. I rubbed my temples. What then? I'd thrown Sir Woolston's head in and..? My mind's eye served up nothing but more flashes. Sheep bells chiming between the pop and hiss of the fire. The rotting head hitting the flames. And then, more a *feeling* than anything else. A giddying tug at my sternum—Sir Woolston—then a rushing, like I'd released an enormous breath. Then lightness. Freedom. Like I could float away. And euphoria. Somewhere between drunk and dreaming, to my mind.

A knock sounded on the bathroom door, then a husky, "Emma, how much longer will you be? Nanna needs a piss."

I started up from the tub. This could wait. I threw my muddy clothes in the wash basket, adjusted my towel and opened the door. Nan stood in the hall, cane in one hand, a towel and a tea cosy tucked under her other arm. "Sorry Nan. I'm a bit of a mess this morning." My gaze dropped to the tea cosy. "Shall I, uh, get you a fresh shower cap?"

Nan waved me off. "Nothin' wrong with this one." She peered over into the steamy bathroom. "Are you finished?"

"Ah, yes, all yours." I stepped aside.

"Thank you, darling." Nan squeezed past me. "But best take off that hat, you look ridiculous," she said and closed the door.

#

I waited in the kitchen, listening for the squeak of the bathroom door opening to signal

43

Nan was out. She had seen the skull. Dad hadn't, but she had. I was not crazy. Two people couldn't share the same hallucination, not to my mind. Not when I hadn't primed her or anything.

But I had to be sure.

I stirred my coffee absently with a spoon and took a sip. It was stone cold. I gagged and spat the mouthful back into the cup and put it in the microwave.

"She's near, you know. That's why she sees it," a voice said behind me. A strange voice. One I didn't recognise.

My hand flew around the handle of a saucepan and I whirled. "Who—"

No one was there. The kitchen was empty, so was the entrance hall and lounge beyond. I frowned.

"I've never seen a Speaker in the flesh before." A man in a faded Guns N' Roses shirt and skinny jeans appeared at my shoulder, eyeballing my profile.

I yelped, stumbled back, stepped on the hem of my jeans and landed smack on my arse. Pain smarted through my coccyx. I choked down a howl of agony and whimpered instead.

The man winced. "Sorry, I always forget how finicky Fleshies are about boundaries." I glowered at him through my pain. He appeared late twenties, though it was hard to tell. He had a look of sickness about him. Sunken eyes, hollow cheeks. No hair. Not even eyebrows. And pale. I could see the kitchen benchtop through him.

Another ghost.

My mind garbled out the first thing that came to it. "Fleshies?"

"That's you, the living folk."

What certainty I'd had about my faculties drained away. Why, yes, a small slice of insanity for breakfast, please, thank you. I swallowed. Everyone had their quirks, right? I tightened my grip on the saucepan, for all the good it would probably do. "You going to possess me?" I asked.

"Me? No. I'm not into that." The ghost snorted and waved my concern off with a gesture that reminded me of Nan.

I blinked, recognition flicking on in a distant memory. I studied his face and saw Dad's eyes and Nan's nose. "You're Uncle Michael."

The man beamed. "You remember me! I didn't think you would."

"Well, it's more that you look like Dad without hair." I eased the saucepan onto the counter but kept it within easy reach. Along with the salt. That kept off spirits, didn't it? It did in movies. Then something else Michael had said wormed through my shock.

"What's a Speaker?"

"You are," Michael indicated himself. "You talk to the dead."

"I *what?*"

"Talk—"

"I heard you. What I meant was *how?*"

Michael shrugged. "I don't know how it all works. Every Speaker is different, so I'm told. You're actually the first I've met. But *that*," he pointed to my head, and it took me a moment to realise he was pointing at the skull, "that's a sure part of it." He came close again, and a cold prickle ran down my arm and shoulder as he leaned in to examine the sheep's head masking most of my own.

"He's cursed you well and good."

My heart thudded into my throat. "*Cursed*? I'm cursed?"

"All Speakers are, one way or another." He cast me a sly look, eyes roving over the bone mask and the half broken horn curling from my temple. "What on Earth did you do to piss that old ram off so much?"

Broke his gate, got him run over. But still, it wasn't like I'd *pushed* him in front of the truck. He'd done that all on his bloody own. And yet... I fell silent, mind returning to the fairy gathering, the dancing and the fire; the rush and joy that had coursed through me when I'd thrown Sir Woolston's head on the flames. It hadn't felt malicious. Not even when Sir Woolston had possessed me. Bloody-minded and stubborn, sure, but I'd not sensed any malice, hard as it was to believe. I chewed my lip. But a curse was a curse, and that meant nothing good, to my mind. "How do I get rid of it?" I asked.

Michael pulled a face, wrinkling his nose. "Hell if I know."

Some use you are, I thought, but didn't say. I didn't fancy another possession and midnight frolic in the paddocks, no matter what Michael said he did or didn't do.

A footstep on the veranda outside made me look up. Dad returning from the hen house, a small bucket in one hand.

"Eggs for breakfast," he announced, plunking down the bucket on the counter. Four small eggs lay inside. I winced. Not many of our hens had been laying well recently. Neither of us could work out why. "Let me do it," Dad said when I made to pick up the saucepan again. He set the pan over the flames, drizzled oil into it and cracked two of the eggs in.

"Emma," he began.

I grimaced. *Here it comes.* The heart-to-heart, feelings and stuff all laid out; exposed with their pants down. I love Dad, dearly, but he didn't know when to let a conversation die. It was like talking to a Goddamn boomerang. I shot a glare at Michael, still standing in the middle of the kitchen.

He held up his hands as if I'd turned a gun on him. "Okay, okay, hint taken." He vanished, but I suspected—no *sensed*—he hadn't gone far; I could *feel* him there, like an itch at the edge of my brain.

"I know it's been tough since Mum," Dad went on. "I'm not around as much as I should be. It's hard for me too."

I blinked. I'd braced myself for another "are you okay?" or even a "maybe you should see a doctor", but this was not what I'd expected. It was worse.

"I miss us," Dad said. "We used to talk all the time, you and me. But now we barely talk at all."

"We talk plenty—" I began.

"I don't mean those 'good morning' niceties, I mean the big things. Where's your head at? What are you feeling? What's new in your life? I don't *know* these things anymore, Em. I miss that. I miss knowing you."

My insides squirmed as I stood there listening. I didn't do feelings. Sure I felt them, languished in some, brushed off others, but I didn't *talk* about them. Because some I couldn't put words to. To try was like picking at a scab. Why couldn't he just leave things be?

"I know selling the farm came as a surprise," Dad said, dropping two slices of bread into the toaster. "I never meant for you to find out like that."

"And when was I supposed to find out? When the 'For Sale' sign got nailed to the fence?" Unfair, I knew, but I didn't care. If Dad wanted feelings, I would bloody well give him *feelings*. Angry ones. "This is my home, and you're selling it out from under me. I *know* it's for Nan." I said, cutting him off when he opened his mouth.

He picked at the eggs in the saucepan; they were nowhere near ready. "It's just a house, Em."

Red rag to a bull that was. My fists clenched and hot rage flushed into my cheeks. "It's not just a house. It's everything here. Everything I know and *remember*. And Mum is—" I stopped. A sudden, exhilarating, Goddamn brilliant thought flashed into my head. Mum. Hope bubbled into my chest, tingling down to my fingers. Mum was *here*. And I could see her.

I barrelled out the kitchen.

"Emma!" Dad shouted after me. I ignored him, breathless as I raced down the hall, out the back door and through the yard. Cold earth numbed my toes as I ran up the hill to the Karri tree and its gravestone.

"Mum!" I cried, coming to a stop under its boughs. I searched the hillside, looking for a pale flicker, a glimpse of movement. She had to be here.

But the leaves were still; the grave silent.

"Mum?" The hope that had been building inside me shattered, shards lodging into my heart and chest. I choked, *feelings* I couldn't name gutting me with a thousand cuts. My lips quivered and I swallowed, fighting down the heat in my throat. Be a turtle, I repeated my old mantra: draw in my soft bits and let the world batter my shell with me safe inside. But it wouldn't work, my mind refused to bend like it had four years ago.

I stared at the grave.

Nothing. Not even the wind.

And then the heat rushed up and out, spilling down my cheeks.

#

"Why?" I asked, when Michael appeared beside me an hour later. I sat, leaning against the Karri tree: the bumps and ripples of its trunk dug into my back. The heat inside me had gone, leaving me hollow and dry.

Michael sat down beside me. "I'm not sure. Some stay, some don't."

"Then you've never seen her?"

46

He shook his head. "Never."

I picked up a dry eucalyptus leaf and folded it in my fingers. The leaf bowed and cracked with little splintering sounds. I folded again. *Crack, crack* it went, brittle, dry veins popping.

"What did you mean before?" I asked. "When you first spoke to me."

Michael cocked his head, a see-through frown pulling his brow together.

"About Nan. You said, 'She's close'."

"Oh, that." He stilled and looked up into the Karri's branches, and I had the sense that he saw more than just leaves. "Her time is coming. That's why she can see," he waved at my head, then himself, "you know."

A gumnut-sized lump clogged my throat. "Nan is—" I whispered.

"Dying. Something in her brain. She's known for a while. Years actually. I've been telling her she needs to tell you, but she's adamant she won't."

His words seeped in. And I couldn't respond. All I could do was stare at the grass. "Why?"

Michael sighed, a scowl playing over his face. "Says she doesn't want to be a burden."

"A burden? She's not—"

"I tried telling her that. But you know how she is."

Stubborn as a certain bloody ram I once knew. "How long has she known?"

"She found out just after your Mum."

My stomach clenched. I imagined Nan sitting in a doctor's office in her clashing colours, hearing the news for the first time. Alone while the rest of us dealt with our own grief. And then choosing to remain alone.

I'd thought the heat inside me spent, but its warm prickle returned to the back of my mouth. "Oh Nan." *You didn't need to do that. Didn't need to do it at all.* Michael came and sat beside me, his translucent body brushing against my fleshie one with a cold tingle.

"You've been with her all this time?"

Michael nodded, and I thought I saw a silvery sheen in his eyes. "It's hard, you know, to only ever watch." He toyed with a blade of grass, his hands slipping through the stalk as if grasping air. "Not to be seen, heard or felt. But then they start hearing you, and that's even worse, you know? Because for a heartbeat you hope that soon, maybe, just maybe, you might not be alone anymore." He bit his lip and stilled his teasing of the grass. "I'm a terrible son," he muttered, more to himself than me, and I wondered if I'd judged wrong, whether Michael might be even younger than I'd guessed. Dad had never said how old he was when he'd died.

The ghost of my uncle met my gaze. "She saw me for the first time three weeks ago, looked right at me. That was when I knew she was near."

Silence parted the air between us, even as my heart quivered in my chest. I swallowed and forced out the question I'd been avoiding. "How long?"

Michael held up his palms. "I'm not a doctor, but she's seeing more and more into the Everywhen. A couple of days, a week maybe."

Less than a week and Nan would be gone. My beautiful, dear, kind, and yes, batshit eccentric, grandmother would leave us—*me*. I tried to imagine the farmhouse without the clack of her cane on the floorboards, or the shuffle of her slippers. No faint snores from the recliner chair in the lounge. No gaudy knitwear or yarn-bombed trees in the spring. My ribs grew tight around my lungs.

It was happening all over again. I clenched my fists and stood. "I won't let it."

Michael blinked. "What?"

I turned down the track, determination in my stride as I headed for home.

#

I slapped the dusty file on the table in front of Dad. "You need to take Nan to hospital."

Dad frowned over his afternoon coffee and picked up the file. "What's this?"

It had taken me all day to find it. First waiting until Nan fell asleep so I could go through her things, second to actually think to check the wardrobe. They'd been buried at the back, in an old shoebox.

"Just read it," I said, fidgeting. I couldn't keep my bloody hands still. I shoved them into my pockets and paced. Dad's eyes scanned the first page, then forgot me as they flicked on to the next and the next, taking in the words I'd read earlier. *May experience confusion, disorientation and other dementia-like symptoms.*

The wrinkles on Dad's forehead deepened into crevasses I could have seen from across the room. I waited until he read the line that had stopped me cold. And there it was. A slightly sharper intake of breath and something like fear flashed over his face.

Inoperable.

Dad was still a moment. Then he swallowed. "Where did you get this?"

"I found it. When I was putting Nan's washing away." A lie, yes, so sue me. Bigger things were at stake. "*Please*, take her to hospital."

Dad's glanced back down at the papers.

"Look at the date," I urged. "It's old. They're finding new ways to treat things like this all the time. Sally from school, her mum had bone cancer and they cured her with some new breakthrough or other."

Dad stared at the sheets as if he didn't understand. "She didn't tell me," he whispered. He rubbed his eyes with gritty fingers.

I sat down opposite and squeezed his hands. "Please. Take her."

He squeezed back but didn't move. "I knew it would happen one day, but so soon..."

"Dad," I interrupted. "It's doesn't have to happen, we'll take her to hospital, get some tests. They'll find a way."

He looked at me then, eyes all wet and shiny and sad. Then his arms were around me, hugging me into the smell of sweat and hay and livestock. He kissed my head. "I'll talk to her."

"No! We need—" I writhed out of his hug. "She's not well. Really not well. She needs help."

Dad stared at the papers on the like a man lost at sea watching his ship sail away. First

Michael, then Mum and now Nan. Everyone was leaving him too, surely he understood. I waited for a nod, some sign of approval. Instead, he seemed to sink into himself, broad shoulders hunching in. "It's her choice, Em. We can't force her."

"We can!" I nearly screamed it. And for a heartbeat I was struck with the urge to bow my head and charge at him; tackle him to the ground and shake the sense into him. "Why won't you do anything?! You just sit there and take it! Every time! Why won't you fight for her?!"

"Em—"

"Why didn't you fight for Mum?" This time I did scream, and hot tears turned the world into blobs of shape and colour. I drew a ragged breath, the words rise out of me, ugly and unstoppable; bleeding feeling. "You could have. But you didn't. You just nodded your head: 'Yes, Doctor, I understand Doctor.' Nothing you can't do, bullshit. You could have waited. Could have given her more time. That's all Mum needed. Just a little more time. But you turned off the switch."

The Dad-shaped splotch flinched as if I'd slapped him. Another dragged breath. This time from him. I braced for the retort, for the barbs to come flinging back at me. Instead, nothing.

A brush of liquid fingers at my elbow; cold tingled up my arm. I rounded on Michael. "What?!"

"You're out of time."

#

She lay in bed, a knitted patchwork pulled up to her chin. One arm was exposed; a blood-pressure cuff wrapped above Nan's elbow. Doctor Patel glanced once at the reading, then released the Velcro.

"Keep her comfortable," was all she said.

Dad and I trailed her out to the kitchen. Dad's face still hadn't regained its colour—not in the 24 hours since we'd rushed into Nan's room and found her unconscious on the floor. I fiddled with the pull cord of my hoodie, vaguely aware of my fingers knotting and unknotting the string. Invisible beside me, Michael hovered. Literally. Every now and then the light would catch his translucent flesh-or-whatever and he'd flicker in the corner of my eye, like the halo of a migraine, to my mind.

"Quit that," I muttered, rubbing my eyes. My head felt tight, like Sir Woolston's skull was squeezing my brain between his horns; a final 'fuck you' from the dead ram.

Michael shot me a glare. "She's my family too." He drifted over to Dad, and the two of them peered at Doctor Patel in earnest, both of their expressions mirroring one another in that oddly familial way.

The Doctor met Dad's gaze. "How much did the hospital tell you?"

That her condition was advanced; something about the MRI showing a tumour obstructing her Temporal Lobe—wherever that was—and pressing against her brain stem. And, more to the point, that there was nothing they could do. Dad said as much to Doctor Patel.

She motioned us to the kitchen table. All three of us sat, even Michael; he balanced on the back of one chair like a whisper.

"It's unlikely she'll wake," Patel said. "But if she does, she will be disorientated and probably won't be able to speak." She studied Dad and I in turn, her brown eyes serious behind her glasses, face neutral. "It would be kinder for her if it's not drawn out." For a heartbeat, a reflection of my ram's skull flashed in her glasses. Then it was gone as her attention shifted to Dad. "Pray for it to be quick and painless, if that is something you do."

"It isn't," I cut in.

"Emma—" Dad started.

Patel held up a hand. "It's fine." She studied me again, lingering on my face before her expression softened. God, I hated that look. Pity. I'd had my fill of it after Mum. I shoved my chair back and made to stand, but Dad caught my wrist.

"Em, please." His hand slid into mine, squeezing my fingers tight, like he was scared of losing me. It was just the two of us now after all. The thought was like a knife between the ribs. I swallowed hard and sank back to my seat, my grip tightening around Dad's. From his perch, Michael stared at our hands, a quiet longing in his gaze.

"What do we do when—" Dad stopped, dragged in a breath, and his next words came out husky. "You know."

"Call me. I'll take care of it."

He nodded and laboured to his feet to show her out. The moment they stepped out to the veranda I got up and padded back down the hall, back into Nan's room. She was still there, still wrapped up under the covers, a slight fall and rise of her chest that said she was still with us. I turned to the silvery ghost sitting on the edge of the bed, watching herself sleep. She still wore the blue hospital-issue pyjamas and the canary-yellow cardigan I'd slung over her shoulders when we'd brought her home.

"You need to get back in there," I told her, pointing at Nan's body.

Nan's ghost blinked, coming out of her stupor. Her form was faint, like a washed-out watercolour, but growing stronger every time I looked at her. "What was that?" Her eyes narrowed. "I thought I told you to take off that hat."

Instinctively, I reached for my head and cursed Sir 'fucking' Woolston under my breath when my fingers met nothing but hair. "I can't," I said. "You need to go back."

A bubble of hope grew inside me as she seemed to consider it. "No," she said at last. "It's all achy in there. And it smells funny."

Trust Nan put it like that. I tried again. "You can't stay like this. It's not good for you."

Nan snorted and rocked back on the bed, cracking her ghost knuckles. She wasn't as solid as Michael; some part of her still tethered to her flesh and bone perhaps. "Feels bloody brilliant if you ask me." She rounded on Michael beside me. "What's that look for?"

Michael hesitated, sharing a look with me. Apparently, this was a first for him too. "You're dying, Mum."

Nan stilled, silent a long moment. "About goddamn time," she muttered.

"Nan," I began, motioning to her body in the bed. "Please. Go back."

She jutted out her jaw. "You never knew how to let things go." She grimaced. "Got that from me I suspect." Her green eyes turned on me, and for a heartbeat I was reminded of the ancient fairy sheep in the field, old eyes that had seen more than anything had a right to. But I wasn't about to be lectured by my grandmother with literally one foot in the grave.

"Nan—" I started again.

"No buts," she snapped. "Your tongue is so silver you could mint a year's currency with it. I'm not listening. It's my last day and I'll do as I bloody well like."

I turned to Michael for help. The hint of a smile that had been playing on his face fell away. "You can't force her. Speaker or not."

Of course not, like a curse could never actually be useful. And here I was speaking to the ghosts of my dead uncle and nearly dead grandmother. Like a crazy person. Fuck me. Perhaps I was insane. I ran a hand through my hair. There had to be a way.

Nan jumped up from the bed. "Walk with me," she said, striding to the end of the room in a way I hadn't seen her do in years. When I didn't move to follow, she crooked an eyebrow. "You're going to deny your old Nan her dying wish?"

When she put it like that, I didn't have much choice.

#

Nan's dying wish turned out to be multiple dying wishes. We headed down the drive, onto the bus and into town. Nan's old bingo hall was empty, but she wandered the hall, drifting between imagined sets of tables. We walked down to the seafront, scattering gulls as we approached. Nan leaned out over the jetty railing and sucked in a breath of sea air—or perhaps it was an imitation of breathing, it wasn't like a ghost had lungs.

"I'll miss this place." She pointed to a rusty lamppost at the shore-end of the jetty. "I kissed your grandfather there, you know? That very spot. Eyed him out at the disco I did, brought him down here."

I cocked my head, suspicious. "And was that all you were doing?"

A grin. More gum than tooth.

"Bloody hell, Nan."

Michael laughed. "You scoundrel."

Nan's grin faded as her gaze landed on her dead son; nearly invisible in the midday glare. "I wished so many times you could have more time to love." She hesitated, then cupped a hand to his cheek. "You were so young."

"I knew love, don't you worry." He looked away and I sensed awkwardness between them. Words left unsaid. "I know you didn't like him, but Will was good to me."

Nan quivered, her whole form rippling like someone had cast a stone into a pond. "I was wrong."

Michael took Nan's hand in his own and held it, staring at their clasped fingers—hers wrinkled and curled, his smooth and young, both of them translucent. A flicker of something, an echo of that longing I'd seen in Michael's face before, mixed with relief perhaps, maybe pain. "I know, I heard you," he said, again. "I thought I couldn't forgive for a long time, but then I saw what you did for him. How you'd visit every other day to make sure he was okay. Talked him into finding love again." A small smile. "I saw it all. I found my peace long ago, Mum."

"Then why—" I started and bit my tongue before I could finish the thought aloud. *Why did you stay?* If Mum had moved on, gone into the—what had Michael called it, the Everywhen?—why hadn't he? Unless... *Nan* was the reason Michael had stayed here? The thought pulled in my chest. He had stayed when my Mum had moved on, or whatever dead things did. I wanted to ask, but that was his business, to my mind. So I kept my mouth shut, and let mother and son have their moment. When I looked at Nan again, her ghostly form seemed stronger somehow, more defined. More like Michael. The lump grew warm in my throat and I left them on the jetty, the pair of them looking out to sea like two clouds who might blow away in the wind.

The bus ride back to the farm was a blur. We walked up the driveway—cutting through Sir Woolston's paddock didn't feel right—and when the farmhouse came into sight, tin roof all lit up orange in the sunset, my throat closed. Not yet. I detoured Nan to the barn. She'd always liked animals.

Banjo greeted me at the door with a rasping mewl and rubbed his face against my leg. When Nan crouched to greet him, the tom hissed and bristled as if he might swipe.

I pulled my leg away from the crossfire. "Can he see you?" I asked Michael.

"I don't think so. But he feels us. A lot of animals do."

He was right about that. The horses stamped and nickered to each other when we passed their stalls, and Billy the sheepdog ducked into his kennel at our approach. Even the chickens stayed on the far side of their coop.

"I'm sorry, Nan," I said, expecting some sort of upset, perhaps even frustration. Instead, she wrapped a hand around my own, chilling my fingers numb.

"They understand," she said. "I'm not supposed to be here."

My stomach knotted. *No, not yet.* The skull squeezed my temples, as if it disagreed. Nan tapped my arm. "It's time."

#

"Where have you been?" Dad demanded the moment I walked through the door. He looked distraught, hair dishevelled, his 5 o'clock shadow well on its way to bristle, bags under his eyes. Neither one of us had slept last night—I probably looked much the same come to think of it.

I'd had it in my mind to tell him about his mother and brother's ghosts padding off down the hall—he had a right to know after all, they were his family too. But when I opened my mouth I chickened out. "I ... needed some air." I shoved my hands in my pockets. I should have brought flowers or something. Then, before I knew what was going on, Dad was drawing me into a hug, smoothing my hair.

"I'm sorry, you're here now. That's what matters."

I took a breath; the sweaty, unwashed scent of his shirt filling my nostrils. My stomach cramped. I had to tell him. This was Dad. If I had to tell anyone, it should be him. I swallowed. "Dad, I—" Again I hesitated, not sure how to put it all into words; Sir Woolston's curse, Michael's haunting, Nan's spirit growing more solid every minute. "I think it's soon," I said. *Fucking chicken.*

His hug tightened, and he kissed the top of my head. "I know."

"Michael's with her."

Dad paused, cocking his head. "I didn't think you remembered him."

"I've become... reacquainted."

"You know, I never said anything to Nan as I didn't want to upset her, but every now and then, I get the sense that he's near." He hesitated, a slight tension running through him arms as he held me. "Sometimes your Mum too."

I stiffened and heard the barely audible intake of Dad's breath. *And I never said anything to you, as I didn't want to upset you either.* The words hung unspoken between us. I forced myself to relax; not to let the hope rush up inside me. The skull on my head tightened, the weight of its horns straining my neck, as if Sir Woolston was back in my head, berating me. I bit back a scowl, forced down the disappointment. Mum was gone, I knew that.

"I'm okay," I said, and winced at the lie, "I mean, I'll be okay." I scuffed a shoe. "I'm sorry, about what I said yesterday."

Dad did what Dad did best, he waited. He was good like that. Patient. He never pushed. I'd always figured it had been from working with animals for so long. Maybe it was, maybe it wasn't.

"I know you fought for Mum, in your own way," I said. And it was true. He'd been the one after all who'd found her, rushed her to emergency, clung to her side every minute of every test until the doctors were sure. All I'd been able to do was stare. I hadn't even been able to bring myself to take Mum's hand. I'd just stood and watched, wishing I'd wake up. I'd hated myself for that.

"I wish I could have been like you then," I admitted and felt my throat warm. Fuck I hated feelings, but this needed to be said. "Nan was right. I'm shit at letting things go." I wanted to fight for Mum, for Nan, but sometimes to fight for someone was to know when to stop. Nan had shown me that. It had just taken a while to sink in. "She told me she's ready." I swallowed a gob of spit and unshed tears and went on before my voice broke. "I'm ready now."

Dad held out his hand. "Let's go."

I nodded and took it.

#

Nan's breath was faint; her eyes still under her eyelids, a halo of grey curls around her head. Dad and I sat on vigil, hunched in kitchen chairs pulled up on either side of her bed. Together we watched the rise and fall of her chest, each time thinking, this one would be the last.

And still Nan stayed.

Her ghost sat at the end of the bed again. She was almost solid, the bedframe barely visible through her. Next to her, Michael appeared dull and milky as he held her hand. I cocked my head at him, confused. She'd said it was time, so why was she still here?

He shrugged, helpless. "I don't know."

When I caught ghost-Nan's eye, she glared back. "Don't ask me. Hell if I know."

I rubbed my neck, trying to ease the tension from the skull. It had grown heavier in these last hours, pulling the muscles tight in my neck and pressing around my brow. It was everything I could do not to rest my head on the covers of the bed and close my eyes for a moment's respite. I shifted and massaged my forehead. Wretched curse. When I died, I would give that ram a bloody piece of my mind, or better yet, a boot up the arse for buggering off to the Everywhen and leaving me with a skull trying to squeeze my brain out my ears.

"You okay?" Dad asked.

"Just a headache," I said. Partly true.

"I'll get an Aspirin," he said, rising.

"No, it's fine," I caught his wrist. "Stay, you don't know when..." I trailed off and glanced at Nan. Truth was, I didn't want to be alone when it happened. Not with her ghost right here watching. It didn't seem right to my mind. None of it did, come to think of it. I opened my mouth to say something, anything, and stopped.

Dad was staring at the end of the bed. At Nan. "Mum?" he said. His eyes flicked to the ghost beside her, his lips parting. "Michael?" He went still, as if scared he might frighten his brother away.

Nan's ghost rocked to her feet, her eyes alive. Michael's head snapped up. Dad gaped. "You're..." his voice wobbled, and he stepped towards them, pulling my grip free of his arm. Then he blinked, looking around the room, confused. "Where did they...?"

It couldn't be. I reached out, touched him again, this time on the elbow. Skin to skin. Dad sucked in a breath and his eyes darted from Nan's body under the covers then to her ghost at the foot of the bed. He swallowed, eyes misting. "This is it, isn't it?"

Nan leaned close, pecked a kiss on Dad's cheek. "Not forever," she said. "But until then, yes, this is goodbye." She grinned at him, more gum and teeth, then kissed his other cheek. "Thank you, my boy."

Michael came forward and Dad ogled at him, unable to get any words out. For a moment, I worried Dad might faint. I shouldn't have. This was Dad, he took it all in stride, even as the tears spilled out of him and he choked out something unintelligible.

"I know," Michael said, and hesitated, then clasped Dad's shoulder. "I'll take good care of her. I promise."

And, like that, something in my head gave—a loosening in my neck. A stitch unravelling around my temples; an easing in my lungs, like a breath releasing. My skin prickled, hot and cold flushing through me—the same as that night at the bonfire with Sir Woolston's ghost. Behind, there was a low, finale sigh from the body in the bed. Before us, Nan's ghost shimmered; her glow fading.

I released Dad's arm. "She's gone."

He nodded, mute. Staring at the bed.

Beside me, the two ghosts hovered. One freshly minted, the other old and well-past his time here on Earth.

"Where to now?" Nan asked.

A soft bleat called in my ears. I shivered, the way becoming suddenly clear; pulling in my chest the same way a pigeon always knows true north. I held out one hand to Nan and the other to Michael. "I know a place."

#

I found my way easily enough. When I stepped into Sir Woolston's paddock, felt wet grass under my feet, the land just *shifted*. I walked, the world twisting itself around me in a blur of trees and hills and sky, until I arrived to where I needed to be. Had I not had two ghosts in tow, I don't think I could have done it.

The field was exactly as it had been. But the figures around the bonfire had changed. They'd thrown off their sheep skins, wearing loincloths of hide and fabric instead. They stood taller, lankier than before, horns gone and hair long; their forms mirroring the human spirits before them. All that said, their eyes remained the same, gold and ancient beyond reason. Perhaps that was the way of things here—them shifting to match the dead who found their way here. Maybe it was a comfort thing. Or reassurance.

Nan, Michael and I stood before the fire, its heat buffeting my hair and flaring our shadows long behind us.

"You're sure about this?" Michael asked.

I shrugged. "It's where Sir Woolston went, and he seemed pretty happy about it." I recalled the rush, the freedom roaring in my bones, and was halfway tempted to step into the flames myself. But no, this was for ghosts like Nan and Michael. I might be a Speaker to them, but I wasn't one of them, not yet anyway. Truth be told, I wasn't quite sure what I was.

Michael and Nan exchanged a glance. "We're ready."

"Then jump," I said.

They didn't. Instead, Nan reached for me, cupping my cheek, just as she had with Michael on the jetty half a world away. "Thank you." She wagged a finger at me. "And whatever you do, don't let your Dad sell the farm."

I blinked. With everything else I'd clean forgotten about the sale. Not that we needed to worry about that now. The thought sucker punched the reality home. This was it. I clamped my jaw, in part to gulp the heat of a sob down and partly to stop anything silly from spilling out. I nodded instead.

"Good girl." She took Michael's hand. "Ready?" she asked.

"Ready."

Together, they leapt into the flames. Their woops rang in my ears, and I felt them go; their departure a sudden lightness in my body, like a part of me was drifting up into the smoke with them. I wiped my eyes with a sleeve. *Bastard ram,* I thought, turning for the trees and back the way I'd come. The ancient figures danced around me, their shadows twitching under my feet.

Sir Woolston sure had pulled one last doozy on me. Michael reckoned it was a curse. But I think he was wrong. It was something, but not that. Perhaps a gift, in Sir Woolston's twisted way. A final "got you" from one stubborn git to another.

With a sigh, I stepped back into Sir Woolston's paddock, the world settling into a familiar rusted fence and paint-peeled farmhouse.

Bloody ram always did get me in the end. One way or another.

A TALE OF HEARTS AND HORNS

Sign: Taurus
Element: Earth
Symbol: Bull
Dates: April 20 to May 20

The frost is thick on the plains when the Hunter sets out. Coals from the campfire are long cold and he dons his cloak of goat hide, takes up his spear, and crunches over the icy grass. He walks into the sunrise, eyes searching, first the ground, then the horizon, hoping for a cloven imprint, a pile of dung or a four-legged silhouette outlined in the sun.

He sees nothing. But then, aurochs are not easy to find. The plains are vast—all he's ever known in his short life—running from the boggy marshes and Ur's towering ziggurats in the south to Sippar's wool dynasty in the north.

It's an impossible task he's been set, and he knows it, but proceeds anyway. Because it's for a girl. One he loves—or thinks he does.

Her price: an auroch. A bull for a bride. Her father will accept no less. A man (or a boy in his case) must prove his worth, that he can provide, said her father when he'd asked for her hand.

Of course, he could have gone to the village cow herder; asked Sumat for his best bull and presented it. But the village head wouldn't go trading his daughter for a mere cow. Aurochs are wild creatures, shoulders taller than the boy's head, girth wider than his reach, and with horns that could fit two of him between their tips. Such a prize could buy him a hundred brides across the plains, but he'll settle for just one. Each night he recalls her smooth cheeks, dark in the firelight, soft hair under his fingers, and a flash of white teeth as she leans in, shedding her day-mask of chaste village girl like a snakeskin.

"Wait for me, Ku-aya," he told her before he'd left.

Back in her mask, Ku-aya had not responded, not with her father watching, but just as the Hunter turned to leave, he'd caught the smile and ever-so-slight incline of her head.

So he hunts and hopes, day after day on the plains. His supplies—a water skin and three loaves of hard flatbread are tied in a sack at his waist—dwindling to a trickle and crumbs. If he does not find his prize soon, he'll have to return. Empty handed. The thought quickens his steps as he follows the Blue River, Id-Ugina, eyes scouring the bank for that elusive hoofprint. Each heartbeat he is disappointed. And in the fading dusk, when the skies open and the rain plummets, turning his boots sodden and extremities numb, the Hunter screams at the heavens, cursing the gods. First Enlil for sending the storm, then Utu for not shining longer.

He cannot get his fire started. The ground is wet, wood damp and the kindling green. His stomach rumbles and he throws down his tools, curses again, and wraps himself in his cloak to wait out the night. Only, he doesn't.

A bray, low and soft and almost lost in the patter of rain, reaches him.

The Hunter pauses, breath turning light in his chest, sure he imagined it. But there it is again. A hum on the edge of hearing, like the murmur of an incantation hymn, the kind En priests sing under their breath in the temples. A shiver passes over the Hunter; hairs prickling in the wet as he clutches his spear and trails the sound.

By the light of the moon, he picks his way along the bank. Pauses, listens, takes three steps then pauses again, until a shadow—a bovine head, black on black—shifts in the dim. It stands under a lone cedar tree, head turned windward. A snuff, and the Hunter goes rigid on the bank, imagining those nostrils twitching, catching his scent, then the twin horns lowering to charge. A heartbeat passes, then two. The auroch brays again, stamps once, then heads for the water. The twin horns lower and a gentle lapping reaches the Hunter's ears. Slowly, the Hunter lowers himself into the reeds, forcing stillness lest he startle the beast. His hands twitch around his spear, energy brimming under his skin. He hardly dares breathe. An auroch. An auroch here. For him.

Godsent, it must be.

A sign.

On the bank, the auroch shivers, the sheen of its black fur rippling like the waters of Id-Ugina before it, and the Hunter is transfixed, eyes lingering on the white fur stripe that runs down its muscled neck. Beautiful in its power.

He must have it. His family might be poor, his lands small, but Ku-aya's father can't ignore such an offer, or the status it would bring. The Hunter grins, imagining the look on her father's face when he leads the bull back into his village. Ku-aya's hand is as good as his.

He uncoils the rope from his shoulder, forms a large loop at one end with a sliding knot. He considers the best approach. There's no way he can match the beast's strength. Its shoulder stands taller than he does. He squints at the long legs, far longer than any cow he's ever seen. Those are legs made for running. If it flees, there'll be no catching it.

Out from the reeds he slinks, creeping for the lone cedar further up the bank, holding his breath as he goes. The auroch, nose deep in the water, wallows forward, emitting another contented bray to the night. The Hunter ties one end of his rope around the cedar; tests the knot. It's a good rope, fresh and well made, but now its weave feels thin and flimsy in his sweaty palms. He pokes his spear into the slipknot at the rope's other end and holds it out at length.

With a quick prayer to the gods, he tiptoes down the bank, soundless, easing each foot into place before shifting his weight. So he goes. Ten paces out from the auroch, the beast snorts and shifts its bulk. It's ears twitch. The Hunter stops, caught mid step, sure he's been seen.

With a huff, the auroch shifts again and settles onto its knees in the water, jaw working as it chews its cud.

It's as if the gods are inviting him. Go on, he imagines Enlil calling on the breeze. Take it.

He steals forward; the rope loop dangling at the end of his spear quivers. One step, two. Easy does it. His feet sink into wet sand, cool moisture pricking between his toes. Closer. Closer. He reaches his spear and rope loop out, arching it over the auroch's head like a snake stretching its body from a tree and drops the loop over one horn, then yanks it tight.

The auroch starts, and with a bellow the Hunter feels in his chest, it leaps up from the water, thrashing and bucking, snapping its head this way and that. Eyes bulge in its head: a ring of white around dark irises.

Attached to the cedar tree, the rope snaps taut, pinging a note into the dark like the string of a lyre. The woven strands creak under the strain, and the Hunter braces for the inevitable pop of it tearing in two. But it never comes. The beast kicks; the white eel stripe down its back bunches and writhes. Water sprays the Hunter on the shore. Another bellow.

It happens too suddenly for the Hunter to react. The auroch jumps, twisting and bucking in the air; the rope catches under one hoof. In half a breath, the line is tangled in its legs, knotting around its knees and dragging its head down. Its nose dips the shallows. Muscles flex. The rope digs in, its grip somehow wrapped around the auroch's neck. The beast teeters, grace and beauty gone. Just a panicked animal on the plains.

Then it falls.

From the bank, the Hunter watches it all unfold. The auroch flails, hind hooves running at the air, its two horns the only part of its head above the waterline. Bubbles rise between them. Fast at first, then slower, and slower again. Part of The Hunter's mind is screaming, telling him to take up his knife and cut the rope. But it is a small part. The rest of him watches from a place outside himself, horror locking his muscles still, mind numb.

At last, the twitching stops.

Still the Hunter stands there, stunned. He counts the rush of his heart in his ears until he runs out of numbers he knows. Then his body is moving without him, finally sliding the knife free of its sheath and sawing through the rope. Water presses cold around his calves as he wades in, reaching for the horns.

A small shake. The head so heavy it barely moves.

Nothing.

The Hunter's hand slips into the water and runs along the beast's neck. The fur is wet fur, still warm, but there's no throb of life underneath. Then his fingers meet rope, welted into a ridge in the animal's flesh and he recoils as if burned.

His stomach folds. Nausea rises in his throat. Inexplicable. He's seen death before. Killed before. This should be no different. Yet his hands shake, sweat stings his eyes. He'd not meant to kill it. One auroch eye meets his; the empty stare accusing, robbed of its lively gleam, and the wrongness of it twists the Hunter's stomach.

He stumbles back onto the bank, reaching it just as his stomach heaves.

#

The Hunter forces himself to rest. Rest and see what the morning brings. Perhaps then he can find a way to salvage the situation. The bull is not alive, but perhaps Ku-aya's father might accept a set of auroch horns for above his hearth, the Hunter thinks as he lies under the cedar, staring through its branches to the dark above, trying to ignore the disappointment lying heavy in his belly. If he stripped the carcass, it would feed Ku-aya's and her family for months—was that not providing? But how would he carry it all back with him? The Hunter rolls onto one side, then the other, unable to find comfort. Once he leaves the bull's body, he cannot return. River eels and scavengers would strip the carcass bare in a matter of days. The Hunter tears his hands through the black coils at his brow, stiff with grit and sweat from the plains, and closes his eyes.

A crackle in his ears snaps him awake. Two arm spans away, a fire burns, flames darting around a log set in a hollow of earth dug in the grass. On the other side, two eyes reflect the orange glow, their light dancing in time with the flames.

The Hunter gasps, comes to his knees, and scrabbles for his knife. The eyes shift, the body behind moving into the light to reveal a face—dark skin, angular cheeks, square jaw.

"My bull is dead."

For a moment the Hunter thinks it is a man, but then for a heartbeat, its features appear delicate, almost womanly, and the grey eyes drink him in. They speak again.

"Why did you kill him?"

The Hunter swallows, licks his lips, but his voice doesn't come. It's scurried somewhere down his larynx. The face shifts again, man, woman, man, features never quite settling. This is not the face of his kind. This is something else. At last, his words return. "Who are you?"

The being on the other side the fire cocks their head. Hairs prickle down the Hunter's neck. They look at him the same way a hawk might study the passage of a rat with passing interest, as if wondering whether or not to swoop. "Men call me Inanna."

The Hunter's blood curdles and his eyes turn nightward. The specks above are as cold and hard as the gaze across the fire. Inanna. God of the heavens. A croak rises in his throat before his voice flees again.

Full lips twitch in the shifting face, teeth flash. "You have heard of me then."

The Hunter falls to his knees, bows his head, prostrating himself in the grass. Heavens and stars. A god. And he'd just killed their bull. "I—" He begins, and stops. Something is wrong with his head. It feels heavy; awkward against the earth. His fingers go to his brow, smooth skin meets his touch, but when they travel left and right they each bump against a ridge of something smooth and hard. Something inside the Hunter squeezes, stealing his breath. His fingers trace the ridges up and out, following their steep curve from his head. Horns.

He lurches up with a cry, hands patting his face—nose, still a man's, chin, the same. His hands curl around his ears. They are long, fur soft. His hands travel down, following the softness. His neck is thick, shoulders hunched with the weight of his head. At his chest, he finds smooth skin again and the Hunter knows a moment of relief before he squints at his feet in the dark. Cloven hooves poke from under his *kanauke* skirt. A flash of movement, and the Hunter spots the tufted tail swish between his misshapen knees. He is full auroch from the waist down.

He screams. A bray rushes out his throat, choking into the night. "Please," he begs. "Turn me back."

Inanna's gaze is unsettling as they study him. "I cannot." In the flickering fire, their features shift and change like fish scales in the sun.

The Hunter tries again. "Please..." His chest itches, and he rubs it but can't shake the sense of emptiness underneath his ribs. "It was an accident. Please!"

Inanna lifts a hand, beckons with a finger. The Hunter stumbles forward, awkward and eager, but a hoof-step behind him stops him still. The auroch melts into the firelight, huge beside the Hunter, the muscles in its long legs twitching. And very much alive. It paces past him towards its owner, leaving no prints in its passing. The Hunter ogles at it.

"But I... what," he tries, falters, tries again. "How?"

Inanna strokes the bull's nose. "I used your heart."

Anger flares inside the Hunter, hot as a crafter's kiln. "You stole my heart?"

"You stole my bull."

The Hunter fights for composure; to not scream and wail at the heavens. After all, the god of heaven is here, listening. He swallows, tasting earth on his tongue. "It was an accident." He forces himself to look into those iron eyes. "Please, I'll do anything."

A pause. "Anything?"

Something in the way Inanna says it prickles in the Hunter's chest, itches at his hollow. *Careful,* it warns. He ignores it. "Anything."

Inanna's smile broadens and they rise, a smooth motion, like water flowing upwards, their body a hymn of skin and corded muscle, power and beauty, man and woman. For a moment, the Hunter forgets himself and gapes, then feels a familiar stirring in his loins. He pries his gaze free and stares at the grass.

Ku-aya, think of Ku-aya!

Inanna's feet stop before him, toes curling in the stalks.

"Bring me a new heart," Inanna's voice issues from above. "And I'll swap it for yours." A finger under his chin tilts his head up and into those iron-studded eyes. The hollow inside him twists, an invisible hand clenching around the space that was. "A good heart, Hunter. Strong, full of life. Like for like. I'll accept nothing less."

The Hunter licks his lips. "And when I find it?"

"I will tell you the words to summon me." Inanna whispers the sounds to him in the dark and makes him repeat them back. "Good," they purr and return to the auroch's side. "Good luck, Hunter."

#

He wakes with a start. A dream. Thank the gods, just a dream. He lifts a hand to his head and his fingers knock against one of his horns. His howl sends a flock of larks into the sky.

Not a dream.

His eyes come to rest again on his cloven feet. Just one morning ago, he had toes. His stomach twists and he averts his gaze. He dares not look at his face in the waters of Id-Ugina, but he imagines what he might find there. A misshapen head; auroch's eyes staring out of his own. A sob catches in his throat and comes out as a soft bray on his breath.

A frantic quacking and a beat of wings from the reeds makes him start: a waterfowl taking flight. The Hunter curses, hugs himself, and tries not to stare at the fur on the back of his hands.

He cannot return like this. The village would turn him out. His family too. And Ku-aya... his stomach drops into that empty space inside him, like a stone down empty well. What would Ku-aya think?

A heart for a heart, Inanna had said. How hard could it be? His eyes track the waterfowl above. Too far away now to bring it down with a well-placed stone. Dazed, as if woken from a deep sleep, he gathers his things, hands going through the motions:

62

coiling the rope back into tidy loops, bundling his last scrap of bread into the pouch on his belt and taking his waterskin down to the banks of Id-Ugina.

At the water's edge, where he will not look at his reflection, a soft hiss rises from the reeds. The Hunter stiffens, years of hunting on the plains and more years of stories as a child have attuned him to that sound. He remains still, eyes searching out the source. There. A flicker of a tongue, a glint of eyes watching from between the stalks. A water snake. The Hunter relaxes a little. Not the venomous cobra, or one of the many cantankerous vipers that strike first and ask questions later. No, this snake is smaller, perhaps the length of his arm and half again, hard to tell with it coiled among the reeds, skin a muddy green, eyes bright.

Full of life.

Might it be that simple? The Hunter hesitates.

Only one way to know.

He strikes fast, faster than he ever has before. His future rides on this. His fingers snap around its neck. The snake emits a muffled hiss, before his hand clamps tight. The long body writhes, knotting over itself, around his wrist.

Crouched in the reeds, the Hunter's free hand combs Id-Ugina's shallows, curls around a rock in the water, pulls it up. He lifts the stone high over his head, then swings it down, bashing the snake's skull in. Mud and river silt splatter his chest. The reptile unknots in his grip. Cool blood drips down his palm.

The Hunter staggers to shore, flops to his knees. He lays the limp creature in the grass, pale belly up, and says the summoning words.

One beat passes. Then another.

A trickle of panic stirs in him. Perhaps he said the words wrong. Perhaps he has not presented his offering to Inanna's satisfaction. Quickly, he draws out his knife, slices the snake open, roots inside its miniature ribs like a mole hunting for worms. He plucks the heart free. So small. A pea in his palm. A plum in miniature.

Size doesn't matter. It's the life Inanna wants. He counsels and says the words again.

A breeze tickles the back of The Hunter's neck, stirring his fur on end. The pressure rises into a gust and shakes the leaves of the cedar, creaks the branches. For a moment he swears he hears, with his cursed auroch senses, a distant laugh.

But no god.

Try again, Hunter.

Any life, it seems, will not do.

He buries the snake, whispering an apology to it and Ningizida, god of snakes and the netherworld, as he turns the earth over the broken body. The smell of it follows him up the river as he walks, tasting copper on his tongue.

He kills a gazelle next. He downs it with a well-placed knife, thrown into the herd before they spooked and fled, leaving the injured doe behind. When he cuts it open he finds a fawn in the womb. He offers both hearts to Inanna, lying them side by side on the ground with bloody hands.

They don't come.

He waits for the breeze. But that doesn't come either. The evening is still; hot and sticky in the long light. Strange this, he wonders as he stares at the hearts, a few nights ago he'd been chafing his fingers together to keep them warm.

When he sleeps, he dreams of returning to Ku-aya, whole and a man once more. Together they sneak into the furthest field and lie in the barley, the golden stalks scratching their skin, tickling their thighs.

"What took you so long?" Ku-aya asks when they are done.

The Hunter opens his mouth to answer, but a bray comes out instead. *No, it can't be.* He is whole. He must be whole.

Ku-aya frowns, her eyes search his face, lingering on his head, his ears. She shifts in his arms, her weight pulling backwards. "What's happened to you?"

"It's nothing. It's still me," the Hunter says. He reaches for her. Black fur ropes his fingers. He snatches it away. But too late, she's already seen. Her eyes drop to his legs, spies his hooves, the tail poking out his *kaunake*. She sucks in a breath and worms out of his hold.

The Hunter scrambles after her. "It's alright, I'll find a heart," he says. He catches her wrist, pulls her in. "Ku-aya, please!"

She writhes. He catches her other hand, holds her still. "Please Ku-aya, it's me. It's still me!"

She bites him. Her teeth sink into his arm, driving deep. The Hunter yelps, pain sparking through him. He pulls away. Ku-aya stays still, eyes locked on his, confused and dazed. She coughs. Blood bubbles over her lips. Then her face slackens, the brightness dims in her eyes and they roll into her head.

The Hunter feels a familiar, horrifying warmth drip from his fingers. He looks down.

Ku-aya's heart is clenched in his grip.

#

His scream wakes him. Night greets his return. The fire has burnt low, the gazelle meat strung up like shadows above it. The Hunter gets two breaths in before his stomach turns and he retches. Gazelle meat and river water slop onto the grass. Shaking, he slumps back and curls into himself, waiting for his breath to slow, the tightness in his hollow chest to ease. Ku-aya's last expression comes to him. So shocked and betrayed, her gaze reaching at him, wondering what she did to deserve this.

Is that what you want, Inanna?

64

Cold dread radiates from his gut, spreading through his limbs like venom. *Not her. Please, Inanna.* The cold presses in, sits on his chest and makes it hard to breathe. *Anyone but her.*

As if in answer, the breeze shifts, buffeting the coals and setting the smoked meat swinging.

The cold in his gut vanishes, hot adrenaline taking its place as a new smell reaches him. He rocks to his hooves, quivering, ears twitching in the dark.

And then he hears the voices.

Words rise out of the night. "Abba, someone's out there." The voice is light and unbroken. A boy's. The Hunter can't make him out yet, but he imagines a finger rising and pointing at his smouldering fire. Imagines the horror creep over a young, beardless face at the sight of him.

No! Don't look. He comes to his feet.

"They moved!" The boy says. "Abba, it's a man."

The Hunter feels for his satchel, then his knife. His hand shakes, fingers sweaty on the hilt. *Please, just go away.*

"I see him." The second voice is older, husky from use. It clears phlegm from its throat, then calls: "You, by the fire, what are you doing so far from the Ur road?"

The Ur road? He'd come further south than he'd thought. The Hunter blinks into the night, willing his eyes to focus. Bit by bit, he makes out two figures, one shorter than the other and barely twelve kush away. He can't make out their faces, he reads the apprehension in the taller figure's frame—something in the stiffness of the shoulders.

A waft of livestock meets his nose, then a faint moo. Cows. Behind the figures, a herd of shadows move. The Hunter's breath catches. Could he..? No, Inanna would never accept a cow, no matter how strong or lively. The god has made their wish clear. But what if he offered a *dozen* cows? Could it be enough? Enough to spare Ku-aya?

For Ku-aya, I'll slaughter a hundred.

The wind tickles his ears, ruffles the hair around his horns. Almost as if it approves.

"Sir? Are you lost?"

The Hunter's mind races. A dozen cows. He could do it. Open their jugulars, bleed them on the bank of Id-Ugina, then present their hearts to Inanna on the dawn. But there was the matter of the cowherd and his brood... how to deal with them?

The cowherd is still talking: "The road to Ur is three uš east of here, off the—"

"Abba!" the boy hisses; he's come closer in the dark. They both have.

They stiffen, some intrinsic sense that warns of danger; the Hunter has it too. Or had it. Briefly, he wonders when that changed. No matter. He shifts his weight, his trembling body stilling.

"Now there, stranger," the taller one begins. "Let's not have any trouble. We'll water the cattle then leave you in peace." One arm reaches out, placating. Away from the fire, the Hunter finally makes out his face, it's thin with a trim beard and crowded teeth hang inside his gaping mouth. The boy beside him is thin too, gangly from growing, and he's staring.

"Abba, it's not a man," he says.

A croak rises from the cowherd. He falls to his knees, pulls his kin down beside him and prostrates himself in the grass. "Forgive us, O'Maskim." *Forgive us, demon.*

The Hunter's ears twitch at the word, his stomach tightens. *For Ku-aya.*

"Careful, Abba, there's no trusting them," the boy whispers to his father.

The cowherd cuffs him. "Be silent," and pushes his son's head harder into the earth. "Forgive him, he's not yet learned to weigh his words before speaking."

They've seen. By En and Enlil, they've seen. The Hunter pushes the panic down. He stamps one hoof into the ground beside the man's head, swats his tail. *Let them see.* He weighs his own words carefully, opens his mouth—

"Whatever I can offer in recompense, I'll gladly give," the cowherd blurts, lifting his head.

The Hunter meets his eye, steels his glare, thinking of Inanna's iron gaze. "Your herd."

"My... herd?" the cowherd gapes and the Hunter swings his horned head closer. The man swallows. "All of them?"

"All."

The cowherd stares aghast, like he might argue. He glances up at the horns again, then down to the cloven hooves. His mouth clicks shut. "Please accept our offering, O'Maskim." He bows low into the dirt.

The Hunter nods. "Blessing upon you." Unsure how to conclude the encounter, he brushes a hand over their heads. It feels right, somehow. Their hair tingles under his fingers; charged, like the air before a storm.

He tries not to think about it as the pair turn and flee into night.

#

Twelve cows. Twelve steaming carcasses. Twelve hearts piled before his fire. And Inanna, at last. A wry smile quirks the god's top lip as they survey the corpses. "This is quite the mess you've made."

"You came," The Hunter says, he tries to clean the dry blood crusted onto the back of his hands. "Is it enough?"

Inanna chuckles, voice turning into a two-toned harmony, like two strings of a lyre plucked at once; one note deep, the other high and tittering. "Skies no," they say.

The Hunter throws his knife down to the dirt, bites back a curse that could land him in even worse straits. "How many?" he demands. "How much more?"

Inanna grins. "Just the one heart, dear Hunter."

Just *one*? ... They couldn't mean ... A slow, cold horror slithers into the Hunter's belly, chilling him to the bone. His breath shudders. "No."

"No?" the god arches a thick brow; orange twilight glints off bronze cheekbones and strong, bare shoulders, but the iron eyes remain cold.

The Hunter gathers his courage and straightens his back. "No. I won't kill Ku-aya."

Inanna's lips press together. "Then a demon you'll remain. They're already hunting you, you know."

The Hunter shifts, hooves sucking into the blood-churned earth. "Who?"

"A cowherd and his boy arrived in Ur at noon today, telling a tale of a maskim on the banks of Id-Ugina. A maskim who took their herd but gave them a blessing. I believe the cowherd later won big in Ur's gambling houses."

The Hunter blinks, ears pricking. "He did?" All he'd done was brush a hand to the man's head.

"Indeed." Inanna's wry smile returns, this time with teeth. They lean close to the Hunter's ear, breath tickling his fur, and produce a bronze coin in front of his eyes. A sheaf of wheat glosses one side. "He was murdered for three shekel."

Cold seeps up from the Hunters gut and around his chest. A shiver passes down his legs; his bovine tail gives a nervous flick. *What did I do?* The coin vanishes back into Inanna's *kaunake* wrap and they step away. Their head turns skyward, and for a beat the god's eyes soften to silver.

"Go home, Hunter. See your lover. Claim her heart, before there's nothing left to claim."

He stiffens. "What do you mean?"

"Go home," Inanna says again.

Fear constricts his throat. The Hunter swallows and forces the words out. "Is Ku-aya sick?" He snatches his satchel from the fireside and starts stuffing his supplies into it. "Well?" he demands, wariness forgotten. When the god doesn't answer, he pauses, looks up.

Inanna is gone. He is talking to an empty night.

#

It is dark again when he returns to his village, sulking from shadow to shadow, trying his best to hide his form as he makes his way through the barley fields. Drumbeats thrum the air and the sound pulses in the hollow of his chest. They're celebrating. As he draws closer to the buildings, he picks out more instruments: flute; lyre; *voices*. Not just any old strangers. There, that's Sumat's drunken bellow, Nirah the basket weaver's smooth notes—he listens for one voice in particular, but can't hear her.

Fear puts a spoon to his gut and churns and he hurries up to the first of the mud-brick homes, peering around its wall into the trading square. Feasting tables line the center of the square, piled with fruit, breads, and cooked meats. A wedding feast. Villagers mill in clumps of two and three, talking and laughing as they sip cloudy *sikar* through reed straws. A whiff of the fermented barley brew reaches the Hunter and he licks his lips, longing for a taste. He stamps down on the desire. *Ku-aya first.*

He searches the crowd, eyes darting from group to group, half expecting to see her figure squatting among the children, whispering mischief into their ears. But not this time. The Hunter eyes a group of unmarried girls, wondering if her sharp tongue has got her sent home; it wouldn't be the first time.

When a child runs past, his *kaunake* skirt cradling a mound of dates from the table, the Hunter ducks back behind the wall, the hollow inside him spasming. Not sure whether the thought of being seen or being recognised scares him more, The Hunter swallows, rubs his sweaty hands on his kaunake and, when he's sure the child is long gone, peeks out—

And spots the newlyweds at the head of the square. Something in the bride's posture is off; her straight is back, chin high, shoulders stiff in the same way Ku-aya's went when she spoke about her father—a rare thing, but not unheard of.

"Let's not talk about him," she'd spat the last time, flicking her hair out of her face with a disdainful finger. "And all he cares about is selling me off to a wealthy husband."

In the square, the bride lifts her hand and flicks a stray lock aside.

The Hunter stares, horror building inside him like a scream. Ku-aya. It's *Ku-aya.*

Beside her, a man lounges in the cushions, talking animatedly to a wool trader from Kish. His head is shaved smooth, eyes alight, and there's no mistaking the grin on the groom's face, even from a distance. The Hunter eyes the groom's coiled beard in envy, fingers brushing the feathery bristles on his own chin as he searches his memory for the man's name. He's a wool trader too, out-of-town, but rich; Ku-aya's father had introduced them once in the market—before the Hunter had asked for Ku-aya's hand.

Sin... Sin-nagar? No, Sin-nasir. The merchant talking to him moves off, and Sin-nasir turns to Ku-aya, gesturing at the figs on the table. His gaze lingers on her lips, then the golden leaves of her headdress, and the Hunter catches the raised notes of a question. Ku-aya shakes her head. The groom slumps a little, puts the fig down, his lips drawn tight, as if he'd just taken a mouthful of sour wine. His eyes slide to Ku-aya, inspecting her figure through her kaunake. She senses it and stiffens.

Why are you just sitting there? The Hunter wants to shout at her. This isn't the Ku-aya he knew. Ku-aya did what she wanted, when she wanted. The Hunter fights down panic, and then the urge to charge into the celebration, knock the tables asunder.

What if she does *want this?* The fresh thought bites into him. *No, she mustn't. Look at her up there.*

A scream pierces the gathering. Shrill. Blood-chilling. And *close.*

The Hunter spins and finds the child—the one who'd been stealing dates from the tables, named Ak something, Akim?—standing at the Hunter's back, a pool of urine darkening the earth under him. His mouth is open, eyes snared on the Hunter, colour draining from his face. He screams like he's seen one of his nightmares come to life. Maybe he has.

Silence smothers the celebration. Heads turn, seeking the source of the noise. The Hunter staggers away, plunging back down the dark road. He startles an elderly couple heading back early to their mud-brick home.

They scream. The man faints. And the woman's shouts hound him into the night. "Monster! Maskim! Be gone!"

And the Hunter flees, crashing through the village fields, flattening crops under his hooves until the sounds of the village fade. At the banks of Id-Ugina he falls to his knees, the hollow inside him aching, and tears at his horns as if hoping to rip them out of his head. His fingers dig into the fur at his shoulders, like he might peel it off—just as he does when stripping the hide of a kill. But all he does is draw blood.

When he screams, it comes out as a long, piercing bray.

Not even the wind responds.

#

It is past midnight before the Hunter dares to sneak back—against his better judgment. *She's married now, there's nothing you can do. Ku-aya's heart belongs to Sin-nasir.* But still his hooves carry him across the fields, heading home, heading to Ku-aya. *One last goodbye,* he tells himself. A last goodbye before he goes west into the desert and dooms himself to monsterhood; to do whatever it is maskim do.

Normally, a groom would take his bride back to his own household, but Sin-nasir has no home here. There is only one place they will be.

The Hunter steals back into the streets, wincing at the soft thud-thud of his hooves and tries to time his steps to the wedding drums. He finds the house easily; he knows the way by heart—or by whatever beats inside him. The square, flat-roofed silhouette throws a familiar shadow over the open courtyard of Ku-aya's family home. All the windows are dark, bar one above the open doorway into the courtyard; everyone has vacated into the homes of friends and extended family while Sin-nasir is in town.

The Hunter sinks into the shadows and listens. No sounds, but the faint hiss of a fire in an oil lamp. Certain the newlyweds are not inside, he approaches, stretches to his full height and places a white poppy on the window sill—as he always had. When last he'd left this message, Ku-aya had found him waiting in the street outside and they'd snuck into the fields to eat the poppy seeds together. He slinks back to the edge of the courtyard. All he can do now is hope she sees it.

69

The moon is full and low in the sky when the drums and music stop. Roused by the silence, the Hunter makes sure his form is hidden in the shadow of the wall and waits. Sure enough, footsteps approach the front of the house. One set is heavy, scuffing on the dirt, the other is faint, light on the ground and delicate, each step carefully placed to make minimal sound. The ache in the Hunter's chest squeezes around his ribs: he'd taught her that. *Like a plains cat on the prowl,* he'd once instructed and marvelled at how quickly she'd picked it up.

In the window, the lamp light flickers as figures cross the room.

"Come to bed, my love," Sin-nasir's quiet urging drifts down to the courtyard.

Ku-aya laughs. "Why the rush, dear husband? We have all night." Her words lance a tendril of fear into the Hunter's gut. *Could she really want this?* Her figure appears at the window, hands find the dead flower. It's too dark to make out her expression; the light of the lamp shadows her face. The Hunter fights an exasperated groan and forces himself still. Wait. Patience.

Then Sin-nasir's arms wrap around her and he nuzzles into her neck. "Come to bed," he whispers, drawing her back. For a beat, the light catches Ku-aya's face. It's wooden; the forced smile she wears for her father. She turns on him, fingers wandering up his chest.

"I'm afraid I've drunk far too much sikar," she says. "I need a chamber pot."

The Hunter holds his breath, ears rammed up at the window. Blood rushes in his head. She saw the poppy. She's coming.

Sin-nasir sighs as Ku-aya pulls away from him. "Be quick."

Ku-aya tut-tuts him and pads from the room. The Hunter quivers and swallows, tongue suddenly thick in his mouth. Her feet, barely audible, whisk closer. He anxiously pats his horns, as if trying to smooth them back like errant curls. They stay rigid on his head and he recoils into the dark, stomach writhing. Her silhouette arrives at the door, then steps out. The Hunter struggles for breath, labouring for the right words as she hurries across the courtyard, heading for the street. *Call her name,* he commands his voice, but it doesn't obey. Fear pumps in his ears. *Call her name!* he wills again.

But she'll see, Fear answers, freezing him in place. Fists clench as he batters it down. *CALL HER.*

"Ku-aya!" It comes out as a grunt.

At the street's edge, she pauses and squints into the dark. "Who's there?"

The Hunter clears his throat. "It's me."

Ku-aya's head snaps around, moonlight catching her as hope and uncertainty clash across her face. "You," her voice shakes. She swallows and straightens. "Where have you been? You've been gone for months!"

Months? That's not possible. The Hunter counts the days as far as he is able. Even so, he's sure he's not mistaken. "It's only been a few weeks."

"It's been four months, you swine!" Ku-aya hisses. She takes a blind step towards him in the dark and the Hunter dances back, grimacing at the clump of his hooves on the dirt. Ku-aya's eyes latch onto his shadow and her anger softens. "I thought you were dead. I thought my father's ridiculous request for a bull got you killed. I even wondered whether he might have had a part in it. En and Enlil, he was insufferable when you didn't come back." She huffs, hands going to her hips, but it doesn't disguise the tremor in her arms. "But you're here now, that's what matters. It's not too late." She reaches for him.

"P-Please." The Hunter throws out a hand to ward her away. "Stay there."

Ku-aya frowns, gaze drawn to his fingers and his black, auroch-furred hand. He snatches it back. Her frown deepens into a scowl. "What are you hiding?" She presses in.

"Don't," he stammers. Quick as a viper, her fingers catch his wrist and she reels herself in until they're chest to chest. Gods, her smell, sweet cedar and cypress. He sways, the oil in her hair wicking up his nose, into his lungs and igniting the ache in his crotch. Her hands find his face, cup his cheeks. She leans in—

And stops.

The Hunter's ears twitch as she snatches a breath. Her eyes, pupils wide and black in the dark, travel up, along his horns, then down to his bovine legs. He expects her to scream, or maybe prostrate herself like the cowherd did and beg forgiveness. Ku-aya does neither. She studies him.

From the window, a snore cuts short. Muttering, then Sin-nasir's groggy coos reach them: "Where have you gone, my dearest?"

Ku-aya's grip tightens around the Hunter's arms. Rage flashes across her face, before she relaxes again. "Just a little longer, husband," she calls. "Lady's business." A grumble responds, but a beat later, another snore rises over the sill. Ku-aya pulls the Hunter to the edge of the courtyard. "En and Enlil, what happened?" she whispers.

He doesn't know where to begin. The story comes out in a jumble. Inanna, the auroch, something about a snake, the cowherd and his boy, his search for a heart, Inanna's demand it be hers. Ku-aya listens, saying nothing until he runs out of words.

"A heart, you say?" she says when he is done. She sits beside him on the wall, fingers lacing with his. She strokes the back of his hand, sending a tingle down his arm. The Hunter nods, stomach knotting. He shouldn't have come here. Not on her wedding night.

"Well, I can't go giving you mine," Ku-aya reasons. She puzzles a moment, dark brows knitting before her eyes snap to his. "You love me, don't you?"

"Always."

She smiles; a secret smile, one she uses when she knows something he doesn't. "Then wait here."

Ku-aya detaches herself from him, the air turning cool at the Hunter's side as she crosses the courtyard and over the threshold of her home. The Hunter starts after her; she shoots him a warning glance. He stills.

"I won't be long," she says. For a beat the dark drinks her in, then she is gone.

He strains his ears, for what he's not sure. His tail gives a nervous swish under his *kanauke*. How far away is dawn? He can't stay much longer. *Shouldn't* stay. This is a far longer goodbye than—

A shout rips from the window: male, loud. Sin-nasir. The Hunter freezes. She's been discovered. There's a grunt, the sounds of two bodies struggling. Then a squeal, like a hen's screech under an axe. Something heavy thuds to the floor. Gasping. Gurgling.

"Ku-aya!" The Hunter is on his feet, blundering through the doorway before he can think. The room is dark, his horns catch on something hanging from the ceiling. Herbs. He thrashes through, scattering dried leaves. Up the stairs. Hooves clatter, slip-sliding for purchase. "Ku-aya!" He barrels into the room.

She's hunched over Sin-nasir. One glance and the Hunter knows he's dead. Blood pools under the body, thick and steaming; it cloys up the Hunter's nose as he draws close. A grinding, grating sound emanates from Ku-aya. Cold spreads down the Hunter's throat, clutching at his hollow. He takes a step, then two, until he can see her fully.

Straddled over her husband, she saws at his exposed ribs with a bronze kitchen knife. A rib cracks, followed by the pop of another and she pulls his rib cage open like a bloody flower.

The Hunter stares, transfixed, unable to move, not even look away.

Ku-aya's hand slides between the bones, her knife flashing deep. Once, twice, half a dozen times. Then she pulls, slowly, bit by careful bit and draws out Sin-nasir's heart. The Hunter chokes down a cry, like it's his heart she's ripping out. Ku-aya, his dear, clever, mischievous Ku-aya. *Why?*

"You've been going about it all wrong," she says, and a smile crooks her lips.

The Hunter tastes copper in the air. Her sweet cedar and cypress scent is gone. His hollow aches; he fights down tears. "... I have?"

Ku-aya paces towards him. Heart cupped in her palms as if presenting a gift. "You've been trying to retrieve your old heart," she says, and he tries not to look at the red flecks on her cheeks. "But instead, you just need to take a new one."

The Hunter quivers. "But my heart—"

Her expression hardens. "Is gone. It's in Inanna's hands now."

"But they said—"

"Gods and their games," she spits. "Do you think you'll really get it back?"

Not unless I trade it for yours. The words whisper through his thoughts, rising the hairs on his neck before he shoves them down. *Never.* Not to Ku-aya. Not even now.

"Did Inanna say you couldn't replace your heart with another's?"

The Hunter thinks back, shakes his head.

Ku-aya pushes Sin-nasir's heart at him, red dribbling down her fingers. "Then take it."

Still he hesitates.

"Do you want to be whole or not?" she asks. "Do you want to be a man again?"

He nods and she places the heart in his hands. It's still warm. He stares at it. His lover's heart or this. Either way, he becomes a monster—this time for real. His eyes find Ku-aya standing opposite in the dark, red ugliness soaking her front. The hollow wrenches in his chest, like a pet monkey banging at the bars of its cage. He can't leave her. The village will kill her for this—and she knows it. He closes his eyes and bites back a sob. "What do I do?"

"Eat it."

He bites it like an apple; forcing his flat teeth through the muscle, tearing a chunk free. It's chewy, with a slightly gamey taste. He tries to swallow quickly, get it over with, but chokes and nearly vomits before he gets it down.

Something at the back of his mind is screaming. Sweat beads at his forehead.

The next bite is easier. He goes slower, it's easier to chew; his teeth are sharper. By the third bite, his skin itches; his legs feel oddly hot. He doesn't look. Bite, chew, swallow. And again. His belly fills, nausea rising inside him.

"Keep going," Ku-aya urges. "It's working."

At the last bite, his gut is squirming. He's so full he can hardly breathe. His chest is heavy, head light; sweat slicks his neck. One gulp and the last lump slides down his throat. He's panting, hands shaking. And feels a heart thud in his chest for the first time in weeks.

He turns his hands over. Smooth skin. He feels for his horns, only to find gritty curls instead. A glance at his feet as he swoons. Toes. He has toes! "Ku-aya, it worked!"

"I know, I see it!"

A slow clap sounds from the window.

They spin, Inanna sits on the sill, long legs crossed under the god like one of the great cats—apex predator of the plains. "Well played, Hunter." They rise and circle Ku-aya, one moment chest bare and proud as an Ur warrior, the next all sultry curves— and then both at once. Briefly, the Hunter wrestles with the duality of it. But then, what does it matter? He was a man *and* an auroch, and Inanna is a god. An entity of the stars. Man, woman, human, monster, such rigid concepts are trivial to them. Perhaps humanity could learn something from their example.

Inanna pads to a stop before Ku-aya. "I see why he likes you." They grin, but their iron eyes are as distant as the Heaven they come from.

Ku-aya's bloody fingers clench into fists. "He's cured now. You have no hold over him," she says. If the Hunter didn't know her so well, he might not have noticed the quiver in her voice.

Inanna chuckles. "I'll give you this one, little snake."

Ku-aya blinks, even more uncertain. "Just like that?"

"It is not every day you surprise a god." Their gaze drops to Sin-nasir, dead on the floor. "Best not linger long," Inanna warns and turns for the window, muscles flexing as if they might spread their arms and take flight. "Take better care of this heart, Hunter." Their eyes fall on Ku-aya, pausing for a long heartbeat. "Be careful who you give this one to."

#

The pair walk into the dawn, putting the village behind them. They carry little; he can hunt what they need on the plains. She bears a small sack of supplies and stolen jewellery to sell once they reach Ur. It should buy them passage across the sea. Passage to a place where no one knows them or has heard of a god named Inanna.

And yet, as they walk towards a new life together, the Hunter can't help but wonder, *If not for Inanna, would we have dared this road at all?*

Behind, their shadows stretch across the fields. When they reach the river, one shadow twitches, as if each throwing off a cloak. The other follows in turn. As one, they reach for the other, their darkness tangling. Their owners walk on, oblivious. In their wake, the shadows writhe, combining into a single mass. Its shoulders hunch, legs deform. The last thing to change is its head: it elongates and grows a set of horns.

Across the plains, the breeze sighs, then chuckles.

Good luck, Hunter.

WE WHO REMAIN

Sign: Gemini
Element: Air
Symbol: The twins
Dates: May 21 to June 21

Part One.

I knew something was wrong the moment Kieran opened the old chest freezer.

His shoulders stiffened. Breath hitched in a strangled gasp.

And he promptly slammed the lid shut.

From across Mum's dilapidated laundry, I crooked an eyebrow. "What's got into you?"

My brother's right hand twitched—a quick flex and shake of his fingers. A nervous tick he'd had ever since we were kids. Being his twin, I knew exactly what he'd do next: he turned to me. "Kirsty, there's a body."

Not 'hey, you should see this...' or 'um, you won't believe what I found...' No, he just launched straight in there. Because I was the 'fix it' twin, and being the fix it twin came with certain responsibilities—namely, not freaking the fuck out. So, I stepped around Mum's haphazard stacks of tinned beans and tomatoes on the laundry floor, over the bolt cutters Kieran had used to break the freezer's lock, opened the lid, and peered in.

My insides shrivelled.

A body. In all its freezer-burned glory.

At first glance, it was more a crusty, ice-caked human hand lying innocently between the packaged mystery meats. But as I stared, the outline of hips, shoulders, and head became apparent in the rise and fall of the frozen produce. A single frost-covered eye peered out from behind a bag of peas.

A body.

In my dead mother's freezer.

A small, distant part of my brain welled with the urge to scream. Recoil. Maybe hurl. Instead, what came out was, "Fucking hell."

Can't say it was the *last* thing I'd expected. The ancient chest freezer had been locked for years. We'd always assumed it contained Mum's booze stash, and both of us refused to touch the stuff. But on the list of things that Kieran and I could have found inside, a corpse was near the bottom. Well, near-*ish*. I rubbed the scar on my chin, forged aged ten at the hand of Mum and a gin bottle.

A lanky shadow fell in beside mine; my twin had found his cojones again and peered into the freezer next to me.

"Is it terrible that I don't feel as surprised as I should?" he asked, his fingers working the broken padlock he still held.

You'd know better than me, you're the one who stuck around, I thought but didn't say. He'd stayed, I'd left. No point arguing about it anymore. Mum was gone and now we had to clean up her mess. If the house hadn't been worth a pretty penny, I would have said burn it to the ground.

"We'll have to report it." I lifted a hand to massage the growing migraine at my temple. "Don't touch anything else."

Kieran nodded along, like he always did, gaze searching the laundry as if taking mental stock of where he'd been cleaning. Then he cleared his throat and surprised me with an actual idea. "What if we... uh, buried it in the yard?" His blue eyes darted to mine, then away again. He sank onto the drier and ran a hand over his unshaven chin. The un-tanned band of a missing wedding ring stared up at me from his fourth finger. "A body means an investigation, which means we might not be able to sell the house straight away." He scratched his head, probably trying to hide the tick in his fingers. "And I could really use the money. Rent's expensive, y'know?"

I squashed the overwhelming urge to shake sense into him. Hard. "No, Kieran, we can't. That's obstruction of justice. It's a seven-year jail term. Don't you even think it."

He held up both hands in surrender. "All right, all right. Call it in." A bit of dandruff floated down to land next to a stain on the t-shirt he'd been wearing for the last two days.

Would it kill him to at least pretend he had his shit together?

I unlocked my phone and dialled, then listened to the line buzz in my ear. This would put a dent in my plans to be back in the city for Monday, but it couldn't be helped. My head gave another throb, and I longed to crawl out of the light, close my eyes, and drift off in the dark.

Instead, the line picked up.

"Yes, I'd like to report a dead body."

#

"She wasn't all bad," Kieran said from one of Mum's musty couch chairs as he flipped through a photo album.

It'd been one day since we'd found the body. I sat on a chair opposite my twin, a cup of truly awful instant coffee in hand as I watched the police forensics come and go, ducking under the fluttering crime tape across the laundry threshold. *Crime scene. Do not cross.* I scowled at the tape. Any hope of quick sale was long gone. Hell, we'd be lucky to sell the house at all.

What the police hoped to find, I wasn't sure. The body had been old, I'd heard one forensic say. Thirty years, another had guesstimated when they'd managed to thaw the ice around the body enough to see more of it and assess its decomposition. They'd carted it off not long after.

Kieran held up the photo album. "See?" He tapped a finger on a picture of us down at the beach. Three, maybe four years old at most. All sun hats and wide smiles. It tickled a faint memory in the back of my mind. I groped after it, trying to bring it into the fore. No good, my childhood memories were notoriously flaky.

"It's your brain trying to forget," my therapist had explained once. *"A coping mechanism."*

With a sigh, I focused on the picture and the grin on Mum's face, searching the crinkle around her eyes for a hint of deception or tell of what was to come, and found none. The Mum I remembered wore a scowl; she'd worn it in death too when I'd identified her body in the hospital morgue. But here, in this photograph, Mum was... not pretty— she'd never been that—but happy. It was like staring at someone else. A stranger.

Kieran flipped the album's page and pointed at another photograph. This one of Mum standing outside the sign for NOVA labs, her white lab coat stark against the red-brick entrance and eucalypts in the background. "She looks so young." And she did. Scarcely past twenty, I'd bet. This time Mum's expression was cultivated, drawn into a tight-lipped, almost embarrassed smile. A scrawl beside it read, *NOVA, March 1987.*

"I wonder who took this?" Kieran mused.

"Colleague probably."

My twin cocked his head, thoughtful. "Perhaps Dad did."

We'd never met the man. Gone from the scene before we could remember, but he'd been a fellow lab tech with Mum. Bernie No-Last-Name. We'd never been able to pry that out of Mum. Not that it stopped us from trying to track him down in our teens—to no avail.

Kieran turned the final page of the album and jumped when a loose photo slid out from one of the album's back pockets and landed in his lap. Frowning, he picked it up. I leaned forward, squinting at the same messy scrawl on the photo's back: *NOVA, Dark Matter Accelerator, 2 November 1990. First successful test.* Kieran flipped the photo around, revealing Mum standing on a scaffold platform before the mouth of a vast tunnel. Wires, panels, and metal tubing ran from the tunnel's opening like the trapping of a cybernetic funnel web. At the heart of it all, Mum smiled. Grinned, actually.

The hairs on my arms prickled. This time, I recognised the smile, fleeting though my experience was of it. The one that didn't go to her eyes. Patently slapped on like gaudy lipstick. Part of the mask she wore to pass for normal.

"Put it away," I told Kieran. With one last look at the image, he did so, slipping it into the back of our half-perused photo album.

Someone cleared their throat behind us, snapping my attention up and to the lounge doorway. A plainclothes policeman stood on the threshold holding a manila folder.

"Is this a bad time?" he asked.

"No, er, no." I rose, wiping my clammy palms on my jeans. *Damn your creepy photos, Mum.* Kieran stayed where he was, blinking stupidly up at the cop as if he was stoned, which, it occurred to me, he could well be. "What can we do for you..?"

"Detective Constable Rob Nguyen." He held out a hand.

"Kirsty," I said, taking it and nudging Kieran into action when he didn't move. "My brother, Kieran," I introduced without thinking, then cursed myself. Kieran might be a deadbeat two-time divorcee, but he had survived on his own without me. Survived Mum. He didn't need me doing his introductions.

At the guilty twinge in my chest, I pressed on, "We were the ones who found the body. Is there anything you can tell us?"

DC Nguyen's dark eyes studied first myself then Kieran, calculating and weighing us both. I knew the look. My therapist used it when debating whether to tell me something I wouldn't like, as if worried I might break—or explode. A flicker of anger stirred inside me. I hadn't made it through eighteen years with Mum and not built up a bit of grit.

I folded my arms. "What is it?"

DC Nguyen handed me a piece of paper from his manila folder. "My condolences."

I glanced over it once. Preliminary medical examiner report. Most of it was incomprehensible jargon but for a few clear lines:

Sex: Female

Age: Unknown

Probable cause of death: Blunt force trauma to head (autopsy to confirm).

All within reason, except for the note at the end of the page.

Fingerprints confirm deceased as Dr. Roza Hackett (DNA test to confirm).

Mum's name. Wordlessly, I handed the paper to Kieran.

"You're mistaken," I told Nguyen. "Our mother died a week ago."

Nguyen's eyebrow quirked, just a little. "We're aware." He tapped the top of the paper in Kieran's hand. "Your mother's fingerprints are on file from... previous misdemeanours. Along with her death certificate. So, you can imagine the confusion when our Jane Doe's prints came back as a match for your mother..." His quirked eyebrow rose another millimetre as he let the unspoken question hang in the air.

I scowled. "It obviously can't be Mum," I said. "If you're hoping for an explanation, you're out of luck." *Your lab screwed up,* was what I wanted to say, but instead I opted for: "Are you sure the body wasn't contaminated? She was in Mum's freezer. For a while, as I understand it."

"Forensics took the prints and ran them twice. Positive match both times."

I shook my head. "I'm sorry, but I can't explain it for you."

"I can," Kieran said and held the paper out to Nguyen. "Mum had a twin." He said it like it was obvious. And, of course, it was. Twins had very similar fingerprints—DNA too. Kieran and I had spent a chunk of our formative years Googling everything about twins. As a fraternal twin, I had about fifty percent of the same DNA as Kieran. Identical twins could be much, *much* higher, and their fingerprints could be as close as a ninety-five percent match. More than enough to fool a crime lab.

Only, Mum had never, *ever* hinted at having anything so much as a sister, let alone a twin.

What the hell, Mum?

But it did make sense and Nguyen was nodding.

"We came to the same conclusion," he said. "Do you know your mother's extended family well? Any aunts, uncles? Parents?"

Together, Kieran and I shook our heads.

"It was only ever Mum and us," I said.

DC Nguyen's expression didn't show disappointment, but it was clear in the droop of his shoulders. "Very well then." He fished in his pocket and produced two business cards, handing one first to me, then Kieran. "If you think of—"

He stopped as Kieran reached for the proffered card. Only then did I notice that Kieran's traitorous photo album had let slip one of Mum's photos to the floor. The one of her grinning before the entrance of NOVA's labs. Mum beamed up at us, oblivious to the surprise on DC Nguyen's face.

"She worked at NOVA?"

Key word: worked, the thought sneered through my head as Nguyen scooped up the photo and examined it.

"Thirty years ago," I told him. "She was involved in a workplace incident. Assaulted another scientist. They sacked her." Everything had gone to shit after that.

The detective's gaze roved the photo, drinking it in. "We've had a lot of complaints regarding previous employees," he said. But he sounded distracted, like the photo had set the cogs whirring in his head.

"Such as?" I prompted, trying not to sound too interested.

Nguyen blinked, as if coming back to himself, and scowled. "I can't go into details. Part of a larger case."

A larger case? Does he mean against NOVA? I'd always thought Mum's bad behaviour had been her taking the loss of her job out on us—back before the alcoholism had started. But what if there'd been more to it?

"Did NOVA do something to its employees?" I demanded.

Nguyen gave me a hapless shrug. "I can't—"

"Go into details. Got it." I snapped and pinched the bridge of my nose where a fresh migraine was starting.

Nguyen cleared his throat. "I'm sorry," he said at last. He handed the photo back to Kieran and gestured to the business cards he'd handed us earlier. "My number's on the card if you find anything else."

We watched him pace down the hall, floorboards creaking as he went.

Kieran sank back onto the couch with a huff. "Like a bull in a china shop. You haven't changed at all." He flipped open the photo album and shoved the photo back inside.

I arched an eyebrow. "Oh, and I suppose *you* would have handled it better? How many joints have you smoked today?"

Kieran's gaze slid along the floor, following the worn edge of Mum's faded Persian rug. "I don't—I'm not using anymore. I stopped after Mel said it was... you know, over." He picked at a callous on his palm and the silence grew between us.

NOVA labs might have killed Mum's empathy, but she'd been the one to beat it out of me. I was a cold bitch. Emotionally absent, my therapist had explained. Had been for as long as I could remember—except when it came to my twin.

Without really registering it, I sank into the couch beside Kieran. It was an old thing, the kind of couch that folded you in half inside its cushions. I clasped my hands around my knees to stop myself sinking and focused on my mouth to shape the word I hated most of all.

"Sorry." The urge to grit my teeth and clamp my jaw shut rose. I battered it down and took a breath. *Say it.* "About Mel. I should have been there for you." I wasn't sure how much of it I believed. Perhaps about half. But it was half more than I'd cared for before I'd started therapy. Baby steps.

Kieran sat there, quiet as always, whether in stunned silence at my apology or brooding, I couldn't tell. Not until his lip gave the faintest twitch of a smile. "Maybe you've changed a little." He fiddled with the corner of the photo album, then heaved a sigh. "I'm trying to be better. Really. Truly." Another twitch of a smile. "Been channelling a bit of you actually. Copying some of that confidence you got from law school, you know?"

It was my turn to sigh. "Don't. I'm a terrible role model."

Part Two.

My phone rang at eight a.m. Far too early. I fumbled for it, heard the *clunk* as it tumbled off the motel bedside table. Swearing under my breath, I roped it up by its charger cord and answered.

Kieran's voice issued across the line. "An estate attorney just rang about Mum's will."

It took a moment for the news to sink in. "She had a will?" The Mum I'd known had never been that organised.

There was a murmur of assent from my twin, then he gave a strangled clearing of his throat. "The uh, attorney said I'm, um, the sole beneficiary." There was an audible swallow on the line. "Mum left me everything."

She what? A flicker of irritation ignited in my chest. Not because she'd cut me out—I was the one who'd gone non-contact after all—but because this was exactly the type of shit I'd come to expect from her. Mum hadn't cared about anyone, but she'd always liked drama. Perhaps she'd thought this would finally drive a wedge between us.

"Bitch," I breathed down the line, then remembered Kieran. "Not you." I paused, then added. "You deserve it."

And he did. Where I'd moved across the state and into the city to get out from under her, Kieran had moved to the next town. He'd visited every weekend to pick up the bottles and run a load of laundry. He'd sent cards and taken her out on Mother's Day and Christmas. For the life of me, I'd never understood why.

"House, money, whatever, I don't want it." I reassured.

Kieran gave a rueful laugh. "The house is probably not worth the land it's on now." His laugh turned into a sigh. "The attorney said Mum left an envelope at their office with a copy of her will. They've had it for years, apparently, so who knows what it's about. But she's on her way over to drop it off. I think you should be here when I open it." He paused, then went on, softer still. "I want you to be here, Kiz."

The fire in my belly brought on by Mum's gall sputtered and went out. Bloody Kieran always knew exactly how to talk me down.

"I'll text you the address." There was an awkward pause on the line. "New flat since Mel and I... you know. In the big apartment block. Can't miss it."

My phone buzzed as the message came through. I glanced at it. Did a quick mental map.

"I'll be there in thirty."

#

The stains on the envelope might have been coffee. Might have been something worse. It sat on the breakfast bar of Kieran's studio flat, leaning against a stack of unwashed cereal bowls. A photocopy of Mum's will lay folded underneath it.

"It's date stamped," Kieran said, sheepishly removing the bowls and putting them into the sink. He pushed the envelope and photocopied will towards me as I sunk onto a stool.

I noted the thickness of the envelope and the slight bulge at its bottom. I ran my fingers around the edges. Some kind of book perhaps? I flipped the envelope over. Sure enough, the date was there below the seal, black ink stark against the orange paper, like one of those old school stamps librarians used to have.

2 September 1992. Kieran and I would have been two going on three then. And the envelope was still sealed, untouched for all that time. I set it down and unfolded the will. Standard fare. Kieran's name printed as executor and sole beneficiary. I glanced at the date and frowned. Same day. *2 September 1992.*

Well, that stings a bit. I'd assumed her cutting me out had been a recent decision.

I went back to the envelope.

"You sure you want me to open this?" I asked. "It's addressed to you."

"I'd rather it wasn't."

I cast Kieran an exasperated look, and found him scrubbing the bowls in his sink and stacking them on the draining board with far too much interest. Couldn't say I blamed him. Who knew what Mum had put inside. Probably something cruel. I fought the urge to hurl the envelope out Kieran's fourth story window and be done with it.

Instead, I took a breath, then another. My fingers relaxed around the paper. This was for Kieran. Logic said the contents would be for him too. All the better I open it. If it was bad, he didn't have to know.

I grabbed a knife and shoved it under the flap. Upended the contents onto the bar.

A clatter, a thud, and final a swish of paper. I cocked my head, saw Kieran do the same from his spot by the sink in our eerie twin synchronicity. A bulky watch lay on the engineered stone, along with a leather journal and a folded note.

Frowning, I snatched up the note and opened it.

Don't let anyone at NOVA have this. Especially if I *ask for it.*

My confusion deepened as I picked up the watch and turned it over in my hands. Rather than a flat glass screen, the watch's face was shaped in a half-bubble, like someone had slapped a miniature snow globe onto a Velcro wrist band. Unlike a watch, there was no one to twelve in a circle. No digital numbers or hour and minute hands. Just a swirl of velvet black dust and a button emitting a green light on one side.

I handed it over to Kieran to inspect.

"What is it?" He tapped the glass dome. The black inside shivered and swirled, coming awake like a fish startled by a tap on its glass tank.

Snow globe was not far-off, I thought as the dust settled. I grabbed the cracked leather journal that had come out of the envelope with the watch and opened it.

12 January 1990, NOVA

We did it! The collider works, but the results are... what's the best way of phrasing this? Perplexing? Unexpected? Unprecedented?

Let's go with that last one. Makes us sound like we know what's going on.

Bernie says I need to keep my own records—he doesn't fully trust NOVA won't bury this or give the credit to someone else. Says he's seen them do it before. So here we are. Hello journal.

Our experiment was to prove the existence of dark matter. Only, the readings were coming back wrong. I was tasked with finding out why. Turned out to be both good news and bad.

The good: we discovered a new particle. Celebration. Much excitement!

The bad: it interferes with all our <u>other</u> readings. Boo! No more dark matter experiment.

We're calling it the Gemini Particle—two-faced thing that it is.

Sorry, I should probably explain how the collider works...

Despite Mum's best attempt, my eyes glazed over words like 'lead-ion collision' and 'particle detectors'. As I understood it, they beamed particles through a long tunnel and smashed them together. Somewhere, somehow, that was supposed to help prove the existence of dark matter. I skimmed the rest of the page as she listed out the various tests and recalibrations her team did. The Gemini Particle kept appearing. A most vexing problem—until things went sideways.

It was the thunderstorm, she wrote.

Forecast said it was supposed to pass fifty kilometres south of us. It didn't. By the time it was overhead, we were already mid test. Best I can guess, we got an extra jolt from a strike to our power station. The collider is only supposed to draw two hundred megawatts, but this time it got more. About 100,000 megawatts more. Whole lab blacked out.

When the power came back on again, there it was, in the detector's beam pipe where we'd been monitoring collisions.

A tear. A crack.

Just a tiny one. A hairline fracture in reality.

Paper thin and barely a meter long, it bent light around it. Looked a bit like one of those carnival funhouse mirrors.

We were beside ourselves. Spent more than a good amount of time in panic mode, I'll admit. Scanning, rescanning, rebooting systems and running safe checks. My nerves were a mess the whole time, all I could think about was the newspaper headline: 'Scientists Tear Hole in Universe'. Of course, now I realise that was silly. There's no way NOVA's PR team would let that happen.

We were halfway through our sixth safety check when our security guard's radio crackled, and a distorted female voice issued from it: "Hello? Does anybody copy?"

We all exchanged a glance; all our security staff were male.

"Perhaps a trucker gone off road in the storm?" Bernie suggested. He gave our security guard a nudge. "Go on, they might need help."

"Copy received," our guard replied, clearly confused. "Identify yourself. This is a military channel, over."

"This is Dr. Roza Hackett. Senior Physicist at NOVA, over."

Everyone looked at me. I'd said nothing. Not even touched a radio. I hadn't even moved.

The guard scowled. Probably thought it was a couple of kids taking the piss. "Identify yourself," he growled into the receiver. "You are not Dr. Hackett. She is standing right next to me, over."

The radio gave a couple more unintelligible bursts of static then fell silent. We waited. Waited until I thought that was the end of it. Prank over. Kids gone home.

With another crackle, the voice returned—clearer and alarmingly more like mine, "I am also called Dr. Roza Hackett..."

There was a long pause.

"I think I'm talking to you from another universe," she said.

She was right.

We'd found another universe.

But it was more than that.

We see binary systems a lot across science. Biology, ecology, astrophysics. Point is, they're everywhere, and waaaay more common that we think. We have binary DNA. We get binary stars and binary asteroids. So why not binary universes?

That's what we found. Our binary.

I put the journal down. A laugh caught in my throat. "Jesus Christ, Mum." This had to be a trick. And still my eyes were drawn along her finely curled cursive.

It's almost identical to ours. We named it Pollux.

Nope, no, not a chance. I slammed the journal shut, making Kieran jump.

At his questioning look I huffed and passed him the journal.

"Obviously, she's lying," I said as Kieran turned the page and crooked his head when he reached the binary universe line. "Or was trying her hand at science fiction."

"Then why the note?" Kieran asked, motioning to the slip of unfolded paper on his breakfast bar: *Don't let anyone at NOVA have this. Especially if I ask for it.*

Why indeed. I picked up the watch he'd abandoned on the drainage board and turned it over, half hoping to find an inscription on the flat of the watch back or inside the band. Nothing. Though, there was a ring of reddish brown in the groove that ran around the watch's circumference. Blood? Surely not. Then again, this belonged to a woman who'd hidden a body in her freezer for thirty years.

Kieran was thumbing through the journal pages at a time. "I'm not seeing any mention of a watch," he said. "Pass it here."

"Hold on a sec, let me look," I jerked my hand away in annoyance when he reached for it. Not quick enough. His fingers brushed the dial, thumbnail catching the rim of the button. With a faint *ping* the button popped clean off. A spring came out with it. He swore, grabbing after the tiny button and spring like they were a bar of soap. Caught them on their third bounce across the breakfast bar.

"Careful, dipshit!" I snarled and regretted my tone as Kieran flinched.

"Sorry," we said to each other in unison. The synchronicity made me want to swear at him again. Instead, I placed the watch before us on the breakfast bar.

"I have smaller fingers," I said. "You hold it while I try to screw it back in."

We crowded over it, heads pressed together as we tried to figure out how to fix the thing.

"Was the light blinking like that before?" Kieran asked as I shoved the spring back into the button's hole and rammed the button back on.

He was right. The steady green light was now blinking. It flashed faster and faster, speeding up with every blink, like a camera's timer counting down to the flash. Blink... Blink.. Blink. Blink-blink-blink. My stomach clenched in sudden warning.

"Kieran—"

The watch pulsed under my fingers. A shock ran through my body, something between a static jolt and the burn from a hit to the funny bone. I staggered against the breakfast bar as Kieran yanked his hand away, hissing under his breath and shaking his fingers.

"Thing packs a punch—" he stopped, hand frozen in mid-air as he stared at his kitchen, face growing paler and paler.

I righted myself and scowled at the line of grime the kitchen counter had smeared across my shirt. "Fuck's sake." Then I frowned. A second ago, Kieran's breakfast bar had been the clean, dappled white of engineered stone. Now, it was smeared in mud and soot.

What in the—

I followed Kieran's stare across the kitchen, a knot growing in my stomach as I took in the dust, the scorch marks on the ceiling, and the open hole in the wall where his cabinetry should have been. Swallowing, I squelched across the mud-covered floor to get a better look at the ruin outside.

A town sprawled below us. But not the one we knew. Roofs were collapsed, fences tumbled, whole houses vanished under ivy and scrub. Black vines wound through the streets, fat tubers as thick as a person undulated over the sidewalks and wrapped around fallen lampposts as if they'd constricted the life out of them.

The whole scene was eerily quiet. Not a soul as far as we could see. Not even a bird call.

A wasteland.

A footstep at my back and Kieran was beside me, gazing down at the sight below. He coughed, cleared his throat, then gave a breathless: "Where are we?"

Not in Kansas anymore, that's for sure. I followed the black vines through the cracked and potholed roads. Same grid pattern. A faded street sign, its letters just legible through the dust, was strangely familiar. Same streets. I'd turned left down it to get to Kieran's block of flats not fifteen minutes ago. I glanced at the journal gripped in my hand and the floor shifted under me again as my head went light.

Binary universes.

"Holy—"

"Kirsty, the floor!" Kieran's voice rose over my stunned silence. He'd no sooner spoken when the muddy vinyl shifted by my left shoe. Something *wriggly.* I snatched my foot up, half expecting a rat, or maybe some big fuck off spider, but no. Just a vine. No thicker than my little finger.

It writhed through the dirt, its foremost shoot questing for my sneaker. I traced its shape through the mud and opened a grimy sink cupboard. The vine curled under the sink and over the S-bend of the drain and was clumped against the powerpoint for Kieran's dishwasher.

Weird. I crouched to examine it. Rather than smooth, its surface was fuzzy. Velvety. I itched to poke a finger into it, but didn't quite have the courage. *Don't go touching shit in fucked up binary universes.* That had to be a rule somewhere.

"Kirsty!" Kieran hissed, skirting around the vine with a scuff of his slippers. He pulled at my shirt. *"The floor!"*

Belatedly his words sunk in, and I swung my attention from the strange vine to the rest of the kitchen floor. *All* of it was moving. Vines popping up everywhere to stretch themselves towards us. Subtle. Slow. Like the first twitch from a Venus fly trap. My gut clenched. I shuffled back, pulling Kieran with me. First it was Mum's creepy photos. Next her batshit crazy journal. Now we'd moved on to unnerving—from the least likely source of unnerving I could think of. A damn plant. And yet instinct drummed inside me to not let those questing vines touch us.

"You think they're carnivorous?" Kieran wondered aloud as we edged closer to the hole in the wall.

Really, Kieran? Now you get curious? I shuffled back another step.

A cupboard banged behind me, and I sensed him rummaging. "If this is universe is anything like mine, then—Yes!" He straightened, fire extinguisher in his hands. He shot me a questioning look, as if seeking permission.

I shrugged. Worth a shot.

Kieran snapped the seal and sent a spray of foam across the writhing floor. The vines recoiled, shrivelling up into themselves as if he'd set a blowtorch to them. Relief pooled in my stomach. Thank fuck.

"We should go," I said, skirting around the vines towards the front door, Mum's journal and watch tight in my grip as I went.

My twin didn't argue. Just followed.

The elevator was out of order. Not that we'd risk it. Stairs instead. Down and down in looping floors. Not many vines here, just tiny tendrils of them concentrated around the busted lamp fittings. At the bottom, we reconvened.

I held the watch in my palm as we crouched over it. The light was blinking red. Blinking was good, right? Time to get out of here and figure the rest out later. Back home. In the right bloody universe. I gripped Kieran's hand in my free one and mashed down the button.

No pulse. No funny-bone tingle through my muscles.

The watch emitted a loud beep then, in a new kind of beyond-the-grave creepy, spoke in a digitised version of Mum's voice:

"Gemini Particles depleted. Please recharge."

"You have got to be kidding." It took everything I had not to kick the stairwell's rickety exit door clean off its rusted hinges.

Kieran sagged onto the stairs. "We're stuck here?"

I growled under my breath. "Absolutely not." I jammed down the watch button again. Same response. Turned the watch over in my hands, and for the first time, noticed the black swirl inside its dome was gone. Beside me Kieran opened the journal on his lap and began searching its pages. Still in a pair of fluffy-white house slippers, he looked even more useless than usual.

"Must be something in here," he said, opening to a fresh entry and reading aloud while I examined the watch.

21 January 1990, NOVA, Castor

The probe made it! Bernie says of course it did. The project had two Dr. Roza's working on it for nine days straight. Even so, the mind does boggle.

There's a way through. Holy freaking Moses!

We knew from our radio transmissions that the Tear led directly into the other universe. We also knew the Tear could transmit radio waves from one universe to the other. But the real question, was whether matter could make it through too—and still function on the other side.

So we packed up a camcorder, instructions on how to use it (this was another universe after all) and sealed it inside an aluminium box.

I shot my twin an exasperated look. "Get to the point."

Kieran scowled. "Blame Mum, she wrote it!"

"Ugh, fine. Keep reading."

No sooner than ten minutes after we pushed the box through the Tear (that was an experience and a half, let me tell you; turns out our little rent in reality is remarkably flexible!) we got our first glimpse of Pollux.

Their lab was almost identical to ours. Different colour wiring, a different brand of lab chairs, but so much the same.

Next step. Living matter.

He finished reading and I pursed my lips. It might explain a few things, but it didn't help our current predicament. "Look for more about the substance inside. Gemini Particles or whatever she called them," I said, trying to pry off the watch's back for the umpteenth time. What we might do if I got into the watch, we never found out. Because from his spot on the bottom step of the stairwell, Kieran stiffened.

"Look," he whispered, pointing at the broken lamp screwed into the brick. The string-like vines clustered around it were wriggling, inching their way down the wall and in our direction.

"They're drawn to us." He said it so utterly non-plussed I wondered if he'd lied about not smoking anymore. At last, a frown creased his forehead, and he flicked through the journal's pages. "But why?"

I harried him to his feet. "Perhaps it's just a species of invasive plant in this universe." *This universe.* Saying it felt strange. Wrong. It made my stomach do weird things I didn't like.

My twin shook his head as I pushed him through the stairwell door and out onto the street. More vines. Thicker vines. Drat it. We'd have to keep moving.

"Look at this. At what it was." Kieran motioned to his neighbour's lopsided fence. "The housing, the streets, they're identical."

"Almost identical," I said, pulling him past the street sign I'd spotted from the hole in his kitchen wall. This close, I could make out the subtle difference. Here they called it Casrial Road instead of Casrial Street. "Same, same but different."

He frowned and glanced at the journal again. "You're right."

"Obviously."

We continued for several more minutes, me following the mental map in my head; him trailing after me with his head in a book. Journal. Whatever.

"Don't fall behind, Kieran," I warned, then grimaced at the old and familiar words. Same warning I'd used when we used to walk to school. I'd looked out for my twin—but I was also Mum's kid. Stick with me or fend for yourself. That was the rule.

"Where are we going?" he asked.

"To NOVA," I said, not realising our destination myself until I'd spoken it out aloud. "Or whatever this universe calls it." The memory of my old town's crowning feature rose in my mind: a hexagonal dome behind a barbed wire fence. "They'll have answers there."

Kieran gave the empty houses a pointed look. "If anyone's even there. This place is a ghost town."

"That doesn't mean NOVA is. The next town up the road is probably alive and thriving."

Part Three.

The next town was not alive and thriving. Night had long fallen by the time we reached its outskirts, our feet blistered and aching. It had been a tedious journey. Stepping over vines as thick as people. Detouring around ones that were too big to jump over. Neither one of us had said anything, but the vines were definitely more numerous here. As if they converged on the place.

Or led from it.

With the image of vines creeping their way across the countryside, we holed ourselves up in an abandoned junkyard on the edge of town. A rundown house with peeling paint served as our abode. Not a single light switch in sight, just a fireplace and a broken gas lantern, which made me breathe all the easier. After seeing vine after vine coiled around streetlights, clumped against transformers, and swarmed around a service station's shop, it was clear the things were attracted to electricity.

"Energy," Kieran had corrected when I'd pointed out a temple of vines around what must have once been a power relay station. He'd flipped back a page in the journal. *"They're attracted to anything that emits energy. Electricity is just the most readily available."*

"Then why are they still here?" I'd asked. "Power's out. Everything's dead."

My twin shrugged. "Vines are pretty thick here. Would take a lot of energy for them to move like they do, so they've probably gone dormant." He'd inspected a vine as wide as my middle running along the side of the road. "Maybe they're all lying in wait for food to come along, like funnel web spiders do."

His words had sent an unfamiliar chill through me. So much so I didn't dare light a fire once we tucked ourselves up on the dusty couch in the junk house. I was just wondering if I could risk pulling out my phone to see if I could get a GPS on where we were—assuming GPS and my phone even worked in this universe—when Kieran placed the journal into my lap.

"You should read it," he said. "All of it." It wasn't that he was uncharacteristically serious, Kieran was often that, it was the way he looked at me. Searching my features as if they were somehow new to him.

I rubbed at the ache at my brow. "Maybe later."

"Read it now," he insisted. "Please, it's important."

"The light's going." I motioned to the sun sinking below the cracked windowpanes.

With a huff, Kieran fished out his phone and tapped its torch on. "Last vine I saw was on the main road over a kay back. I think we're good." He handed it to me, then sat down and watched. Waiting for me to start.

I rolled my eyes. "Fine." I snatched the phone off him, wincing as my head pounded with the beginnings of a fresh migraine. "Keep a look out just in case."

15 February 1990, NOVA, Castor

Ten tests. Ten dead lab rats. In under a month no less. That must be a new record for us. There's something about the Tear and living matter that's incompatible. We've tried sedation. Tried jacking them up on adrenaline. Tried sealing them in a lead box. Sealing them in plexiglass. Nothing works. They're all dead the moment they pass from this universe to Pollux. The answer is in how we shield them. It has to be.

The Tear emits very low radiation—nothing more than anyone would experience on a plane trip—and Gemini Particles. It's pumping them into our lab like some binary universe aircon. The lab is covered in them. Health and Safety have us wearing hazmat suits every time we enter the lab, with full scrub down procedures when we exit.

The solution to shielding our rats has something to do with Gemini Particles. My gut tells me so, even if my brain doesn't know why.

For the time being, Dr. Roza-Pollux and I have been exchanging stories over the radio, comparing our childhoods and formative years to understand our similarities and differences. What's funny is we're both with Bernie, only over there, Bernie is currently on a six-month secondment in Melbourne.

I remember my Bernie going for that job. He didn't get it.

20 May 1990, NOVA, Castor

Solution found. I can't believe it took us this long. At first, we thought the rats were being exposed to <u>too many</u> Gemini Particles as they went through the Tear. But it's the opposite; they're exposed to <u>too little</u>. The particles are our proverbial shield. They are our lead box/plexiglass equivalent to stopping whatever it is about the Tear that kills our rats.

The next question is finding a way to collect enough particles and ensuring our rats carry them through the Tear.

In other news, Health and Safety are talking about running more tests on the Tear. They're worried about the amount of Gemini Particles it's producing. As if we hadn't already run every test imaginable!

I paused at the end of the entry, lifting one dubious eyebrow at Kieran. He wasn't perturbed. Just gestured at the journal.

"Keep reading."

With a sigh I readjusted the phone's torch and turned the page.

25 June 1990, NOVA, Castor

Bad news today. Despite our safety protocols, the Gemini Particles are no longer isolated to our lab. They're everywhere at NOVA. In the air we breathe. The tea we drink. Health and Safety are freaking out. They're worried about what exposure will do. All projects related to the Tear are on hold. The lab is sealed off and the rest of the facility undergoing a purge.

Thankfully, we still have radio communication with Pollux. What's curious is they're not reading the same level of Gemini Particles over there. The "stream" (that's what we're calling it here) is one way. My theory is the space-time rupture happened on our side first—by a millionth of a millionth of a second. But that might as well be eons when we're talking quantum physics. Had it been the other way, Pollux would be the ones with their lab locked down.

For now, I've sent all our data to Pollux. We might be on hold, but they are under no such restrictions.

31 August 1990, NOVA, Castor

She bloody well did it. The most astonishing bit? She managed it in just a few weeks! Part of me is a bit jealous she cracked it, but in a way, she is me. More or less. I'm sure I'd have figured it out if I'd been in her shoes.

Our lab monitoring equipment detected a new probe coming through the Tear this morning. The Gemini Particles always give a little spike before something physical comes through from Pollux. So, as usual, I hazmatted it up to go inside the lab and retrieve it. It was a probe, but not the usual kind. This one was small and brown. For all the world it looked like a taped up cardboard box. Then I was close enough to see it wasn't like a cardboard box, it was one. Back inside the lab, Bernie and I opened our parcel. A watch lay bundled up inside, Styrofoam packaging rustled around it as we pulled it free to examine it. Underneath it was a note.

Press the button to start charging and leave somewhere with high concentration of Gemini Particles, *it read. Then underneath in parenthesis.* (Give it time. It might take a while.)

So that's what we did. It took a long while to charge. We left it in the lab for a whole week. Sure enough, over the course of the week, a simmer start to build up inside the watch's domed face. On the seventh day, I arrived at work to find the light on the watch's side shining a solid green.

"Now what?" I wondered aloud to Bernie.

He shrugged. "Put it on a rat and send it through," he said, and reached for my radio to notify Pollux of our plan.

Twenty minutes later, I was carrying a white lab rat inside a plexiglass box into the detector's chamber—once again in hazmat suit. Outside the Tear, I opened the box, strapped the watch around the rat's middle, and pressed the watch's button on the rat's back, then prepared to shove the whole box through the Tear.

Only I didn't need to. The rat gave a squeak of surprise, an odd shiver that turned its hairs on end, and vanished. Poof! Gone. Like a bloody magician's trick. Leaving me standing before the Tear with an empty box with a couple of rat droppings rolling about in it.

A heartbeat later, the radio on my belt buzzed. "Successful transmission, Castor." Dr Roza-Pollux's voice—my voice—issued from the receiver, positively bouncing with excitement. "I repeat, successful transmission!"

One day I'll write a paper on the intricacies of how it works, but in essence, Pollux built us a Gemini Particle magnet. A proverbial carrot on a stick those little suckers can't resist.

The catch? The watch needs to be here in Castor to collect enough Gemini Particles to work. We're the universe with the high concentration. In theory, a watch on Pollux could collect enough particles, but would take years. Decades even. Here on Castor, it's days. So that's what we're working to. One watch to travel to Pollux. One to travel home. We've already put in our order with Pollux. They'll send a set of watches through the Tear; we'll charge them up. Divide and conquer. How's that for cross-collaboration? Take that HR. Bernie and I are going to be the first humans to visit another universe. Assuming Bernie even wants to come, he's been real crabby of late. I think it's the workload; he's been putting in crazy hours. I tried talking to him about it, but ... you know what, never mind, I'm sure it's nothing. Besides, there's a trip to Pollux to look forward to now! (Note to self: arrange babysitter).

I'm particularly interested in testing the range of the watches in proximity to the Tear. Do you have to be standing close to the Tear or can you blip from one universe to the other from your living room? So many things to trial, I can't wait!

All that remains is getting Health and Safety over the line. God help us.

I put the journal down on my lap and released a long breath, trying to wrap my head around it all. If my day had not already involved being sucked into another universe and chased by energy-sucking vines I would have thrown the book across the room and cussed Mum every which way and backwards. Actually, I still wanted to do that. Desperately wanted to. But we were in another universe, and it was dark outside, and I needed to keep my shit together because, holy fuck, we were in another universe. A half-crazed laugh bubbled up my throat. I couldn't help it.

Kieran was still watching, probably thinking I was having some kind of psychotic break. His fingers fidgeted his lap as he waited.

My laugh died. "You want me to keep going?"

He nodded.

The lump that had been growing in my gut hardened into a rock. "There's more?"

He gave me a grim smile that turned my hairs on end. "There's more."

29 September 1990, NOVA, Castor

We did it. A month of pushing that Health and Safety boulder uphill, we got there. New decontamination installations. New safety protocols. Dozens of forms. Signatures. Doctor's approvals. The lab is open again.

We're going.

My gaze snapped up to Kieran as a vision of the frozen body in Mum's freezer flashed through my head. "Is this when—"

"No, keep going."

2 November 1990, NOVA, Pollux

Pollux is...not what I expected.

And it is.

I've been anticipating this trip for weeks. Imagined it like an upcoming holiday to somewhere far away and exotic. But now that I'm here, it's just... so familiar. Yet at the same time, it's not. Small changes, some almost imperceptible, keep reminding me that this is not my world. Dr Wyndham has a moustache. Pollux's Ms Baumer has a birthmark above her right eye that ours does not. My lab tech, Dr Mizushima, is Dr Okumura here; they never married.

And the me of this universe? We're almost the same, but for a couple of infinitesimal differences. Different haircut, a scar from an old graze on her elbow she said was from coming off her bike in her teens. A freckle in one eye. A mole on her cheek.

Psychologists have a term called Uncanny Valley. It's where a robot or a doll looks too human but at the same time not human enough. People find it unsettling; familiar and frightening all at once. This is like that, but on a larger scale. An uncanny universe. Like being outside the world rather than part of it.

Had Pollux been vastly different, perhaps this sense of uncanniness would be less.

Roza-Pollux has a unique take on it. She reckons it's not the likeness of Pollux to Castor that unsettles me, but that my purpose—the 'role' I fill in the universe—is already taken. By her. Turns out this other version of me got an extra helping of spirituality. In a weird way it makes sense. In this universe, the theory of relativity was not discovered by Einstein, but by David Hilbert. Nonetheless it was discovered. Roza-Pollux claimed it was Hilbert's role to discover it here, while in Castor it was Einstein's. She cited a bunch of other histories where events match, but the people involved were different.

"That our lives happen to match so completely is a stroke of uncanniness," she said.

Each to their own, I suppose.

In all, it was an uneventful trip. I suppose that's a good thing.

Note to self: Now we have lab access again, tell the techs to do a deep clean. It's been unkept for months and it's starting to show. When we came out, there was mould on the accelerator's wiring and computer terminals. Mould! Of course, Bernie tried to clean it himself to spare the techs, but that stuff needs proper chemicals and a scrubbing brush, or it'll keep coming back.

Uncanny universe.

Can't deny how those words sent a prickle down my spine. *Like being outside the world rather than part of it.* I knew that feeling. That sense of unbelonging. I'd felt that all through my teens. I'd chalked it up to angst and raging hormones coupled with Mum's deterioration. But what if it hadn't been? *What if—* Gooseflesh spread over my arms, and I turned over the page, searching for more.

5 November 1991, NOVA, Castor

It's hard to believe it's been a year since I first stepped into Pollux. Things have been, hectic to say the least. I'd almost forgotten about you, Journal. Sorry. I'm going to have to back fill later but, for now, know that this entry marks an important occasion.

Roza-Pollux visited Castor for the first time today.

It's taken nearly a year to convince her to come; my other me is much more cautious. It's been good to return the hospitality. Though, I suspect she felt the same discomfort as I did on my first trip. I assured her it eases with more crossings and time. But I couldn't bring myself to tell her it never fades completely.

Of course, she asked how I was doing since the breakup... since Bernie. (God, it hurts just to write his name. But I can't help it. It's like picking at a scab.) Her Bernie never came back from his secondment, so I suppose she knows better than most how I feel. All the same, I wish she hadn't asked. Her Bernie hadn't changed. She hadn't witnessed something shift inside the man she loved. Hadn't been beaten black and blue. She hadn't had to get a court order to keep him away. Didn't have to delete the HUNDREDS of voicemails and text messages from him demanding she let him see his child.

Most of all, she doesn't have to answer Kirsty's constant 'When is Daddy coming home?' questions.

Even now, it doesn't feel real.

In the end, Roza-Pollux's visit was a comfort, even if some of her questions weren't. We speak a lot over the radio. Even more on my trips to Pollux. This trip has involved a lot of late nights in the lab, sharing a bottle (okay bottles) of wine. She always asks after Kirsty, and I about Kieran. Being a single parent is hard, and she gets it. Is it weird to have a best friend that's also yourself? Hate to think what that says about either of us. But you know what? Screw what people think.

Note to self: order hospital-grade disinfectant. Damn mould is back with vengeance.

Holy, fucking... *fuck*! I stared at the journal. Read the entry again. Next to me, Kieran stiffened, sensing the part I'd reached and the revelation in its paragraphs.

She always asks after Kirsty, and I about Kieran.

I read the line again. Then a third and fourth time.

What the actual—

My twin. Only my twice-divorced, can't-hold-down-a-job, doormat of a brother wasn't my twin. He was another version of *me*. The journal slipped from my hands, and I stared into space, mind spinning. My brother was not my brother. My brother was me. He and I were the same person.

Almost.

I clung to that thought. Held it tight. I was not my brother. Our 'roles', as Rosa-Pollux had theorised, were not—could not—be the same.

I was a success. *I* had a job. A career. A house. Okay, townhouse.

I'd fought for what I'd wanted.

I had got away from Mum.

Kieran shifted, not meeting my gaze. "There's more after that," he said, stooping to pick up the journal that had slumped to the floor of the junk house. "I haven't finished it, but I thought we could read the rest togeth—"

I snapped up a finger, migraine flaring afresh at my temples after sitting still for so long. "No, and don't you dare read it aloud. My mind has no more room for fucked up shit right now."

My twin—the male me, Pollux me... yea no, that creeped me out more; I was going to stick with twin—he shut his mouth, paused, as if thinking it over, then nodded. *How the hell was he so calm?*

"Tomorrow then."

So, we slept. Or tried to. Squeezing two adults onto one lumpy sofa is not a recipe for comfort in any universe, and the bombshell from Mum's journal kept me awake well into the early hours.

Through it all, three questions kept spinning around in my head in time with my pulsing headache. Which Mum had we buried last week? Which Mum had been in the freezer?

And who had been the cuckoo in the nest, Kieran or me?

Part Four.

I would have liked to say that when I did sleep, it was deep and dreamless, with the kind of slow waking reserved for Saturday mornings, combined with the aroma of coffee from the neighbours. It was anything but. Sleep, when it did come, was light and on high alert; trained into me from living with Mum. Waking was not slow either, but a sudden lurching upright, tripping over my feet and then the sofa as the junk house door swung in and the barrel of a gun thrust in our faces.

This was how Kieran and I learned we were not alone in the universe. At least, not in this one. And the aroma that met us was not so much coffee but B.O.

"Clear. They're human." the lead gunman said. "Apologies for the surprise." He lowered his gun and stepped away, giving us space to stumble to our feet. The two gunmen at his back followed his lead, though I couldn't help but notice these two kept their fingers resting on their triggers.

"I'm Sergeant Nguyen," the lead gunman rifled through his pockets, and handed us each some sort of freeze-dried protein bar. "Our instruments picked you up yesterday, but it took us a while to reach you."

"Your instruments?" I asked, trying not to stare at this universe's version of DC Nguyen. Less clean shaven. A scar on his cheek. Older by at least twenty years, which was weird. And yep, that was his odour de Homo Sapien filling the room. Lovely.

"We detected a surge in particle energy." Nguyen said, waving my question away. "But before I answer any more questions, answer mine: did you touch any vines?"

Confused, I shook my head. "What does—"

"No," Kieran said. "We didn't."

"Didn't brush against one with your clothes?" Nguyen went on. "It's fine if you have," he added quickly. "We'll just need to destroy your clothes."

"No," Kieran answered for us again. *Weird seeing him do that.* He paused, gaze dropping to his decidedly less white and less fluffy slippers. "Except for our shoes."

"We'll deal with those later," Nguyen assured. "But first, there's someone who wants to meet you."

One of the gun-bros stuck his head out the door and motioned to someone else outside. Footsteps scraped across the veranda and a shadow passed next to the window, the panes too grimy to make out more than a figure. Tall but stooped in the shoulders—someone older, who'd probably spent too much time hunched over a desk.

If it's a Mum from a third universe I'm going to lose my shit.

It wasn't Mum.

He stood in the ramshackle doorway, green army fatigues and grey hair going wispy. But unmistakable. He had Kieran all over him. Looking at him was like looking at my twin—no, the male *me* from another universe—aged seventy years. Same eyes, same nose, same jaw. The only difference between them was a smattering of freckles on this old man's cheeks and his height. He was taller than Kieran by half a head, even with his stoop.

But it wasn't Kieran he looked at. It was me.

"God damn," he breathed. "You look just like her."

My mouth opened. Closed. Of all the ways I'd imagined meeting Dad, this particular scenario had never crossed my mind. I opened my mouth again, forcing words out.

"You're Bernie," I said, dumbly, and my insides wanted to curdle. *Well done, Captain obvious.*

His gaze switched to Kieran, then back to me. He swallowed, nodded, and we watched with growing horror as his face crumpled, tears welling under the hand he'd pressed against his eyes. "Yeah," he croaked.

"Which one?" Kieran demanded. "The one who beat the shit out of Mum or the one who ran?"

"Kieran!" I rounded on my twin. *And people called me the cold bitch.* He really was taking this whole channelling me thing seriously.

"No, it's fine," Dad said, wiping a snotty hand on his fatigues, and drew in a shaky breath. "I'm Bernie Pollux." He swallowed. "The one who ran."

That meant he wasn't *my* dad. He was Kieran's. I glanced at my twin, waiting to see if he'd put two and two together. From his carefully impassive expression, I guessed he had. Which had to mean—

"This is Pollux?" I spoke the realisation aloud.

Bernie shook his head. "This is Castor."

Kieran and I twinned again, tilting our heads to the left in sync, neither one of us understanding.

"I've been trapped on this side of the Tear a long time," Bernie said. He pointed at the watch I'd strapped to my wrist for safe keeping while I'd slept. "That was once mine. The Roza from Castor—*your* mother—" that part he directed pointedly at me "she stole it from me and fled to Pollux."

#

All in all, it was a simple story. Okay, perhaps not simple, but not difficult to follow. While Bernie-Castor became a wife beater in this universe, Bernie-Pollux had been on secondment in his own world. Or rather, selling the discovery of the binary universe to a NOVA labs competitor.

"I made a terrible mistake," Bernie admitted.

Too right you did, I thought, but said nothing. The message had already sunk in without my input.

"The money was too good to turn down," he explained from the wobbly dining room chair Nguyen had fished out to give the old man a place to sit while he told his story. "I gave them everything I knew. But they were never able to replicate the Tear. Breaking through to a binary universe requires effort from both sides. That the Tear happened at all was one in a million-billion chance. More than."

According to Bernie, what they did succeed in was recreating Roza-Pollux's watch. They produced a handful and sold them back to NOVA. For half the price—and access to the Tear. If NOVA hadn't already been hounding Roza to produce more watches, they'd probably have sued.

"My Roza, Pollux's Roza, was furious. Didn't want anything to do with me after that," Bernie said. "We worked separate shifts. Roza and NOVA took the day, Pinnacle Labs and I did the nights. But by then, things were starting to go wrong in Castor." He gestured into the air. "I was part of a team sent across to try and help fix it. Didn't work. Some were killed, some died. Some made it back, some were trapped here when their watches broke or were stolen."

Kieran had nodded at that, clearly understanding something I didn't. In another universe, I might have forced the issue out of him, but Bernie's words pulled at my thoughts. What had he meant by 'some were killed, some died'? I was about to open my mouth and ask when Kieran jumped in.

"Why didn't you build another watch to go home? Clearly, you know how."

There he went again. *What has gotten into him?* I gave my twin a glance; he'd come alive in a way I'd never seen before. Like he'd woken up from a dream. And here I was desperately trying to stay afloat in this nightmare.

Bernie gave a wry grin. "Ah, well, there's the rub." He ran a hand over the two-day bristle on his chin. "Of course, I tried. But you need substances from *both* universes to make it work. Pollux's machinery. Castor's Gemini Particles. We used to make the watches in Pollux then send them through the Tear to charge up here on Castor. It was a good system until Pollux's bass got wind of the outbreak on Castor and shut it down. By then, I was already here.

"And then Mum stole your watch and escaped to Pollux." I finished.

Bernie nodded. "She did. Pollux refused to send another watch."

Kieran gaped. "So they, what, *marooned* you here?"

"Contamination protocol. Said they'd sent more watches through once the Gemini outbreak on Castor was contained." He scowled at the memory. "You can see how that went."

At my raised eyebrow and Kieran's frown he went on. "'Watch' is not really the right term for what that device is." He motioned to the machine on my wrist. "Compass is more accurate. Only it works between universes. Without something from Pollux to tell it which way is true it can't take you anywhere." He looked between us again, gaze fixing on Kieran and turning bright and teary in a way that made my muscles tense.

"By the time I realised my predicament my team had burned, lost or discarded what we'd brought over with us. It's almost impossible to build a new watch without Pollux materials."

Until we showed up. The realisation hit me full force. No wonder Bernie's armed escort of us—or rather, the armed escort of the watch on my wrist. This wasn't a rescue mission. This was a retrieval. I glanced down at the watch and had to stop the urge to hide it from sight. A night in Castor had refilled its particles somewhat, a small velvety dust pile had gathered inside the dome. But the light on its side still blinked red. Relief puddled in my legs. Still time. For all we knew, that was the only reason why they hadn't swept in and taken the watch from us.

A hiss of static on Sergeant Nguyen's radio made Kieran and I jump. "Movement on the perimeter," came the warning from the receiver. Nguyen sighed and straightened. "Best we walk and talk. It's not a good idea to stay so still this close to ground zero."

Kieran stiffened. I frowned. *Ground zero?*

"NOVA labs," Bernie said, reading my confusion. "It's about ten clicks out, but even so, the vines are sensitive enough to sense us here. They'll be inching towards us even now." He pulled the handgun holstered on his belt and peered through the stained window. Nguyen took the door; his two fellow gun bros fanned out across the veranda.

"A gun's not going to be much use against a bunch of vines," Kieran pointed out.

Nguyen gave a knowing smile. "They're not for the vines."

My twin's face fell, and an expression close to horror flitted across his face. "People still live out here?"

"In a manner of speaking."

"Two puppets, ten o'clock. Two hundred meters," one of Nguyen's gun bros spoke up from the veranda as we gathered our things, not that there was much to gather. Just my jacket left on the arm of the sofa and a pair of mismatched boots we'd scrounged from the junkyard to replace Kieran's slippers. The soldier who issued the warning peered through the sights on his gun—rifle some part of my brain registered—tracking something through the scrub.

"Keep eyes on them, but don't engage," Nguyen said. "They're probably just patrolling."

Bernie, Nguyen and the soldiers marched us down the rolling gravel driveway and back onto the road Kieran and I had been following the day before. Sure enough, the vines we'd left at the roadside had crept a good ten meters down the turn off to the house. There, Nguyen handed us a pair of respirators from his camouflage backpack.

"For the vines," he said. "They might seem too slow to feel like a threat, but their speed isn't the danger, it's their spores."

Kieran turned to look at Nguyen. "Spores?"

"They're not really," Bernie said. "But 'spores' is the analogy people are most familiar with. The vines release high concentrations of Gemini Particles that change people if they breathe too much of them in."

Alarm spiked through me, and I did a double take of the nearest vine. *That thing is made up of Gemini Particles?* My chest tightened. "Changes them how?" And how much did we need to breathe in? Could we have been exposed in Kieran's apartment?

"It starts with moodiness, then progresses to irate behaviour, and then to violent outbursts," Bernie explained as we walked. "Paranoia is common. The particles hijack the frontal lobe of a person's brain."

The knot in my chest tightened. *Just like Mum.* And she'd been at the heart of this binary universe business. It'd been a while since I'd studied any form of human biology, but I was pretty sure the frontal lobe housed our executive functioning abilities. Logic, reasoning, decision-making, etcetera. Nguyen confirmed it a moment later when he translated Bernie's science speak.

"It twists their thoughts," he finished.

My gut gave a guilty twitch. Last time I saw Mum she'd lost much of that higher reasoning; I'd blamed it on the bottle in her hand.

"I see," Kieran said, and when I glanced at him, it was clear he did. There was a look of understanding on his face, an intensity in his expression as he mulled the information over. When he caught me looking, he fished out the journal he'd folded into his back pocket and palmed through the pages. "Here," he said, handing it over, page opened to 18 June 1992. "You should read the rest."

"*Now?*" I asked, with an incredulous glance at the road. Admittedly, it was almost empty. "Just give me a summary."

There was a long pause as Kieran considered my suggestion. Then he shook his head. "I wouldn't know where to start." From behind his respirator, he lifted a mocking eyebrow. "Besides, you're Ms. Hot Shot Lawyer. Multitask is your middle name."

I huffed and snatched the journal off him.

18 June 1992, NOVA, Castor
I'm worried.

It's been seven months since my last entry and eight months since Bernie and I split. I'm trying to keep you updated, Journal, yet it's so bloody hard to find the time. But it's past midnight and I can't sleep; I need to write this out. I'm sure I'll look back on this and laugh at how crazy I sounded. Earlier this week, I got a call from our old landlord. She was raging. Screaming at me down the line. Something about Bernie not paying his rent for three months before skipping out and leaving the apartment in a right state. She sent me photos. And it's bad.

It's the mould. The stuff from the lab. We've been keeping on top of it here, but Bernie's been in the wind three months, and who knows how long he let it go unchecked before then. I've lived in my share of dodgy rentals, but I've never seen mould like that. Stuff's coated the floor. The walls. The fridge. Landlord says it's covered the house's wiring and is causing the power to trip.

I reported the containment breach to work yesterday, and the news has gone all the way up the chain. Health and Safety are having an absolute field day with it.

Is it possible Bernie or I brought back an invasive species of mould? With our two universes being so similar, we thought it unlikely anything like this would happen. But we were still careful. We'd shower after every crossing. Scrub our shoes down afterwards. Wash our clothes at the lab. We didn't even bring food back with us. However it got out, it's got a foothold in Bernie's apartment.

Have I unwittingly unleashed the Cane Toad of moulds on my universe?

24 June 1992, NOVA, Castor
I haven't been able to get into the lab all week. Health and Safety have put it in lockdown. Bernie's apartment is under quarantine (the landlord loved hearing about that, let me tell you), and from what I've heard, it's spreading. Yesterday, the mould got into the fuse box and shorted the whole apartment block. They've moved everyone out until they have it contained. More unhappy landlords. Which has translated to quite a few of NOVA's upper echelon's breathing down my neck for answers I don't have.

I've been on the radio with Roza-Pollux every day. They have no record of any mould like what we're seeing.

I'm too afraid to say out loud what I suspect. I haven't even told Roza-Pollux. If she's me, maybe she already knows.

To top today off, fucking Bernie left me a 20-minute rant on my answering machine. The guy is absolutely off his rocker.

25 June 1992, NOVA, Castor

Tests came back this morning. It's not mould. It might have the state's biologists stumped but not us. We know what it is.

Gemini Particles.

Our tests confirmed it.

We knew hundred to the billions of them were congregating on our side of the Tear. But we completely underestimated how quickly their numbers would intensify. If my theory is correct, we have more than the Tear to blame for this. At some point when particle quantities reach a critical mass, their behaviour changes; they start interacting with the environment and replicating somehow.

Funny thing is, our watches charge at about the same speed as they always have (not that we're permitted to use them). But it makes no sense. Higher particle concentration should mean a quicker charge. It's like the particles are avoiding the watches. Since the lab lockdown, the mould's turned up on the computers again. Tendrils of black roping across the screens. Around the phones. And the microwave, God they love that thing. Whole contraption looks like a fungal growth on the cameras.

Stress is getting to people too. Fights are breaking out daily. Just yesterday I had to step in before fists started flying between Mizushima and Wyndham. The reason? Mizushima took the last chocolate mousse at the cafeteria. Seriously. What are we? Three? My own daughter knows better and she's only two.. Took everything I had not to knock sense into the both of them.

And of course, there was another incoherent message from Bernie waiting on the machine when I got home. Likely ranting how I can't cut him off from Kirsty. I deleted it without listening. I am DONE with people today.

"Where are we going?" I asked Bernie as we traversed a particularly vine infested street. Too infested to risk reading and walking at the same time.

"NOVA," Bernie said, grimacing as he stepped over a foot-high vine to an accompanying pop and crack of his knees. Not much access to painkillers in the apocalypse I guessed.

"We're going back to where it all started," he said.

I frowned as I followed him. *I* had headed to Mum's old labs because they were the logical place to find a way out of this mess—before Bernie and Nguyen had come along and given us this bracing reality check. But why on earth—

"Time to get up close and personal with Zero," said one of Nguyen's gun bros; Freddie, I'd heard the others call him. I sensed him grinning at me underneath his respirator.

Bernie grimaced again, but this time I was sure it wasn't his knees bothering him. Regardless, I didn't understand. Did Freddie mean Zero as in *ground zero*? My stomach twisted and I stumbled to a stop. Kieran gave me a worried glance, but I ignored him and stared at Bernie like he'd gone mad.

"We're going *to the Tear?*" There was no keeping the 'what the fuck' tone out of my voice. "Why?"

The old physicist shrugged and kept walking. "I want answers."

I stared after him. What could be more important than getting the hell out of here?

Kieran gave me a nudge in the side to keep moving. "Let it go."

I whirled on him. "Are you kidding? This nutter wants to—"

"Kirsty." The sharpness in his voice turned me still. Like a parent warning a child not to wander too close to a cliff. "*Let it go.*" My twin nodded to Freddie and the soldier's two compatriots—Kasey and Lorne, I'd learned. All three gripped their rifles with a fresh alertness they hadn't shown before. Nguyen watched on, looking impossibly tired.

"We need them," Kieran continued. "And they us. We need to work together."

I scowled. Kieran the peacekeeper to the rescue. All too willing to bow and scrape to get himself out of the remotest confrontation. With a huff, I closed my mouth and stomped past another vine, taking comfort in the weight of the Gemini watch on my wrist. As soon as it turned green, I was transporting Kieran and myself out of here—with or without them.

The thought made me pause.

If I could vanish the moment the watch was ready, why did I still have it? Either Bernie, Nguyen and the rest had *way* too much faith in me (unlikely) or they knew something I didn't. Like that the watch wouldn't work. Or it needed some other thing in this universe to operate.

Shit.

I snuck a glance at the device. It still blinked red, but otherwise no cracks or scuffs. Of course, I was no expert.

Lucky break, asshat, I thought after Bernie's retreating back. *Looks like we're in this together after all.*

26 June 1992, NOVA, Castor

Another fight today. A bad one. Roux stabbed Mizushima with a knife from the lunchroom. Police and ambos were called. New lab's a mess. Blood everywhere.

I'm starting to wonder if there's more to it than stress. I asked one of the interns to get a blood sample from Roux before the police took him. Sent it to one of the biologists we consulted when we first considered travelling to Pollux, asking them to test it. Nothing to do but wait now.

I really hope my hunch is wrong.

29 June 1992, NOVA, Castor

It's not stress. It's the damn Gemini Particles. They're in our blood. At least, they're in Dr. Roux. His veins were positively teeming with them. I ordered all of us tested. Lots of grumbling about that. To no surprise, we all have varying levels of particles. Baumer has the highest—she's been on mould clean up all week and been mighty snippy about it. My levels are low, but still. It's unsettling to know there are particles floating around in my veins doing who knows what.

Health and Safety has put us all under quarantine. We're to stay on site under observation. Which is all well and good if you're not a single mother of a toddler. Honestly, the sitter has already called the lab twice asking how many days I expect to be here. I don't think she's coping. From the screaming on the other end of the line I know Kirsty is not.

1 August 1992, NOVA, Castor

Fucking fuck! Mizushima went full lizard brain this morning. Then Baumer. It was Mizushima's turn to clean the mould this week, but Baumer chipped in yesterday when Mizushima broke down about not being able to go to their little boy's track day. Never mind that none of us have seen our families in over a month.

All of NOVA's labs are off limits. Particle concentration is too high inside, and the mould too dangerous to be in contact with.

7 August 1992, NOVA, Castor

Hard to believe it's only been a week since my last update. All hell's broken loose here. Parts of town are being evacuated. Word is the mould escaped the state's quarantine and has found its way into the power station.

The footage is something else. Wyndham and I were huddled around our quarantine TV, watching the news. It's engulfed the power station. Just a black smudge from the TV news helicopter. Turns out Gemini Particle mould goes ropey if left to replicate long enough. We saw it too though our lab cameras. The Tear looks like something out of a B-grade sci-fi movie, tendrils all feeding into it like some weird Gemini Particle pipework. The last thing I saw before the cameras failed was the Tear, Gemini tendrils coiled around it like a walnut. I could have sworn the thing was pulsing.

Power's out for the whole town. We've got generators, so does the hospital, but I imagine everyone else is running on torches and candles.

I tried ringing the sitter. The line didn't even go through.

I'm scared.

Oh God, Kirsty, please be okay.

It was strange to see myself through Mum's eyes. Stranger still because I had no memory of these events. Even at two going on three years old, wouldn't I remember *something* of this? Instead, all I had was a dim haziness. Was that normal? Could normal people recall that far back? My therapist said trauma affects memory. Was I not remembering because I had been young or because of something I'd experienced?

I shuffled over to Kieran, flashing him a glance of the page I was on. "Do you remember your life before I came to Pollux?"

He frowned. "Not much. Flashes of people and places mostly."

"You don't remember meeting me?" I probed.

He pursed his lips as he considered. "No." He frowned again and scratched the day-old bristle on his chin. "You were always there." He tapped the journal. "Even though I know now you weren't. Not at the start."

In hindsight, I should have expected his answer. He'd had a rough time of it from Mum too, so it stood to reason that the details of our earliest years would fade into obscurity. All the same, it bothered me as I flipped open the journal to continue where I'd left off.

8 August 1992, NOVA, Castor

Twenty-four hour update: Still no word from the sitter. I'm going out of my mind.

To make things worse, someone broke into the main lab last night. Security cameras and the swipe card checkpoints are totally shot from the mould, so we have no idea who it was. I know it's illogical, but I can't shake the feeling it was Bernie. Like he was trying to find me or something. I'm not allowed to go into the lab to check if anything's been taken or damaged. IF it <u>was</u> a burglar, joke's on them. The equipment is caked in mould. In other news, NOVA has decided to move us. Not sure where. Brass are being real cagey with information—so shit has hit the fan big time. Hundred bucks says the mould's found the generators.

9 August 1992, Everland Motel, Castor

Motel. We're in a God damn motel. Not a lab, not a sealed facility. A motel. With people coming and going outside the window. Their only precaution? They've locked us in. Like we're in a damn prison. Pretty sure Wyndham in the room over just kicked down the door and left. Heard sirens and saw police manhandle him back inside. Now he has a security guard outside his room. Don't blame him either. If the sitter hadn't called, I would have been right there with him in his escape attempt.

Okay, the story with the sitter. She claimed she called and called the lab but wasn't getting through. (Mould probably in the phone lines). Anyway, someone from NOVA finally contacted her when they were moving us and gave her my motel number. She finally got through this morning to let me know my sister came by and picked Kirsty up. I nearly hit the roof, and I was seconds from screaming down the line that I didn't have a sister when it clicked.

Roza-Pollux. She must be in Castor. Nice of NOVA to fucking tell us. When NOVA said they had help coming in they must have meant a team from Pollux. How long she's been here I have no idea. I'm fuming—last time I hire that sitter! You can bet NOVA is getting an earful once this blows over too. I keep telling myself Kirsty is okay. She's with Roza-Pollux, so she's with me, in a way.

It's not helping.

"Puppet, one o'clock." The warning came from Freddie, snapping my attention back to the road we walked on. The group stiffened, and Kasey and Lorne lifted their rifles, training them on the front yard of a dilapidated house. I had to squint to make out the figure shambling behind the peeling picket fence. A black and white tie-dyed shirt hung from his tall frame, and he swayed as he walked.

"Keep sights as we pass," Nguyen instructed. "Only shoot if it follows."

"Don't want it spraying more spores," Lorne said to me with a wink, which left me cold.

We moved down the street, keeping to the opposite sidewalk. The puppet and its yard grew closer, close enough for me to make out the traces of tattoos on his arms and neck. A damp smell clung to the air, like clothes left in the washing machine too long, and I imagined the Gemini spores washing against my respirator, fighting to get in. I checked the respirator was still properly in place and sped up.

"Why do you call them puppets?" Kieran whispered to Bernie as we moved past. Then the puppet turned, and it became clear.

The tattoos weren't tattoos. They were vines. Fuzzy tendrils spread across the puppet's face, diving in and out of his skin like worms through peat, weaving through his face, his head, his arms. The puppet's jaw opened and closed like a goldfish as we stumbled past, unable to tear our gazes away. His eyes were bright and alive in his vine-infested face, but they rolled in his head—like Mum's had after two bottles of gin—all red rimmed and unfocused. He moved again, jerking back around to do another lap of its yard, and I glimpsed the wrist-thick vine running along the length of the man's neck.

Like some sort of prosthetic spine.

Whatever the hell it was, it was creepy. Tendrils ran off the vine, digging *into* the man's neck and upper back before vanishing underneath his shirt—which, I realised, was not tie-dyed but white and covered in patches of black mould.

"That's what direct contact with a vine does," Bernie said. "It grows on you and eventually takes over. We're talking weeks rather than months."

Because of course—*of course*—the universal black mould Mum had unleashed turned people into zombies. *Why the hell not?* I fought down a hysterical laugh and took stock of all the encounters we'd had with the vines. I definitely hadn't touched one, had I?

"Looks like its guarding the transformer," Nguyen said, nodding to a rectangle shaped growth of vines next to the puppet's fence.

"If there's still juice in that thing, I'll eat Freddie's crusty socks," said Lorne.

"This used to be a well-to-do area, lots of private solar panels. They might still be feeding power into the grid," Nguyen said.

Whatever the reason, the puppet didn't leave its post. Just watched us with its rolling eyes. The hairs stayed up on my neck all the way to NOVA labs.

10 August 1992, Everland Motel, Castor

They're releasing us today. Thank fuck. Forty-eight hours in this bloody motel is forty-eight hours too many. Although, 'release' is a loose interpretation. NOVA's got other, more pressing concerns on its plate. Namely, the state breathing down their necks. They've had to lock the entire town down. Gemini mould is popping up everywhere. In people's houses. Gas stations. At the hospital. Everything and everyone is now in quarantine. Police blockades on the roads in and out. The town square has turned into tent-city with people who have been forced to leave their homes. So, yeah, it's bad. In the grand scheme of things, letting two scientists go home after nearly two-weeks in isolation probably doesn't even register as a blip on their radar. It's not like we're going anywhere.

My bag is packed. Motel bed stripped. Dishes washed and left to dry in the sink (minus the one I broke) and sofa shifted to cover the hole I kicked in the wall yesterday when NOVA wouldn't give me the radio to contact the Pollux team. Good thing I have a radio at home.

But for now, all I can do is sit here.

Hurry the hell up NOVA. Kirsty is waiting for me.

I turned over the page, expecting to see another date, place and universe. Instead, it was a frantic scrawl. My mother's carefully crafted letters had turned jagged and stretched over multiple lines.

She's taken her.
Roza-Pollux has taken Kirsty.

She had the gall to leave me a note saying she's 'evacuated' Kirsty to her universe. What utter bullshit! And NOVA let her. The real kicker? They've shut down all binary universe travel until the Gemini mould is under control.

If this rage is the Gemini Particles inside me, well and good. I need all the rage I can get. God help Pollux when I get over there.

No one steals from me.

No one.

Part Five.

Under the shady gumtree of our rest stop, I closed the journal and exhaled. The end. Or rather, end of that particular chapter of Mum's life. I'd read it twice. Again, I flipped the empty pages after the last entry and let out an exasperated sigh.

I could more or less guess what had happened. Mum must have sought out the Pollux team. Stolen Bernie's watch. She'd travelled to Pollux and found Roza at some point, because her watch and journal had ended up in Roza-Pollux's will nearly a month later. Perhaps they'd lived together. Perhaps that had been Roza-Pollux's intention all along. I wondered how long it had taken for Mum to get restless, to feel the uncanniness of a universe she didn't belong to sink in. Perhaps Roza-Pollux sensed danger. Perhaps she simply wanted to stop Mum from returning to her Gemini-infected world. Whatever the reason, she'd taken Mum's watch and journal and hidden them—in her will as it had turned out. How long had Roza-Pollux survived after that? One week? Two? I imagined how my mother, in one of her rages, might have snatched a pan from the stove—or perhaps a gin bottle—and swung it at her other self's head.

On second thoughts, definitely a gin bottle.

But guessing was not the same as knowing. And there was no way to know—at least, not here on Castor. It was infuriating. Maddening. Teeth gnashingly enraging. A giant middle finger from beyond the grave. A vision of Mum laughing at me from her bottle-festooned sofa rose in my head and anger sparked inside me.

I curled the journal into a roll in my hands. *You know what? I don't need to know.* I placed it down in the dirt and gave Kieran a prod. "Got a light?"

He frowned, opened his mouth as if to say no, before catching my expression. Sheepish, he fished out a lighter from his pocket and held it out.

I snatched it up, swiped down on the spark-wheel. Flame sprung from the lighter's hood and I rounded on the journal lying in the dirt.

And like that, my anger fizzled out. My hand quivered. Unable to traverse those final few inches. To set alight the last bit of Mum—*my* Mum—I had.

Kieran cleared his throat. "Are you—"

"I'm fine! Just... give me a minute."

A minute came and went. My hand went on quivering. I drew in a breath, then another, and willed my hand to move. It wouldn't. Even dead, she still had power over me. Then Kieran's fingers fell over mine and my twin took the lighter from me. Wordless, he sparked it in a smooth, practiced motion, opened the journal to its middle and pressed the flame to the paper pages. It caught easily, spiralling smoke up between us.

"There," Kieran said. "It's done." A pause. "Do you want to say anything?"

"No. She was a two-faced murdering bitch." I spat. I'd intended to leave it at that, but my mouth kept moving. "She was awful. I *shouldn't* care. I don't *want* to care. If not for her—" *If not for her Kieran would still have* his *mother.* The one who had cared—for however short a time it had been.

"She was still your Mum—*our* Mum."

I fell silent and stared at the flaming pages, lips pursed tight. His hand found mine.

"Bye, Mum," he said, and looked at me expectantly.

I swallowed hard. Gritted my teeth. *Say it.* "Bye, Mum." I meant to sneer the words at her crumbling journal, but instead they came out as a whisper, a release.

Bye, Mum.

Neither of us said any more. Just stood side by side, watching the journal smoulder. A buzz at my wrist made me glance down.

"Gemini Particle containment at 80 per cent," Mum's robotic voice issued from it.

Kieran choked on a laugh, even as the irrational urge to yank it off and throw it on the fire boiled up from inside me. *Of all the fucking times!* I rounded on the blasted thing.

Despite the swirl of particles in its globe, it still blinked red. I frowned at it. The journal had said it should recharge in a couple of days. And it'd *been* a couple of days. So why wasn't it ready yet? Maybe the particles were *avoiding* the watch like Mum had suggested.

We're in trouble if that's true. My earlier doubts returned. Why had Bernie let me keep the watch? True, it was no use to anyone yet. But the thing was valuable; it was our ticket out of here. Why allow me to keep it on my wrist? Me, a new and untrained entrant to the world of Castor.

A new insidious thought wormed up. *What if it's not about the watch at all? Perhaps he doesn't need it. Maybe he doesn't give two shits about it.* That would track with what I'd seen so far.

I frowned and chewed my lip under my respirator. *Then why bring us with him?* If there was another watch or some other way of getting to Pollux, why had Bernie and Nguyen sought us out? Why were *we* here?

My face must have given something away because Kieran cocked his head from his seat next to me and leaned closer. "What is it?" he whispered.

I shot the rest of the squad a look. Nguyen patrolled while Bernie and Kasey rested against their packs. Freddie and Lorne had vanished two hours ago carrying a portable generator and a jerry can between them. They'd it dug up from under one of the eucalypts. I had to hand it to them, they were nothing if not prepared.

I leaned close to Kieran, lifted my respirator, and whispered into his ear. "Did Bernie tell you *why* we are heading to NOVA? About the answers he's looking for?"

Between the revelations in Mum's journal and the exhaustion from hours of walking, I hadn't spent much time thinking about Bernie's insane plan to visit the Tear. But now, with the NOVA labs in spitting distance, the reality of what we were about to do was sinking in.

Kieran's respirator tilted as he cocked his head the other way, and his gaze grew distant, clearly pondering his answer. "No," he said, slowly.

Damn. Bernie mentioned something about going back to where it all started. But what did that *mean?*

Think Kirsty.

My brain limped. Could have been that I hadn't slept for more than a few hours in the last forty-eight. Could've been the Gemini Particles had weaselled their way into my brain. Was I paranoid? Correction: more paranoid than usual? Who the fuck knew. Paranoia was one of many pandora's gifts Mum had instilled.

The knot of anger inside me twinged. *Oh no, don't you dare start feeling sorry for her now.* My empathy might be a bit out of whack, but I still knew right from wrong. I'd built a career on it. Knowing what had happened to Mum didn't excuse what she'd done. She might not have had her full faculties at the end, but she sure as hell did at the beginning. Her hubris had started all of this.

And still that knot twitched.

Damn emotions. Should never have let Kieran hold that quasi funeral for Mum's bloody journal. *Focus, Kirsty.* What did Bernie hope to find at the Tear?

God, it could be anything. Study findings, equipment left behind, the proverbial silver bullet to our zombie problem.

Or something about the nature of the Tear itself.

Ground zero. Where it all began.

Was he looking for some kind of closure? I blinked. *Or a way to close the Tear?*

I glanced at Bernie resting in the brown grass, head propped on his pack for a pillow. Yeah no, that was too altruistic for a guy who'd abandoned his family. He might be smart, but he was selfish through and through. If this was just about getting home, all he had to do was fix my watch and wait for the particles to refill it. He didn't need to be at NOVA Labs to do that. No, there was a reason he was out here risking his neck.

"Only one way to put this to bed," I said, and stomped over to the old physicist. Judging from the rise and fall of his chest, he was still awake anyway.

Kieran scrambled after me, hissing "Wait! Kirsty, hold on!"

I kicked Bernie's boot with my sneaker. Not hard. Just enough to get his attention. I was getting an answer, one way or another.

His watery blue eyes blinked open. Furrowed his brow, briefly confused. Then, seeing my expression through my respirator, relaxed into resignation.

"What the fuck are we doing, Bernie?" I demanded. "Why are we here? What are we looking for?"

With a sigh, he sat up. "I suppose I owe you that." He said it more to Kieran than me. "But you'll probably wish you hadn't asked."

"Spit it out."

"Please," Kieran added.

Bernie's gaze fell on his son, his *biological* son, and there was a softening around his eyes. He checked his wristwatch. "All right. Guess we have time for this." He ran a hand through his hair and fell quiet, clearly collecting his thoughts.

After a full minute of silence, in which I nearly prodded him again, he finally started.

"Have you ever wondered why we haven't encountered Gemini Particles and our binary universes before?"

Dumb luck, I thought, but Bernie didn't wait for us to respond.

"In a binary star system, the orbit of the stars is usually stable but not always. In those instances, the stars slowly get closer and closer. Eventually one is absorbed by the other. Same goes for binary black holes. They eventually merge. It takes billions of years, but it happens."

Kieran sank down opposite Bernie in the grass, crossing his legs to listen. "You're saying our universes are merging?"

Bernie cleared his throat and held up two fingers. "The way I see it, we are in two possible scenarios. The first, we're in a true binary universe; like a pair of binary suns." He clenched his fists and manoeuvred one around the other in a circle, mimicking two suns orbiting each other. "But something has upset the balance between them and how they're closing in on one another."

Something like ripping a Tear between universes? I wondered. But no, that couldn't be right. Bernie was talking on the universal scale. The Tear was an infinitesimally small thing by comparison. A hair line fracture. Less than. Blaming the Tear would be like blaming a single atom for the rampage of an elephant.

"Over time we've come closer and closer and are now on the verge of merging," Bernie continued to explain, bringing one fist closer to the other with each circuit until his knuckles bumped. He mimicked an impact and tangled his fingers together. "In this scenario, the appearance of Gemini Particles is a sign one universe is getting close to another." He swallowed and dropped his hands to his lap, a flicker of fear crossing his face before it was quickly hidden. Kasey lifted his head from where he'd been resting it against his pack. "In layman's terms, Castor is about to crash into Pollux," he said. "And we'll go down with the ship if we don't get out."

Bernie shot Kasey a 'zip it' glare. The soldier sighed, rolled his eyes, and fell silent.

I pursed my lips behind my respirator. He told a good story, but I wasn't buying it. "How does escaping to Pollux help then?" I asked. "Either way, we're fucked."

Bernie held up an arthritic finger. "We are. *If* we're in scenario one."

"So, the second scenario?" Kieran prompted.

"The second is that our universes are more different than Roza thought," Bernie continued. "Instead of a sun-sun equivalent, Castor and Pollux are more like a sun and a companion black hole. In this theory, Castor is acting like the black hole, sucking matter from Pollux. Feeding off it, as it were."

Oh joy. Now we're in a vampire universe. Great, just great.

"What are the Gemini Particles in this scenario?" Kieran asked. "The digested parts of Pollux?"

"Something like that."

"But there's nothing wrong with Pollux," I blurted. "It was fine when we left. No mould. No vines. Nothing."

"There wouldn't be. Not yet. The incoming particle stream of particles was always strongest here in Castor. How old are you?"

Next to us, Kasey sat up from his pillowed pack, apparently very interested in my answer. Intensely interested. Like his future was riding on it. I tried to ignore the soldier as I answered.

"Thirty-five."

There was a collective silence as Kasey and Bernie exchanged a look. Why did it feel like the second scenario was suddenly the more likely of the two?

Bernie gave a grim smile. "We already guessed based on how you look, but..." he trailed off and gave a shrug. "When you left your universe, what year was it? 2024?"

Mute, I nodded, still not following. What did the year have to do with anything? A glance at Kieran said he wasn't any the wiser than me. I opened my mouth to say so when Bernie heaved a sigh and said, "Time dilation."

The words tickled a long-ago memory from one of my high school physics teachers. Black holes were so powerful they warped space-time. And there was something about time slowing down the closer you were to a black hole's centre. Is that what he meant? Would that stop Pollux from noticing the effects? Could a universe devouring matter from its sibling also warp that universe's sense of *time*?

As if reading my mind, Bernie gave a slow nod. "In Pollux, it's 2024. Thirty-two years since the Castor lab breach." He's grey eyes met mine; rheumy with the start of a cataract in one. "Kasey, what year is it here in Castor?

The soldier blinked, clearly surprised Bernie had brought him into the conversation. He cleared his throat. "2046."

"Twenty-two years difference." Bernie confirmed. "For you it's been thirty-two years. For me, it's been fifty-four."

Kieran and I stared. Fifty-four years trapped in Castor. Jesus. But it did explain his and Nguyen's older appearances.

"Then the second scenario is—" Kieran began, but I cut him off.

"That's not the right question." I fixed Bernie pale face with a hard stare. "Even with the time dilation, both universes are still screwed. So why cross to Pollux at all?"

Bernie's expression turned stony. Next to him, Kasey shifted, uncomfortable.

Let me guess, here comes the part we won't like.

Behind us, someone cleared his throat: Nguyen back from patrol. "To have more time," the Sergeant said.

I raised an eyebrow. Not following, as usual.

"Time dilation could mean Pollux lasts another fifty years, maybe even one hundred," Bernie explained. "Enough to live out our lives." Then he added, more rueful, "More than enough to live out mine."

"Make it the next generation's problem, is that it?" Kieran concluded with a scowl.

When he put it like that, he was right. It was pretty fucked up. But hey, it wasn't like humanity hadn't done it before. And who was I to judge the old physicist? He'd lived more of his life in the wrong universe than in the right one. If I had a chance to escape this shit hole and spend my few precious remaining years cocooned in Pollux's time dilatation, I'd jump at it too.

After everything I'd seen and heard in the last few days and the winking out of existence alternative, this news was practically sunshine and rainbows. We had time.

So, why weren't they happy about it?

My lips press into a hard line behind my respirator, and I fought to keep the glower out of my eyes where they'd see it. Questions warred in my head; I went with the most pressing. "Where does the Tear fit into all this?"

Bernie gave one of his wry laughs. "Isn't it obvious? One watch means one shot. And there's seven of us"—he pointed to my wrist— "That watch was designed to transport one person—two in an emergency." He held up his hands as Kieran opened his mouth. "Now, before you panic, I've built a device to enhance its output, but the closer we are to the Tear, the greater our chances of all of us making it through."

I narrowed my eyes. "I thought you wanted answers?"

"Yes, that too."

Two birds one stone, was it? He spoke as if everything was perfectly obvious and under control, even though it wasn't and not all of us were physicists. And, back up, what was this 'all of us' business? *That* sounded like some of us might not survive the trip. My mind turned back to Mum's description of the dead rats they'd tried to send through. Was that what awaited some of us?

My stomach gave a flutter. The 'wish you hadn't asked' was beginning to make more sense.

An alarm sounded on Bernie's wrist, making us all jump.

"Time to move," he announced and nudged Kasey, who'd gone back to resting against his pack. "Walking in ten." Kasey muttered something about drill sergeants and vine dust and rolled to his feet.

I sidled up to Kieran as we waited for Bernie and his gang to pack up the site and check their rifles. "You believe him?" I asked.

Kieran was silent and I knew he was pursing his lips behind his respirator. "I don't know. I want to, but..." He trailed off. Shrugged.

"Yeah," I said. "I know what you mean."

It was Bernie. In one universe, he was the father who walked out. In another, an abuser. A different me might have accepted his explanations at face value. But for me of the here and now, it all seemed... too convenient.

And it still didn't explain why I'd been allowed to keep the watch. The thing felt heavy around my wrist. I itched to take it off, but didn't dare. Only an idiot would think Kerian and I wouldn't blip out of this hellhole the moment the watch reached full charge. And Bernie wasn't an idiot. Which meant, there was more to getting back to Castor than simply mashing the watch's button once it was full. *But what?*

"Keep an eye on them," I told my twin.

Kieran smirked—or at least I think he did, I couldn't see his mouth from behind the respirator. But it was there in the tilt of his head and the way one cheek bunched around his eye. "Read my mind," he said.

#

We stood before the barbed wire fence of NOVA's facility, watching Nguyen run a finger over a tattered, hand drawn map held together with duct tape.

111

"We're entering from the north side," he said, pointing to the nearest building from our position on the map. "Skirt around A Block." His gloved finger dragged across the map, pausing between A Block and the larger hexagonal building that dominated the centre of the page. It dominated the view before us too, its hexagonal dome rose through the gumtrees like some sort of tarnished sun. "There's a maintenance hatch about two hundred meters south-east of A Block. That's our entry point. With the generator as bait the accelerator's tunnel will be clear." Nguyen gave an appreciative nod to the sweating and still puffing Freddie and Lorne who'd re-joined us at the fence line.

"We should have a straight run through to Zero," he finished.

The gun-bros nodded and checked their weapons and respirators. From their cavalier attitude, I guessed they'd been through the plan before. This little show and tell was for Kieran's and my benefit.

Bernie leaned over the map, gesturing to the entire NOVA grounds. "This place is filled with puppets. The flares Kasey and Lorne set in the south-west will be drawing them and the vines away, but it's no sure thing." He fixed Kieran and I with a beady stare. "So, watch your footing and no more talk until we get inside."

I couldn't take it anymore. I had to know. I lifted my hand, and not waiting for Bernie to acknowledge it, blurted. "And what *is* the objective?"

Bernie's gaze roved over me, steel blue eyes sharp and cutting. Dang, now I knew where I got it from. Beside me, Kieran shrank away as if he'd been burned.

"Main lab, three stories down. *That* is our objective. *That*'s where Zero will be." There was a ferocity in his voice that made the hairs on my arms stand on end. An intensity. Not crazed. Focused. Like thirty years of planning had come down to this moment and, by God, we were not to fuck it up.

I raised my hand again. "And what *is* Zero? I'm beginning to think that word means something different to you than it does for me."

Bernie's gaze snapped to Kieran then me, and for a heartbeat, his intensity dimmed. Hesitation. Doubt. Fear. Each flickered through his face in quick succession before the final one: guilt. Goosebumps broke across my neck, and Bernie's expression hardened again, determination returning double-fold.

"It's a brain," he said. When neither Kieran nor I showed a sign of understanding he added, "A mass of Gemini Particles encased around the Tear. It controls all the vines."

"The seed," Kieran breathed from beside me, so soft I almost missed it through his respirator. "Mum wrote about it in her journal."

...the last thing I saw was the Tear. Gemini tendrils coiled around it like a walnut. Like a seed. And I could have sworn the thing was pulsing...

"It's a lot more than a seed now," Freddie grumbled.

At my stunned silence, Bernie gave a nod, and apparently satisfied, folded the map up, and tucked it in his front pocket. He motioned to Nguyen. "Let's go."

I sucked in a breath, trying to settle my whirling thoughts as we fell in behind the soldiers. *Okay, okay, okay.* So, the Tear was Zero *and* the brains of the mould apocalypse.

And we were gunning for it. Quite literally. I glanced at Nguyen's figure as he cut across to the silhouette of A Block, Bernie and the gun-bros in full stealth mode behind.

I still didn't understand *why*.

Or what Bernie wasn't telling us.

Maybe they really did want to destroy it. Yet, Bernie's gaze had unnerved me. He hid it well, but fear was an old friend in my house. Bernie's intensity was no eager anticipation of a fight; it was his amygdala barely being held in check.

The man was terrified. Down to the bone.

And we were headed straight for its source.

Every survival instinct said to turn and run. Abandon ship. But we couldn't. This universe was on the cusp of collapse, and the bastard was our only way out.

Kieran's hand closed around mine. Reassuring in its warmth. "For better or worse," he said.

With a sigh, I gritted my jaw, tightened my grip around Kieran's fingers and pressed on after them. He had the right of it, of course. When you're stranded in a world that's ended, what other choice was there but forward?

Part Six.

The plan went off like a plan thirty years in the making—without a hitch.

I didn't like it. Not one bit.

We found the hatch. A squirt of oil from one of the gun-bros saw it swing up and open with ease and only a faint squeak from its hinges. Down into NOVA's underbelly we went, scrambling hand over hand down a ladder, headlamps dotting the wall of the shaft. Above, the hole of moonlight from the open hatch shrank with each descending step until Lorne, last in the line, slammed it shut and sealed us in so no stray puppets could follow us down.

Five minutes later, we landed on a walkway running along a high circular tunnel. Next to it ran a metal tube the width of an arm span, like a giant water pipeline, only, instead of water, it contained a vacuum like outer space. Particles had once hurtled through that pipe at 99.999 percent the speed of light before crashing together. Mum had crossed out a lot of the technical stuff in her journal, but I'd understood that much.

Nguyen took the lead, rifle stock pressed tight against his shoulder, his boots *clank-clanking* on the walkway as he advanced down the tunnel. Freddie and Bernie followed, then myself and Kieran, while Kasey and Lorne covered our rear—or our escape, depending on how you looked at it.

I found Kieran's hand again, feeling childish but calming at the warmth of his grasp. On we walked, the sweat of our palms growing slicker the further we went. We'd been moving close to fifteen minutes when the tunnel opened into a room the size of a cathedral. The pipe we'd been following ended in a disc of machinery the size of a Ferris wheel. At least, I assumed it had been some kind of machinery. I could only make out glimpses of the various panels, cables, circuitry, and metal underneath the vines constricting the thing.

"One of the detectors," Bernie said, answering our unspoken question. "This was where we collided particles to see if we could discover any new ones." He pointed back down the circular corridor with its not-water pipeline. "Flew those particles around our racetrack and smashed them together. Then sat back and watched." His finger shifted to a small alcove to one side of the cavern. I couldn't be sure from this distance and the mould covering the station, but it looked like a set of desks and computers. "Eight hundred million collisions a second," he went on, gazing at the abandoned station in what I could only describe as a fatherly fondness. Misplaced, obviously.

Kieran cleared his throat. "This is what detected the Gemini Particle?"

"This is where they first uncovered its presence, yes."

The hairs prickled on my arms again. He made it sound like the particles had been lying in wait for thousands, nay, millions of years, for the right moment to awaken. Forty-eight hours ago, I would have scoffed, but I'd seen the predatory nature of those particles up close. Cold shivered down my spine. I checked the Gemini watch on my wrist. Still red. But the blinking light had sped up. Almost there. Had to be.

Next to Bernie, Nguyen checked one of his instruments. Looked a bit like a dive gauge with a couple of dials on its front, but no tube connecting it to an oxygen tank.

"We need to get a move on. Particle concentration is going up," he said, tapping one of the dials.

Bernie nodded. "As it should." He started towards a set of stairs that ran up the face of the enormous wheel and... my gaze scaled the stairs, following them to a narrow scaffold that led into a man-sized tunnel at the wheel's center.

"You can't be serious," Kieran said. "We're going *inside* it?"

"That's where Zero is," Nguyen said with a shrug, following Bernie up the stairs.

A nudge from Freddie got me moving. With a scowl, I moved up the steps, doing my best to ignore the ache in my feet and the part of my brain whispering, *This is too easy.*

"Have you seen the Tear?" I asked.

Nguyen nodded. "Once. Before we met Bernie and realised we needed something from Pollux to successfully cross."

We arrived on the scaffold. The mouth of the 'Ferris' wheel loomed ahead.

Kieran stopped. "Something from Pollux?" he repeated. His hand gave a nervous twitch.

I froze. That hand tick. Why now? What had him spooked? My gaze snapped to the tunnel and the vines and mould covering its walls. Thankfully, it was big enough that we wouldn't have to duck our heads. Creepy as fuck, sure, but Kieran's gaze wasn't on that. It was on Bernie.

Something from Pollux.

"Keep moving," Freddie spoke from behind us. He gave me another nudge. Not hard, but firm enough to make me lurch forward.

Something from Pollux.

The cold that had been growing in my limbs crept into my gut, settling there in a hard, icy block.

Kieran.

I was from Castor. But Kieran... wasn't. What was it Bernie had said? The watch needed materials from Pollux to work. How *much* material were we talking here? Could one watch provide enough Pollux material needed to guide seven people to its universe—or did it need more?

We rounded the lip of the tunnel mouth. And there, as I took in Bernie standing before a knot of vines in the middle of the tunnel—a knot that glinted yellow-white from the objects entwined within—it all came together. Bones. Pollux bones. The remains of his original team. I'd bet my life on it. A skull grinned at me from amongst the shrine. My stomach recoiled; nausea crept up my throat. They'd found the materials for their compass all right.

My hand snapped around Kieran's wrist, and I locked my knees, refusing to take another step. Was it me or were those vines pulsing? Skin crawling, I peered into the dark expanse beyond the mound of bones and couldn't see a thing.

"The actual f—"

"It's not what it looks like," Bernie interrupted, holding up his hands for peace. "They were already dead. We didn't kill them."

How reassuring... I took a step back; bumped into Freddie. "So you, what, dug them up?"

"Easy." Freddie's hand clapped down on my shoulder. "Wasn't like they were using the bones. And we really needed Pollux material. No harm, no foul." His fingers tightened around my shoulder. My hand clenched tighter around Kieran's wrist in turn. I wouldn't let them take him.

I expected a comment from my twin at that, but instead he frowned. "If you had the materials all along, why haven't you left yet?"

Bernie and Nguyen exchanged a glance, then Bernie cleared his throat. "Things have escalated since your Mum was here."

"Escalated?"

Bernie hesitated. Now that he was here and staring down the barrel of whatever it was he'd planned, his intensity had fled.

Like the coward he always was, part of my brain sneered. *Surprise, surprise.*

The old physicist wiped his palms on his khaki jacket and stepped forwards, fingers splayed, almost... pleading? "You have to believe me when I say we had no choice," he began.

I stepped between Kieran and him, fists clenched as I stared him down. "What are you talking about?"

"We made a bargain," Freddie spoke from behind us.

I rounded on him. "A bargain with who?" I demanded, flaring my arms to keep Kieran safe behind me. They had guns, true, but old habits and all that. Freddie shot a glance at Nguyen and Bernie, then shrugged, and pulled a thin grey tube from his belt. Glow stick. With a crack like a spine popping, Freddie set it off and a green glow suffused the tunnel. I got one look at Bernie and Nguyen's faces, all haggard lines and deep circles under their eyes, before the glow stick sailed past them and the bone pile and into the dark of the tunnel beyond.

It hit the vine-covered walkway with a soft thud.

The *floor* moved. Vines shifting and rolling towards the sphere of light. Far faster than anything I'd ever seen. And there, in the darkness, an unmistakable knot of vines.

The seed.

Another crack and a second glow stick joined the first. My jaw dropped as I made out a silhouette held aloft in the knot like some sort of zombie Jesus. Vines wrapped around desiccated limbs, coiled through an exposed ribcage, trailed from a mummified head.

"Sweet, mother of—" Kieran began. He took a half step forward. I grabbed him to stop him getting too close All the same, my jaw stayed open.

It looked like Bernie. An older Kieran, aged 105. Same jaw, same nose. My heart lurched. *It couldn't be.*

"Oh my God," Kieran breathed.

Not *like* Bernie. It *was* Bernie. Bernie *Castor. My* Dad.

Nguyen shifted again, his finger hovering over the trigger of his rifle. "Meet Zero. *Patient* Zero."

I stared at the thing encased in the vines. A brain, Bernie Pollux had called it. *The* brain of the Gemini Particle plague. I'd imagined something more like a root system; a network of vines all leading back to its single seed source. I hadn't pictured a person—or what was left of one.

Zero.

I swallowed. "Is he..?"

"It's not him. Not anymore. He's not alive, not really." Bernie Pollux said. "But the Particles have absorbed part of who he was." The vines shivered and pulsed again. The glazed stare of my father's dead eyes fixed on me. Don't ask me how, just know that I *felt* it. As sure as I felt the shudder run through Kieran beside me. I stared back, unable to tear my gaze away. *Literally.* My eyes wouldn't move.

At the back of my mind, a small bud unfurled. Like it had always been there. Maybe it had.

Hello, Kirsty.

Part Seven.

I stumbled back, the words in my head snapping me out of the primal freeze that had taken over my body.

"I can hear it! Why the *fuck* can I *hear* it?!"

"Kirsty?" Kieran. Alarmed. Crouched beside me, one hand on my back. Pain twinged in my knees from the walkway grate and I pulled my hands away from my ears. When had I sunk into a ball?

I glanced back down the tunnel to the *thing* at its end. Those empty eyes snared me again and the presence unfurled in my head once more.

Look at you, all grown up. Your Daddy is so proud.

I clapped my hands over my ears and tore my eyes away. *Oh God, make it stop.* "What is this?"

Bernie Pollux tapped his respirator. "Gemini Particle exposure."

My hands flew back to my respirator. The damp-clothes scent of a puppet had crept inside. I'd been so distracted by the tunnel's revelations I'd not checked it again. I launched up and rounded on the man, shoving him in the chest. "Bastard, you gave me a faulty respirator!" Asshole barely moved, damn it. He was stronger than he looked.

Bernie shook his head, gaze firmly down and not looking at the body wrapped in the darkness. "It's not. More likely from your exposure as a child," he whispered. "Enough to hear Zero, not enough for him to turn you into its puppet. "It's the same for Nguyen, Freddie and I. We're not sure why."

"That's Zero for you," Nguyen muttered.

Kasey gave a grunt. "Sometimes I think I'd rather be a puppet."

"Wait, you're saying it's speaking to you?" Keiran asked, the disbelief in his tone morphing into horror as he peered down the tunnel at the half-corpse.

"You don't hear it?"

"He won't, not for a while," Nguyen said. "He wasn't as close to ground zero when it all kicked off. Minimal exposure, like Kasey and Lorne." He gestured to the two soldiers.

"First generation born after the breach." Lorne said, voice sour. At my confusion he tapped his respirator. "Been wearing these the moment we came out of our mamas. Lucky us."

Kieran cocked his head, the wrinkle of doubt in his forehead slowly smoothing over. He swallowed. "And this Zero, you said you made a bargain with *it*?"

Bernie nodded. "The Gemini watches worked before the particles became sentient. Before the breach fifty years ago, we could pop back and forth with just a handful of particles and the material of the watch to guide the way. But now? Now, Zero controls who comes and who goes."

"It stopped you leaving the first time you tried," Kieran said, understanding crossing his face.

They all nodded. By the light of the glow stick, I saw the fear. *This.* This was the source. The thing that terrified them. Terrified Bernie. A sentience who barred his way, trapping him in this dying universe.

I licked my lips, cleared my throat, tongue thick in my mouth. "What was the bargain?"

An achingly long silence followed my question. Until Nguyen cleared his throat and said, "It wants you, Kirsty."

Me? It was as if my brain had hurtled headlong into a dive, only to bellyflop instead. Not Kieran? But *me?*

The presence tugged at my mind. *Knock, knock, Kirsty. I know you hear me.*

I clenched my fists. However Zero was doing it, it had its hooks in now. But I'd not survived thirty years of Mum's bullshit to be railroaded into submission now. "How did it even know I was here?" I growled through my teeth.

Bernie tapped his head. "Zero sensed you arrive and commanded—" he broke off with a shudder, and I guessed Zero had whispered something into his mind "—Zero *asked* us to fetch you," he amended.

Kieran glowered at his Dad, his anger palpable. His body quivered with it. "You're no better than the puppets. Worse, even. They don't have a choice."

Nguyen came to Bernie's defence, stepping between them with hands outstretched, as if he might ward off a blow. "We've been waiting for years for Zero to come to the table. Decades searching for something we could bargain with. Your arrival gave us this chance. We have to take it."

I unclenched my jaw, rage and disbelief boiling inside me. "But *why?* Why *me?*"

"Because it was your Dad," Bernie said.

I've gone to a lot of trouble to see you again, baby girl. Least you could do is look your Da-da in the eye.

I flinched as Zero's voice spoke in my head but kept my gaze down, just like Bernie, Nguyen and Freddie were doing.

"It has his old thought patterns. Learned those pathways," Bernie went on. "He died wanting you. So now Zero thinks it needs you too."

We'll do great things, you and me. We'll devour universes whole.

I clenched my teeth against Zero's whisperings and rubbed my ears. No good. Kieran's hand fell across my shoulders, and my twin's face loomed in my peripheral vision.

"You okay, Kiz? What's it saying?" His eyes were large behind the respirator, but instead of the fear I'd seen in the others, there was fire. Hot anger. I frowned.

It starts with moodiness, Bernie had said about Gemini Particle exposure. *The particles hijack the frontal lobe of a person's brain.*

I rarely knew my twin to be really, truly angry. That was my job. I was the one who fought—whether in the schoolyard or the courtroom, I'd never backed down. Kieran had never had that inclination. At least, not until recently. He'd always played peacekeeper, always grovelling and gophering, doormatting himself to Mum's every whim, then drowning himself in whatever drug he needed to numb it afterwards. Was this just him trying to mirror my confidence or was he showing early signs of Gemini Particle exposure? Not enough to hear Zero, but enough to give him the confidence he craved.

Either way, anger was still a far cry from action—and an even further cry if you were Kieran.

With an effort, I glared at Zero down the tunnel, fixing my gaze firmly on its withered ribcage. "Fine, you got me here. Now what?"

Join me. Become me.

"Like hell I will."

Bernie wiped his palms on his jacket again in what I was beginning to recognise as his nervous tick. "Actually, that's exactly what we need you to do. Giving you to Zero is the price of our passage." He tried to arrange his face into something earnest. "Not just for us. This world still has survivors. The way would stay open for anyone wanting safe passage to Pollux."

"Pollux is doomed too, you said."

"Time dilation. Enough to live out our lives," Bernie reminded. "For everyone who crosses."

Ahh, there it was. Selfishness wrapped up in selflessness. The ol' 'don't think about me, think about the hundreds of people you'd save' yada, yada. Meanwhile, he'd get to cross into Pollux and go on his merry way while my mind and body were sacrificed to the zombie mould.

Yes, come to Daddy.

Shut up.

I was about to tell them all where to shove it, when Kieran stepped between us, squaring his shoulders and meeting Bernie eye to eye. Okay, more like eye to Bernie's chin, but he tilted his head and held his old man's gaze.

"Don't listen to them," he said to me. "If there's another way, we'll find it."

"There isn't," Bernie snapped, a flicker of intensity returning. Or desperation. Probably desperation. "Zero controls the Particles. He controls the way through. What part of that don't you understand?"

Kieran quivered, and for a heartbeat, I thought my twin might take an uncharacteristic swing at him. Until true form reasserted itself and he relented, looking to his mismatched boots. "There has to be another way," he said to the pile of bones at his feet. "*Please, Dad.*"

Ooof, way to play the Dad card.

Bernie Pollux flinched. Beside him, Nguyen hesitated.

"You're sure there isn't another way?" Kieran asked.

Bernie shook his head. "This isn't a logic problem we can fix. It's an emotional one," he said, jabbing a finger at the corpse down the tunnel. "Bernie Castor's last wish before the Gemini Particles took him over was to be with his daughter again. The Gemini Particles now carry that wish."

Nguyen waved his dive device at us. "Hate to be the bearer of bad news, but the readings are getting higher. We can't stay here much longer or we'll *all* end up puppets. Respirators or not."

Bernie stepped around Kieran, clasping my hands in his. "If not for us, do it for Kieran," he whispered. "He will cross with us. Safely back to Pollux. I promise."

"What? No!" Kieran tried to push Bernie out of the way. The old man didn't budge. Dude had more strength than I gave him credit. A second later, Nguyen and Freddie were wrestling Kieran away, one arm locked around each shoulder.

"Stop, Kieran! Just... just let me think," I said to Bernie.

"Think faster," he said. "This universe is on the verge of collapsing. Pollux is the only way any of us survive this and you're the only one who can get us through. Now, I know you probably don't give one whit what happens to us, but your sacrifice will save your brother too. You've always taken care of him, haven't you? I see it." He nodded to Nguyen and the gun bros with their stranglehold on Kieran. "They see it. This is how you save him. Him and us." He gave my hands a squeeze. Just how Kieran always did. "We'll remember you. Honour you for as long as Pollux holds."

That was how he was putting it? Framing me up as noble and brave. A sacrifice for the greater good. Anger flared inside me, even as my palms turned clammy and my heart drummed high and fast in my throat. I forced a trembling breath, then another. Call me a selfish bitch, but I didn't want to die. I glared at Bernie. At his wiry frame and sun-blasted skin born from fifty-four years living in the apocalypse. Maybe he deserved to go home.

But so did I. My hands curled into fists at my side.

I was about to tell him where to shove it when my gaze fell on Kieran, still locked in Nguyen and Freddie's hold. I stopped, anger falling away like a stone dropped down a well, and my stomach did that squeeze that only Kieran could make it do. My twin. My brother. The only family I had in any of these fucked up universes. He was the one who cared. Who nurtured. Who screwed up over and over but still found a way to pick himself up, dust himself off and try again.

He was the one who'd stayed.

And, like that, Bernie's words made sense. What was there for me to return to in Pollux anyway? I was the fighter; Kieran was the lover. I'd fought with fists, fought with words, fought to leave Mum's shadow and then for my career. Left to my devices, I'd have kept on fighting. Gone back to work. And every day I'd return home to an empty house, empty calendar, and a social media feed void of genuine connection.

I drew in a shuddering breath. "Okay."

"Kirsty, *NO*." Kieran's shout echoed through the tunnel.

The old scientist-turned-solider nodded and released my hands. "Let her say goodbye," he instructed Nguyen and Freddie. They relaxed their hold on Kieran and let him stand properly, though Freddie's grip remained on the cuff of Kieran's shirt.

"Don't do this," Kieran pleaded, looking between Bernie and me.

I stepped in close and wrapped my arms around him. I couldn't remember the last time I'd hugged him. Should have done it more.

"Make something of yourself, eh?" I whispered to him. "Maybe ease up on the weed a bit though." He let out a hollow laugh that choked into a sob. Kieran had always been comfortable crying. Didn't care who saw. I wish I could have been like that.

"You don't have to do this," he said.

"I do."

I released him. Didn't dare look at his face when I did or my resolve would shatter. Instead, I stared down the tunnel at Zero. "What do I have to do?"

Come to me. Together we'll unmake this universe.

It was doing a pretty good job of that on his own. Bernie was right where emotion was concerned. Often logic wasn't involved. Just a want. Right now, that want was me. But the fighter part of me wanted a better explanation.

"Then what?" I demanded. "You get me, finish devouring our worlds. What then?"

I expected something like, *'And then we die', or 'We end' or 'We stop existing',* because that made sense. Even the Gemini Particles needed a universe to exist in. Zero's answer was none of these.

Then we go back to sleep and wait for the next universes to call us.

I blinked, my brain giving an odd warping sensation as all the implications of its words resounded through my head. It would *sleep*? Sleep where? What kind of entity could exist without a universe? Without reality? A glance at Bernie and Nguyen confirmed they'd heard Zero's answer too and were as baffled as I. Only, Bernie's face was morphing into one of abject horror.

What? I wanted to scream at him.

He got it wrong, Zero chuckled our heads. *We are so much more than these universes.*

Understanding dawned, and that block of ice in my belly surged through my veins, turning my entire body numb. The experiment Mum had been running that started all of this had been in search of dark matter. Naysayers and fearmongers had warned she might unleash a blackhole on our world. But what if she'd unleashed something worse? Knocked on the doors of reality only to have something beyond knock back? The Gemini Particles *weren't* of this universe—they weren't of *any* universe. They were something *un*-real.

Next to them, Freddie jerked Kieran's shirt collar. "Move along," he said. His free hand tapped the dive gauge. "Some of us are on a time limit. Your bro included."

Kieran stiffened, that hot anger returning to his eyes like he might whirl and tackle the soldier holding him. Then he deflated, arms going limp, and Freddie relaxed as he relented.

That's it, play the peacekeeper, I willed. *Stay alive.* My chest tightened, twinging in the way that only Kieran could make it. *Go home. Live. Laugh—*

The fire flared in Kieran's eyes again. Quick as a viper, he rounded on Freddie, lunged for his belt. His fingers found the holster, wrenched the gun free and offloaded it. Into Freddie. "Run Kirsty!"

The soldier didn't so much as grunt. Just slumped to the walkway and stared—as if stunned Kieran had actually done it. My twin rounded on me, adrenalin turning his eyes huge and dark. He gulped once, caught his breath, then screamed at me again.

"Run!"

I stumbled back two steps, the heel of my sneaker squelching into Zero's bone shrine. I glanced down. Vines slithered under my foot, and I jerked my shoe away.

Bang.

I hit the deck as the second gunshot sounded. Caught a glimpse of Nguyen's upraised rifle as I went.

Bang BANG.

Those from behind. *Kasey and Lorne.*

I rolled over. Kieran stood over me. He swayed. Shifted. Locked his knees to stop himself from falling. My heart stopped. Three bullet shaped holes had ripped through his shirt. Burrowed deep in his chest. Blood ringed the wounds, soaking through the fabric in larger and larger splotches.

Zero chortled from the back of the tunnel. *Come to me, baby girl.*

No, no, no.

I launched upwards, grabbing Kieran as he swayed again. Too late. He fell sideways. Slipping through my fingers and landing against the wall, which woke with a surge of vines. Tendrils sprang to life, wrapping Kieran fast. His respirator was knocked askew, and our gazes met. Terror and triumph all at once. He gave me a lopsided grin.

"Couldn't let you do it."

Idiot! This was not how it was supposed to go. I grabbed Kieran shirt and pulled. *Pop-pop-pop* went the fabric until it tore free into my hands. I tried to grab for him again, only to snatch my fingers away as a vine coiled around Kieran's middle and pulled him deeper.

Yes, that's it, baby girl, come to me! Join me! Zero crowed.

Confusion rose in the midst of my panic. Did Zero think Kieran was me?

Something DC Nguyen had said back in Pollux rose through the panic. *"Positive match both times."* I thought of how the police had puzzled over freezer Jane Doe's fingerprints—*Roza Pollux's* fingerprints. I'd assumed Kieran and I were too different to ever have the same mix up; Kieran had a Y chromosome after all. But since then, we'd learned we were not fraternal twins but the same person from different universes. Perhaps our DNA was more alike than we thought. Yet, as I thought it, a line from Mum's journal filled my head.

My place—the 'role' I filled in the universe—was already in use.

Perhaps it wasn't about DNA at all. Perhaps we matched one-to-one in some other, unknowable way. Some shared intrinsic nature.

Perhaps Zero was simply too far gone to notice his error.

I didn't care. Zero was taking my twin. My *brother.* This was not how it was supposed to go. I was the fighter. The protector. That was how it'd always been. *Shithouse timing for finding your spine, bro.* My hand closed around his hair, gripping tight.

"Let him go!" I screamed.

Kieran's eyes grew distant. Blood gurled in his throat. Dimly I was aware of the soft, slow smile spreading across his face. *Don't smile you—*

Then he was ripped away. Vines closed around him, forcing me back with nothing but a bloody clump of hair in my hands. Gone. Consumed.

I sank to my knees. This couldn't be happening. "It was supposed to be me."

Baby girl. Daughter dearest, Zero murmured, cooing like a dove. I scrubbed at my ears, desperate to block it out. *My one, my only... Daddy missed you so much... Wait, you're not—no, who are—*

Deep in the tunnel, Zero's body twitched. The vines holding Bernie Castor's body to the wall sagged then clenched, like the death grasp of a giant hand.

Stop. Get out! Zero's shriek reverberated through my skull. Something in my head swelled, throbbed, one hundred times worse than my worst migraine. Gemini Particles; had to be. It was as if Zero was clawing its half-dead fingers down the inside of my skull.

Go away! Zero screeched.

Bernie gasped, hands instinctively flying to each temple. Nguyen curled into himself with a grunt. Already on the walkway, I hugged myself into a ball. Zero continued wrestling with something inside my head. Like two versions of itself were in a boxing match over my brain.

"Sir! Sergeant!" Kasey yelled, running to Nguyen's side while Lorne tended to Freddie. They dragged them onto their shoulders.

Go away! Zero screamed again.

Too late, motherfucker. Kieran. Inside my head. Holy shit. My twin was inside my head. Not dead, but wrenching control from Zero. What in the actual—

I glanced at the remains of Bernie Castor. Its ribs were crushed, desiccated limbs askew. Broken. A faint 'beep' sounded from my wrist. The watch. Glowing green for the first time in days.

Go. Go now! Kieran sounded in my head again. *I can't hold it back for long.*

My brain churned, trying to make sense of it. My twin was inside Zero. Boots clattered behind me as Kasey and Lorne dragged Freddie and Nguyen towards the end of the tunnel where something ... *shimmered.* I squinted. No, wasn't my eyes. The air itself was warping, like heat haze on a baking summer's day. Everything shifting and swaying. Zero's face in the vines distorted, but I could have sworn the vines were bulging next to it.

"Wait!" I shouted at the gun bros. They needed the watch. Needed Gemini Particles to shield them and something from Pollux to navigate the way. At the same time, Bernie Pollux's voice rang through the tunnel. "Hold on, Sergeant!"

The old scientist staggered to his feet, swayed once as if he was drunk, then dug two gloved fingers into one of the skulls in the bone shrine. With a curse, or perhaps a prayer of forgiveness, he wrenched it free of the vines. With a grimace, he straightened, then reached into a pocket and pulled a battered Gemini Particle watch out. Even from where I stood, it was clearly a cobbled together thing; it looked more like a walkie talkie with a bubble imbedded where the speaker should be. But underneath the glass, I glimpsed the swirl of Gemini Particles.

Sneaky bastard did have a spare. I eyed another bone poking out of Zero's shrine. And plenty of scavenged Pollux material. He'd accounted for everything—except for sentient particles barring his way. But no longer.

Bernie tossed the skull to Lorne and the watch-turned-walkie-talkie to Kasey. "You'll need those."

Lorne caught one, Kasey the other and with a nod, grasped the bleeding Freddie and wobbly Nguyen. With a nod to Bernie, Lorne mashed down the walkie talkie's button. As one, the party vanished.

Bernie Pollux's hands fell around my shoulders. Hauled me up. "Now us," he said.

Hurry, Kieran whispered in my head.

"Why?" I mumbled, struggling to get my legs to work. Felt like whatever signals when from my brain to my limbs had been scrambled. How Bernie managed to move at all was beyond me. The old dude was tough. I'd give him that.

"I'm not running away. Not this time," he said, the tendons in his jaw popping as he pulled me all the way to my feet.

My gut twinged. First time anyone other than Kieran had made it do that. I glanced back at Zero and my chest spasmed again. A new face had emerged from the bulge of vines on the wall. Kieran's. His eyes—still sea blue, but deeper... darker—found mine and pinned me.

Go home, Kirsty. For me.

Pain pricked in my palms. My nails digging in as I clenched my fists. "That's not fair. You don't get to do this."

Bernie frowned as he steadied me. "I know you're upset, but there's no knowing how long the ability to cross will stay unimpeded. We have to go—"

I ignored him and focused on Kieran. Gemini Particles clumped on his cheeks, down his throat, across his forehead. I bit my lip to stop the hot tears gathering behind my eyes. "God damn it, Kieran, you don't get to do this."

I do. My twin's eyes crinkled around the edges as he gave me a sad smile. *I couldn't let you go through with it. You always looked out for me. Protected me when Mum wouldn't.*

Until I didn't. Until I left! I wanted to rage. Or scream. Or cry. Where was the ice queen when I needed her? Everything was falling apart.

Bernie tugged at my arm, pulling me closer to the Tear. I dug in my heels. He reached for my watch. One press, and I'd be through. Back home.

Only, it wouldn't be home. Not anymore. Everyone I cared about—the *only* person I cared about—was here.

And like that, I knew I couldn't do it. Couldn't leave. Everyone who might have ever cared for Kieran had left. His Dad. Both Mums. His wives. And me—and I'd nearly done twice. I wouldn't leave my twin alone in this dead universe. I reached for the Gemini watch on my wrists, flipped off the strap.

"I left once. I won't leave again." My mouth formed the words mechanically, like I was watching through someone else. Bernie forced another step out of me. I don't even know if he heard. Not that it mattered. My mind was made up.

"Do something with the time you have left," I said, and pressed the watch against his wrist, mushed the Velcro straps together, and hit the button. Bernie's grey eyebrows shot up, a surprised gasp escaping him. I pushed him hard, and at last, the bastard moved. He stumbled back a step, then two. The watch beeped. And he vanished.

Kirsty, go home, Kieran's voice sounded sharp in my head. Half commanding, half pleading.

"I *am* home."

I pushed up my sweater's sleeves and pressed my hands into the vines. They were softer than I expected. Fuzzy and kind of mushy.

When the vines reached for me, I didn't fight. If Kieran could take a turn as the fighter, I could be the peacemaker. I leaned into the wall and closed my eyes. When the tendrils picked me up and drew me in, they were tender. The pressure in my head built again, but instead of pain, it was a release; a lifetime of tension falling away. Falling into the system that was Zero.

A universe of awareness winked to life inside me. Hundreds of vines, billions upon billions of spores. Millions of puppets milling to and fro, mindless and waiting for my command. How was I here and not one of them?

"I'm still getting a grasp on it, but it's something to do with Bernie Castor." Kieran said from beside me. Not physically beside me, of course. There was no seeing. No bodies in this place. But somehow, I knew he was next to me. Maybe more figuratively than literally. *"Your Dad's desire to have you meant the Particles didn't try to control us but sort of merged with us instead."*

"No, get out. Cheating, lying, bastard—" Zero/Bernie-Castor seethed, pushing at my twin. I sensed them wrestling for control of the system. Kieran's hold wobbled as the more experienced operator gained ground. I reached out my figurative hand, bolstering Kieran's will with mine and our hold stabilised.

"No, daughter, baby girl, don't do this."

I shoved him down, wrapping my will around the parts of him in Zero. Kieran's will joined mine as he sensed my intention. *"You're no father of mine."*

Our wills synchronised. *"GET OUT,"* we bellowed, and gave Bernie/Zero one almighty shove. Mid-scream, the presence that was Bernie/Zero snuffed out. I felt a body encased in vines pop out of a tunnel wall and clatter to the walkway. Quite dead.

Silence followed. Hours, days, weeks, we couldn't tell. Time was a thing for universes, and we'd become something beyond that. All the same, with great effort Kieran gathered himself and probed the edge of the Tear.

"You think they made it though?"

"I like to think so," I replied. I stretched out my awareness, feeling through the Tear to its furthest edges in the other universe where our particles were slowly gathering. Building in number to herald our arrival. *"You ready?"*

I sent him a flicker of assent and grasped my figurative hand around his once more. Our minds set and synchronised, we stretched ourselves out across the universes. Felt where our tendrils burrowed. Bit by bit, we pulled them back. Bernie/Zero had been greedy. Full of want. Zero/Kirsty/Kieran would not be like our forebearers. This much we vowed.

Gently, we retreated into the Tear to buy our worlds time. How much is anyone's guess. Our awareness doesn't work on human timescales anymore. Here, in this place between universes, we're alone. But together. And here we'll stay, elbows locked together, wills overlapping, holding our particles at bay.

Holding until time is no more.

KARKINOS

Sign: Cancer
Element: Water
Symbol: Crab
Dates: June 22 to July 22

Water presses cool against my face. Below, the seabed is quiet; a sweet stillness broken by the faint 'click-click' of parrotfish biting away chunks of coral. I drag in a lungful of air and bubbles hiss up from my tank. God, I love this place—I should have come back sooner.

With a kick I surge forward, heading for the wreck on my underwater horizon. It's even more overgrown with coral than I remember. Fish dart in and out of portholes and between rigging laden with seagrass. The visibility is superb. Thirty meters at least. I haven't seen it like this since...

Since Mary.

We never found out what happened. Not for sure. She went out for a snorkel one day—not far, she said, just off the beach—and never came back. Then noon trickled into evening and I called the island police. Searched everywhere. Other bays, the reef, the wreck—no sign. Hit by a boat, some said. Taken by a shark, said others.

And my Mary was gone. Cut from my life clean as a doll cut from paper, with nothing but a Mary-shaped hole left behind. I scoured that beach of five years, hoping against hope I would find some clue, a trace, an answer, anything. I looked for her in the faces of strangers every trip into town. Nothing.

Keegan talked me into the funeral. *"You've got to move on Dad."*

Shortly after, at Keegan's insistence, I picked up my shattered pieces, closed the door on our family home of forty years and left for Broome.

I hadn't been back since. Not in eight years.

A school of angelfish scatter as I glide down to investigate a table coral. Its colour is vivid, orange and pink. I hang there, suspended, feeling the faint pull of the current. *What would it be like,* I wonder, *to simply float away?* To forget the aches and pains of the world above and drift?

A dart of movement draws me back to the wreck. With a flick of fins and a scooping of hands, I turn, an ungainly whale of neoprene and air tank. It's a crab; nestled down in the broken hold. Its blue carapace glints through the weed and coral fingers, and I drop closer and closer again, hoping for a better look. Its shell is at least the width of my splayed hand. Perhaps bigger. A good size. *A good supper.* I snatch at it. My gloved hand gives a faint tremble before my fingers clamp around the crab's abdomen and pull it from its cranny. Its legs kick, pincers writhe, antennae whirl. I drop it inside my dive net.

It stares up at me, black eye stalks forlorn through its prison net. My stomach gives the tiniest of guilty twists. Circle of life, buddy.

Let it go. A memory of Mary visits me. It's the height of summer and I'm fishing off the town jetty; she's ridden her pushbike up to see what I've caught. She doesn't know me then, not really. But she frowns when she peers into my bucket and sees the crab I've netted from the muddy shallows.

"Let it go," she says at once.

I stare at this girl—almost a woman, but not quite—who tries to tell me what to do with my catch. *"No way,"* I say. *"That's dinner."*

She wrinkles her nose. *"It's mean."* Her eyes settle on me and glint with a hint of mischief I'll come to know well. *"And..."*

"And what?"

The corners of her mouth tick up, like she's suddenly letting me in on a secret. She leans in. *"And I don't much fancy crab for dinner."*

I blink, astonished, then grin and hold out my hand. *"Name's Roy, Roy Quin. Pick you up at seven?"*

Like that, we met. Over a crab. Fifty years married we would have been, come tomorrow. When she didn't come back that day, when she must have inevitably sunk to the seafloor, the crustaceans probably picked her corpse—

I wrench my mind away, bubbles belching from my regulator as my heart flips in my chest. Don't think it. Not of her... not like that. My eyes burn behind my mask. I check my dive gauge. Half a tank left, but my enthusiasm has waned. It's been enough for this old man. I turn to go.

A metallic gleam from the hole I pulled the crab from catches my eye. I stop, squint and push some weed away, revealing a crusted—I pause, not quite able to believe it—handle? I feel my fingers further into the hole, trying to discern whatever it is that's lodged inside. Despite the algae and barnacles, its shape is unmistakably rectangular. I dig my fingers around it, brace my fins against the bones of the deck and pull.

The crab in my dive net kicks and twitches, waves its pincers like angry fists.

A box slides out the hole—covered in rust and baby coral. I stare, recognising what it is at once.

A safe.

#

The safe is heavy and I'm puffing by the time I haul it along the beach, up the sand track, and place it on the rickety table in the living room. Water puddles across the dry wood, bringing the smell of brine and seaweed with it. I eye the lock, or what's left of it: a barnacled knot of metal and cemented sand. One decisive blow with a hammer could snap it clean off, but I don't have anything like that here. I left it all with Keegan back in Broome. If I call him now, I'll get a lecture about diving alone. He'd not been keen on me moving back here as it was.

"Are you sure, Dad?" he'd asked, hazel eyes earnest like Mary's. *"It's a long way from anywhere. And with your health..."*

I'd told him, in no uncertain terms, that that was the point. *"I'm dying. Nothing you or me or the doctors can do about it. I'm doing this while I can."*

My son had sighed, looked like he'd wanted to say more, until Zoe had run into the hallway, begging her father to see the model train set she'd assembled. With a meaningful glance as he was pulled away, he'd said: *"I'll check up on you every other week. Call if you need anything. And take your pills."*

I turn the safe around on the table, ignoring how the barnacles scrape gouges into the wood. The safe is small, not more than a box really, and barely a hand deep. I rummage through the kitchen drawers, my shaky hands scattering the cutlery until I finally catch a butter knife. Back at the table, I wedge it through the lock's arched shackle and twist. The pressure builds, and the disease trembles my hands. I growl and adjust my grip, leaning my weight on the knife. The silverware bends instead. And just when I think it is going to fold in two, the clasp of the lock snaps. With a ping, sand and flakes of rust scatter across the table.

"Ha!" I bark in triumph and reach for the lid. And stop.

A scratching, clicking sound comes from the kitchen.

Frowning, I leave the safe untouched and go to investigate.

It's the crab. Crawling across the floor, dragging my dive bag with it. The critter has pulled itself up and out of the kitchen sink and made a break across the tiles. Its plate-sized shell gleams a stormy blue in the evening light. The eye stalks swivel on me; pincers snap up.

And it charges.

Yes, *charges.* Crab-runs sideways at me it does, pincers raised, legs skittering over the tiles. I step out of its way. I'm barefoot; I don't fancy one of those pincers around my toes.

The crab follows. Still coming for me.

"What in the—" I backpedal, a familiar stiffness tinged with pain turns my gait awkward and ungainly, like my legs don't belong to me anymore.

Still the crab comes.

I lunge for the sagging sofa, near falling onto it, and with effort, heave my feet up after me.

The crab stops. Its antennae twitch, eye stalks shift from me to the dripping safe on the table. And there it stays. Watching.

Slowly, I uncoil on the sofa, lower one foot on the floor, then the other, and wait. The critter doesn't move.

Get ahold of yourself Roy, it's just a crab.

With a groan, I haul myself onto my feet. My muscles spasm with the effort. I miss the water already, the weightlessness of it, the freedom from my shaking. How easy it is to move again.

I approach the crab, thinking to scoop up the end of the dive net and return it to the sink, but as I come close, its pincers rise, claws open. I take one step towards the creature and it thrusts its pincers out, warding me off. When I try to grab the dive net, it scuttles around and lunges for my hand. I snatch my fingers back, cursing. Little cretin nearly got me.

I back up and the crab settles, squatting into itself like an irate spider.

"Think you've won, eh?"

The crab, for its part, jerks its antennae like it's flipping me the bird.

I grind my teeth and think of the bucket under the laundry sink. How I might thump it down over the wily crustacean and jostle it back into my sink, and then into a pot.

When I do thump said bucket over the crab, it goes ballistic. Its legs scrabble, sounding like a rat under the floorboards. It claws bang against its plastic prison, and the bucket skitters across the floor as it tries to free itself. I heft a dusty, spine-split Macquarie dictionary with both hands from the bookshelf. My muscles quiver as I carry it tight against my chest, then drop it on top of the bucket to hold it down.

With a sigh, I shuffle to the table where I'd left the safe. I hold my breath as my hands clench the lid—a strong grip to stop the tremors—and push it up. It opens soundlessly. Not so much as a squeak. I blink. I'd expected a shrieking of rusted hinges, a groan of metal, but the lid swings open like it's freshly oiled. Strange.

Thunk, thunk, thunk. The crab bashes its bucket.

I look inside the safe.

I don't know what I was expecting. A few corroded coins, perhaps a quill and inkpot, remnants of a journal, though the pages would have disintegrated years ago; maybe a pocket watch.

Thunk, thunk, thunk, goes the crab.

I stare. Hot and cold flush through me. My belly curdles.

It's a heart.

#

It's not a human heart. Too big. Far, *far* too big. Four of my fists in size at least. And it's metal. Cogs and gears and springs are enclosed behind a glass carapace. Brass funnels curl out of its top and side: the aorta and main arteries. A clock face lies over one ventricle—strange and impossibly small symbols are carved where the numbers should be, each one a series of dots and lines. Twelve in all. The clock itself has two hands: one is normal looking, the other has a tiny orb at its end painted half black, half white.

But that's not the clincher.

The clincher is that *it's moving*.

Deep within the heart, the fine gears slowly turn. It takes a long minute for me to be sure, but yes, there it goes, a tooth in the largest gear clicks over.

A breath shudders out of me. "Incredible." How has such a thing survived the sea? Waterproof. It must be. New too, surely. There's no tarnish of age. But what about the state of the safe? All appearances suggest it has been underwater for tens of years, if not hundreds.

With tentative hands, I lift the heart out of the safe. It's heavy. I tighten my grip on it, feeling the tell-tale quiver in my fingers. The brass and glass surface slides in my grip. It's still wet. Slippery too.

And *warm*.

I swallow.

Then the heart beats. The metal doesn't shift, not like a heart of flesh might, but *something* shivers through my hands, up my arms.

I nearly drop it on the table.

That's when I see the reverse side. Another clock face. Only this one has various shaded circles depicted on it; its single hand pointed at a waxing circle, almost full. *It's the moon.*

Thunk, thunk, thunk. I jump as the crab starts up its banging again. Stronger than before. The bucket scrapes across the floor, gaining a few centimetres. I consider my find on the table a moment longer, then go out back to retrieve my dive gloves. They're still wet, but I pull them on and head into the lounge. The bucket has moved another half metre.

With a sigh, I lift off the dictionary, remove the bucket and scoop the crab up in the dive net. I take it outside and sit on the back deck to untangle it. It is tedious work; the crab's pincers chomp down on my gloved fingers and don't let go until I pry its claws apart. I curse. Several times. The thing's like a bloody limpet. And every time I loosen a claw, its antenna thrash furiously. I can almost imagine it swearing at me.

At last I get it free. I pull myself up on the handrail and shuffle across the yard, past the leaning picket fence and along the sandtrack through the dunes.

"You're in luck today, crab." I tell it as I set it down on the beach. "Any other time and I'd have eaten you."

I release the crustacean. But instead of scuttling off, it stands there. Pincers lax and open. Almost as if I've surprised it. I roll my eyes at the thought. *It's a crab, for Pete's sake.* I flick a bit of sand at it with my toes.

"Go on, off you go. If you're so keen to live, go get on with it."

When it doesn't move, I shrug, turn and creak back over the dune. A smile crooks my lips as I walk.

That was for you, Mary.

#

Plink, plink.

I wake to the sound of coins clinking together. Coins? I'm imagining it, surely. Half asleep and with the stiffness holding my limbs to ransom, I open my eyes and listen.

Plink, plink, it comes again. And when I strain my ears: rustling, scratching, clicking. I stare into the dark, my stomach shrivelling into a gristly knot. The darkness isn't the still, quiet dark I've always known. It's moving; shadows within shadow shifting and rolling, and my mind fills with the thought of bugs carpeting the floor.

I claw my body up, levering myself on the bedside table. My muscles shudder—they're always particularly bad first thing in the morning before I take my medicine; like Tin Man left out in the rain. Fingers find the nightstand lamp, tap it on. Light flares.

And my floor moves. Blues, reds, browns and oranges, scuttle away from the lamp. The yell rises in my throat and gets lodged there. A hacking, spluttering cough comes out instead.

Crabs. Hundreds of them. Different shapes, sizes, species: there, a mud crab found in the local estuary, and there, a golden ghost crab, and over there a lopsided fiddler.

Plink, plink. I round on the sound coming from the foot of the bed. A mound of metal sits at my feet, covered in algae and dripping a puddle into my sheet. As I gape, a hermit crab, no bigger than my palm, crawls over the foot of the bed and drops a gold coin onto the pile. Despite the coin's green corroded tint, I spot the unmistakable markings of an Australian dollar.

"Consider this payment." A small voice rises from my nightstand.

I spin, heart buoying up my chest and into my throat.

There's a crab on my nightstand. A familiar crab. The very one I'd set loose on the beach some hours ago now, I'm sure of it. Big and blue and...

I hesitate, suddenly not trusting my eyes.

... Not a crab?

I mean, it's a crab, but the longer I look, the less crab-like it becomes. It stands erect on three sets of legs, one of which taps as if its patience is thinning. The next pair are folded, like a set of arms, and above that thrust its claws, gesticulating to get my attention.

"Yes, down here. Good, you can hear me properly. At last."

Gobsmacked, I lean in. The eyestalks on its head change, looking more and more like an odd armoured helm. Its antennae and mouth shift too, until a strange humanoid face stares back at me; antennae like a living beard on its chin.

"What... what... is—are..?"

The crab-man gives something of a little sigh, his shell shrugging. "I am Guardian Tasi, and we—" he waves his claws out to the room— "are karkinoi."

My gaze follows Tasi's claws and as it does, the crabs before me change too. Each one turns into tiny humanoids with armoured bodies and antennae on their chins.

I'm hallucinating. That's it. Only explanation. I flop onto my pillow, rub my face, check the nightstand again.

He's still there.

Fuck. All right, think. First thing, call Keegan. Tell him I've gone crackers, full kitchen sink nuts. Though, truth be told, I'd always thought my independence would be claimed by disease, not insanity. The thought boils inside me. I feel cheated. This was supposed to be my last hurrah. Sunset years while I could still have them. And I'd barely been here a week.

"You're not crazy. You folk always seem to think that. Now, to business." Tasi snaps his pincers. "We wish to trade."

"Trade?"

"Yes, we have brought you gold and coins given to the sea. A small fortune, yes? We wish to trade it for the Heart."

"The heart?" The clockwork heart on my lounge table flashes into my head. *That* heart? But what could these probably-just-my-imagination karkinoi crab folk want with it? "Why?" I blurt.

"A sea witch trusted it to our keeping long ago. It was our—*my*—duty to guard it—" he glares at the edge of the nightstand, not meeting my eye— "to keep it safe."

Despite the scene of crabs in my bedroom, I lift an eyebrow. "You didn't do a very good job of it, if you don't mind me saying."

Tasi's leg stamps hard on the nightstand. The mottled blue of his shell darkens. "I *do* mind, but what's done is done."

Seems I hit a nerve.

Tasi folds his claws. "Landfolk usually don't see us or our treasures at all. But somehow you did. You took it and bested me. So now I am here to trade for it."

I blink at the karkinoi, thinking of how the crab had bashed at the bucket when I'd opened the safe. How it had thrashed and bit when I'd freed it from the dive net. He was right, I *had* bested him. But if I were to set my chin on the nightstand, he'd barely come up to my brow. Hardly something to be proud of. To him I am giant; monstrous; a Goliath in the extreme. And still he stands there, annoyed, granted, but ready to barter. Got to admire the courage of the fellow. To think I'd nearly put him in a pot. But something Tasi said comes back to me and I frown.

"You said I saw you, but I didn't. Until tonight you looked..." I hesitate, wondering if saying 'crab' might be construed as derogatory, the same way 'monkey' might to a human. "Not like you do now." I amend.

"You saw the lockbox, and Tasi in his guise. Before you touched the heart that is," a new voice wheezes from my elbow. I start and look down. The hermit crab, the same one that'd dropped its coin at the foot of my bed, has scuttled up without my noticing. It's barely a third the size of Tasi as it stands on its back pairs of legs. Its features are finer still; the shell on its back reminding me of a giant snail's. But when I look closer, there's markings—tiny writing—all over the shell.

"If I were to guess, I'd say you were partially sighted," the hermit crab says, and scratches one claw to its scraggly antennae-beard as if thinking. "It is rare among landfolk, but not unheard of." Its voice is rasping and higher pitched, like it might be an old female hen. But it's a guess at best. I'm hardly the expert.

"Lorekeeper Wehi." Tasi acknowledges the newcomers with a bob of a claw. Wehi returns the greeting.

"But I've never seen you before or the safe," I point out. "And I've dived that wreck hundreds of times."

Wehi shifts, her shell cocks to one side. "Mmm, the gift comes and goes, it's said. Most common in children. And sometimes the elderly when..." she trails off, and I sense hesitation; something in the way all her legs suddenly still. "Are you ill, man of land?"

The weirdness of it clicks together into an odd logic and I sigh. "Call me Roy, and yes."

"Is it terminal?"

I shift in my sheets. It's not something I like to dwell too much on. "Yes. But with any luck, not for several years."

Wehi scratches her antennae again. "Then that explains it."

Tasi's leg taps twice on the nightstand, clearly impatient. "As curious as this is, Lorekeeper Wehi, Roy of Land, I would ask we stick to the topic at hand: the trade." Tasi motions a pincer to the mound of coins. "Are you willing to accept this in exchange for the heart?"

I wave his words off. "I have no use for gold. I have everything I need here. And in a few years it won't matter at all. If the heart is so important, please, have it."

Tasi and Wehi stare at me aghast.

"We cannot do that," Tasi says. "There must be a trade, it is our law."

"It is our way," Wehi adds.

"I can't just give you the heart back?"

"No, you won the heart. Tasi must either best you to win it back or make a trade. And frankly, his chances aren't high at winning—" At this, Tasi stiffens, his tapping leg stamping hard on my nightstand. "—we karkinoi are not fighters, we rely on stealth and remaining hidden," Wehi explains.

My back aches, but I ease myself up and Wehi scrambles further down the bed as I swing my feet to the floor. "What if I, say, happen to leave the heart on the beach for you? Conveniently lose track of its whereabouts?"

Tasi's claws shoot up, pincers opening wide like he's ready to charge at me. His mottled carapace darkens. "I would *never* stoop to such dishonest—"

"Forget I mentioned it," I say quickly.

"Tasi must trade. Anything else and he forfeits our claim to it." Wehi climbs back over the sheets, stopping a hand's breadth short of my thigh. I glance over at the pile of sea-crusted coins. What harm could it do really? I could send them back to Keegan, perhaps he'd find them worth something.

"Then I suppose I accept your coins."

Tasi throws his claws in the air again. "Should have said it the first time!" His snaps his pincers shut, evidently exasperated. He paces back and forth on the nightstand, muttering something too quiet for these old ears to hear.

"Is there a problem?" I ask Wehi.

The hermit crab's shell rises and falls, as if she has heaved a great sigh. "You have already refused his first offering, now he must find something of greater value. It is..."

"Your way," I guess, and now it's my turn to sigh. "Look, there really is nothing I want or need—"

At that, Tasi makes an odd sort of squeaking cry, and his pacing turns frantic. Wehi and I watch him scuttle back and forth on the nightstand. Any second now, I swear he'll wring his claws together.

"Hold on, I'm not finished." I lift a hand to placate him. Tasi's pacing slows, but only a little. "Seeing you, *learning* the karkinoi exist is a gift in itself." And it's true. If only Mary could be here to see them. She would have loved this, not scream and nearly wet herself like I had. She's always been the more adventurous of the two of us. A familiar ache spreads across my chest. I swallow it down.

"Sadly, a gift is not the same as a trade." Wehi says.

Damn. "All right, what if..." I begin, thinking quick. "Would you teach me about the karkinoi and the Heart in exchange for it?" I am nothing if not curious.

A quiet takes hold of the room. Tasi stops pacing.

Beside me, Wehi falls silent, her antennae-beard still. "That is a big request."

"It's beyond my rank to authorise," Tasi adds.

"Oh." I chew the inside of my cheek, thinking.

"But I will take you to someone who can." Tasi adds, brightening—if light blue quickening through his carapace is anything to go by. "Yes, this will do." He bobs his claws—some sort of affirmative gesture I'm realising—and scurries down the electrical cord of my nightlight.

A faint tug on my pyjamas turns my attention down again. Wehi has a pincer clamped around the leg of my pyjama bottoms. "If you'd be so kind, could you return me to your floor, Roy of Land? Not all of us are as spry as Guardian Tasi."

I oblige and scoop her up, my quivering muscles jolting her about on my palm until I cup my other hand over her and deposit her to the floor. When I stand straight, the rest of the crab entourage scuttle into the corners of the room. They are right to fear, I suppose. Humans eat crabs all the time. Catch them by the pot-load. My stomach twists. *I* had eaten my fair share of crabs over the years. Had some of them been karkinoi? But not many humans could see them, right? Mary's words to me all those years ago come back again. Strangely insistent.

Let it go.

A ludicrous, insane thought crosses my mind. *Had she known?*

The sight of Tasi dancing back and forth on the floor pulls me back to the present. "Come, come, Roy of Land."

I frown. "Just Roy is fine. Where are we going?"

"Why, to see Karkinos, of course, the Crab Queen."

#

"Are you sure I won't drown?" I ask, standing on the beach with the waves lapping my ankles. The sky overhead is the dim purple of pre-dawn.

"Lorekeeper Wehi's charm will protect you," Tasi says, his voice gargling as the water washes over him, turning his blue body into a faint blob of shadow under the whitewash.

I examine the symbols the hermit crab has scratched on my chest, between the curling white hairs. They looked little more than a bunch of squiggles. She'd tried to do it on my hands, but the persistent shake of my muscles had ended that before she'd even started. I hold my fingers up in the moonlight, the shake is noticeable to the naked eye. Today would be a bad episode. I should go back home, rest, take my medicine and sleep the worst of it off.

But the wave washes back out and Tasi scuttles forward, beckoning me.

And I follow, clenching the safe containing the Heart to my chest.

The water is oddly warm. Not too hot or cold. A comfortable temperature. A shiver prickles through me. Is it Wehi's charm that's doing this?

"Good, breathe normally," Wehi instructs from my shoulder as I wade in up to my chest. The water stings the fresh cuts of her spell in my skin. Definitely not dreaming. I'm unsure if the thought is comforting or terrifying. The safe weighs me down, anchoring my feet to the seafloor as the water reaches my chin. I lift my head to keep my mouth and nose above the surface, suck in a breath—

"No, breath normally." Pain fires through my earlobe. Wehi's pincer. I yelp, my footing slips, a wave buffets my face, and before I can think I suck *in*. And the water feels light, warm in my throat. It slips into my lungs, effortless, and then it rises again, exhaling through my nose. I blink. The world below is as sharp and clear as the world above.

"Incredible," I whisper, then frown. I sound not quite normal. My voice is deeper and less husky than it is on land.

A small chuckle from my ear, and the pressure on my earlobe releases. Wehi drops from my shoulder and swims for the sandy bottom to wait beside Tasi.

"Come," Tasi beckons. His voice is deeper underwater, more resonant. He curls a leg at me, encouraging, and I catch a gleam of runes there. More karkinoi magic. But before I can wonder what it does, the answer becomes clear. Tasi shoots off across the sea floor. In a heartbeat, he's a good pool length ahead.

"Wha—but—I," I stutter. There's no way I can keep up with that.

"Swim like normal," Wehi advises. "My charm will do the rest." Her voice too has dropped in pitch. If I close my eyes, I can almost feel it wash over my skin.

I tuck the safe under one arm, and kick off the bottom, doing an awkward half breaststroke as I kick my legs. The water rushes past. In half a dozen strokes I've caught up with Tasi. Unbelievable. A tapping of tiny legs follows us, like a cascade of marbles hitting stone. I check behind me, and a wave of crabs flows over the rocks, hundreds of bodies streaking across the seabed.

"Come, come." Tasi waves me on. "I've sent a messenger ahead, Karkinos is waiting."

The seabed drops away, turning to rocks and coral and patches of seagrass. But there's no time for sightseeing. Faster we move, the seafloor formations turning into a blur.

Bit by bit, the number of crabs with us drop away. When I ask Tasi about it, he shrugs one claw. "They're going home, of course," he says. "We live all over."

"All over where? The reef?"

"Of course."

"This Karkinos you're taking me to, he rules the karkinoi of your reef?"

"No, Wehi is the leader of our colony. Karkinos rules all karkinoi."

"*All* karkinoi? Everywhere?"

"In all oceans, yes." Tasi says simply, as if such a thing is obvious.

I slow my swimming. Where in the world were they taking me then? The thought of going for hours, possibly even days chills my limbs. "How long will it take us to reach him?"

"Not long now, she is on the other side of the reef," Tasi says.

"The Crab Queen lives on *this* reef?" I ask, incredulous. Here, of all places? I might be a gullible old man jetting across a reef on crab magic, but that seems farfetched—too coincidental—even to me.

"Karkinos has paths to every colony," Wehi says from behind and sensing my confusion adds, "you'll see soon, Roy of Land."

And I do. We round a coral atoll and there's a cave burrowed into one side of the underwater island. I gape. The mouth is dark and wide enough for three people to swim abreast through the opening. All those years with Mary diving this reef. How did I not know this was here?

I swing back to ask Wehi, only to catch the smug little smile of Tasi's miniature face. Oh, right, karkinoi magic. Of course.

Tasi puffs himself up, rising onto his back legs as he lifts his claws. "Roy of Land, be sure to show respect. Karkinos rule is absolute here. She made us and can unmake us just as easily." He taps a pincer on his chest. "Wehi's charms keep you alive here, but they can be undone. Remember that."

She *made* them? Wait, does that mean all karkinoi are her offspring? My mind spins at the thought. Better mind my Ps and Qs then. I swallow, the warm water around me suddenly stifling.

"I will guide you." Wehi's voice sounds in my ear as the prick of legs settles on my shoulder. "Follow Tasi."

I obey.

The tunnel is not overly long, but it is dark. It's all I can do to follow Tasi's blue shell. We round a bend and a pool of light appears high above us. It shimmers like light reflecting on the sea on a sunny day. I frown. That can't be right; we should be deep in the middle of the atoll by now. As we near, the light shifts and moves like shadows moving across a mirror—or behind it. A prickle runs down my legs.

"Go on," Wehi urges.

I take a watery breath and push through the pool.

Air meets me on the other side. I cough, exhale, water gushing from my nose. My fingers find sand and I heave myself out, dragging the dripping safe with me, and stare.

I'm in a clearing. Tropical palms dot the sand. Humid air laps my skin. Overhead, a full moon sheds sliver light on the scene. My mouth drops. There are pools everywhere! Hundreds of them. A scuttle to my left and a crab—legs as long as I am tall, its body the size of my head—drops into an obsidian-black pool with a 'plunk' like a stone into a well.

"Come," Tasi calls from my feet. "Watch your step."

Another crab emerges from a muddy pool to my right. Stops, stares at me, then scurries away.

"They're portholes," I realise aloud.

"Yes," Wehi agrees. "We call them paths. Quickly now, we should not leave Karkinos waiting."

I squelch after Tasi, wishing I'd spared a moment to change out of my pyjama bottoms. To take my mind of it, I try counting the pools as we go but they stretch off between the trees, far beyond my sight. Do they all lead to other karkinoi colonies? That thought makes me marvel all the more. Another twinge in my chest, snatching my breath. I wish Mary could see this.

Tasi scuttles around a hedge of palms, I follow. And stop. My stomach drops to my knees.

We've stepped into a large clearing as long as a football pitch. Palms and ferns line the expanse, walling the sandy throne room in. There are no other crabs in sight, except one.

And it's the largest crab I've ever seen. Ever heard of. Could even imagine.

Coral red, its body would dwarf my house, front yard *and* back yard combined. Its back legs are tucked under it, its mid-legs—thick as palm trees—are relaxed on the earth. But its two pincers are spread wide, claws open, in greeting or affront I can't tell.

Tasi waves a claw at me, indicating I should follow. My legs turn weak. Now, of all times for an episode. I shuffle forward, cool sweat mixing with the warm seawater on my skin. We stop short of the Queen, and what I took to be beady eye stalks from across the room, reveals itself as a crown of eyes and thorny shell.

"Remember to bow," Wehi whispers in my ear.

I pull my stare away and drop to one knee. *What do I say? Should I say anything?* I clear my throat, open my mouth—

"Welcome, Landwalker Roy."

The voice surprises me. I'd expected it to boom; to rattle my bones and reverberate in my chest. But instead, it's smooth, soft; pitched exactly as it needs to be and not a decibel higher.

"It-it's an honour, Queen Karkinos." I garble out, heart in my mouth.

"Rise, come, I want to see you better."

With more effort that I'd like to admit to, I struggle back up. Then I suck in a breath, look up into her face and step closer.

Her features are similar to Tasi's. A strange, but humanoid face in an arthropod head. With her this big, I'm able to make out details that I hadn't seen before. A hooded brow, eyes slightly further apart than I'm used to. Instead of skin, her face is all armoured plates, which don't allow for much expression. On her chin, her antennae-beard is long and each one flicks about, reminding me of a snake's tongue scenting the air. One of them reaches out, touches my head.

I freeze again, holding my breath.

"You bested my Guardian," the Queen says.

I try not to cringe. "It was an accident," I say, then add a hasty, "your majesty." And dip my head.

"Nonetheless, beat him you did. And the messengers tell me you have refused to trade." Her attention shifts to Tasi, who shrinks into the sand. "*Why?*"

Wehi tugs my earlobe. "Set me down, Roy of Land, if you'd be so kind."

I lift her off my shoulder, cupping her in both hands and place her on the sand beside Tasi. My fingers shaking something chronic as I do—whether it's from nerves or disease I'm unsure. Mix of both probably.

"Queen Karkinos, if I may," Wehi says. "Roy of Land here has little need in the items we offered. He is ill, not long for the landwalker's world. But he does wish to trade."

"Oh?" That's got her attention. Karkinos shifts, a brief rise of her back legs as she moves her bulk forward a foot and leans in. And as she does, a face—a *different* face—comes into view on the crown of her carapace. It's male, judging from the bristle on its cheeks. His eyes are closed, brows relaxed, sleeping-like. Or dead. My jaw slackens, but I manage to keep my mouth shut.

"What is it you seek that my karkinoi cannot give, Landwalker Roy?"

I'm too dumbstruck to answer. *There's a human face on the crab Queen's head.*

"Knowledge," Wehi speaks for me. "Roy would like to learn about the karkinoi. In exchange, he will trade us the Antikythera."

Antikythera? She must mean the heart. But I'm too distracted to do much else than stare at the Queen's shell.

Karkinos settles again, and as she does, I spot a new face, this one behind her foreleg, practically curling around the lip of her carapace. How many of them are there? Why? My stomach shrivels. What have I gotten myself into?

"Very well, Landwalker Roy. You may ask me three questions. Will that suffice?"

I drag my eyes away. "Y-yes." I place the safe on the sand. "I accept your trade."

"Very well," Karkinos gestures a giant pincer, and I try not to think about how easily her claw could wrap around my head and crack it like a walnut. "Please, ask your questions."

"I, uh..." I hadn't thought this far ahead. I search for inspiration and my gaze lands on the safe at my feet. "The heart, your Antikythera, what is it?"

Karkinos rocks back on her legs, her claws snap together with a 'whump' that I feel in my belly. "It is the heart of our people," she says. "The Antikythera measures the stars and moon, so we may work our magic."

I frown. "It's what allows you to use magic?"

"Is that your second question?" The Queen asks, tilting her body and head to one side. I glimpse another three faces on the back of her shell before I pull my eyes back inside my head.

"No, no!" I say quickly. Should I ask about the faces? Would that be rude? I still have two questions. I decide on another. "Tasi said a sea witch entrusted the Antikythera to you. Why?"

"It was she who made us. Long ago, she took us from the waters and taught us magic to help her." Karkinos' voice turns wistful, and her black eyes unfocus. "She was a marvellous teacher." She starts and shifts again, more faces flashing into view on her shell. "But even witches cannot live forever. Her life dwindled. She knew we needed a source to draw from to continue her work, so she forged the Antikythera, infused it with all her magic and gifted it to our keeping."

"I see..." No wonder it was so important to them. So why hide it in a wreck? Did they think it safe there? I'm tempted to ask, but I can guess the answer. No one really comes to our beach. Town was an hours' drive away, and Broome, the closest city, another four after that. Our beach has no facilities; no picnic or camping. Just a dirt road to the little house in the dunes Mary and I shared. But part of Karkinos' answer sticks in my mind. *The sea witch's work.* What might that be? Did they call up storms on unsuspecting sailors? Turn the tides? My eyes light on the face at the top of Karkinos' carapace and my last question tumbles out of me before I can think.

"Why are their faces on your back?"

Karkinos turns her shell to me and I suck in a breath. My arms fall slack at my sides. I'd expected another face or two protruding from her back like the odd pimple. But this was... they were... immeasurable. Her shell is covered in them. Every last millimetre. Men, women, children, young, old, small, big. Hundreds, possibly thousands of faces. All of them sleeping.

"These are souls who were lost at sea," Karkinos says. "They are waiting to be reborn as karkinoi."

Somewhere in my throat, my voice croaks. Because my gaze has caught on a face in that mass of noses and cheeks, brows and chins. My vision narrows to a pinprick. Tasi, Wehi, the lockbox, even Karkinos, fade away; my focus is only on that face.

Impossible. My brain says.

Please let it be. My heart replies.

I swallow, the shake renewing in my hands. I flutter closer, drawn inexorably in. Fall to my knees. Is it?

It is.

"Mary?"

#

Karkinos moves before my hand can brush my wife's cheek. "Do not touch them."

And like that, Mary's turned away, out of sight. I stagger to my feet.

"Please, let me see her! Let me talk to her!"

"I cannot." Kariknos says. There's a slight edge in her tone—still soft, but firm, a warning not to argue. I try anyway.

"But—"

Pain shoots up my foot. I yelp, glance down, and find Wehi has one pincer clamped around my little toe. Once she sees I've stopped, she releases her hold. "I am sorry, Roy of Land, but it is not possible. All the soul's on Karkinos' back must sleep until they are reborn. They suffered in their last moments. It would be cruel to wake them as they are."

I imagine what it might be like to drown at sea and wake up trapped on the back of a giant crab. No limbs. No body at all. Perhaps they have a point. I slump into the sand, a hot ache spreading through my chest, up my throat. They are right. But Mary, my Mary, is there. Right there. And God, I miss her so much. So much it hurts.

My head presses into the sand as I prostrate myself before the Queen of Crabs. "Please," I whisper.

The responding silence cuts deep and twists in my stomach. Tears distort my vision. *Please.* I can't leave Mary behind. There must be a way. I search frantically. Mind whirring. "A trade!" I blurt. "Anything you want. Anything to free my wife."

That's what karkinoi are about, isn't it? An exchange of equal value? Eye for an eye. Or maybe ... a soul for a soul?

Karkinos heaves a sigh, sinking down onto her legs again. "I cannot trade her freedom, Landwalker Roy," she says. "Would you have her haunt the seas? She is to be reborn, as a karkinoi, as all karkinoi are."

As all karkinoi are? I blink. All karkinoi are born from souls lost at sea? I look to Wehi and Tasi for confirmation. Both of them nod. A new pain rises inside me, this one cold and bitter. Mary will be reborn while I am soon to die. Forever apart. No matter which way. I wipe my eyes. "Do they remember who they were?" I ask, turning to Tasi and Wehi crouched in the sand. "Do you remember?" *Would Mary remember me?*

Wehi's shell rocks from side to side, as if she's debating her answer. "I was cast off a cliff," she says at last. Her voice is so quiet I have to lean close. "I couldn't swim."

She leaves the rest unsaid, but it's enough to chill me to the bone.

Tasi scratches on foreleg with a pincer. "I was a cabin boy on a Dutch ship. We ran aground."

"I am sorry," I say. I shouldn't have asked. But I'd had to know.

Tasi shrugs his mottled shell. "When I hatched it was very fresh. Very painful. But now," he pauses, claws opening and closing as he thinks. "Now it is like remembering a story I heard long ago. There is no more pain."

"I see." And I do. If Mary has the chance to live a new life, one that helps ease the shock of her death, who was I to take that away? The ache in my chest builds, but I know I am right. My eyes sting and I swallow, try to speak again, but a sob labours out instead. Get up, I tell my body. Take your leave. This is for the best. For Mary. But all my failing muscles do is shake. I am drowning, but not in water. My fingers clench the sand into fists. Why is it so hard?

Something cool falls on my hand. A mottled claw. Tasi, his blue shell bright in the moonlight. "Would you be willing to make a different trade, Roy?" he asks.

"A different trade?"

Tasi beckons Wehi with a foreleg. She scuttles over and they bow their shells together as words too quiet from me to hear pass between them. Wehi nods, murmurs something; Tasi pauses, then shrugs his claws.

"Very well," Wehi says, and they break apart once more. She turns to Karkinos. "We wish to propose a new trade."

Karkinos rocks back on her hind legs and one massive claw strokes her antennae-beard. "Go on."

"Roy of Land has proven himself a formidable force," Wehi says. "What is more, he has shown himself honest and respectful of our ways."

Where are they going with this?

Tasi rises onto all his legs. "I, we, wish to employ his services to protect the Antikythera."

I stare at them. "I'm just an old man—"

Wehi's claw shoots out, pinches my arm. Hard. Shut up.

Karkinos eyes her two subjects, then me, and the air turns heavier under her scrutiny. "What do you propose in return?" she asks.

"Turn him into a karkinoi. Let him be with his beloved when she hatches."

Wait? What? My heart thuds in my chest. Me? A karkinoi?

The Queen is silent, her claw still stroking her antennae. "This is no small asking," she says. Her body shifts, sending shivers through the sand as she turns on me. "And you are not a lost soul."

My insides turn to ice. Do they mean to drown me? I might be dying already, but I don't want to drown. But... if it meant I could be with Mary again. Could I go through with it? Hope and terror set my heart racing. This is moving too fast.

"It is not enough," Karkinos announces, "and it is not our way to take life," she adds with a glare at Tasi and Wehi.

Just like that, in a few words, the little flame of hope I'd been cultivating splutters and dies. With a mute nod, I pull myself onto my feet. My legs shake, but I manage it. Sensing my time is up, I bow. "Thank you for hearing me out, Queen Karkinos."

Karkinos rises, this time to her full height, dwarfing me in her shadow. "Walk with me, Landwalker Roy," she says suddenly and starts down the sandy throne room.

I blink, sure I heard wrong. Walk with her? A glance at Tasi and Wehi and they bob their claws in the affirmative, and gesture for me to follow. I hurry after the Queen. Her gait is slow, methodical; every step considered. Even so, I have to coax my muscles into a shuffling jog to keep up with her.

She leads me past the pools, her legs picking and placing between the ponds with care, until we find ourselves on a beach. Gentle waves lap the shore, and Karkinos lowers her bulk onto the sand with a sigh.

"I am willing to grant you this trade," she says, without preamble. "But I need you to do something for me."

From this angle, the moonlight catches her face and I'm struck by how tired she looks. I sink down beside her, unsure of the protocol here.

"If it means I can be with Mary, I'll gladly do it."

"Careful, Landwalker Roy, you don't know what I'm asking yet."

My chin lifts. "I meant what I said. Grant me this wish and I'll do anything you want."

The weight of her gaze returns as she inspects me. "Karkinoi are born from souls lost at sea," she begins. "But not all of them can become a Queen like me. In fact, very few can."

I tilt my head. Where's she going with this? "Why not?"

"Because they did not choose this life," Karkinos says. "We give it to them, and many are happy to take it, but they don't choose. Queens like me chose this; we agreed to our fate before we died."

The heft of her words sink in. *Before she died.* Like all karkinoi, she too, had once been human. I open my mouth, not sure I want to ask my next question.

"Are you saying..?"

"I want you to take my place, Roy." Her black eyes fix on me. "Become Karkinos."

"But I-I'm not even female."

The Queen laughs, an odd gurgling noise through her mouth. "Male, female, it does not matter. What matters is that you are willing. That when your time comes, you go peacefully."

My mind gallops to catch up. "You mean... you *won't* drown me?" I can't help but feel a glimmer of relief at that.

"A violent death would mean you could not soothe the souls on your back as Karkinos."

Cool sand presses on my palms as I lean back to think. I'm no leader. Hell, I've barely a handle on my own life. Managing things was more Mary's talent. She had a way with people. My gaze slides to Karkinos's shell, landing on the face I've missed every day for the last thirteen years. I'm no leader, but if I agree to this, Mary will be there to guide me.

Perhaps she's been guiding me all along. To here. Now. This choice.

"What will happen to you?" I ask Karkinos.

Her foreleg traces lines in the sand, and suddenly I see the shape for what it is, dredged up from a memory of Mary and I sitting on our veranda one night, and her pointing the constellation out to me. Cancer, the crab. "I will move on," she says. Her eyes turn skyward. "My love is up there now, and I wish to join her."

A pang rises in my chest. I know that pain.

Rising to my feet, I brush the drying sand off my pyjamas and rest my hand on her enormous claw. "I'll do it."

Five years later.

I wake to a tap-tap on my nightstand. Open my eyes. Tasi. Strange. He's come early this month, he normally doesn't visit before the full moon.

"What is it?"

Tasi spreads his pincers—a karkinoi's smile. "It's time," he says.

I sit up. "Oh." Hope quickens inside me. "Really?" I sit up. My body feels good. Fresh. "Should I bring anything?"

A shake of his body. No. "Just yourself. She's waiting."

Excitement bubbles inside me and I swing out of bed. No pain. No aches. A good sign. I leave the lights off as I move through my home. Finding my way by moonlight has become habit these last few years. I steal across the lounge, wincing at the creak of floorboards. A soft snore comes from the guest room; Keegan and Melissa haven't roused. I'm sorry to leave them like this, but it can't be helped. I step out onto the veranda.

"Grandpa?"

I turn. My granddaughter Zoe stands on the threshold in her nightie, blinking away sleep. She's small for a nine-year-old, but every day she grows more and more like Mary. Headstrong. A girl who knows what she wants.

"Where are you going?" she asks.

I drop to one knee, and grin. "Off to be with your Grandma. Be good to your parents, eh, kiddo?" I rustle her hair. "I love you. Don't you forget that. Now go back to bed, before you wake your Da, eh?"

A frown creases her forehead, but she nods, and shuffles back inside the house.

I pace across the dunes, over the last rise and stop, not quite believing my eyes.

Crabs *cover* the beach. Every inch of it. Thousands, perhaps tens of thousands. All shapes and sizes and species; shells glinting and gleaming in the moon. I step out past the high-tide line and they move, parting like a curtain to bring me to a familiar looking hermit crab waiting with Tasi at the water's edge.

"Wehi," I say and bob my arms in an imitation of a karkinoi greeting.

"Roy," she says, returning the gesture. "It is good to see you again."

We walk into the water, Tasi, Wehi and I. Wehi on my shoulder, Tasi perched in my palm. The water surges around my legs, pulling me deeper, and I feel the urge to look back. I hesitate. Then a claw pinches my ear.

"Mary has something she wanted me to tell you," the hermit crab whispers.

I cock my head. I'm listening.

"Let it go."

Tears spring to my eyes. "Yes, I will."

I step into the waves. Close my eyes and the sea sweeps me up.

I'm coming Mary.

Back in the beach house, my body cools. Heart attack, the doctors will say. No mistaking that pain in my chest last night. My memory wanders along the hall, across the patio to the shore. There's a small parking lot here now, and a boat ramp; a couple of science research vessels are shacked up on trailers for the night. It took a lot of work and lobbying to get them here, and the discovery of a loggerhead sea turtle nest in the area, but Keegan and I managed it.

A path leads from the boats down to the beach. And as my spirit quickens and hardens into its new shell, I smile, thinking of the sign planted on the shore.

Mary Quin Marine Reserve. Fishing strictly prohibited.

LIONESS

Sign: Leo
Element: Fire
Symbol: Lion
Dates: July 21 to August 22

You found me on the plains sleeping with my cubs. A shot from your weapon sent us scattering into the bush, but not before one of your iron balls lodged in my chest. I remember the pain, the searing burn that curled through my ribs as the pride ran, as fast and far as we were able.

But it wasn't fast or far enough.

You followed. Tracked us down through the noon when the heat is worst. When we had to stop to let the little ones rest.

Aya sunk down beside me, licked the wound your iron left. "How is it?"

"It hurts, a bad hurt," I said, whimpering as the wound flared afresh.

When dark came and it was time to hunt, I couldn't move. My body was heavy, my legs weak, claws and teeth blunt with fatigue. When my cubs came to suckle, they bumped the wound and I snarled at them to stay away.

Nussa nudged them back with her nose. "Be off Seyha, Senga. Let your mother rest."

The next morning, my world was dim and I couldn't lift my head.

"Nurse them," I begged Nussa. Her cubs were older, but she still produced milk.

"Do not fear," she said. "They will not go hungry." She dropped down beside me, the warmth of her body seeping into my cooling one. "I will take care of them."

"I don't want to go."

Aya nestled in too. "Rest. Go with the Earth."

But I did not rest. Because you found me. We heard you coming in your cars. They rumble like rain season thunder. Impossible not to hear when we're alert. We were that time, not like the first. Your weapons and shouting did the rest. My family broke for the horizon, vanishing into the haze with nothing but paw prints in their wake. I yearned to follow, to hunt the nights away with my mother, aunts and sisters; to play with my cubs. But my body ached, the pain deep, blood oozing. So, when you pointed the barrel at my head, I was ready. Soon it would be over.

But I did not go to the Earth. I stayed.

I watched you pose with my body. You splayed me out on my belly, put your boots on my back as if I were a mountain you'd conquered, not the mother you'd caught unawares as she rested from feeding her family.

I consoled myself. Death is the way of things. My meat will feed another family. Another mother, another cub. They will grow strong. My strength will become theirs, just as my prey had strengthened me.

But you took my body away, far away, and paid a man to remove my skin. He dumped my meat and bones in the dirt and left them there, a free meal for the vultures. You thanked him, rolled me up like an armadillo and stuffed me in a suitcase.

This is the end of it, I thought. I can go. Earth take me.

But then came the sounds. Rumbling engines, whining turbines—I have names for these now, I have done a lot of watching while you've been away. You took me to your homeland on the other side of the world, far from my beloved grasslands. And when light returned, you rolled me open; unfurled me on your floor. And there I've stayed. Waiting, watching, longing for the earth of my home.

There are no antelope here, no wildebeest migration to follow. Just an old cat who hisses at my skin when he's allowed into your study. There are books though. I read them over your shoulder—that took some seasons to learn. But when you read aloud to your cub, it made it easier to grasp. He's quite the sweetheart, isn't he? All blue-eyed and chubby. What's the phrase you people use? Could eat him right up? Yes, a gorgeous cub.

But shh, hush now, stop struggling, let me finish.

I learned many things in your room; I might have been happy to stay there. To watch and haunt that space. Until you did *that.* A holiday, I thought. You've had a few over the years. But this one was longer. Not your weekend getaway to the Hamptons. It doesn't take a baboon to work out you'd gone abroad.

Day in day out, I paced, my spirit rustling papers on your desk. I've been getting good at that, you know? That chill your wife complains of in the lounge? That's me prowling past. The creaking floorboards that wake your son at night? I'm there in his room.

Then you returned. You opened your suitcase and I saw a new skin. Tan fur, rounded ears, lips pulled back into a snarl. You spread it out beside mine. Golden fur; mouth forever frozen in a snarl. A young lioness killed in her prime.

And I knew rage.

I know my kin anywhere. My cub. My baby. My Seyha. Gone to the Earth too soon.

"Murderer!" I snarled, and the walls shivered. You felt it, oh yes, I saw how you jumped. You called out to your wife: "Did you feel that?"

She put your fears to rest. "Feel what?"

And like that, you shrugged and dismissed it.

Dismissed me.

You should not have done that.

Quiet now, it'll all be over soon.

You were tired from your trip, see? Thought to do some work before dinner, but exhaustion got the better of you. I sang you a lullaby I once sang to my cub now lying there on the floor. Your eyelids drooped; you rested your head on your desk. And I took my chance.

I pounced. My skin wrapping you tight, muffing your scream. We fell to the floor you and I, a tangle of skin and fur. My teeth found your throat and I *squeezed*.

And now here we are.

You writhe, but I writhe with you, learning how you move; how all those bones and muscles work together. My skin sticks to your back, curls around your belly, pulls over your face. There's a crunch of bones breaking and remaking. Our vision darkens. Our body drops to all fours.

Your screams fade.

Hush now. This lion is done sleeping.

MAIDEN'S DAWN

Sign: Virgo
Element: Earth
Symbol: Maiden
Dates: August 23 to September 22

Part One.

The dragon came for me at dawn.

Wrists shackled, I stood on the clifftop, the waters of the Madra Sea churning below. A glint of scale flickered in the purple clouds as Draugr's twin suns rose; wings a lapis blue to match the sea. Even then, watching my fate bank and circle over the cliffs, she stole my breath away.

T-minus 22 seconds. I pushed away the part of my brain calculating the distance and the dragon's speed. It wouldn't go away.

Behind me, villagers gasped as the dragon's shadow swept over us, blotting the sun. Someone screamed. Fear prickled through my belly. *T-minus 20 seconds.* I pulled at my manacles. A hopeless effort tethered as I was, iron cutting into my wrists.

"Father," I pleaded, throwing my gaze to the familiar figure standing before the mob, his face firm, resolute. "Please, don't let them do this!"

He remained stoic, staring past me to the descending dragon, my words flowing over him like he hadn't heard them. The only sign he felt anything at all was when the dragon alighted on the grassy top and his hand clenched white around Cella's shoulder as my sister shrieked, "No! Don't hurt Astraea! Let her go!"

"Great Dragon," Gauron, the village wizard, spread his arms wide and bowed. "We offer you this sacrifice in exchange for our land and our freedom. Honour our accord; take her and leave us in peace." He bowed again, golden headpiece dipping low.

The dragon leaned in, reptilian head as big as a cottage and held up by an enormous, roping neck and chest. Turquoise scales glinted in the sun, each one the size of a dinner plate. A wave of crisping heat buffeted me as she scented. I swallowed my tears. *Don't cry.* I bit down on my lip, the sting of pain strengthening my resolve. *No screaming,* I vowed. *Do not scream.* Gauron would find no quarter of satisfaction there. Instead, I counted in my head, taking refuge in the numbers and their patterns, seeking the calm they so often brought. But when the beast opened her jaws, and a hot, oily breath blasted the hair from my face, I faltered, mind tripping as my heart thudded into my throat.

This was it. My end.

Do NOT scream.

I shut my eyes, braced for pain.

But she didn't bite. The giant mouth opened again, filling the air with an odd, hissing, screaming whine, so loud it buzzed in my chest. Then incisors snapped down on the iron stake that tethered my chains and manacle to the clifftop. She sheared it clean in half. A great foreclaw the size of a boulder encircled my waist, glossy talons as long as my arm closing around my pinafore. A fresh blast of wind set my ears ringing. My head span; feet lifted from the ground.

"Astraea!" Cella screamed my name.

The world fell away. My father's upturned face pale and on the edge of terror and Cella's screaming one was the last thing I saw.

#

"Wake up."

Something warm brushed my cheek. I cracked open frozen eyelids to darkness. Was I dead? A cool breeze washed over my skin, prickling the hairs on my arms. Apparently not. I sat up, patted myself down. Hands, arms, legs, all there. My ribs felt a little bruised and one arm a bit tingly, like I'd fallen asleep on it.

A hand fell on my shoulder. My yelp echoed through the dark and I scrabbled to my hands and knees, wheezing as I tried to settle the heart that was trying its darndest to escape up my windpipe. "Who's there?!"

"It's all right, I mean no harm. You're safe."

I squinted into the black and could just make out a shape standing over me. "Who are you? Where's the dragon? Did it take you too?" The words tumbled out of me in a rush.

A laugh, a bit shrill, but it sounded genuine. "One thing at a time, eh? First some light. I forget your eyesight is not so good without augments."

I frowned. My eyesight was perfectly fine, thank you very much. Better than Cousin Banta's and a lot better than Macey Grayson down the lane. My stomach twisted at that. They'd been my family, my friends. Not one of them had lifted a finger when I was taken. *Except Cella.* Heat returned to my belly, boiling as anger stirred there. I didn't need them anyway. The pang in my chest said otherwise.

With a faint hum, light flared above us, crisp and white—I'd never seen light like that before. Beside me stood a woman, ridiculously tall, at least two heads more than me, and I'd never thought myself small. Her hair was dark, and perhaps it was the light, but I swear it had a blue sheen to it.

"Who are you?" I demanded.

The woman bent down, her green... *suit* I guess you could call it. Though, it was all sewn together. If it hadn't shimmered like light reflected off the sea, I would have called it a pair of long johns. I took her offered hand, and she pulled me to my feet. "Call me Cora."

"Cora?" I repeated, testing the name on my tongue. She nodded.

"Good. Do you remember how you got here?"

I scrunched up my face. "The dragon took me. We flew over the ocean, and I remember being cold. *Really* cold." I made no mention of those initial moments as we'd careened over the waves. The sums had spun across my vision thick and fast, working out elevation and impact force. I'd briefly deliberated the merits of a quick drop versus a dragon's jaws before opting not to struggle in the monster's grip. After that, it was blank. I squinted up at the light; it emanated from an orb humming above Cora's head. "I guess I fainted," I grudgingly admitted. "What happened? Where are we?" I searched the dark. "Where'd the dragon go?"

"Don't worry about the dragon," Cora said. "It won't bother you again."

I eyed the woman. A full head-to-toe-to-head appraisal. Tall she might be, but she was slight. Willowy. Was I supposed to believe that, what, she'd *scared* it off? I caught the snort in my throat, which turned it into a gagging sort of grunt. Fortunately, my new friend took it as a sign of assent.

She motioned me to follow her. "I'll show you around."

"Around?" I echoed as I followed. My feet clattered over something rough and perforated, like a grate.

"We're on my ship, the *Spica*."

"A ship?" I stopped, listening for the creaking of wood and rigging, but found a soft hum instead, along with the faintest exhalation, as if the walls were breathing. Cora and her orb-light moved away, stopping at the entrance of what I could only describe as a tunnel. I put my hands on my hips. "Strangest ship I've ever sailed on."

Cora smiled, a pinched, thin-lipped thing that screamed she was trying to hold back a laugh. My skin prickled. *She knows more than she's letting on.*

"The *Spica* does not sail, per se," she said. "Not on the ocean anyway." At my confusion she added, "It's not a ship as you know it. But it is very old." She reached into the tunnel and there was a pop followed by a quiet whine that vibrated the floor and walls. Light flicked overhead, like firelight in a draft, but without the heat of a flame behind it. A chamber flooded into view: smooth grey walls—were they iron?— high ceilings bearing lights too bright to look at head on, and below, sure enough, a grate-covered floor. Where in the gods was I?

"Ah, that's better, eh?" Cora said. "Come." She motioned to me again. "You'll catch cold if you stay down in the hangar too long." With that, she turned along the tunnel, the orb at her head—a shiny, metallic thing the same colour as the walls— bobbing along next to her.

I staggered along behind, my legs still halfway numb. "Did you really save me from the dragon?" I asked.

"One question at a time," Cora replied. "Let's get you settled first."

Settled?

The tunnel ended in a closed door—an arch, really—wide as a cottage and at least twice my height in size, like it was made for something or *someone* a lot bigger than either Cora or me. Or a whole lot of smaller someones perhaps. I did a quick calculation. In the blink of an eye, you could have a small army pass from the tunnel into whatever lay beyond.

Cora pressed her palm to the wall, and the door *slid* open. Slid. On its *own*. I swallowed my gasp, turning it into a cough instead. Once we stepped through, I glanced back at the door's other side. No person manning it, no cog or crankshaft, *nothing*.

"You're a wizard," I breathed, staring at Cora, unsure whether to run for my life or throw myself on the floor and plead mercy. I rehearsed the words in my head: I hadn't meant to touch the relic in Grayson's field, honest, hadn't ever dreamed it would actually *turn on*.

"I'm an astrobiologist." Cora replied, her tone clipped.

Shit, she's offended. Quickly! Change the subject. "What's an astro bi-gologist?" I blurted. *Seriously? Gods, just kill me now.*

Cora didn't skip a beat. "Biologist. I study other worlds. Planets just like this one. Or at least, I did."

I stopped dead. Come again? "So, you're telling me," I said, slowly, shoving the metal stream of numbers in my head aside to wrestle my whirling thoughts into order. "You study world*s?* In the plural? As in more than one?"

"Yes, Draugr is one of many worlds I've studied."

In the wake of my stunned silence, she turned, and I realised I'd stopped walking to openly gape at her. She gave me another tight-lipped, holding-back-a-laugh smile. Not a mean smile, just knowing. Like she had secrets to spill. I hurried after her again, curiosity seizing control of my mouth.

"Have you *been* to these other worlds?" I asked. "What are they like? Are they hard to get to? I suppose you'd need magic or—" I followed Cora as she opened another door and stepped through. I'd anticipated a lair, or a dungeon with magical runes scrawled on the walls, maybe a giant bubbling cauldron. But no.

It was a sitting room. How perfectly... ordinary.

Granted, it was bigger than my father's entire cottage. Plush chairs draped in furs sat before a crackling fire. Impossibly large windows ran the length of the far wall while the adjacent wall contained a floor-to-ceiling bookshelf. I veered towards it, eager as a cat to a milk bowl, and read one of the spines. *Géométrie Algébrique et Géométrie Analytique.* I frowned. What language were these in? Either way, they were near illegible. I sighed.

"This is the common room, you're welcome here any time," Cora said, gesturing to the chairs.

I went to the window and looked out. A short rocky cliffside lay beyond, scarcely a few paces wide before it dropped into a pink and orange sky and a view of mountains and rolling hills. To my left hung one sun low against a set of peaks—due west then. In the east, the frosted mountain slopes eased to rolling pasture. My eyes traced the fields all the way to the glint of sea just on the horizon.

"Your house is at the top of a mountain?" I asked, more out of disbelief than any real confusion, but Cora answered anyway.

"More accurate to say it *is* the mountain," she said. "*Spica's* been grounded for eons. We built the mountain around her to protect her."

"I see." I didn't, not in the slightest. *Did she mean from the dragons?* I peered out the window again. Not a trace of wing or scale in the sky.

"We are safe up here. *Spica's* well hidden," Cora reassured. "Shall I show you your room?"

I pulled my gaze away from the sunset. "My room?"

"This way." Cora indicated a door in the west wall—wood this time and no bigger than the front door of my cottage. With a twist of its brass knob, we stepped into a hall. Doors lined either side; an ornate red rug ran underfoot. Cora stopped at the third one along, opened the door and motioned me in.

It was a simple room. A bed in one corner with a trunk at its end, a desk in the other wall, and an empty shelf beside it. A window—its glass polished to a mirror sheen—hung on the far wall like a painter's frame, its subject the same pasture and sky view as the common room. On the desk a vase held a single yellow flower—one I didn't recognise.

I flicked the petals with a finger. "Nice touch."

"It's a sunflower," Cora said. "From my world."

I cocked my head. "Which world is that?"

A slight pause. "Earth." Cora hugged herself, her sea-green eyes going distant. "It was lost three thousand years ago, if the computer isn't malfunctioning."

I frowned. Computer? What in the gods was that? And three thousand years? If she was born on that world, she must be *old*. I studied her. Her body reminded me of a twig on a winter tree. Thin cheeks; pointed nose and chin. No lines of age. She didn't look a day older than my twenty years. In fact, she even looked *younger*.

My eyes narrowed. It was a jest. Surely. No one looked that good after three thousand years. Even if she was from another world. It was a lie. A fantasy made to pull on my dreamer heartstrings. But why?

Cora shook herself. "I'll let you rest," she said. "The *Spica* is a lot to take in. We'll talk more in the morning."

With that, she began a retreated, turning for the door.

"Astraea," I blurted.

She paused, and I felt an inexplicable flush creep into my face as her green eyes landed on me, questioning. One of them had a fleck of hazel in the iris. I caught myself staring and forced my gaze back to the sunflower.

"My name," I blundered on, feeling my cheeks grow hotter. "You gave me yours so... I thought..." the words left me so I shrugged and let my explanation lurch to a stop. In all truth, I didn't know what I'd thought. Only that I wanted her to know it.

Cora smiled. Truly smiled. It spread across her face, dimpling her cheeks and crinkling her eyes. As it did, my heart did the thing I'd long dismissed as a girlish fairy-tale fancy.

It fluttered.

"It is nice to meet you, Astraea."

I'm not sure what I said in response—or if I said anything at all. But as soon as her footsteps faded down the hall, I sank to the bed and stared at the wall, heart and head still whirling. Only when it belatedly occurred to me that I hadn't heard any click or latch of a door lock, did I rise to check it. It wasn't locked. And, more to the point, I wasn't locked in. But when I opened the door to examine the bolt mechanism, all relief drained away as my gaze landed on Cora's orb floating on the threshold. It's 'eye'—a single round socket half the size of its body—blinked a rapid green.

I slammed the door shut again, swallowing hard. What the in hells was this place? More importantly, was I a guest or a prisoner?

#

"Sleep well?" Cora asked when I emerged into the common room.

"Yes, thank you," I lied. I'd tried to plump my cheeks in the mirror and unrumple my slept-in clothes before leaving my room, but it hadn't done much. She probably saw straight through it.

"Come, sit down, eat," Cora insisted, rising from the table. "There's eggs, toast, porridge..." She pulled out a chair for me.

I ran nervous fingers through the folds of my pinafore and sat, trying not to ogle the spread on the table. It was more food than I ate in a week. I chose a piece of bread from the table and smeared something that might have been jam onto it. Cora watched every move like an eagle watching its chicks. I cleared my throat. She started and looked away, apparently flustered.

"What is it you want?" I asked.

She blinked at me. "Whatever do you mean?"

I put my uneaten breakfast down on the plate set before me, my stomach doing cartwheels. *She's a wizard, Astraea, are you mad?* But my mouth blurted, "You saved me from the dragon? Why? You must have had a reason."

Cora's lips quirked, her knowing look returning from yesterday. "You can do calculus in your head," she said, then at my frown, added, "The numbers, Astraea. I know you see them."

I felt the blood drain from my face, down my throat, and coil into a knot under my ribs. The jam knife slipped from my fingers and clattered to the floor. She knew. *How in the bloody sky gods did she know?* "But..." my lips parted, about to whisper *How?* before I bit down on my tongue. The last time I'd confided in anyone about my numbers, it had... well, it was part of what had got me tied to a cliff as a sacrifice. That secret had been quick to spill after I'd activated the relic in Grayson's field. I swallowed the ball of grief and stinging betrayal and clenched my fists into the folds of my skirt.

"You are not like other people," Cora went on. Her eyes, deep green this morning, glinted like cut glass. "Surely you noticed? I couldn't let them kill you for that. Not before you understood how special you are."

My heart galloped in my chest. "I'm not a witch."

"I never said you were—"

"I don't dance naked around a fire in the woods, I don't eat babies, I don't conjure spirits—"

"I know you don't." Cora sipped her tea. Entirely too calm.

I dragged in a breath, feeling as if the massive common room were squeezing me in, smothering me in its books and plush furniture. As a pre-teen I'd had nightmares of walking naked through the village, desperately trying to hide my pubescent body— this was a hundred times worse. I was stripped bare and in a way I hadn't thought I could be. "How did you know?" I whispered.

"I've had the computer scanning for people like you ever since I woke up."

Since she woke up? Scanning? And there was that word again. *Computer.* What did it all mean? I folded my arms, lifted my chin. "Show me."

This time the tea in Cora's hands quivered, sending little ripples across the surface as she set it down. "I'm not sure that's—"

"Show me." I demanded. "Or am I your prisoner and this—" I gestured to the walls and window "—just the gilded bars of a cage?"

Cora met my glare, then her gaze fell away from mine to the floor. "You are never a prisoner," she said, shrinking into herself in a very un-wizard like way. "You are too important for that, you're free to come and go as you like."

"Really?"

Then my saviour/captor did something very odd. Her eyebrow quirked and her gaze darted up to mine. In that moment, she too was unmasked, her expression naked. There was confusion there. And hope as she stared at me. Hope *in me.* Of all things. Me. Why? A smile flickered across Cora's pointed face. "Really, really."

Heat rose up my neck, threatening to spread to my face.

"Come," Cora said. "I'll tell you everything."

She led me away from the wood-furnished walls of the common room and back into the steel tunnels. Our footsteps echoed in the passageways. Figures popped into my head. Fifty-two meters long, four meters wide, three and a half meters high. Seven hundred and twenty-eight metres cubed. I blinked and pushed the calculation away. *Get out. Shoo. You've caused enough trouble already.*

The passage ended and Cora stopped outside one of those sliding doors again, punched the button. It opened into a windowless box. Barely 12m³. She motioned me in, and the doors closed behind us with a quiet hush.

"Stasis chamber," Cora announced to the air, then turned to me. "Hold on, the magnetism can be abrupt."

I frowned. "Wh—" The box plummeted. My stomach folded into my sternum, and I threw my hands for hold on the wall. *We're falling. Dear gods, we're going to die.* My fingers scrabbled over cold walls, searching for a way out. I opened my mouth to scream.

Warmth wrapped around my hand and gave it a reassuring squeeze. "Astraea, it's fine. It's just a transport pod. We're okay," Cora said. "Trust me." She gathered both my hands and held them close. "Breathe with me." She counted numbers aloud—*in the Fibonacci Sequence.* "Zero, one, one, two, three, five…"

"Eight, thirteen, twenty-one…" I echoed as she searched my face, her deep ocean eyes pausing when they met mine. And stayed.

That was when I knew that there was something special about Cora too.

My heart slowed, the panic rolling off like beading sweat. Then the pod's deceleration kicked in, pulling my stomach into my pelvis and jangling my nerves stiff. The door slid open.

"This is where it all began," Cora said.

We stepped out onto a platform. And I gawked. We were standing in the biggest, gods-bloody cavern I've ever seen. Though 'cavern' was something of a misnomer. Grated gangways ran from the platform like the spokes of a wheel for as far as I could see. A ladder to one side drew my eye down, and I saw the same hub-and-spoke walkways replicated below, and another one below that. Whole levels. I glanced up. Same above.

I turned full circle, mouth ajar, taking it all in. "What is this place?"

Spaced two meters apart on every walkway, giant cylindrical orbs were rigged up, a mass of piping extending from their tops, like fruit hanging on a bizarre metal tree. Cora led me to one. It was smooth like the walls of the transport pod had been, featureless but for the small glass porthole, conveniently positioned at my eye-level. Cora motioned me to look inside.

After a moment's hesitation, I peered in. A shape lay on the pillowed surface—or rather, the absence of one. A hollow where a shape should have been, like an imprint left in snow. A human imprint. A Cora one—right down to her narrow neck and shoulders.

"This is where I woke up," Cora said. "One year ago."

I tore my eyes from the interior of the orb and stared at her.

"It's a stasis capsule," Cora went on. She rubbed her nose, shifted on her feet, clearly uneasy. "It puts its occupant into a sort of slumber while they travel across space."

I placed a hand on the capsule, wonder tingling across my skin. *A means to travel to other worlds.* "This is how you got here?"

"The ship got me here. But I wouldn't have lived to see the trip through without the pod."

I wrinkled my brow. "Hang on, you said you've been here for three thousand years."

"I have." Cora indicated the pod. "I was just asleep in there for most of it."

So, she wasn't a wizened crone disguised by a bloody good bit of magic—if one believed in that sort of thing. Which I did. You didn't grow up on Draugr *not* believing. Not when the wizards performed miracles all the time. Not when a single sky-god relic could wipe out an entire village in a plume of ash. Magic infused everything to do with the gods. And only the wizards were permitted to handle...

My hand slid from the capsule. A croak rising in my throat. It was Cora's turn to frown.

"Astraea? What is it?"

I tried to speak, but nothing came out. My knees wobbled, and I swallowed. "You're one of them." *How had I not realised earlier? Gods and starry skies, how could I have been so stupid?* "You're a sky god."

I clamped my hands to my sides like one of the village guard coming to attention before wizard Gauron. "Forgive me, I have trespassed on your hallowed grounds."

Cora caught my collar as I made to bow, jerking my prostration to a stop. She yanked me upright.

"I told you already, I'm an astrobiologist. A *bi-olo-gist*." Her voice had turned clipped and pink blotches had formed on her cheeks. Was she angry? Embarrassed? Both? I stared at her, baffled. When I'd pictured the gods as a child, I'd envisioned beings of poise and perfection, beautiful creatures who radiated power like a hearth. Not this blotchy, rake of a woman with blue-tinted hair and spraying spittle.

Cora released me with a huff. "I'm no more a god than you are," she said. "Put it out of your head."

I didn't, but I let her say her bit.

Cora brushed hair from her face and straightened. "As I was saying, the *Spica* has been here nearly three thousand years. I was in stasis for most of it."

"Until a year ago."

"Until one year ago," she confirmed.

My gaze travelled past Cora and along the walkway, noting the number of pods stretching out as far as I could see. It was the same on every spoke—above and below. My mind ran the numbers without thinking.

Ten thousand, four hundred and fifty capsules.

Ten thousand, four hundred and fifty sky gods.

I was standing in a tomb. The thought made my skin turn cold. "There are more of you here?"

Cora shook her head. "They're all empty."

"Where did they go?"

My saviour/captor rolled her eyes. "Isn't it obvious?"

I stared at her, expectant as a child before a teacher. But instead of giving an answer, Cora shrugged and turned.

"Tell me when you figure it out." She waved for me to follow her.

She funnelled me out into another tunnel that opened out into a room—if you could call it that. Helm might have been more apt. While there was no wheel, the walls were riddled with screens and dials, most of them dead. In the middle, and looking terribly out of place, was a polished wood table. Smooth with age, it was not unlike the one used by the village council in the town hall, I thought as I ran a finger along it. Not a speck of dust. How was that possible? One person couldn't possibly maintain this enormous place on her own.

"Welcome back, Cora A-Astraeus."

I started as the voice sounded out of the forward wall. Neutral in tone, I couldn't place it as male or female.

"Please don't be a-a-alarmed citizen Astraea." A search found the point in the wall the voice resonated from, a small funnel like one of the orator relics that Gauron sometimes used to preach to large crowds.

"Who are they?" I whispered to Cora.

"That's *Spica*," she said. "Or, I should say, her A.I. An artificial entity who runs the ship. It was damaged not long after we landed. Her personality is intact, and a few key operating systems—life support, food printers, and stasis—but the rest..." Cora sighed. "Let's just say *Spica*'s been grounded ever since."

Heart slipping back down my throat, I followed Cora to a screen. I'd seen others like it before—but unlike the ones we unearthed from fields and found collecting dust in the basement of a dead relative, this had no blemishes. No cracks or scratches or bits of glass flaking off at the corners. When Cora motioned a hand over it, the image sprang to life as crisp and clean as gazing through a window.

"This the command center," Cora said. "It's where the crew monitored the ship while it travelled to Draugr. They took turns in ten-year shifts while everyone else stayed in stasis."

"What about..." I wrinkled my nose, trying to recall the right word from my brief excursions to the harbour. "The tillerman?" At Cora's frown, I added, "The one who controls where it goes."

"Ahh, you mean the pilot. They sat further down in the hold. In a special chamber that let them interface directly with *Spica*."

Okay, I hadn't followed most of that. I was about to ask more when something from earlier nudging its way into my thoughts. Cora *Astraeus*, that strange -'Aey-Eye'- voice had said. Astraeus sounded like a family name. The hairs prickled up my arms.

"I named you after the gods," my first mother once told me, not long before she died. *"I named you Astraea so they might see fit to bless you."*

My mother hadn't been alone in that thought. Astraea was a common name in the county. There had been two of us in my village alone.

Opposite, Cora tapped on the screen and began pressing a series of buttons on the wall. I scowled. *Not a sky god my arse. We name our children after you.* Pass it on from parent to offspring. An ancestral name handed down through the ages—

I stopped. My last thought circulating through my head again. *An ancestral name. From parent to offspring.*

Offspring of an empty stasis chamber.

Holy freaking sky gods.

I whirled on Cora. I was right. Gods and stars, I *knew* I was right. The knowledge of it buzzed in my blood, as if I'd always known.

But I didn't get time to tell Cora. Because the moment I opened my mouth, an alarm went off.

\#

We ran down the tunnels, my saviour/captor/ancestor swearing under her breath.

Two turns along and Cora's orb met us. The alarm ceased.

I slowed, sucking in lungfuls of air. "What was that about?" But Cora and the orb didn't stop moving. I swore, hiked up my skirt and hurried after them. *Who knew those skinny legs could move so fast?*

"What's the emergency?" I huffed.

"SOS beacon. Everyone who comes to *Spica* has one," Cora replied, not slowing. "Is it Michael's?" This she directed at the orb.

"Affirmative."

Cora cursed under her breath. "How far away?"

"T-two hundred and thir—ty kilometres, east-northeast," the orb crackled and stuttered. I ogled at it for a painfully long heartbeat. *The Aey-Eye was inside this thing?*

My brow pinched together. *Could've bloody said something sooner, like, say, when it was hanging ominously around my door.*

Cora put on a burst of speed and, gasping, I lurched after her, cursing gods—well, ancestors I suppose—and my stupid skirt. What had possessed me to think dying in a dress was the right way to go? What had I expected? To seduce a dragon with a frock? Not likely. We clattered into a massive chamber. I stumbled to a standstill. Giant sky god relics lined one wall.

Machines. I slowed, staring at their sleek, hawk-shaped bodies, glass eyes, arms tucked under their bellies and outspread wings embedded with turbine engines. Dragons. Not of flesh, like the one I'd encountered. These were metal. Titanium-alloy. Just a scrap from one of these could buy a village.

"Gods be," I murmured, before Cora's hand clamped around my wrist and pulled me over to one, right under its wing. She pressed a series of buttons on the belly of beast. It beeped and with a *phsst,* a door popped up and open.

"You wanted to see it all, this is your chance," she said.

She was right about that. I clambered in after her. It was a small space. Six chairs, surrounded by a wide glass view port and a dashboard full of screens and buttons—a smaller version of *Spica's* command centre, only this one had a stick set before the forward chair—a bit like the tiller on a dingy.

A flump of cloth landed on a seat beside me, making me jump.

"Put that on while the engines warm up. They'll stop you passing out." Cora said, motioning to a green pair of pants she'd thrown onto a chair. I plucked at the leg of the thing, it was heavy. But they were pants. And that was an improvement on my current wear. I stripped down to my undershirt and slid them on.

"Make sure they're tight," Cora added. "If we go supersonic, we'll be there in ten minutes."

Supersonic? The words trickled through my brain and a faint pressure built behind my eyes as my brain worked the numbers.

Two hundred and thirty kilometres. In ten minutes. 1254.55 kilometres per hour. *Holy—*

More numbers sprang into my head. Draugr's radius, mass, gravitational constant, rotation, probable flight vector, headwind—*wait, where in the gods was this coming from?* The sums swirled before my eyes, and like a jigsaw, the final number snapped together. Predicted acceleration speed. I beheld it a heartbeat, a flicker of panic shooting needles into my gut. *Oh gods.*

I vaulted into the chair next to Cora, grappling to buckle myself in.

"Are you sure about this?" I couldn't keep the tremor out of my voice.

Cora didn't look up from the dashboard. "Very sure." She flicked a switch.

Under us, the beast's engines screeched; billowing air buffeted the other craft down the row. The sound vibrated through the seat, up my back and into my teeth. It was almost like being inside a real dragon's belly. Minus the squidgy bits and being chewed into mincemeat first.

Perhaps following Cora had been a bad idea.

"Hold on," Cora advised and yanked the tiller up. *Too late now.*

My gut lurched, worse than the transport pod. I clung white knuckled to the arms of my seat. Through the bulbous forward window, the floor fell away, and the steel curtain of a giant door [one hundred and fifty meters by fifty meters—*damn it, brain, stop*] parted.

"Engaging in three... two... one." Cora rammed the tiller forward.

My body slammed into the back of the chair. A force pressed on my chest, pushed through my ribs and hard against my spine. My skin dragged backwards. Around my legs, my new pants clenched, squeezing the blood out of my throbbing limbs. I sucked in a breath, gods it felt like someone was sitting on my chest. My vision dimmed, narrowed to a pin prick. Panic thudded in my throat. I fought it down. *Think about something else.*

"I figured it out, by the way," I managed through clenched teeth, blinking back the darkness.

"Figured what out?" Cora asked. She too was pressed into her seat, but where I felt like my face was peeling off, she was all focus and forward intent on the sky.

"Everyone on Draugr is descendant from the sky gods. You're our ancestor." The weight on my chest eased off. The craft was reaching maximum velocity.

Cora eased back the tiller and sighed. "We're not sky gods. Just human."

The pressure relented. I wiggled in the seat; blood surged through my limbs again and I flexed my hands.

" *We* could be related," I realised out loud.

Cora snorted. "I was in stasis for three thousand years. I'm no more related than you and a stranger on the other side of Draugr is."

We levelled off and Cora leaned over the controls, twizzled a few dials.

"Where are we going?" I asked.

"Illia county," Cora said, eyes narrowing at the screen. "I have a ... companion on the ground. He triggered his beacon."

I blinked at her for a long moment. "I thought you were..." I began, but realised she never actually *had* said she was alone. Having more than one sky god awake at a time made sense, why not give them some company while they guarded a dead, well half-dead, sky ship? I frowned. Were they guarding it though? Why?

"Cora, why did you stay on the *Spica*?" I asked. "I mean, there's a whole planet here." I gestured at the green fields and blotches of forest whizzing past below.

She stiffened, spine straightening, shoulders pulling taught. If not for the rumble of the engines, I swear I'd have heard her suck in a breath and release it. Her hands fell lax on the controls.

"Do you not wonder why your people stopped being sky gods?" She glared at the screen before her.

Your people. Not 'our' people. Your. The distinction burned bitter in my mouth. And yes, I did wonder.

"There was an uprising," Cora said, still talking to the control panel. "A coup. Ten years after we landed. They killed the crew families. The very people who spent years of their lives bringing them here." Her fingers found the tiller and squeezed, and I sensed her biting back tears.

I swallowed, not sure if I wanted to know the answer to my next question. "Why?"

Cora shrugged. "Draugr wasn't so hospitable then. People got sick easily, died young, or were eaten by the native fauna. They blamed us. Said it was our fault for bringing them here, even though they volunteered." She gave a bitter laugh. "Like the Earth we left was any better." Cora sighed and sank back in her chair, deflated. "When the coup happened, our new settlement burned to the ground. The crew families tried to escape on the *Spica,* but the enem—*others* infiltrated the ship and—" her voice hitched, and she dragged in a breath— "killed the pilot while he was interfaced."

"You knew him," I guessed.

Cora nodded, her eyes squeezing shut. Another laboured breath. "My dad."

Oh.

"We crashed. The survivors went into stasis after that. With *Spica*'s AI damaged and the wizards looking for us, one person stayed awake to care for the rest and watch the world, waiting for a time to come when we'd be welcome again. Now here we are."

Here we were. I reached over and put my hand on her shoulder. Patted awkwardly. I'd never been very good at playing comforter, but something in the hunch of her shoulders and the wobble in her voice made me want to wrap my arms around her. Hold her. Shield her from my world. "We're not like that, not all of us. Not anymore. I swear."

Cora's lips pressed into a line. "Seems you've forgotten what they tried to do to you. All because you have a bit of crew ancestry in your veins."

I blinked. *A bit of what?*

"Worst of all, they all *watched*," Cora practically growled the last word, her jaw clenching together as the fury sparked in her eyes. "And now they're after another of us. I *won't* let that happen." She gripped the tiller tighter. "Hold on, I'm about to decelerate."

Godsdamn. I grabbed the base of my seat, and the force threw me forward into the seat's harness. My pants clenched around my legs again and my bladder sloshed.

"Target five hundred and —hirty-four metres and closing," *Spica's* Aey-Eye announced through the orb.

"Engaging holoflague," Cora said and pressed a button.

The steel cabin shimmered for a heartbeat, then snapped clear again. I frowned and peered through the bulbous window. Spotted the scaled wings stretching out on either side of us. My mouth dropped open. "You're kidding me."

Cora flashed me a wild grin. "I don't kid."

The sun caught the illusion's scales, glinting lapis blue back as us through the window. We were a dragon. A bloody sky gods dragon!

"But—wh—*how?*" I garbled.

"We never put stealth tech in our crafts, didn't think a colony ship would ever need it," Cora said. "But when we arrived, the local fauna kept attacking our crafts. So, we created a work around. Disguised our ships to mimic the biggest and baddest creature in Draugr's ecology."

I gazed through the window, admiring the detail of the wing membrane, right down to the dew drops collecting on the scales.

"Target two hundred and twenty meters," *Spica* announced.

Cora took the tiller and stared through the windows. "Look for a crowd," she said.

"There!" I jabbed a finger. Some hundred meters east and hundred and fifty-four meters below were the tiled rooftops of a village. A group of people gathered in its market square. Even from this far away, I could make out the flashing gold of a wizard's ornament on the lead figure's head. Every wizard wore one of those golden bands—a relic given only to the wizard's order and a symbol of the sky gods' blessing. Supposedly it took years of training for an apprentice to earn the right to wear one.

The wizard in question was gesticulating at another figure bound to a stake; male, I thought, squinting through the dragon's forward window. Old too, if the frizz of white hair on his head was anything to go by. As we neared, a rock flew from the crowd and struck the captive on the head. He sagged against the bindings.

"Animals," Cora spat and jammed the tiller forward. We lurched down, engines screaming. The crowd saw us coming and scattered like a flock of birds.

Cora bore down on them, hands flying over the controls. At the press of a button, a holo-display of two mechanical arms appeared above the console. Cora shoved her hands into them, her fingers and thumbs taking the shape of its pincer grips. Outside, a scaled leg whipped out at her command. Claws sliced through the rope binding the man, caught the body as it fell, gripping our charge in gentle claws.

"Be off beast!" a muffled shout sounded from outside the ship. The wizard. His robes were covered in dust kicked up from our arrival, his gold headpiece askew. "Take this sacrifice and return to the sky!"

Cora snorted, flexed her hands in the holo-display and a dragon leg knocked the wizard head over heels. Then she was pulling her hands free, holo-display vanishing with a beep of an instrument, and she gripped the tiller again. "Let's not outstay our welcome, eh?"

The craft whirled. I caught the flash of robes and gold again as the wizard struggled to his feet, fumbling at his waist. "Away, I command you! Take this heathen and leave these grounds!" he screeched. It was almost comical until I caught sight of the relic he lifted and pointed at the breast of the dragon—right at our window.

Cora saw it too. "Shit!"

"By the sky gods, I will *smite* you. Be gone!" he screamed, spittle flying. And fired.

The laser pierced the glass like a needle, searing across Cora's side before punching a finger-sized hole in the metal wall behind her.

"Guh," Cora grunted, jerking in her straps. "Fuck!" She pressed one hand to her side; it came back bloody. "Shit!" she swore again and yanked the tiller. We shot upwards, pressing my backside hard into my chair. The engines roared, and I fumbled for my straps and clicked myself back in.

Insane. Part of my mind was saying. *This is utterly, gods bloody insane.*

We ascended to two hundred meters and slowed our pace to one hundred kilometres per hour. Cora eased away from the tiller with a groan.

"Is it bad?" I asked.

Cora grimaced and showed me the bloody gash just above her hip. "Hurts like a bitch, but I'll live."

"Do you have miracle relics on *Spica*?" I asked, not thinking. Cora cast me a frown, and I rephrased. "Devices that heal."

Cora nodded. Her face had gone a shade of grey I'd only ever seen on a corpse. I unbuckled and scrambled over. "You don't look so good."

My captor/saviour/ancestor swayed, clutching her head. Red had soaked her green-glinted suit down to the knee. "Might need you to take over," she said. "I'm not feeling great."

"Come again?"

"It's not too hard," Cora said, closing her eyes and leaning back with a wince. Her fingers gripped her side. "*Spica's* Aey-Eye will give you everything you need."

"I can't fly this thing." My voice pitched into a squeak. "I don't even know where to start!"

"Interface with *Spica* and you will." She motioned her free hand at the orb floating over us.

"But I'm not a pilot. Not like you."

Her brow creased and she sighed. "Astrobiologist. I keep telling you. I don't have the right genes to work the numbers like a real pilot." She opened her eyes, trapping me in those bright irises. "But you do. You *see* the numbers. All *Spica* pilots see them." Her hand found mine, squeezing it tight. "Being a pilot is in your blood."

I swallowed. *Gods be, this was too much.* I was just a girl. Just a girl who was good at math. Okay, *really* good at math. Who'd dreamed equations before her teacher ever wrote them on the board. Who'd showed her best friend her notebook of workings, from the mass of Draugr to its distance from the twin suns, and got strung up as a sacrifice for her effort.

"Just try," Cora urged. "I'll talk you through it, but I'm in no condition to land this craft. My head is spinning."

I hesitated, then nodded. But Cora had shut her eyes again. I cursed under my breath. Sky gods, what was I doing? "All right."

Cora's lips quirked. "Okay, take hold of *Spica's* comms relay."

Um...

"The floating ball," Cora amended at my silence.

I plucked it out of the air and held it out. "Now what?"

"*Spica* create new profile. Username: Astraea. Code: pilot." Cora said.

The orb beeped. "Ready for scan."

I glanced at Cora, about to ask what next, when pain bit into my thumb. I yelped and released the orb. It caught itself mid-air and whirred itself back up to eye-level. A dribble of blood oozed out my thumb and I put it in my mouth.

<Gene-modifier detected. New user accepted. Welcome online Pilot Astraea>

My head exploded. Well, that's what it felt like. Codes of numbers flew across my vision. Figures, sums, equations, flight paths, star maps. Knowledge I couldn't possibly know streamed into my brain. Half-blind, I groped for my chair, found it and sagged into it. *Gods and starry skies, this was... incredible!* My brain gobbled the information in, digested it, and fresh understanding rippled out.

I opened my eyes. The control panel lay before me—suddenly no longer an alien wall of strange knobs and screens. I touched one screen. *Altimeter.* And that: *vertical velocity indicator*, and this: *radar.*

Gods be. Maybe I could do this.

"You okay?" Cora whispered. Her face had turned even paler. I had to get her back to the *Spica* and fast.

"I'm good." I sank down next to her. "I'm going to move you."

She managed one nod before I lifted her out of the flight seat and half dragged her to mine. She uttered a grunt, clenched her jaw and forced her legs to move, one step, then two, until we collapsed into her seat. All of it without a word of complaint. I buckled her in. "Hang tight," I said. "We're going home."

Cora smiled. "I'd like that. But let's bring in our passenger before he freezes."

<Open hangar door?> The question reverberated through my head *Spica's* neutral tones—minus the hiss and crackle of the orb.

"Yes, *Spica.*" I flicked a switch, bringing the craft's holo controls online again. A heartbeat later, our rescue dropped through the door, puddling onto the floor in a mass of rags. Unconscious too, an egg the size of my fist on his forehead.

Double damn. Time to get out of here.

<Set course for flagship?> *Spica* queried, making me start. This was going to take some getting used to. I sighed. "Yes, *Spica*."

#

I leaned over the man on the gurney. After a bit of guidance from Cora and the *Spica*, I'd landed the dragon back in the hold. A second communication orb had met us as soon as we opened the craft's door—two floating stretchers in its tow. Had it been any other day, any other time, I would have gawked, but I had no room left for surprise. With some manhandling I got both Cora and our rescue on each and let the orb lead me through the maze of tunnels. What would it have been like, I wondered as we walked, to travel these halls while *Spica* was in space? Would it have been lonely being one of a dozen awake while the rest of the gods—*humanity*—slept?

The orb directed us into a white-walled room, capsule beds lining its walls. I recognised them. Far newer looking, and not to mention cleaner, than the one I'd seen back in my village. I swallowed back memories of seeing my first mother climbing out as haggard as when she'd gone in. I pushed the memory away. These ones still worked—*Spica's* connection confirmed they did. But I couldn't shake the sense as I closed the lid on Cora that I might come back to a body instead of a healed person.

Our rescue was in better condition, apart from the lump on his head. I dabbed it with a concoction from a set of drawers *Spica* directed me to, rubbed some sort of salve into the cut the rock had left, and left him on the stretcher.

He woke within the hour. A hoarse croak rising from the stretcher. The orb zipped over to him, hovered an arm's span above his head.

"*Spica*," the man rasped. "You made it."

I approached. He was middle-aged going on old, the lines on his face like wrinkled clothes. His hair more grey than black, but his eyes were bright and dark, just like Cora's. Haggard sprang to mind. He frowned at me.

"You're new," he observed.

"I'm Astraea."

He managed a nod, winced and pressed a hand to his head. "Cora?"

"Healing," I said, motioning to the healing pod. His gaze followed my hand and landed on Cora's pale figure behind the glass, something flashed in his eyes. Anger, sadness, or maybe regret? He heaved a sigh. "Name's Michael," he said, easing himself up into a sitting position. He held out a hand.

I took it, feeling gnarled calluses under my fingers. Working hands. Not the hands of a biologist.

"Cora said you were her companion?" I asked.

167

"Companion?" He choked on a laugh. "We're from the same crew family." He smirked at my surprise, cracked lips parting. "Cora is my sister."

Huh? My eyes flicked to Cora, to Michael, and back to Cora again. No way. "You're related? But you're—"

"Old?" His face gave an odd twist, like he swallowed something sour. "*Spica* woke me up twenty-five years ago when the last steward died."

I see. And I did, if only just. I cocked my head, studying him. What kind of family had I gotten involved with here? "If you don't mind me asking, what were you doing so far from the *Spica?* Cora said it wasn't safe for people like you."

"Checking up on a few ... things." He paused, measuring me the same way Cora had, as if debating what he might say—and what he might not.

I scowled and set my hands on my hips. "Enough secrecy, I'm not about to run off and tell a wizard. Be straight with me."

The man grinned at that. "I think I'm going to like you," he said. "What village did Cora pull you from?"

I blinked. That I hadn't expected. "From Marantha, Rigal county, three hundred kilometres west of here," I said, and paused as coordinates spun across my vision. Gods be, this interface was distracting. Surely there was a way to turn it off.

<*Deactivate visual aids?*> *Spica* prompted in my head.

"Yes, *Spica*," I said, not thinking and turned back to Michael.

His face had turned slack, shock dropping his mouth open. Then his expression lit up, the beginnings of a crooked-toothed grin spreading on his face. "Can't be... You're a pilot?"

I shrugged. "So I'm told."

"Cora said she thought she'd detected someone with strong crew heritage before I left, I never..." Michael smacked a hand to his thigh, delighted, then winced and put a hand to his head again. "Here I was thinking there weren't any of you left." He shifted his legs over the stretcher, and heartbeat later he was up and shuffling for the drawers built into the wall. He pulled open one, then another and rummaged. I trailed behind him, not sure if I should stop him or not.

"If you're awake, why is Cora too?" I asked. "I thought it was only one of you at a time."

Michael pulled out a silver-sealed packet from a drawer, ripped off the top and knocked it back. "Excuse me, but I'm starving. They don't feed you in those village prisons, you know?"

I clenched my fists around the hem of my undershirt, forcing the memory away. "Yes, I do actually."

Michael grimaced. "Ah, they caught you doing calculations I take it?"

I shifted, an uneasy twitch in my stomach. To speak so openly about an ability I had spent years hiding made my insides go taut. "Something like that." I nodded to the miracle relic Cora lay in. "Your sister saved me."

He slowed in his eating. "Sorry it came to it," he said quietly, his expression turned sombre, as if the years had settled their weight onto him again. "Descendants like you are hard to find. We're constantly scanning villages, but you're not easy to detect until your abilities develop. We try to monitor as best we can but when you get in trouble," he broke off with a sigh. "Sometimes we can't extract you in time."

It took a long minute for his words to sink in. Descendants? "There are others like me?" I asked. "How many? What happened to them?"

Michael abandoned the drawer and drew a stool over to Cora's pod. He rubbed his face as he sank into it. "To answer your first question, I woke Cora up. I needed the extra help—we've had to extract a lot of you recently."

"Eight since you woke me," Cora muted voice spoke from underneath the glass. Her lips barely moved, and her eyes stayed shut.

"I used to get one or two every year, but the numbers have risen." Michael scowled at his lap. "The wizards are getting better at detecting descendants."

"Could they have found a new bit of tech?" Cora asked from her bed. "Maybe from an old escape pod?"

Michael shrugged, but his face pinched like he'd just drunk sour milk. "It's possible they've started experimenting with what they have."

Noticing my confusion, Michael explained, "The wizards' power comes from leftover *Spica* technology. Relics," he added when my confusion didn't abate. "They hoard them. Use them. Charge you for their use and abilities."

I cocked my head as a new question rose in my head, one that should have occurred to me a while ago: "But why are they hunting descendants?"

They both looked at me like I'd asked if the sky was green. Then Michael heaved a sigh.

"Descendants are born with abilities that can challenge that power. Once your existence threatened their status. Today, I fear, they see you as a threat to their worldview."

"Doesn't take much to frighten small minds," Cora muttered from her pod, a half grimace, half sneer pulling one corner of her mouth as the pod worked its miracle.

"*They* are afraid of *me*?" I couldn't keep the incredulity out of my voice. The idea was ridiculous. Back home, Wizard Gauron had my whole village falling over themselves to do his bidding. The bastard had practically beamed in his glee as he'd chained me to that clifftop. And now Michael and Cora were saying he had been scared of me?

I shook my head, still not able to believe it. "What would have happened if you'd not come?"

"Death by stoning. Torture. Hanging. Any one of a dozen different ways once no dragon appeared," Michael said.

I cocked my head, not following. Michael read my expression and went on.

"The dragon sacrifice tradition is due to an old accord we once had. *Spica's* crew were once notified to pick up a descendant and remove them from the wizards' territories. Negotiations broke down thousands of years ago, but the tradition continues, even if they've forgotten why."

My sister's screaming as Cora had carried me away rose into my head. How my father had done nothing but grip her, numb and white knuckled. "Being eaten by a dragon is a powerful deterrent for any would-be troublemakers," I said, understanding.

Michael nodded and tapped the glass of Cora's pod. She opened her eyes. "Have you given her the choice yet?" he asked.

Cora gave a slight, almost imperceptible, shake of her head.

Michael huffed and his attention shifted back to me. "I'll lay it out for you then," he said. "You have a choice. You can stay here, or we'll take you to a new village, far away from your old one. It'll be a fresh start where no one knows you."

Ah, so that's what had happened to the others. New lives all over Draugr.

"You'll need to keep your head down and stay away from the wizards," Michael went on. "But if you manage that, you'll live a peaceful life."

I folded my arms and bit down on a smile. "Oh no, I'm staying."

Cora's eyes snapped open, fixing on me with a glare. "Astraea, give it more thought." Her gaze softened, but I could have sworn I saw a spark of hope in it. "Please."

I shook my head. "This is the most interesting thing that's ever happened to me, I'm not walking away." I pushed out my jaw, daring them to argue with me. My mother had always said I had a stubborn streak. "I don't want to hide any more. I want..." I paused wondering if I might sound silly to these two people from another world. "I want to be a sky god. I want to go to the stars."

A smile tugged at Michael's lined face. "I knew I'd like her," he said to Cora.

Cora, however, looked unsure. "It's lonely work," she warned. "And often thankless. Not everyone adjusts to learning who and what they are as well as you have."

"She can always change her mind," Michael assured, more to Cora than to me.

"I won't." I folded my arms. "I have something to prove."

The two of them frowned, and in that moment, I saw the familial resemblance. Same frown, right down to the way their foreheads wrinkled, even if Michael's furrows were far deeper. "What's that?" he asked.

I levelled my gaze to Cora's. "That my people can change."

Silence at that. Michael and Cora exchanged a long look. It went on for so long I began to wonder if sibling sky gods could communicate mind to mind.

"Well?" I pressed.

A faint shrug from Cora's shoulder, but her lips were pressed tight, trying not to smile. Michael had no such reservations. He grinned and spread his arms, and for a horrible second, I thought he'd hug me. He didn't, thank gods. Instead, he swept his arms wider and gestured to the air.

"Welcome home."

Part Two.

I float inside the Spica. *My senses ripple through long halls, along wires and across metal hulls. The ship hums, its engines a steady pulse. Comforting white noise.*

The hushed whispers of my crew carry their anxiety through my titanium, to me in here. My orbs follow them, and through their lenses I see the shared glances; their hurry from room to room as they batten down anything not secure.

<Launch in T-minus ten minutes> I send the command through the ship and listen as Spica *echoes it through every orb and comms station.*

Banging and shouting from the hangar pulls my attention back outside. The mob has swelled, their yelling tinny through Spica's *systems. They've swarmed at* Spica's *doors.*

"Traitors! Cowards!" they chant. The air flashes with a shot from a plasma rifle aimed at the doors. "Let us leave!" The impact from the plasm rifle shudders through my metal. It might be half a metre thick, but it won't hold forever.

I clear my throat and activate Spica's *exterior comms. "We can't leave." My voice is low, masculine. "There's not enough power to put you back into—"*

They drown me out. Plasma shots rain at my speaker until it cuts out with a crackling hiss.

<Launch in T-minus four minutes>

We are nearly free when the crowd parts. Two men shove a small, cylindrical cannister at my door. Somewhere, deep inside the Spica, *my gut turns cold. No. It can't be. God preserve us.*

It goes off. No explosion. No sound. But the pulse surges through Spica's *systems— through me. Neuro-links fail. Synapses break inside and out.* Spica's *senses go dark. Pain burns in my head. Blood fills my mouth. I scream.*

"Dad!" Someone shouts. Hands pull at me. "No, please, not now!"

It hurts to breathe. Why can't I see?

"Dad!"

I recognise the voice this time.

"Cora," I whisper. Once. Somewhere outside my mind does an odd twist, like seeing double, but in my own head.

Cora.

The thought rocks through me, pulling my senses free of the memory, and I find myself nose to nose with the ghost of Spica's pilot pod. Dark green eyes, so much like his daughter's. Black hair with a curl at its ends; a scowl of confusion quickly turning to anger.

"You again? Get out!" he spits. "This is my place. My pain. Leave me be."

"I'm not—" I begin. Too late.

Pain explodes behind my eyes and the world ends...

I woke to my own screaming and the electric blue interior of *Spica's* pilot pod. Tears stung my eyes, partly from the memory, partly from the frustration. Again. How many times had it been now? I'd lost count.

"I can't do it." I yanked the sensory cables off my temples. "I can't get past him."

"You'll find a way," Michael said. "*You will,*" he insisted at my doubtful glare.

"Every time I interface, I'm there, reliving it with him." I said, pulling myself out of the pilot pod. "All the way through the... the... what did you call it?"

Michael winced and his arms stiffened—the way they did when he clenched his hands together behind his back. "Electro-magnetic pulse."

Gooseflesh spread across my arms. "It all went dark. Everything."

"That's what EMPs do. Even a small one will knock out electronics for miles; permanently damage them even."

I hugged myself. "He was so afraid." I glanced at Michael and for a disjointed second, I was back in the pilot pod with the ghost standing over me. They had the same eyes. Same nose. And there, same crease in the brow. Then I realised what I'd said, and what the ghost had meant to him. "Sorry."

With a sigh, Michael eased onto the chair stationed on the platform outside the pod. He'd brought it down from the common room—just a simple dining chair—but the sight of it jarred every time I walked in to find it still there. For its part, the pilot pod was perfectly round and hung in a gyroscope so it self-balanced no matter what the ship was doing. Not that it mattered now, grounded as *Spica* was.

"Take a break," Michael instructed, rubbing his forehead with one hand. "We'll come back to it after lunch."

I'm not sure who found whom more exhausting. Him for my constant questions or me from his mostly incomprehensible answers. In the last six months I'd spent half my time rummaging through *Spica's* bookshelves and querying her digital library hunting for answers. The rest of the time had been with Cora, exploring her closer than any of Michael's assigned readings combined.

It started as an innocent invite to stargaze. Cora had packed an old-Earth telescope in a bag, and we'd sat on the edge of the cliff beyond *Spica's* common room for hours.

"That one," she'd said, pointing the telescope at a cluster. "There's a planet around one of its stars that has the beginnings of alien life under its ice. That there—" she gesturing to a long strip of space dust visible to the naked eye that my people called 'The Murk'— "has three habitable planets. Actually, technically one is a moon, but it's the same size as Mars."

"What's Mars?" I'd asked, and Cora clucked her tongue.

"Sorry, I forget you weren't taught about Sol System," she'd said, "Mars was a planet near Earth. We colonised it briefly." She proceeded to tell me about her home system. About a planet with rings and one with a storm that had lasted for centuries. I'd listened, enchanted, in part by her stories but mostly at the way her face lit up as she described her universe.

"I wish I could see the worlds you have," I'd later sighed, pulling back from the telescope to gaze at Cora's upturned face just visible in the starlight.

Her green eyes met mine and there was a longing there that I didn't think was just for her lost stars. My gaze fell on her lips—the same lips I'd been staring at for months— and watched, half mesmerised, as her mouth moved.

"If you want it, go for it," she said.

I'd blinked and jerked my gaze away, suddenly thankful for the dark as a flush crept into my cheeks. Then I realised what she'd meant and nearly snorted with laughter. "Me, a space explorer?"

"Of course. You're our pilot now. It's your job to fly *Spica*."

I'd not thought much on what it meant to be a sky god, or to see the stars. It'd all been too big. Up until that point, I'd only thought about *getting* to space. Not what came after.

My belly did a little twist and flip as Cora's words sunk in. Me, a member of *Spica's* crew. Together with Cora. Exploring worlds.

I knew a moment of budding joy before reality intruded.

Except I can't fly Spica *yet.*

And the ship was entombed in a mountain.

That brought me back to Draugr with a bump.

"What is it?" Cora, ever observant, noticed my sudden quiet.

I sighed and leaned back to look into the sky. "I've still got so much to learn."

Without realising it, we'd shifted closer, and so she'd rested her head against my shoulder. A blissful heat spread down my side from where her body met mine. "Perhaps, but I'll help you."

When I'd glanced down at her, and found her watching me, I'd realised she might not just be talking about *Spica*.

Tentatively, I'd lifted a hand and stroked a lock of her blue-black hair away from her face, marvelling in its softness. My thumb brushed her cheek, then her lips. The moment it did, doubt flared inside my chest. Surely I was reading this all wrong. I was a country girl who didn't know anything. And Cora was so clever, so patient, so, so...

Her ocean eyes found me and swallowed me whole. This close, the hazel fleck in her right iris was large, bright. Sun-like despite the dark. Slowly, her head tilted, lips turning for mine.

Cora's words from earlier came back to me. *If you want it, go for it.*

I wanted her. So much. My heart, mouth, groin ached for her.

Our lips brushed.

"Are you sure?" I'd whispered.

"Skies, yes."

My first touch was gentle, then as she'd responded, we met in a hungry crush. As if we had three thousand years to make up for.

#

With the latest rejection of *Spica's* ghost pilot still stinging, I sought out Cora's hydroponics lab. Sure enough, I found her there, her latest seedings from *Spica's* seed vault lined up in rows along the wall. *Trinidad Scorpion (chilli)* read one of the labels in Cora's neat lettering. Soon these would go into the garden she'd set up at the base of *Spica's* mountain to grow beside her cabbage shoots and onions. As for the girl, her hands were deep in a barrel of muck, the sleeves of her ship suit rolled up to her elbows. I didn't ask. She'd mentioned recycling more than once, and I'd long decided this was one thing I was better off not knowing. I waited until she'd cleaned her hands under one of *Spica's* light showers before handing her a sandwich.

"You made this?" Cora guessed, eyeing my concoction. One end of the bread was thicker than the other from where I'd sawed off the slices instead of letting *Spica's* machinery do it. Something about having all our food prepared by machines had never sat right with me. *Food comes from the heart,* Mother had always said. I loved *Spica,* but the AI's food production lacked human touch. The meals always tasted bland; their flavours dampened to meet everyone's tastes.

At that, my subliminal connection to the ship activated, and chemical equations jumped into my field of view, offering up earnest suggestions. I blinked them away.

"*Spica* interrupting again?" Cora asked, her lip quirking at my sudden pause.

I sighed, slumping down next to a row of budding cabbages. "I'm not sure if I'll ever get used to it."

"You will," Cora assured.

"So you and Michael keep telling me."

"It'll click," Cora insisted. "Just like piloting the dragons remotely did. What's your range now? Four kilometres? Five?"

I closed my eyes, questing my senses out to the dragon I'd landed on a nearby mountain pass that morning over breakfast. Despite my frustration, a smile pulled at my mouth as Cora's instructions from months ago rose in my thoughts. *Feel the dragon. Be the dragon.* She'd been teaching me how to fly at the time, her hands wrapped around mine at the dragon's tiller, showing me how to pilot the dragon by feel alone. Little had she known her advice would be the breakthrough I'd need to remote pilot the dragons as well.

I reached my mind for the dragon on the mountain pass. Felt the systems ping me back, flooding my vision with readings. At the beginning it had been overwhelming. Now, I took a breath, letting it all settle until I could sense the machine's intake of air through its metal belly, the twitch of its wing flaps. Then I calculated.

"Four point six kilometres," I replied, pulling my mind away and opening my eyes again.

Cora crooked a knowing eyebrow at me. "See?" She went back to inspecting her sandwich, turning it this way and that as if expecting a frog to leap out of it. "You've already come so far. Your knowledge of physics exceeds mine now, Michael's too." She lifted a bread slice to examine the cheese tucked in its middle and frowned. "Where did you get this?"

I shrugged. "Asked Michael to pick some up last time he went to Arma." Anything dairy was hard to come by on *Spica*, let alone anything fermented.

Cora scowled. "He goes out too much," she said. "He's going to get himself caught again."

I sighed. "If he keeps his head down and watches what he says there's nothing to worry about. Most folk don't care much for relics or sky gods. *"Unless there's a wizard about.* The unspoken words hung between us, and I motioned to the sandwich. "Are you going to eat that or not? Because I'll take it if you're not interested."

Cora gave the snack a doubtful look, then took a bite. Chewed slowly. Her face lightened. "This is good."

I snorted. "Of course it is, I made it." *With love,* as my mother used to say. I studied the face I'd come to know so well. My captor/saviour/ancestor/lover arched an eyebrow.

"What is it?" she asked.

"I—"

Screams from her father's memory sliced through my head. *Dad! No, please, not now!* I sucked in a breath, gritted my teeth, and forced it away.

"*Spica's* really done a number on you today," Cora observed into my silence.

I closed my eyes and nodded. Every time I climbed into the pilot pod the memory replayed. An imprint, Michael called it. The result of a pilot disconnecting without following proper procedure. Disconnect. He'd said it so clinically. I suppose he'd had twenty-five years to come to terms with it.

"The system is still coded to the last pilot. It will rewrite itself after you interface," he'd assured, more than once. *"You've just got to push through."*

Goosebumps rippled up my arms, and I hugged my knees, right there between the rows of cabbage. Regardless of whether it was a ghost or interference from old system settings, something of her Dad was still inside the ship. If I succeeded, I'd wipe the last piece of her parent away.

Cora's hand found my arm, gave it a brief squeeze. "Is something wrong?" She asked, an edge of worry in her voice.

Did she know? Had Michael explained it to her? "Just some feedback issues in the pilot pod," I said. "Michael and I are working through it."

Cora studied me a long moment, and for a terrifying heartbeat I thought she might call me out on my half-truth. Then she nodded and went back to her sandwich. Guilt crawled into my belly. I should have told her. But what if she asked me to stop? What if she forbade me from wiping the last trace of her father from this world? Because I knew if she asked, I would stop. And I'd never become a pilot. What use was I then? Dead weight on a half-dead spaceship. Better not to have her ask at all.

Yea, I was a selfish cow. I stood, brushed the non-existent dirt off my uniform— blue for pilots. The thrill on Cora's face when she'd handed it to me from the *Spica's* clothing printer still made my heart swell.

"See you at dinner?" I asked.

Cora leaned in, pecked a kiss on my cheek. "Dinner," she agreed. "This time I'll cook."

#

The boy's name was Alto. A skinny, too-small fourteen-year-old in need of a meal or ten. White hair. Grey eyes. Michael pulled him from a village in the North—all bluffs and jagged coastline, not far from where the real dragons once flew three thousand years ago, according to *Spica's* records.

"Come in, come in," Cora ushered him and a bedraggled Michael into the common room. Sat them down at the table.

"Rough trip?" I guessed, taking in the bags under Michael's eyes. He shook his head. *Not now.*

I sighed and watched the boy pick at the meal I'd placed before him before Cora showed our glazy-eyed rescue to a fresh room.

"He doesn't talk much," Michael said.

"Are they always like that?" *Had I been like that?*

"No." Cora had returned from the hall and her eyes snapped to her older brother, her glare pinning him to his chair. "What happened?"

Michael dragged a hand over his face, rubbed grit out of his eyes. "The wizards were prepared for me," he muttered, and stared into his lap. "They had relics ready. Tried to bring the craft down. Nearly did."

A tense pause. "You mean," Cora swallowed. "A trap?"

Michael nodded. "He—" his gaze darted down the hall where the boy had gone "—

176

was bait. They *knew* I'd come."

My gut tightened, the words whistling out of my throat as it constricted. "They know about us."

Michael heaved a sigh, sank deeper into his chair. "Seems so."

"Were you followed?" Cora asked.

Michael's head jerked up, a rare flash of annoyance over his face. "Who do you take me for? Of course not." His scowl faded. "If they did, I'd be surprised." I took in Michael's sagging frame in the chair, his filthy, sweat-stained jumpsuit.

<Spica> I sent. <*Check status of Dragon Two*>

<*Dragon Two is offline*> came the ship's reply.

I stared at Michael, my jaw working open. What could kill a dragon craft? And with no AI systems to guide him, no pilot to fall back on. How had he made it back here?

<Spica, *last known location of Dragon Two*>

<*Twenty-five kilometres north-northwest*> A series of coordinates trickled through my vision. Well, that explained it. He hadn't managed it. And he and Alto had *walked* the rest of the way here. No wonder they'd arrived dead on their feet. I queried the location of Alto's village and was relieved when *Spica* reported it close to one hundred kilometres away. No wizards would be following us here.

In the common room, Cora blew out a breath from her cheeks. "We're going to have to be careful. Lower our profile."

I straightened, blinking away *Spica's* responses. "What if there are others? You can't leave them. The wizards *will* kill them." In the most painful way possible. *Like they'd almost done me.*

Cora's gaze snapped to mine and I knew that look. "I'm not about to risk what's left of my family."

"But—"

"No!" Cora's fists clenched, her cheeks turning their familiar angry pink. This wasn't our first argument, not even our tenth, but I'd never seen her temper so quick to flare. Then she sucked in a breath, and I heard the sob rattle in her chest. *Ah, not anger. Fear.* With one hand, she furiously wiped away a tear. "I said no." Her gaze roved over Michael, his two-day stubble, the scuffed holes in the knees of his suit. "I can't lose you."

And with those words something wrenched in my chest. Pain followed by a blossoming anger. I bit back a '*What about me?*'. Who was I kidding? I had nothing on family. When it came to the crunch, I was relegated to the outside, a stranger looking in. What did Cora's media call it? Yes, that's right.

A third wheel.

I swallowed hard. These last six months I'd finally thought I'd found my place. My family. Cora and Michael and me. The thought of losing any of them make my stomach clench. But now, a new creeping chill wound into my belly.

Had I been mistaken? If push came to shove, would they cast me off like an old, ill-fitting sweater like my first family had? My father's face swam out of my memory. Deaf to my shouting. Eyes averted as I was hauled away and strung up for a dragon by Gauron's men. The old pain twanged awake in my heart.

Suddenly the common room, with all its vast shelves and sweeping windows, was too small. Claustrophobic. I backed from the table.

Michael furrowed his brow, concerned. "Astraea? What's wrong?"

"Oh, nothing, nothing!" I floundered. "Something I ate earlier didn't sit well with me. Think I'll turn in early."

A terrible lie. They saw straight through it. But when I turned down the hall to my room they didn't stop me, which was even worse.

I turned into my room, the one I hadn't used in months. With a click, the door shut. I pressed my back to it and slid down to the floor. The tears wouldn't stop.

#

<Crew member distress detected> Spica's voice jerked me out of a dreamless sleep. I rubbed my raw eyes, blinked twice to see the map *Spica* was projecting into my vision. Nanoids in the blood, Michael had once explained to me how it worked. Passed down from my mother's side. It took a full minute for me to work out what I was looking at.

This map wasn't of *Spica's* interior. It was of Draugr. Specifically, the northern continent. This continent. A small signal winked on and off the other side of the inland sea. As I focused on it, *Spica's* map zoomed in, detailing trajectories, flight paths and— I stopped—the name of the town.

Marantha. My town.

I was out of bed and banging on Cora's door before the next minute was out.

"I see it," Cora's voice called from beyond the door. When she opened it, her usually straight hair was tangled and there were bags under her eyes, like she hadn't slept at all. Her jaw tightened at my expression. "We can't do anything, not right now."

"Why not?" Anger tinged those words and my heart gave a little twist. I didn't want another argument. Not here. Not after our last. But I wanted her to *see*. If we didn't act, no one would. "Michael might not be in any condition to go, but that doesn't stop us."

Cora heaved a sigh, rested her head on the door frame and shut her eyes. "It's too risky, Astraea. You heard Michael." She opened her eyes again and gazed imploringly into my face, as if trying to reach into my soul and change my mind. "They're out to catch us. And they've figured a way to detect crew genes. For all we know, it's a trap."

I stepped in, meeting her gaze with my own. "What if it's not? What if it's someone like me?"

178

"Are you willing to risk everything to test that?"

I hesitated. I didn't want to lose Cora, or Michael, or the place I'd found here. But at the same time, I couldn't sit on my hands and do nothing. Not when we *knew* how to help. When we might be the only ones who could. The wizards might be the villains here. But if we turned out backs, where we any better? I opened my mouth, wanting to explain, to urge her to action.

Cora beat me to it with a sigh. "You're too good to them."

Them. That word again. My temper flared. "There is no them. They're people. *My* people, *your* people. And you're going to let them die." I thrust a finger down the hall, aligning it with the flight path *Spica* had overlaid on my vision. "The people you save aren't "them", Cora. They're sons and daughters. Friends and cousins. Brothers and—" I faltered, horror crawling up my throat "—sisters." I finished in a whisper. *Gods and stars, please don't let it be that.*

"Astraea?" Cora's voice brought me back. My heart thudded inside me, fear turning my blood cold.

"I-I have to go," I stammered and without waiting for a reply, turned and ran down the hall.

Through *Spica's* labyrinth I went. Left turn, straight, two rights, another left, until I emerged in the hangar. Dragon-craft lined each wall, their forms looking like true beasts in the dark. I hurried along to the last in the row, opened the hatch. I didn't know what I'd do once I got there. Strategy was more Cora's thing. But I'd figure it out on the way. I clipped myself into the chair and initiated the start-up procedure. Cora was no doubt regretting giving me lessons right about now—she'd thought it'd help me get familiar with *Spica* and her pilot pod. It had. Until her father's ghost had gotten in the way.

I snorted and started the engines. They roared under me, rattling the craft as if lifted into the air. I'd be lucky if Michael let me back inside *Spica's* pilot pod after this. I'd probably just lost my chance to see the stars. But if I was right, I couldn't leave her... not the one person who'd stood by me. *Cella.* My father might be dead to me, but Cella. My sweet, little sister didn't deserve that. She'd never shown any of my uncanniness, so I'd assumed her safe. But I'd been wrong. If my time on *Spica* had taught me anything, there was more than one set of crew genes expressed through the generations. There were hundreds, if not thousands of permutations.

I punched the throttle, zoomed for the doors.

And pulled up short.

The doors were still shut. I frowned. They should have opened as soon as I powered up the dragon.

<*Spica, open hangar doors*> I commanded, drumming my fingers on the pilot's stick. *Come on, come on.* A clank from within the wall. The door groaned and parted

open, the sliver inching wider, then wider again, then stilling.

<Command overruled. I.D. Caretaker Michael Astraeus>

"What?"

<Caretaker Michael Astraeus has initiated lockdown procedure. No one may leave the Spica*>*

"Cora," I growled under my breath and jabbed the comms button. She must have roused him as soon as I'd run.

"Let me out."

"We can't, Astraea. It's too dangerous." Michael's voice cracked from the dragon's speaker, old, tired, and so gods bloody reasonable.

"You're not going. *I* am. I have to go." I cringed as my words turned pleading. Pleading never helped anything. I'd learned that well. And yet... "It's my sister. I have to help her."

"There's no evidence to suggest that."

"Screw your evidence, I *know* it's her. I'm going." I flicked the switch for the dragon's claws. The holo-control arms appeared before me, and I thrust my hands into them. I'd claw my way out if I had to.

"Astraea," Cora's voice sounded through the dragon's radio. "You're being reckless. Stop, *please*. Don't leave."

Her voice cracked on the last word and my stomach did a little flip. *No, don't do that, oh gods please don't.* I spoke into the radio, hoping Cora would understand.

"She's my family. I can't lose her."

Without waiting for a response, I flicked the radio off and flexed my fingers in the holo controls. My dragon's claws snapped towards for the doors, clamped the slit—

The doors rattled open of their own accord, giving me a path to the sky.

<Lockdown overridden>

I blinked. *They'd really listened?* Then I spotted a small, too-skinny figure standing at the edge of the hangar doors. His white hair glowed electric, and one hand was pressed against the control panel in the wall.

Alto.

My dragon's comms crackled on. *<Go>* A strange voice resonated from the speaker; robotic, similar *Spica's* AI but half a note lower. Across the hangar, Alto's lips didn't move. A nanoid-skill like mine, I guessed. Maybe even another pilot.

Doubt wormed into my heart. If he was a pilot, would Cora and Michael even want me back? I quashed a twinge of jealousy and pushed the throttle. *Deal with it later, Astraea.* Right now, Cella needed me. My dragon shot through the gap, following *Spica's* projected flight path.

"Thank you," I spoke into the empty cabin, wondering if Alto had a way to hear me.

Silence. Then, *<Save your family>* Another pained pause. *<I couldn't save mine>*

\#

I had twenty minutes to formulate a plan. Cora and Michael were probably right about the wizards. Chances were, it was a trap. I initiated the dragon holoflague, admiring the sight of the scaled wings stretching out on either side of the craft before putting my scraped-together plan into motion. I approached Marantha from the backcountry, keeping the dragon low to hug the rolling hills. Even with holoflague, there was no way to hide the craft from sight. Not completely. The old colonists hadn't anticipated the need to cloak their craft. The dragon holoflague had been adapted from *Spica's* onboard tech to study the true dragons in Draugr's north.

"We weren't looking for war. We were a ship of refugee scientists and thinkers. We were looking for a new home." Cora had said once.

I snorted at the memory. How wrong it had all gone.

I landed the dragon five kilometres from Marantha in a small ravine of tumbledown rocks. Cella and I used to picnic here as children, tossing pebbles over the edge and counting the number of times they'd bounce down the boulders. On impulse, I bundled up the dragon's toolkit and slung it over one shoulder. *Spica's* dragons might be scientific vessels with no weapons, but a laser cutter would do in a pinch.

The walk into town was a long one, but I didn't dare take the dragon closer. Besides, I needed time to find a few items to blend in. I crept through Greyson's farm, stopping at Mrs Grayson's washing lines to secure a faded lavender frock and a cloak, which I pulled over my ship suit. Fingers crossed I wouldn't have to run in this get up. From there I followed the road into town. The trek left blisters on my heels. Gods bloody ship shoes. Should have grabbed my boots before I left.

Familiar scents found me as the village rooftops came into view. Smoke from the hearths, warm bread from the bakers, and with a twinge I realised it was close to mid-winter festival. I'd been gone for nearly eight months. A pang rose in my chest. Cella would be turning thirteen soon. How's that for a birthday present.

"Happy birthday, sis. You're descendent from an ancient crew that was stranded here three thousand years ago. Oh, and the wizards want you dead."

That last bit was probably obvious by now. *<Spica, show trajectory of the Descendent>*

A map overlaid my vision and my mind whirred through the numbers in a blink. 302.18 meters. My stomach clenched as I recognised the location. The village square. I hurried on, zeroing in on my target as pulled my cowl lower and kept to the sides of the street. Down the back alleys, zig-zagging my way in.

It was market day. The square should have been brimming with a crowd bartering and moving from stall to stall. Organised chaos as Ma used to call it. Sure enough, the square was full of people. But not a trace of produce. No stalls, no fruit or grain or vegetables. No cloth or weave. Instead, people stood in three lines, heads bowed, the odd whisper passing from neighbour to neighbour.

At the front of each line, I caught the telltale glint of a wizard's gold ornaments. *Three of them.*

I shrank into the shadow of a wall, spitting curses under my breath. *Stars be, what was going on?*

A quick search found an abandoned shop. I ducked inside and made my way up to the second home story. Looked out the window.

Blood drained from my legs.

In the field behind the town square stood a freshly erected gallows. Wizard Gauron's body hung from the noose. I stared. Gauron was dead. Executed. *Why?* My attention tracked back to the lines of village folk. One by one, each of the wizards pressed a relic against the splayed palm of a villager at the head of the line. My breath caught as Draugr's suns caught a single 'eye' embedded in one of the sphere-shaped relics.

A *Spica* orb. Gods and starry skies, they'd found a stash of comms drones.

One by one, the orbs emitted a beep and their scratched lenses flashed red.

"Crew not found," one hissed, the words crackling as though its speaker was under water. The villager was allowed to step aside, and I watched as a few members of the village guard guided them into the communal hall.

My gut clenched. Michael had wondered how they'd been finding descendants so easily. Here was the answer. The drones could detect the crew gene. One prick was all it took. I scanned the village—Marantha had never been particularly big. Fifty people at the most. Double that when all the farmers came into town for market day. Like today.

This wasn't a trap. This was an exposure. An ousting. The wizards were trying to unearth Descendants. And Cella—I searched the crowd, hoping to find the familiar scraggly mess of blond hair. Nothing. <Spica, show Descendant>

Faithfully, the image popped across my vision. The green blinking signal was still there. A trickle of relief flowed through me. Maybe my gut was wrong. Perhaps it wasn't Cella. Maybe my sister was safe after all. Then guilt flickered. It shouldn't have made any difference whether it was my sister or not—and yet, it did. The more I searched, the more certain I was that Cella wasn't down there in the lines. Could she already be in the town hall? Cleared of any crew gene?

Then my father stepped to the front of the middle line.

My breath snagged. *It couldn't be.*

"Palms up," the wizard before Father snapped. He was a skinny fellow, his robes hung off him like a sack and his golden band was slightly too big and slid down his forehead as he sweated. A hand-me-down if ever I saw one.

I frowned. I'd never thought to question it, but why did all wizards wear the same gold ornament? Always around the head.

<L.I.D.>

"What?" I remembered just in time to whisper it.

<Limited interface device. Designed for non-crew members to interface with Spica's *components>* A series of hardware specs flashed up along with rows and rows of code. I went cross-eyed trying to read it. I was no technician. It was beyond me.

Below, the wizard thrust the battered-looking orb into my father's hand. My father started when the orb pricked him. I held my breath, waiting for it to flash red. *Please flash red.* I'd assumed my crew gene came from my mother. She'd been brilliant in every way. Clever, funny, smart beyond her station. But what if—

Across the quiet square, the orb crackled. "Gene modifier detected. Welcome crew member."

"Seize him!" the wizard snapped, and two guards swept in.

My father dropped the orb. It thudded onto the cobbles like a rock. "I'm not—" he began, whirling on the spot. "It's wrong. It's got it wrong!"

The villagers wouldn't meet his gaze. Instead, they eased away from him as if he were diseased. A familiar pang of knowing, pulled at my chest. I knew that look. Father had cast that very same one at me, right before he'd let Gauron into our cottage to take me away. A curl of hot anger roped through my gut. *How's it feel to be on the receiving end, eh, Da?*

But when my father's knees gave and a begging sob broke from him as the guards hauled him away, the feeling evaporated and guilt squirmed up in its place. No one deserved the wizard's wrath. Not even Da.

The village guard dragged him out of the square and into the lock tower. And unmistakable *clank* of a metal door followed.

"Keep scanning!" The wizard who'd uncovered my father barked, and he and his two fellows busied themselves once more.

Faces peered through the windows of the town hall—Marantha's citizens trying to see the unlucky soul who'd been arrested. I imagined Cella among them, wondering why her father hadn't come to find her. My insides gave a little twist at that. Whether I acted or not, she might never see him again.

As much as I wanted to let Da stew for a while longer in his own medicine, I couldn't. The wizards wouldn't give him the chance. Descendants who were *awake*, as Cora called it, were a danger to the wizard's order. A threat to their power.

"They'll string up an awakened descendant just like humanity did to the witches of old," she'd once said.

If *Spica* had detected awakened abilities from my father, that meant he had to be aware on some level of what he was, as much as he might deny it. I muttered a curse and slipped down the stairs and into the street.

It took another ten minutes to circle the square—giving it and the wizards a wide berth—and approached the lock tower from behind. Adjacent to the town hall, it was an old stone building, lopsided like perhaps a real dragon had once alighted on its roof. It was old as Marantha itself, built back when the village was founded. I searched through the bared windows until I found the tower's sole occupant, hunched on an upturned bucket, clutching his arms around himself.

He'd never looked less like a father. Just a scared old man with greying stubble on his cheeks.

"You *liar*." I'd not meant to say those words. But they came tumbling out of me, the anger waking in my belly again.

Da spun at my voice, snatching up the bucket like it were a shield. Or something to hide behind. Then he blinked, recognition washing his face. The bucket drooped. "A-Astraea?"

I straightened at the window, lifting my chin to glare at him down my nose and recited something I'd once heard Cora say. "In the flesh." I made a deliberate show of studying him. "Looks like you're in a bit of a bind, *Da*." I was being petty, I knew, but damn if I didn't feel vindicated.

"Astraea, please." The words came out tired, but wary. "You have every right to be angry—"

"Don't *please* me," I hissed, and he flinched as if I'd slapped him. At the sight of him cowed, I bit back the tirade I desperately wanted to let loose. That could come later; I had more pressing matters. "We have to get you out."

"You should not be here." Da's gaze hadn't left my face. It was as if he were drinking the sight of me in and growing more and more worried by the second. "You need to leave, before they find you."

I squared my jaw. "I'm not leaving."

"Astraea, this is no time to be stubborn." His voice strengthened, almost like the Da I knew before it all went wrong.

"Think of Cella," Da urged. "She loves you. I was a brute for making her watch your sacrifice. Don't make her witness it again."

"And witness *you* sacrificed instead?" I folded my arms and glowered through the window. "You're right, you are a brute." I pressed my face to the bars. "Listen up, no one is getting sacrificed. You got it?"

"Astraea, you can't—"

"I can, and I will." I pulled a laser cutter from my belt. "I'm getting us out of here. All of us. Now shut up and get ready to move."

I set the laser cutter to the bars and after a few tense minutes, they snapped clean and *thunked* to the floor of Da's cell.

"Quickly," I hissed at Da, leaning through the window to offer him my hand up.

"Are there others?" he asked, scrambling over the broken bars. "Is Michael here?"

How in the gods did he know about Michael? I shook my head. Not the time.

"He's not here." I said, hurrying him away from the lock tower. "It's just me."

"What about Cella?" Da peered about us, as if expecting my sister to appear around the corner and deflating when she didn't. "Do you have a plan?"

"Not yet." I returned his scowl with a glare. "I'm figuring this out as I go, all right? Be glad anyone came at all."

We scurried low along the town hall's wall, keeping our heads below the windowsills. "We can't leave Cella," Da hissed at me. "The wizards will—"

"I know, I know," I grated. "Just let me think." Crouched there, I racked my brain. Drawing blanks.

"Can't you call for backup?" Da asked.

"No, I can't." Not after my fight with them. They were too busy cowered up in their sky god fortress. We were on our own. But... A grin crossed my lips. "I have an idea."

I concentrated, flinging my awareness out to the dragon hidden in the gully. I'd never remote operated a dragon from this far out, but how much more difficult could it be? My nerves tingled. Miles away, I *felt* the turbines begin to wind up; their faint heat in my sides like the stretch of dormant muscles. The engine's air intake like a breath into my lungs.

As it turned out, remote piloting a dragon from so far off was a *lot* more difficult. As the dragon rose into the air, a gust caught it, pitching it earthwards. Sirens blared in my brain, my head spun and, crouched below the window, I sagged into the grass.

"Astraea!"

I ignored Da's gasp and shut my eyes. *Concentrate. You can do this.* I narrowed my mind as if squinting into the distance. Da, the village, the world around me dropped away as I lasered my focus to a single point.

"Feel the dragon," Cora's words sounded in my head. *"Immerse yourself in its senses.* Be *the dragon."*

I relaxed my mind as much as I could and let the information pour in. Altimeter data. Wind speed. Thrust. More and more and more, until—

I opened my eyes to a fresh scene. The gully. My body tilting for the earth. I *was* the dragon.

The sheer wall of the rocky ravine filled my vision. Without thinking, I punched my right turbine. Adjusting its output to the wind. My body righted, and with a surge of thrust shot skyward, missing the lip of the gully by 1.24 metres. Far away, curled in the grass under the town hall windows, I grinned.

To Marantha.

#

It took less than five minutes for my dragon to reach the town square. Five hundred meters out, I unearthed some old sound recordings in the dragon's electronic files and blasted it through the external speakers. A biting, shrieking, metal-on-metal roar pierced the air. Below, the villagers scattered, breaking out of their ordered lines to flee like mice before a cockatrice.

Unfortunately, the wizards required more convincing. One of them raised a projectile—just like the one that had shot Cora all those months ago. I gnashed my dragon's holoflague teeth and angled a blast from my thrusters at them. Windows exploded along the shop fronts. Two wizards were knocked to the ground and a third reeled backwards as he screamed and clung to his relic to stop it slipping from his head.

The dragon couldn't laugh, but down on the grass my old body giggled. And like that, I snapped back into myself. I whirled on Da. He stared up at the holoflagued dragon hovering above us, mouth ajar. "Astraea, are you doing this? Did you call it?"

"I'll explain later." I forced him up and into a run for the town hall's doors. "Go, quick. Get Cella while I have the wizards distracted." I opened the door and shoved him through. "Go to the tanner's banks, I'll bring the dragon down there."

"What about you?"

I faltered. I hadn't thought about how I'd get myself there. Could I control two bodies on the go? No choice but to find out. I turned on the steps, reaching for my dragon again. One moment I was in flesh. The next metal. And below, the wizards had regrouped, and were hauling out something from a store front between them.

This couldn't be good.

I aimed another thruster blast at them. But they braced themselves into it, the weight of whatever it was they carried anchoring them down. A barrel turned up, trained on my belly.

Oh no.

"Behold, beast, the might of wizards!" Shrieked the haggard, stick of a wizard who'd interrogated my father. "We fear you no more."

The three of them each placed a hand to the device's metal body. I'd seen pictures of ones just like it in *Spica's* archives. Seen it in the movies I'd curled up to watch with Cora.

A rocket launcher.

No, no, no. I slammed on my turbines, the whine of them rising over the blasting wind. I was too low. Too close. The launcher fired. I rolled sideways, engines screaming. Yes! It'd miss—

The projectile curved mid fight, re-adjusting its course.

—And slammed into my flank.

Data streams exploded through my head. Warning blared in my ears, scrolled across my vision. *Pull up, pull up, pull up.* My vision teetered. I screamed.

And suddenly I was back in my real body. Hunched on the steps, shaking. My skin on fire as I watch my dragon sputter, its holoflague blinked once, twice, then went out. Then with a groan of metal, it slipped out of the sky and plunged into the first row of shops lining the square. Behind me in the hall, villagers started screaming.

"No," I whispered, staring at my fallen dragon. The craft had been my way out. My way *home.*

A hand grabbed my wrist and pulled. Da. With Cella in tow and ogling the wreckage.

"We have to run," he yelled over the screaming. I blinked stupidly, half dazed as they pulled me along. Da holding my wrist, Cella at my rear, her hands pushing at my back. "Run, Astraea!"

It's over, I wanted to say. *I lost the dragon. We can't outrun them.*

Our flight from the village was a blur of running at a crouch through the streets, hiding in garden beds, and diving behind stone fences at the sound of footsteps.

Idiot, I berated myself as we went. *What were you thinking, bringing the dragon so low? Stupid, stupid, move.*

We made it out of the village and were moving north through one of Greyson's fields before we saw the wizards again. The first I knew of it was Da yanking me to the earth, fingers pressed to his lips as I rounded on him, furious at his manhandling. He pointed to the fence-line ahead, where two glinting ornaments had caught the sun.

More wizards. Waiting for us. As if they knew we might come this way.

"They're on the hunt now," Da muttered as we watched the two wizards move along the fence line. "They've called in reinforcements."

Or the reinforcements were already lying in wait, I kept the thought to myself, not wanting to explore what that might mean, and tightened my grip around Cella's hand. "Get ready to run again."

Cella wasn't listening. Instead, her gaze was fixed on the sky. Her hand shot up, pointing skyward. "Look," she whispered, then with growing excitement, "Look!" We followed her finger and my heart stumbled into my ribs with a thud. It was still far away—a speck mingled in the clouds—but I knew that shape.

A dragon.

It couldn't be.

Hope surged inside me, and I flung my mind out—reaching as far as I could. And found titanium and turbines and two siblings arguing with one another.

"Hurry up, bring it down, before we're spotted!" This from Cora.

"I need the altitude to scan for her!" Michael snapped back from the pilot's seat.

They came for me. The realisation hit me so hard, my real body staggered in the street. *They really came for me.*

<*Crew member detected*> a *Spica* orb sounded from next to Michael's shoulder. "Ha, at last!"

<*Welcome aboard, Pilot Astraea*> The orb said. And as my awareness slid into the dragon's system it added. <*Transferring control to remote pilot*>

"Michael, she's here, she's in the ship!" Cora's mouth dropped open. "Astraea?"

<*That's me. Re-directing your course for pick up*> I confirmed through the speakers. <*Meet me at these coordinates*> I pinged them on the screen.

"And the descendent we detected?" Michael asked as I relinquished control and reeled my mind back in.

<*I have him*>

Then I opened my eyes to Da.

"Have what?" Cella asked. I blinked, realised I'd spoken my last words out loud as well as through the dragon.

I grinned at Cella, hugging her to me. "Help. Help's coming. We just have to get to them."

We doubled back through Greyson's farm. In the distance, the village bells tolled, and smoke billowed from the village centre. My gut wrenched. I'd caused that. How many buildings had my fallen dragon destroyed? How many livelihoods put out of business?

I'd find a way to repay them, I promised as we turned down a farm lane and ran the length of the rutted roadway. Not far now. Over a fence, through a familiar bramble patch and then down into our childhood gully. I heard the dragon before I saw it. The whoosh of its rotors; rumble of its engine as it idled. A sound to pull at heartstrings.

The craft had forgone its holoflague. Its titanium wings cast sharp shadows on the gully floor. And there, waving at us from the open cockpit door.

Cora.

"Hurry!" she shouted. "The wizards will have seen us land. Move, move, move!" This she shouted at Da who was bringing up the rear.

I pushed Cella in first, then Da, before I took her offered hand.

"You came for us," I said.

Cora's gaze dropped to her feet. "Couldn't let you face them alone," she said. "That's not what *people* do to each other. *Any* people. Especially not family."

The little ball of hurt and anger that I hadn't even known I'd been holding onto loosened in my chest. Then melted as Cora pulled me close and held me there. "Next time, we go together. I promise."

I swallowed hard. Nodded. In the relief of their rescue, I didn't trust myself to speak. Cora withdrew; gave the okay to Michael. I turned to face my biological family.

"Uh, you might want to buckle in," I warned them, and helped Cella thread her arms through the straps while Da clipped himself in with a precision I hadn't expected. *He's done this before.* How much more hadn't he told me? I leaned back in my own chair and breathed out as Michael lifted-off, slowly accelerating so my family wouldn't black out. I closed my eyes. For now, we were safe. There was a familiar pull on my limbs as the dragon accelerated. Followed by an even more familiar squeeze of Cora's fingers around mine.

I squeezed back, unable to shake a nagging feeling in the pit of my stomach.

Hadn't this all been a little too easy?

I pushed it from my mind. Marantha was behind us now. We were free. My family—both families—were safe. That was all I cared about.

#

I thought I'd have to corner Da to get an explanation out of him. But as it turned out, he sought me first. He and Cella left with Michael to get settled in while Cora and I had done the dragon's post-flight checks. I hadn't expected him to return to the hangar, let alone on his own, but he was there, milling at its doors when Cora and I exited.

"We need to talk," was all he said.

"We do," I agreed. Beside me, Cora paused, casting Da a dubious look before her green eyes turned on me, silently asking, *Do you want me to stay?*

I sucked in a breath and shook my head. "It's okay. Go on without me."

The tension melted from her. As I'd suspected, she hadn't wanted to be in the room while Da and I had this conversation, but she'd been prepared to do if I'd asked.

"Call if you need me," she said, and with an uncharacteristically nervous swallow, drew closer. "I'm sorry about before. You were right." For a moment all I could think was a bemused, *about what?* until I remembered our argument in the command centre. About going to the aid of a crew member. Gods, it felt like days ago.

I drew her into an embrace. Da be damned, he could wait. "You were there when it mattered," I told her. For a long second we held each other, breathed each other in. Until Cora drew back again, wiped a tear from her eye, and brushed a kiss on my cheek. "Go easy on him. We all make mistakes."

My heart did a little squeeze as she left us in the corridor.

Da cleared his throat. "She, uh, seems nice."

I gave myself three heartbeats to gather my thoughts before I turned to face him.

"Did you know? About your blood. About mine?"

"Astraea—"

Anger flared inside me. I thrust my wrist out and slapped the veins on my forearm. "Did. You. *Know?*"

My father's eyes dropped from my face to *Spica's* grated floor. Then he said something I never expected. "It was the only thing I could think of."

My body stiffened. "What?"

Father rubbed his scuffed elbows, his face going vague as he recalled something I couldn't see. "I couldn't lose you too, not like your mother. Not to them."

Somewhere deep in my chest, something pulled tight, threatening to snap. Da opened his mouth, and the horror built inside me. *No, I don't want to know.*

"With your mother's lineage and mine, I'd always knew you carried the genes. You and Cella both. But once your gifts were awake, the wizards would have discovered you eventually. And I, well—" he ran a hand through his greying hair "—I'm not much of a descendent. Barely a gift to speak of. A bit of mathematical know how. But *you.* You were everything they needed and more. I couldn't teach you. But Michael..."

This was too much. Both Mother *and* Father were descendants? And Da had known Michael after all. He'd known about *Spica. Known they'd come for me if I were in trouble.*

I gazed at him in the corridor, speechless. He gazed back, face taut; strangled as if from holding all this back for...years.

My sacrifice had been his game plan. His way of getting me to *Spica.* To safety. By putting me right in the line of fire. I wanted to scream at him. Why? Why put me through all that? Why not tell me? I could have played along. I would have done it. I would have listened.

Instead, all that came out was, "What do you mean you lost mother *to them?*" My voice shook.

It was like I'd taken a knife to his gut and twisted. Da grimaced, his interlaced fingers clenched white. He took a breath and spoke to his lap.

"The illness didn't kill her." His voice cracked on that last word. "The wizards did."

I remember that day like it was yesterday. Me returning from lessons. Barely ten years old. Dad meeting me at the door with the news. Me screaming and running to the empty bed, curling into a ball in the blankets and refusing to leave. For days I stayed like that, breathing in the last of her smell until the sobs of three-year-old Cella drew me out. We held each other then. Grieved together.

A tentative hand on my shoulder snapped me out of my revere. "I should have told you," Da said. "I'm sorry."

I'm hearing those words a lot today.

Part Three.

The introductions went smoother than expected. Da didn't so much as blink as Michael explained the history of the *Spica* to Cella. My sister drank it all in with an intensity I'd never seen before. She studied the stasis chamber with far more interest than I'd ever shown them, asked questions about the *Spica's* medical facilities and the food printers—and was not satisfied with a simple, "That's just what they do" to which she'd replied with, "Yes, but *how?*". For the first time, I saw the woman she was fast becoming. A curious mind that wanted to unravel the making of things. With every question answered, a dozen more took its place. And she delighted in Alto's company. More than once, he sent *Spica's* orbs into aerial patterns to Cella's enthusiastic applause.

If she ever struggled in her new home, I never saw it.

As for Alto, it turned out the boy had a knack for circuitry. Anything with an electrical current he could manipulate. An engineering gene originally intended to help crew keep the power in *Spica's* ion drive steady, Michael had said. Of course, without a crew with the gene to keep the drive steady, it hadn't been powered up in millennia. Instead, *Spica* took its power from solar cells installed long ago in the mountain's sides.

"We might really be able to do this," Cora said once, as we bent over an energy meter to test how much electricity Alto could channel.

"Leave on *Spica?*" I'd guessed.

She'd nodded, showing Michael the reading. "This is off the charts."

"Don't get your hopes too high," Michael had warned. "We'll need to do a lot of testing. Who knows what issues we'll find."

A crackle sounded next to my head as Alto connected to the comms orb hovering beside us. *<But it is possible?>* his robotic voice asked. It was hard to gauge his tone through the machine, but I thought it carried an edge of eagerness. But unlike Cora and I, his excitement was strained. Closer to desperate.

"We've got a pilot to guide us and an engineer to keep the drive stable, so maybe," Cora said. "And you'll both need to double down on your training."

"Baby steps," Michael reminded.

<Give it to me. Everything> the orb said. *<I'll do it>*

That time there was no mistaking the steeliness in Alto's expression. Or the way he curled his fists.

Michael had scratched his chin. "I suppose we could start you off with a basic engineering course from *Spica's* libraries. It'll take you a few years to get through."

<I'll do it in one>

There had been a short, stunned silence, before Cora gave a grin. "I'll send you the files. Astraea can help you with the math."

"Hey!" I'd complained as she volunteered me. Even so, fresh excitement bubbled inside me. We were inching closer to the stars. Bit by bit. All the same, I made a mental note to ask Cella to see to it that Alto got out from behind his desk at least once a day. A fourteen-year-old needed time to be fourteen.

"Why do you want to see the stars so badly?" I'd asked him one morning when we'd bumped into each other on the way to breakfast. It's been a week since Cora had sent the course data packet to him and the bags under his eyes were so pronounced it looks like he was nursing bruises from a fight.

<I don't> his orb said, matter-of-factly.

I'd blinked. "What do you mean?"

His grey eyes fixed on me, far too serious for his fourteen years. *<Any planet with a wizard is a planet I don't want to be on>* he said. *<If there's a way off this rock, I'm taking it>*

He'd tapped his throat, indicating the scars there. *<Wizards did this. They killed my family. Took my voice>*

I winced. I'd long suspected the wizards had been behind his injury, but to have it confirmed made it worse in a way I couldn't explain. The brutality of it. The callousness.

"They really hate us, don't they?" I sighed, looking out the window to the mountain peaks as we arrived in the common room. "I wish they wouldn't. It shouldn't have to be this way."

<It shouldn't. But the only language the wizards speak is power. So long as they have it, nothing will change. You can take a wizard's crown, but they just'll replace the crown>

I'd pursed my lips. "I don't believe that." Then I'd paused, following the thought through a little more. "They just have no reason to change... What if we gave them a reason?"

Alto cast me an incredulous look, which on the face of a too-serious, fourteen-year-old boy, came off as more like a constipated sneer.

<There's just six of us> he'd pointed out.

Six of us against the world. Even if we had the help of the descendants Michael and Cora had rescued over the years, I didn't need any mathematical ability to know the kind of terrible odds those were. My blasted pilot brain worked it out anyway. I ignored the number as it flared in my vision.

<Better to leave> Alto concluded, taking my silence as a submission to his argument. He sauntered off to the breakfast table. But even as he went, my brain still lingered on the thought our conversation had sparked. *What if we gave them a reason to change?*

#

Da was the strangest to watch settle in. He and Michael hit it off as if they were old friends, which was doubly strange. Only when I cornered him in his room did I get the story out of him. Not much to tell, he'd said, and ran a gnarled hand over his growing beard.

"I spend a couple of months on *Spica* when Michael first picked me up," Da said.

"How did he find you?"

An embarrassed smile. "I, uh, tried to steal a wizard's relic, one of their L.I.D.s." At my aghast look he shrugged. "I was barely out of my teens and starving; common sense wasn't high priority. I thought it would make a good pay day."

A hell of a good pay day, I thought, not quite able to reconcile the thief my father had been in his youth to the timid Da I'd grown up with. "And they caught you?"

He nodded. "They did."

"How? The L.I.D. is made for non-crew members, it shouldn't have reacted to you."

"Oh, it didn't. But the holo-display next to it did. It was an old control screen pulled from a dragon. Turned on when I picked it up." He gave a wry laugh. "I'd thought I'd won big. Two relics in one night. Didn't even make it to morning before they found me." He sighed. "I seem to have a knack for ending up on the wrong side of a cell door."

I snorted. Not once, but twice imprisoned by wizards. "Michael got you out?" I guessed.

My jailbird father smiled. "He did indeed. I spent a winter here. Met your mother when she came and the rest you know."

I sat up. "Wait, you met Ma here?"

"Of course. Michael found her a month after me. Helped us relocate to Marantha. Back then it was safe. A village out in nowhere. No wizard to speak of." He scowled. "The arguments we had when Gauron turned up. Did we stay? Did we go? Where would we go? Would we alert them if we ran? In the end, it didn't matter."

Because Ma died anyway. Neither of us said it. Instead, we let the silence of a shared mourning fill the space between us.

"I couldn't bring myself to uproot you and Cella. Not when you showed no signs," Da eventually went on.

I stood. "You should have told us." Memories of the dragon descending upon me swirled in my head. The bite of the iron shackles on the clifftop; the terror, the betrayal so deep it ached. I paused at the door. "I understand why you did what you did but I'm not ready to forgive you. Not yet."

Da stared at me from his desk chair. At last, he nodded, accepting my decision. "I'll wait."

#

We had a month. One short, wonderful month, before it all went belly-up, as Cora would say. It started with Michael's voice blaring through the intercom.

"Cora! Astraea! Get up, meet me in the command centre," he sounded like he'd run all the way up from *Spica's* lower levels.

Beside me, Cora groaned. Her green eyes squinted into slits. "What now?"

I rolled out of bed. "What's happened?"

"Not what. *Who.* Get dressed. We don't have long," came Michael's curt reply, before he cut the intercom off.

"That can't be good," Cora observed from over my shoulder.

It wasn't. When we arrived at the command centre, Michael showed us an infrared scan on one of *Spica's* monitors. We huddled around the screen and stared. A stony silence lengthened between us and grew heavier by the second.

"I don't understand. What are we looking at?" Cella asked at last, frowning to Da.

"Look at the shapes," Michael offered, zooming in and singling out one of them with a finger. "What do they look like?"

Cella considered. "Like people." She tracked the shapes across the screen as Michael zoomed the scene out again. "A lot of people."

"Five h—dred and fifty-six people," crackled *Spica* through a speaker beside one monitor.

A low-grade pain was building in my hand. When I looked down, Cora's fingers were clenched around mine—white knuckled. I glanced at her face, grim and ashen. A prickle of fear dug into my gut.

"It's an army," she said.

Michael nodded.

"Of wizards," I guessed.

He nodded.

Dread pooled into my legs. *They've found us.* I studied the screen again, read the distances. A red mass of bodies twenty-five kilometres off our western border. Not one wizard, or a few. Hundreds. Maybe thousands.

"We have to run." It came out of me before I could think.

Cora whirled on me, a glint of anger on her eye. "Run *where*, Astraea?"

Anywhere but here, I thought. We could take a dragon. Fly as far as we could.

As if reading my thoughts, Cora's hand tightened around mine and her tone softened. "With their new detection capabilities, they'd eventually find us. And away from Spica, we'd be at an even greater disadvantage."

I swallowed the lump in my throat. Damn, *damn.* She was right.

Cella stared at the screen, a crease in her brow. "What do they want?"

Cora scowled. "To loot our tech."

"To smite their ancient enemy," I offered.

"Power," came Michael's answer.

We exchanged a glance and shrugged. Probably correct on all three counts. But there was no way to know for sure unless someone went down to speak with them.

"How did they find us?" Da asked.

Cora's scowled deepened, and she opened her mouth. I sensed an accusation coming.

Michael jumped in. "Any number of ways. Perhaps they unearthed an old comms system with an uplink to *Spica* or pulled coordinates from one of our downed dragons—or triangulated our position from our rescues."

Or all three. I recalled how the wizards had been waiting for Michael and Alto, how they'd had a *Spica* orb and a rocket launcher in easy reach when my dragon had appeared in Marantha. How they'd had reinforcements close by... Those hadn't been attacks. They'd been the precursors of an enemy carefully feeling us out. Determining our capabilities, our strengths, and our weaknesses.

And now they were ready.

"Leaving *is* the safest course." Michael's tone was gentle as we took in the approaching army. "As a temporary measure," he added when Cora balked and opened her mouth to argue. His gaze shifted to Alto, then to Da, Cella and me. "I will stay. But if any of you want to go, you need to evacuate now, before the confrontation starts."

A long pause as each of them considered. Alto was first. He shook his head and stepped forward and rested a hand on Michael's shoulder on a show of solidarity.

All eyes turned on my family. Da took Cella's hands in his own. "We cannot hide like we did in Marantha. If we leave, we will always be running," he said to her. "Always moving." His fingers pressed tighter around my sister's hands. "But if we can face this, if we have enough courage to stand up and hold strong, we'll force them into a siege. They'll have to sit outside and wait for us to come out. And we can survive that. We can survive for years." He glanced at Michael. "That *is* what you're thinking, isn't it?"

"We could survive indefinitely," Michael corrected. "And yes. If we withstand their initial assault, there's a good chance of turning it in our favour in the long-term."

"We've done it before," Cora murmured.

Cella's grip tightened around his and she gave him a short nod. Her mouth pressed into a determined line. My father straightened and faced Michael. "We do not want to run." Then to me, "We won't abandon you again."

My heart wrenched; the old, knotted wound there loosened. Wet splashed onto my cheeks. I blinked, my vision turning blurry.

"No, Astraea, don't cry! We just said we're staying! We're staying!" Cella rushed to me and wrapped her arms around my shoulders. Her face was almost level with mine. *She's grown,* I thought and wiped my eyes.

A rough hand found my shoulder. I glanced over Cella's head. Michael, and Alto beside him. Michael gave me a grim smile. "We're in this together." He arched an eyebrow at Cora, questioning.

My captor/saviour/ancestor/lover tore her gaze away from Da. Indecision creased her brow. She chewed her lip a moment, then released a sigh. "All right," she said and grimaced. "Let's do this." A pause, followed by a softer, "All of us. As people." She said that last word to me.

My heart sang and I longed for time to stop so I could soak in this moment forever. Two families finally coming together. Acceptance. Relief.

Things happened quickly after that. I'd already done the math, but Michael informed us we had a day. Less than that if they had transports—we wouldn't know until they came closer.

After consulting Michael and Cora, Cella set to printing some sort of substance in the food printers. What exactly I wasn't sure. But it made my eyes sting when I went into the kitchens to scoff-down breakfast. Alto set to sealing and barricading the doors, and Da and Michael went to lie a series of mining charges in the mountain slope above *Spica*.

"A last resort," Michael had said. "If all else fails."

The thought of the mountain coming down and burying us alive made my lungs turn tight and breathless, like I was being crushed already. I pushed the fear down.

"We don't have any weapons. Not real ones like the wizards have," I said, as I threw the last of the dragons' toolkits down to Cora. I gazed across in the half-empty hangar. After the loss of Michael's dragon and the one I'd taken to Marantha, we had four dragons left. For all Da's familiarity with *Spica*, he'd never learned to fly a dragon. That left Michael, Cora and myself, so we could have up to three in the air at a time. But to do what? Drop rocks on them? For all our talk of fending off the wizards' assault and forcing them into a stalemate, we didn't have much to work with.

"Leave it to Cella," Cora assured. "That girl's got more cunning than you give her credit for."

I cocked an eyebrow. "Was that admiration I just heard?"

Cora snorted. "I'm just saying we're not as helpless as all that."

I took her word for it. I had my own last resort to plan—and I needed to confront a ghost about it.

Down into the heart of *Spica* I went, right into the pilot's chamber. When I opened the door, the room wasn't empty. Alto was waiting for me inside, legs crossed under him on the floor. A comms drone hovered at his shoulder.

"You got my message?" I asked.

He nodded. *<You said you needed my help?>*

"Do you remember when you said you can take a wizard's crown, but they'll just replace the crown."

His brow furrowed, confused. *<I do>*

"What if we rendered *all* their crowns inert? No crowns mean no more wizards."

He cocked his head, clearly curious about where I was taking this. I lifted a hand to the pilot's chamber. "I have an idea."

\#

Michael went as emissary. He had to try, he'd said. But our slim hope died when his dragon limped into the hangar dented and scorched thirty minutes later.

"Went well, I see?" Cora remarked as Michael opened the craft's hatch.

"About as well as expected," Michael admitted. "I got a better look at their numbers. There are not as many wizards we thought." His stony expression didn't make it sound like good news.

"And?" I prompted, waiting for the rest of the axe to fall. "What is it?"

"They've recruited common folk. That's why there's so many. About ten folk to every one wizard. I counted fifty-six wizards before they fired on me."

Tension pulled at my gut. Fifty-six wizards. Against three dragons.

"What about their weapons?" Cora asked. "Did they have"—she swallowed, a haunted look crossing her face—"radiation cannons?"

Michael shook his head. "Not that I saw. It's unlikely any would have survived the millennia; they need regular maintenance to keep working."

Cora shoulders relaxed.

"But I saw numerous projectiles and launchers. *New* ones," he added.

I looked between them, a new surge of panic rising. "You mean they aren't relics?" A single launcher had grounded my dragon in Marantha. Throughout our preparations, I'd taken comfort in the knowledge that the wizards wouldn't have many such relics—and that they'd be forced to use what ammunition they had sparingly. But if they'd found a way to make new relics and ammunition... My blood chilled. "How?" I whispered.

"Does it matter?" Cora asked.

It does to me. What did that mean for the ordinary people of Draugr? If we failed and the wizards wiped us out and plundered the *Spica* of all her relics, what then? Who would they turn on next?

Michael scrubbed his eyes. He'd not paused to rest since *Spica* had detected the wizards' approach. None of us had. "If I had to guess, they either found a printer, or cobbled one together out of working parts. From what I could tell, a lot of them were wearing new L.I.Ds too."

Explains the increasing number of wizards, I ground my teeth. *And of course, they'd only bequeath that power to those they deemed worthy; whose beliefs aligned with their own. Who would willingly go forth and hunt descendants to cement their power.*

"This has to end," I muttered.

Cora took my hand, her sea eyes meeting mine. Her brow and lips were set in a determined line. "Then let's end it. No more running, no more hiding."

"Strong words, but we won't know until the day is out," Michael said.

My grip tightened in Cora's and I nodded, not trusting myself to speak. If she and Michael knew what I was planning, they might not let me go through with it. Instead, I swallowed the fear and counted the Fibonacci in my head, just as Cora had done for me all those months ago in the transport pod. I gazed into the face of the woman whom I'd come to cherish, thin and pointy nosed; eyes that glinted when she laughed. Her lips, which always betrayed her mood, were pressed tight in a mix of worry and resolve. I soaked the sight of her in, committing her to memory, right down to the cowlick on her fringe-line.

"Cora, if I, we..." I began, not sure how to phrase my request. "If I d—"

A *boom* shook the hangar. Lights flickered. The floor rattled.

"It's started," Michael announced. "Astraea, get to the command centre. Cora, with me."

And like that, my captor/saviour/ancestor/lover pulled free and ran to a dragon waiting on the far wall.

A tramp of feet, and Alto and Cella barged into the hangar.

"They're firing launcher rounds at us," Cella said, breathless. "So far, *Spica's* holding."

Michael nodded. "You know the plan. Get them to back down. Show them *Spica* is too much trouble to take by force." He abandoned his damaged dragon and ran to a fresh one. Beside it, the engines of Cora's dragon roared to life. A heartbeat later, the roar doubled as Michael's dragon warmed up. Then a third joined them as I flexed my mind out and connected with the last craft and initiated its start up.

Alto ran to the hangar door, pressed his hand to the controller—busted since the Marantha incident—and sent a prickle of electricity through it that made my hairs stand on end as he forced the doors open.

Turbines blasted the hair from my face. I closed my eyes, concentrating as I lifted my dragon from the ground and had it follow Cora's and Michael's through the door.

A tug on my sleeve. "Astraea, Da's waiting for you." I nodded, and set my hand on her shoulder, eyes still shut.

"Lead me."

Back through the corridors we went. I kept my eyes shut, senses tuned to my dragon. Wind buffeted the craft as it surged skyward, and the mountain fell away. My dragon's sensors indicated Cora and Michael were in formation with me—and if I stretched my mind, the hum of their dragons' systems brushed against my thoughts. All it would take was another reach of the mind and I could wrap my thoughts around them. But I didn't.

Instead, I let Cella guide my body to the command centre and followed Michael's lead through the sky.

"We're here," Cella announced.

I opened my eyes and caught a flash of the command centre, its screens lit and Da standing over them, analysing the approaching force. Cella sat me down in a chair beside him. Then I closed my eyes again to concentrate on our task.

"Astraea, you're here, good," Da's voice sounded in my ear, along with the sound of a switch being flicked in the control panel. "You ready?" This last question echoed through the *Spica* orb inside my empty dragon—like it would through the orbs with Cora and Michael.

<Affirmative> from Michael.

<Ready> Cora responded.

"Yes," I said and tightened my grip around the arms of my chair.

Michael initiated the dive to bring us into range. We needed to get close, uncomfortably close—and quickly, before they could aim their launchers. Below, the wizards' army came into view. First, it was a mass of indistinct shapes, before it rapidly focused into individual groups, then individual faces as they turned their heads skyward at the roar of our approach. The army scrambled but didn't scatter like I'd hoped. Wizards gesticulated, shouting orders as three launchers were thrust skyward.

Shit. This was going to be close.

"Hurry!" one of the wizards roared. Next to him, a launcher trained on Michael's craft.

"Michael! Look out!" I shouted, my warning echoing through the *Spica* orbs a millisecond before,

<Dropping payload>

The hatch to Michael's dragon swung open and there was a hiss and water sprayed from the dragon, splattering the men below. The launcher wavered, then fired.

"Mi—" I didn't get the rest out.

Michael's dragon lurched sideways, one wing tip dropping perilously close to the earth. Men below ducked. And the projectile passed over the cockpit.

<Quickly Michael, before it circles back!> Cora cried over the radio.

"Don't forget your payload, Cora," Da reminded from beside me.

I caught a muffled curse and imagined her clambering out of the pilot seat and unscrewing the cannister facing her hatch. The distinct hiss of spray releasing sounded over our comms.

Success.

Then the army started screaming. They huddled into themselves, clawed at their eyes—wizards and common folk alike.

In the command centre, a grin spread across my face. Cella was a genius. Well, she and Cora. Cella had been the one who'd had the idea. From Cora's fledgling chilli plants of all things. And with Cora's help they'd used the food printers to isolate the compound that made them so spicy. From there it was a matter of printing as much of it as they could and condensing it into a couple of medical cannisters. They'd only had enough for two. My dragon carried something different.

"A last resort," Michael had said.

I just prayed to the stars I'd never have to use it.

My dragon hung back, assigned to a support and emergency evac role, as Michael and Cora swept over the army, the wind from their thrusters flinging the spice-mixture into the men below.

<I'm empty> Cora announced.

<As am I> Michael added a moment later.

"Michael, incoming at your nine o'clock!" Da called.

The rocket launcher missile had re-corrected its course and streaked for Michael's dragon. He surged his dragon around and took off for the sky.

"Cora, four o'clock!" Da warned. Cora weaved in the air, dodging a laser as it shot from a huddle of wizards in the army's centre.

<Assholes!> her spiting curse hissed through *Spica's* command centre.

"Astraea, behind you," Da signalled.

I throttled my dragon out the way of a grenade. It sailed under my belly and thudded into the crowd. A yell went up. Men dove aside, and the grenade exploded into chunks of earth.

"Thanks Da," I whispered into the quiet room.

"Don't mention it."

I cracked open an eye and found Da hunched over the screens, gaze darting across their running figures, assessing and calculating on the fly as he tracked the encounter. He might not be a pilot descendant, but he would have made a fine military commander had he been born in the right era.

"Your spray missed the eastern flank," Da informed us. "They're regrouping there."

<Copy that> Cora's dragon whirled and shot eastward.

"Michael, watch that mob—" came Da's panicked shout. My gut went cold.

<Shit! Cora, Astraea! They've—> An explosion bloomed in the sky above us and Michael's comms cut off. Bits of titanium spattered down, before a smoking wreck dropped from the clouds and careened into the wizard army. Its impact shook the trees, the craft squashed a dozen men in a blink, rolled twice and shuddered to a stop in the middle of the opposing force. Black smoke glugged out its shattered windows.

<Michael!> Cora's shriek through the *Spica* orbs made my head spin. She dove on them, headfirst, and ploughed into them, the belly of her craft scratching across the earth. *<I'll fucking cream you!>* Men leapt aside, some quick enough, some not. Blood and bodies smeared the earth behind her. This was wrong. All going so wrong.

"Cora, stop!" I cried rounding my dragon after her, heart in my mouth. She was too close to them. All it would take was one, well-aimed launcher.

As if reading my fear, my systems pinged as a too familiar barrel levelled at us in the distance. Right at Cora's rampaging craft.

"Astraea, ahead!" Da warned.

"I know!"

I did the only thing I could think of. I charged Cora's dragon. Rammed her hard; heard her scream. I angled the nose of my craft under hers, flung my dragon's mechanical arms around her cockpit, and slammed down the throttle. We shot skywards.

<Astraea, what are you—>

"Get out of here!" I yelled through the comms.

<But Michael—>

"It's too late." My eyes grew hot, and I gritted my teeth. "Please, Cora. Come back."

My system pinged again, alerting me to the energy signature of the launcher firing. I imagined it streaking towards us, all hatred and prejudice and rage. Why? There had to be a better way. A better end to all this.

"Astraea—" Da again.

"I know!" My grip tightened on my chair. I shoved Cora's dragon away. "Go!" I told her and whirled my dragon around and charged.

Right into the oncoming missile.

Red. White. Pain.

My mind caught the edge of the explosion as I pulled free of the dragon. My vision blanked. Pain seared in my head. I yelled and fell free from my chair, muscles spasming with the memory of my titanium body crumpling, then exploding into fragments as my payload detonated. A distant rumble shook the floor under me.

"Astraea, we're here, I'm here." Hands closed around my wrists, holding them tight until the seizure eased. I blinked open my eyes to Cella standing over me, breathless and pale. She released her grip.

"Are you okay? Can you sit up?"

Gingerly, I pushed myself upright. "I'm okay," I croaked. I looked for Da; found him with his eyes fixed on the displays. He punched buttons, swiped screens, searching, I realised. A knot clenched my gut.

"Is Cora?" I asked.

"Safe and on-route back," Da said. "Alto's waiting to open the hangar."

Cool relief washed through me, then clogged in my throat as another question came to me.

"And Michael?"

Da didn't answer. Instead, his hands worked the controls a few beats longer. A long minute passed, each second turning more frantic as Da searched and searched again.

"Gods damn it!" he slammed his palm against the screen. The image flickered, then stabilised. "I can't find any sign of him," he swallowed. "He didn't make it out of the crash."

Silence filled the room with dread on its heels.

On the screens, the army spread out. From what I could tell, we'd halved their number. But that still left a couple hundred left. And five of us.

We'd failed.

There has to be another way, I wanted to say. But we'd lost two dragons—and the fertiliser bomb. The bomb had been our last play. And it had gone off mid-air, far above the heads of the army. Apart from the odd piece of falling shrapnel, it hadn't done anything to stall the tide of bodies coming for us. I covered my eyes and hung my head in my hands. I wanted someone else to have another answer. To swoop in and know what to do. But as the silence lengthened, the certainty grew in my stomach and churned itself into dread. My plan was the only plan left.

As if on cue, our *Spica* orb crackled and Alto's robotic tones rang through the command centre, *<Cora's back. Door's sealed>* A pause. *<She's pretty shook up>*

I got to my feet. I needed to be with her. Before the end came knocking. A last few precious minutes to ourselves. My feet led me through the corridors. Strange how I'd come to find comfort in these metal halls. To think how odd I'd first thought them. I tramped over grates, arrived at a door, and pressed my thumb to the pad at the wall. A smile flitted my lips. To think I'd thought Cora a wizard because of an automatic door. My throat closed tight at the thought, and a hot burn stung my eyes. To think I'd find the woman I wanted to spend my life with only to have death marching towards us far too soon.

The hangar was dim and quiet as I entered. Then, over the soft whine of turbines winding down, I heard the sobs. It didn't take long to find her. Cora was huddled in a corner of the hangar, clutching an empty flight suit. My breath caught—the suit was one of Michael's, probably pulled from a storage locker. Alto stood over her, rubbing her back. At my approach, he lifted his head, his too-serious eyes meeting mine, and I saw the glisten of his own tears. He extracted himself and, with a nod to me, left us, his *Spica* orb floating after him.

I sank to my knees and pulled Cora close. "I'm here. I'm sorry," my voice cracked and the truth of it hit me like a blow to the gut. Michael was gone. Really gone. My teacher, friend, brother. Family. We'd understood the risks of going out in the dragons, but it didn't make the gaping hole Michael had left behind any easier.

In that moment, I knew I couldn't avoid my plan. I tightened my hold of Cora, breathed the scent of her in. Sweet and earthy. Jam and watered soil. For a long time,

I held her, stroked her hair as the sobs shook through her. I imagined what it would be like to wake up on an alien planet after three thousand years to find everyone else you'd ever known was dead and gone and your only relative aged half a lifetime. And then to lose that person in a hail of violence. I pressed my lips to her forehead and let my own tears fall.

#

The first strike came late, on the cusp of nightfall. It clanged on the hangar door, the sound jerking us apart.

"They're here," Cora murmured. No fear, only resignation.

I pulled her up. "Get the dragon warmed up."

Her sharp eyes studied me. "You've got a plan." Not a question.

"An idea," I corrected. "I don't know if it will work. But I need everyone inside the dragon."

Cora considered me a moment longer, then gave an exhausted nod and turned for the craft. I caught her hand before she walked.

"If it goes... badly," I managed, and the fear rose in my belly again. "I'm glad."

Cora's eyebrow quirked, an echo of her old self crossing her face. "You're glad we're going to die?"

"No. *No*! That's not what I meant." *Gods and stars, say it properly Astraea.* "I meant, I'm glad I met you. Glad you saved me." I squeezed her hand. "Glad I got to love you."

Cora stilled, her expression softening. Then she drew me into an embrace. "Saving you was the best thing I ever did." Her lips found mine for a heartbeat before she drew away, the fire back in her eyes. "Promise me you'll keep fighting for as long as you can. Hold on for me as long as you can. Because I'll rescue you again if I have to."

Her second kiss was soft, warm and all too fleeting. A bang against the hangar doors pulled us apart. "Call everyone down here," I said. "Have them ready to evacuate when I say."

Cora nodded and turned on the *Spica* orb hovering quiet behind her. "Everyone get down to the hangar. Astraea has an idea."

#

I ran to the *Spica's* heart. Down, down through her slumbering cavity to the pilot's chamber. Alto was waiting for me.

<*Took your time. I was worried you might not come*> The orb as his side spoke.

"It's all we have," I said, clambering into the pilot's seat. I sucked in a breath and pulled the helmet on. Its hum filled my ears, and my vision turned white as my mind melded into the machine.

I float inside the Spica, senses rippling in the memories. Bangs and shouts ring through the hull from outside.

"Traitors! Cowards!" cry another mob from another time.

No*, I think.* We don't have time for this.

The memory of the pulse slams into me. It throbs through my head. I grit my teeth. Breathe. Work through it.

"Dad!" the memory shouts.

"Cora," the ghost inside the ship whispers.

I brace myself for what I know is coming.

Pain explodes behind my eyes and the world darkens, spinning into a jumble of numbers and sound.

Hold on, *I will. I fight the panic, the suffocation.* Hold on. *I think of Da and Cella inside the last dragon. Of Alto waiting outside. Of Cora and the touch of her lips on mine.*

Hold on.

Bit by bit, the world stills. My spinning senses stabilise. I open my eyes...

The ghost of Cora's father stood over me. Just as he had every other time. He was the spitting image of Michael—but younger. Full head of hair, less wrinkled, and pale from barely knowing the sun. The ghost's eyes fixed on me with a familiar glint of Cora stubbornness.

"Get out."

"Let me through," I said. "It's really important."

"Leave. Before I make you." The ghost unfolded his arms and stalked towards me. I knew the gesture well. It was how all our exchanges had gone. But this time I held my ground—no more evading, no more trying to sneak past the system. This time I'd face him head on. I would destroy him if I had to.

"Everyone's going to die," I said. "*Everyone.*"

The ghost faltered. His image flickered with uncertainty. "You're lying."

I scowled. "I'm not. Go on, we're interfaced, you can see it all in my head." I held out my arms—or my virtual approximation of them.

He scowled in return. "This sounds like another of your tricks. I won't fall—"

"It's not a trick!" I snapped, exasperated. "Just *look!*"

Michael had always insisted that the link to *Spica* went both ways. I gathered up all my rage at the wizards, grief for Michael, hope for Cora and thrust it at him. It wasn't pretty—I wasn't the most skilled at this and my training was minimal. But if it was possible for a ghost to blanch, this one did. His mouth cracked open from its pressed line, his eyebrows rose. And his advance stopped.

"You understand?" I asked. "Check your sensors if you still don't believe me. If you don't let me past, we're *all* going to die. Me, my sister, my father, and Cora. *Your daughter.* She's the last of your original crew."

His surprise quickly morphed into horror. "And Michael?"

I swallowed, nervous at what my answer might do. But for the first time I'd made him listen. I couldn't afford to lose this thread of trust now. "He's gone. They killed him."

The ghost's expression darkened, and fear prickled up my arms in a slow, spider's creep. If this was just the memory of the man, he must have been something to behold when alive. I searched for something to say, trying to find words to convince him not to turn on me.

"I'm sorry," I said. And thought I'd only meant to say it to fill the silence, the sincerity turned my throat raw. I was sorry I had to bear this news to him. I was sorry we had to fight for our lives. My lip trembled and I bit down the sob. And I was so, so sorry than my friend was gone.

"Come," the ghost said.

I blinked, sure I'd heard wrong.

He motioned to me. Numbly, I stumbled closer. "We do not have long," he said. "They will breach the hangar soon."

My stomach clenched. "Already?"

Colour and sound flared around me, it filled the room—immersing me entirely. I reeled, arms flying out for balance until my brain comprehended where I was. Outside. The light dim in the fading twilight. I stood on a familiar rocky path, and I recognised the crags of *Spica's* mountain—and the outer door of the hangar encased in the rock. A footfall made me spin, expecting the ghost, but found a stranger instead, a gold relic around his head.

I yelped and staggered back. But before I could get out of the way, he walked straight *through* me.

"This is a live feed," I realised aloud.

"It is," the ghost agreed. "Look."

"Hurry up, get it up here!" The wizard barked into the night. Bit by bit, a group of people emerged up the trail all huddled and hunched over, as if carrying something heavy.

The wizard pointed at the hangar door and issued further instructions. The group shuffled closer and dropped something down at the base of the door. It was cylindrical and scuffed metal. My breath caught, heart cracking into my ribs. That shape. *Shit. Oh shit. Oh shit.* Hours of reading and watching all that old Earth history came rushing back. The mushroom clouds, the scorched beaches, shattered homes, disfigured people. I'd wanted to understand who the sky gods had been. What their—*my*—legacies were. And this had been one of the worst.

This one was old and flecked with rust, like it had been hidden away somewhere dark and dank for years untold. *A sky god bomb.* A chill spread over my limbs. It could blow away the mountain, *Spica*, and the wizard's army all.

I rounded on the ghost. "I thought *Spica* wasn't a military vessel."

As quick as it had come, the vision vanished, and the white room returned. "We weren't," he said. "But we didn't know what else was out here. So we brought a small supply of weapons with us to be safe. And one warhead. Mutually assured destruction if it was ever needed. When the coup happened some of our crew took it from the *Spica* and hid it."

"And now the wizards have it." With just enough knowledge to work it, but not enough to know how dangerous it really was. Anger boiled inside me, and I cursed under my breath. For all their smarts, my ancestors had been a bunch of bloody idiots.

A prickle ran down my shoulder: the ghost's touch. I flinched, bracing myself for the vision of his final moments inside the pilot's chamber. That was how it always went. One touch and I'd hurtle into his memories to be churned up and spat out—again.

Nothing happened.

I blinked open my eyes to the ghost's face in mine. His grip tightened on my shoulder—a feather-light pressure. Insubstantial. My stomach curdled as the realisation fully sank in. He wasn't *here*. He never had been. This was not a man trapped in a machine. That man was dead. This wasn't even a man, just a memory. As for whose memory—

My breath caught. It wasn't Cora's father I was talking to. It was *Spica*. I stared into his face, and as I did, the features shifted; moved further away from the mask the AI had been wearing.

"I failed him," *Spica* said. "He died horribly, and I felt it all. Still feel it, even now."

"I know."

"I don't want him forgotten. He deserves better. To be remembered."

"I know."

A pause, then. "I don't want it to happen to you."

My heart squeezed. After all this time, was that what the ghost's issue with me had been about? *Spica* had been trying to protect me from the same fate as its last pilot? I gave it a sad smile. "That's not your call to make. You need to let me in. The living need us."

A long silence followed, and I sensed the ship struggle with itself, until at last, it nodded. "Help me end this pain."

I clasped its hand and nodded. "I will."

For the second time in my life, my mind exploded. The first time it had been an influx of information, a gigaton of understanding surging into my brain. But this time it was an expanding—an unfolding and awakening. My senses raced outward, leaving my body behind. Numbers became sensations—a belly pulsating with an ion drive, the mountain side an itch on my shell; equations of escape velocity, thrust, drag and wind speed became my vision skyward. The stars my destination.

And suddenly I understood. The true *Spica* wasn't one entity—*we* were two. Man *and* machine. Machine for our efficiency, processing, and logic. Human for our imagination, drive and creativity. It was a perfect pairing. But with no one to replace our human half, we'd been paralysed. Clinging to a memory to fill the emptiness in us as our surviving systems eroded.

But no more. We might be old and damaged, but there was still one thing we could do.

<Are we sure about this?> we queried.

<We have never been more sure> we answered.

We turned our minds to the sky and fired up our engines.

#

It took a lot of power to break our mountain casing. More than we would have liked. Even with the help of the last resort mining charges Michael had left.

We didn't care.

We broke free like a butterfly from a chrysalis. Our engines roared with the sound of a thousand dragons, and we laughed as the wizards cowered beneath us. A small moment of victory as we left the ground.

"Astraea! Is this you? Are you doing this?" Our saviour/captor/ancestor/lover/kin cried into our ears from her dragon nestled in the hangar. We grinned.

<It is us>

Our bones rattled, but we were not worried, we were built for stronger gravity than this. But we were worried about our jets, two of them were not firing properly. We'd been buried too long without maintenance. No matter, this would be a short flight.

<We cannot maintain this for long> We sent to the dragon in the hangar, then to Alto hanging onto the edge of the pilot's chamber. A small surge through our systems undid his electrical lock on the hangar door. We cracked it open. *<Be ready to fly>*

A dozen *Spica* orbs flew through the gap—the wizard's old Earth warhead supported between them.

"Holy shit, you're bringing it inside?" Cora shouted.

<A temporary measure> we assured. Soon it would not matter.

Below, the trees had shrunk to pinpricks; the wizard's army a mere blotch on the earth.

<Ready, Alto?> We asked the boy outside our human's chamber. He jumped as our voice sounded from his orb, then nodded.

<Once we leave the atmosphere, you'll only have a few minutes of zero gravity to get to the hangar> we warned him.

<I understand> his orb croaked.

We powered upwards, nose pointed to the stars. Bit by bit the drag lessened on our shell. A weightlessness filled our belly just as we cut our engines.

With a flare of will, we threw our hangar doors open and shunted the wizard's bomb through the gap with four of our orbs. The bomb floated away, its battered metal casing catching the suns glares once, twice, before it faded into darkness. In four hours and fifty-two minutes, it would explode harmlessly somewhere between Draugr and its moons. Assuming it still worked.

We let the relief lap our senses for just a moment. Then our attention swivelled to Alto still clinging to our chamber, his feet floating off the floor from the shift to zero G. One final mission left. Plan Z.

Alto met our human's gaze and gave a single, short nod.

<Initiate stage two> we told him.

Alto flattened one hand against the chamber's metal side.

<In five, four, three, two, one—>

The surge he sent through us felt like a static shock at first. A sharp prick, then a tickling inside our core. Then his surge doubled, tripled, quadrupled. Pain fired through us. Splintering into our systems. Alto flooded power into the ion drive in our belly. We gasped, our mind lighting up as sparks splashed from the chamber.

The energy built in us like a wave. We directed it into our drive—pulsing it around our power source. Our muscles screeched, every joint and fibre on fire. We gritted our human teeth.

<It's not enough. We need more Alto>

A fresh surge, then another.

Other parts of the ship shut down as Alto funnelled energy out of them and into us. Into our core. Our drive. In the midst of the pain and the power, a memory from our previous pilot filled us—

Two men shoved a small, cylindrical cannister at my door. Somewhere, deep inside the Spica, my gut turned cold. No. It can't be. God preserve us.

It went off. No explosion. No sound. But the pulse surged through Spica's *systems—through* me. *Neuro-links failed. Synapses broke inside and out.*

Spica's *senses went dark—*

"*Electro-magnetic pulse,*" Michael had said.

<More!> we roared to Alto. We would end this once and for all.

Three more bursts and Alto pulled away, huffing, drops of sweat rolling off his forehead to float in the air.

Inside, our bones sang. Hummed with the power pulsing inside us, threatening to overload. *Not yet,* we urged, clamping down our teeth. *Not yet.*

<It's enough. Now run> we said to Alto. *<They may need you in the dragon>*

He managed a nod, bunched his legs under him and shot for the door, sailing through it and into the hallway beyond. *<Good luck>* said his orb as it followed.

<*Thank you*>

"*Astraea, what are you doing? What's happening?*" Da's voice this time. Our family had sensed something amiss. The sparks arcing across my hull might have given it away.

We didn't answer. Instead, we clenched our jaw and tracked Alto on our internal sensors. Down the hall, right then left, left, and he was at the hangar.

"What the hell is going on?" Cora demanded from a dragon's hatch.

<*No time. Get inside*> Alto's orb hissed.

She hesitated, but when a panel above them blew and showered sparks down on them, she forwent the interrogation and launched herself for the tiller. We watched Alto climb in, seal the door.

They're in your hands now, Cora.

We closed our eyes, shut off our sensors and fixed our attention inward. A quiver of fear. We pushed it down. *Stick to the plan.*

Our human had looked up EMPs in *Spica's* database and libraries. Read about them and old Earth ion drives in detail over the last few months as she sought to understand. We knew what to do.

One breath to calm us. Held for a count of four. Exhale.

We released our control of the ion drive. Took all the extra energy Alto had channelled into it for us and forced every last scrap into our core.

Sirens screamed. Numbers flashed. We ignored all of it, instead focusing the last of our control into our belly to direct the overloading drive downward for a single, devastating pulse—aimed right at the coordinates we'd risen from.

Please, let this work.

Electricity arched through our halls. Across our hull. Our systems flickered and died. Senses blacked out, turned numb.

<*Thank you*> *Spica* whispered to me.

And I woke to darkness and the sensation of falling.

\#

I jerked in the pilot pod. *What in Draugr?* The AI had kicked me out. Severed our connection, carved me out of our shell and thrust me back into my own body at the last second.

"*Spica?*" I tapped my helmet. "Are you there?"

No answer. Through the visor the darkness was absolute. No blinking lights, no screens, no anything. *Spica* was completely offline. Maybe forever.

The thought made my throat go tight, and I swallowed hard. *Don't go falling apart now. Spica gave you a chance, now use it.*

I yanked the helmet free, and it tumbled away in the air. Fumbling, I found the straps holding me down, released them and kicked away from the pilot pod. With no gravity, I careened forward, and my head collided with the edge of the chamber. I grunted. Nausea rose; I forced down bile.

Now what? I hadn't planned for this. Hadn't thought beyond setting the electromagnetic pulse off. But maybe... just maybe—my heart did a little flip in my chest as I calculated the route between the pilot's chamber and *Spica's* hangar. Three floors. Three floors between me and the hangar where my family was secured in the last remaining dragon. Could I reach it before *Spica* hurtled back to earth? Was that what *Spica* had intended when it shut me out?

I pulled myself out the chamber and along the corridor, my fingers finding handholds in the walls. I'd always wondered what those had been for. Mystery no more.

The quiet was the most unnerving. No hum of machinery, no drone of air filters, nothing but the sound of my own breathing and thud of my heart. I found my way by memory, shutting my eyes in the dark to imagine the corridors I'd walked down a thousand times before. Yes, left here, then right.

A groan reverberated through the ship. Then a faint rumble. I froze, listening, palms turning slick with fear. The rumbling grew louder. And a vibration ran through the wall I clung to.

The atmosphere. We're re-entering.

Time was closing in. I swore and propelled myself down the corridor. Get to the dragon, find Cora.

Heat built inside the corridor. *Would* Spica *survive the re-entry?* The trip up had been rough. Down another corridor. Almost there. The rumble grew to a roar, like a beast prowled outside *Spica's* hull, snarling its challenge. A crack reverberated through the ship—something breaking free? I hurried on. Another crack, then a shudder and I imagined *Spica's* hull peeling away like an orange rind. Starry skies, how much further until the hangar?

My hands found the door. Felt along the smooth surface and found it firmly shut. I punched the access pad without thinking. No response. Fear dropped into my stomach. Of course it was locked, the hangar's outer door was still open. I searched the dark corridor, making out the shape of an open wall locker and flight suits strewn in the air. Alto. He'd been here, and he'd found a way through.

For an energy manipulator like Alto, the locked door would have been a minor obstacle. Not so for me. Not while I was disconnected from the ship at any rate.

Another jolt through *Spica* threw me into the door. Light flared. I cursed again and peered through the door's portal. My breath caught.

The dragon floated askew in the hangar. They were still here! A whimper rose in my throat. I wiped my eyes. They hadn't left me. Gods and stars, they were still here.

But why weren't their engines on? I stretched my mind out, hoping to connect with the craft—but nothing. It was dead in the air.

My belly tightened. Had my pulse fried everything inside it? My heart quickened again, and I swallowed down nausea. I'd been so careful to funnel the pulse downward. Had it not been enough? I'd been prepared to go down with *Spica*, but not for Cora, Da, Cella and the others too.

"No!" I banged my fist on the door. "Come on!"

The door didn't budge. The dragon didn't move.

Calm down, Astraea. Breathe. Think. I scrabbled over to the locker, grabbed a suit, and pulled it on. If I managed to get in there, at least I wouldn't asphyxiate first.

A shriek of metal tearing away from metal rang through the ship. Something heavy pulled in my gut. Not dread, I realised as my body was *pushed* into the door.

Gravity.

Shit.

"Come on Alto," I whispered, staring through the portal. "Make it work."

The dragon slid across the hangar floor. If I squinted, I thought I could make out shapes scrambling around in the cockpit windows. A flash of blue light. Electricity! Hope surged. Another flash.

"Come—"

The dragon's engines choked, then sputtered. Turbines began to turn. I lunged my mind out. The dragon was there, but my sense of it felt muffled somehow, like I'd walked into a dark room. No altimeter readings popped into my vision, no flight paths or trajectories. I groped around the dragon's systems, found the one I wanted.

<*I'm here. Behind the door*>

"Astraea!" Cora voice rang through the cockpit. "Thank the stars. We're coming, we're—"

A jolt bucked *Spica*. My grip was ripped away from the door, and I slammed into the opposite wall. Pain flared down my back. My head spun.

"She's gone, I can't see her!" Cella's cry from inside the dragon bounced through my head.

<*I'm still here*> I coughed and pushed myself back up to the portal. <*Hurry. There's not much time. Spica's breaking apart*>

"We're trying, but the pulse froze the flight system. We've had to reboot." Da. I'd never thought I'd be so glad to hear his voice. "Alto, try now."

Another flash of blue light. In my mind, the room's light flared on. Numbers flooded my vision; my brain predicting our fall speed and impact force. The dragon pulled into the air, bee lining for my locked door. The side hatch opened, and Alto leaned out, one suited hand grasping Da as he reached for the door's control panel. His fingers brushed it, electricity arced and—yes, the doors cracked open.

A *boom* shuddered through *Spica*. The hangar pitched and the dragon's hull slammed into the door, denting it.

"Alto!" Cora yelled.

"He's fine, I got him," Da assured.

I scrambled around the door, inspecting the damage. It had buckled inward, one door shoved off its runners. There'd be no more moving it. I studied the gap split down the middle and sucked my teeth. Thirty-two centimetres at its widest. *Shit.* This was going to be a squeeze.

"Can she fit?" Cora asked, twisting in the dragon's pilot seat. Her face was flushed through the visor of her suit.

<*I have to*> I returned. <*Give me more space. If* Spica *pitches again I don't want to get squashed like the doors*>

Cora pulled the dragon away, and I slid one leg through the gap. So far so good. My hips followed next, then my torso as I shuffled past. The doors squeezed around my ribs, and I exhaled. Air hissed as my suit caught and a rent tore through its chest. *Shit.* I pushed harder, before a hand closed around my wrist and pulled. Another hiss and tear, then yes, I was though!

"Get us out of here!" Da yelled, releasing his grip on my wrist.

Cora didn't need telling twice. The dragon whirled, and the faint pull of g-forces tugged in my belly. I heaved another breath. Still not enough. Hands found me and hauled me up, then slumped me into a chair and strapped me in. Air continued to hiss from my suit. My vision dimmed.

"Lower," I gasped. "Get lower."

Another gasp. Another heartbeat. My lungs heaved, screaming for air. I fumbled for my suit, trying to assess the damage. One tear gaped across my chest; another had split around the seam under my arm. Two more clicks sounded behind me: Da and Alto buckling back in. A thud signalled the dragon's hatch locking shut. Air blasted from the machine's vents, re-oxygenating the hold. *Thank the gods.* I just had to last long enough to—

A punch hit my gut as Cora accelerated the craft. The last air in my lungs left in an 'oof'. My vision narrowed to a pinprick. I fought for another breathe, willing my lungs to fill. But there was nothing to suck in. No air. No substance. Just empty.

I coughed, gagged, and heaved again. Nothing.

Darkness closed in.

Please, don't let this be it.

I clung to my sense of the dragon. But the numbers blurred in my head. And then, like water falling through open fingers, my mind slipped away.

#

I woke in a bed. Soft sheets, soft pillow—too soft to be the foam bedding I'd come to know onboard *Spica.* I frowned and blinked my eyes open. The wooden rafters of my old room greeted me.

Marantha. I'm in Maran—

I started up. The wizards, *Spica*, the pulse! My gaze darted to the bedside and onto a familiar figure hunched at my bedside. Relief sighed through me. *Thank the stars.*

"Cora."

At the sound of my voice, my saviour/ancestor/lover/kin lifted her head, the imprint of her sleeve on her cheek. Her green eyes studied me a long minute, then crinkled into a smile.

"You made it back."

I rubbed the sleep out of my eyes. "What happened? How long was I out for?"

"About thirty-six hours. As you can see, we made it down. Bit of a bumpy landing, but we made it."

At my furrowed brow Cora added, "The dragon took a few knocks in the hangar. Damaged the power cells. Thanks to Alto we had juice to get us down, but I doubt it'll fly again."

I dropped my gaze to my palms, curling and flexing my shell of flesh. "And *Spica*?"

Cora grew quiet. "She crashed. Deep in the mountains." She stood and pulled open the curtains of my old window. A yellow haze filled the air, turning the Draugr suns blood red. "The dust will settle in a few weeks."

I didn't dare meet her eye as I pressed on. "And the wizards?"

A smile twitched Cora's lip. "They're not going to be a problem."

My belly turned to butterflies. "You mean—"

"It worked," Cora beamed at me, reaching for my hands and squeezing them as if she longed to dance up and down. "You freaking did it! Your pulse knocked out their relics. *All* of them."

I gaped. "Wait. All?"

Cora nodded. "Their army is in retreat. We're getting reports of villages and towns revolting. No relics to keep them in line. People are standing up to them, storming the wizard strongholds to free the prisoners inside. Their power is crumbling." She fell quiet, her smile turned sad. "I wish Michael could have seen it."

We lapsed into silence and I leaned back into my pillow. "I'm sorry." My breath caught and I choked on the next words. "I destroyed them all. *Spica*. Our home. Every tie to Earth. Your past. It's all gone. I'm so sorry."

Cora's arms wrapped around me, held me close. "It's okay," she whispered. "You do not need to be sorry. We're free. I'm free. Besides—" her lips cracked open, flashing a grin "—there is no them, remember? Just people. Perhaps it's time I embraced Draugr, just like you've embraced me."

A laugh bubbled up before I could stop it, and my heart swelled. I wiped my eyes. "Now what?" I wondered aloud.

"Your father has dispatched messengers to arrange peace talks," Cora said. "He's hoping you'll attend."

I nodded slowly. If Da was going to broker a peace to last, he would need all the help he could get. And I'd give it my all. I'd managed to bring two families together. Perhaps there was hope for two peoples. My future was about to get very busy.

"What about you?" I asked. "What are you going to do?"

Cora considered. "I don't want my people to be forgotten," she spoke hesitantly, as if sounding out an idea to herself as she went. "I want to pass on their knowledge, their stories, even their mistakes so Draugr's people will learn from them." She straightened, eyes brightening. "I'm going to start a school; a place of learning for all."

I grinned. "I know the perfect name for it."

Sixty years later.

A crowd had gathered in Spica University's field. At the edges, families from the Spica township had spread blankets and lean-to tents across Cora's orchards, while at the centre of the gathering they clustered in groups to exchange pleasantries, drink a mug of ale and gaze across to the opposite shore of Crater Lake.

I watched them all through the ship's display, cleared my throat and rasped down on the comms relay. "Launch in T-minus ten minutes."

Across the lake, people straightened as the announcement reached them. Heads swivelled; hands rose over brows to squint over the water. My heart quickened, my nervous energy taut as wire as I counted the numbers down on my end.

"Pre-flight checks complete, initiating start up sequence," Pilot Indra's voice rang through the ship. Demeter we'd called it. An old Earth goddess of spring and harvests. Cora had warmed to it instantly.

"Fitting," she'd said with a smirk, "given how much of *Spica* we had to collect and scrounge together from across the mountains. Harvest indeed."

Scrounged and built, parts and pieces trialled and failed and trialled again under the university's collective. Cora had long ago retired from teaching, but this had been her passion project; she'd work on it until the day she couldn't. *A project to bring people together,* she'd described when she'd first pitched it to her students nearly fifty years ago.

But really, she did it for me.

"It's your turn." I swivelled the microphone in Cora's direction, watched as her arthritic fingers pressed the broadcast button.

"T-minus five minutes."

A small cheer from rose from across the lake. If I squinted, I thought I could make out Cella's floral pinafore and grey bob on the shoreline. And there, that shock of white hair, was Alto—mayor of Spica township now—signing silently to a group crowded before him, a human translator at his side.

Cora's gnarled hand curled into mine. "It's really happening," she said.

I turned on her, taking in her weathered face, eyes flush with an excitement that mirrored my own. "It really is."

Back to the stars. Even if it was a brief trip. A short out and back by spacefaring standards. But my heart fluttered as the engine fired up, sending a roar through the command centre.

"Fission core is stable," came the report from Caden in engineering. A genius in fission technology, having spent years studying it from *Spica's* salvaged archives—that had been a real find. A lucky one too. We'd never had made it this far without it.

Pilot Indra's voice rose from the heart of Demeter. "Strap in ladies."

We fumbled our way through the half-forgotten strapping mechanisms, clicked ourselves in. I closed eyes and opened my mind to the ship. Its senses flooded into me. The roar in her belly, the quiver of her metal. It took my breath away. After so many years, I'd forgotten this. A faint nudge from Indra and I bowed out, I was too old to pilot—it was Indra's calling now. I was just here for the ride; being an ambassador had its perks.

"Do you want the honours?" Cora asked, pushing the microphone towards me.

I shook my head. "It's your project."

Her lips quirked. "It was your dream first."

We paused a moment, then grinned like we were twenty again. "Together," we agreed and leaned in as much as our straps allowed.

"Launch in ten, nine—" I stared into Cora's face, recalled the girl I'd met in the dark of *Spica's* hangar and the story she'd told me. We were really doing this. My gaze flickered to the flight screen, assessing the flight plan for the umpteenth time. Draugr was one of many worlds, Cora had said when we first met. We'd always known there'd been other colony ships like *Spica*. It was time to return to the stars and find our lost peoples.

"Three, two, one."

Time for to take our place among the sky gods once more.

THE SECRETS SHE EATS

Libra
Element: Air
Symbol: Scales
Dates: September 23 to October 23

Not all secrets are given willingly. Sometimes I have to hunt them from street to street, town to town. They run, scramble, try to weasel their way out of my grip, slippery things that they are. Often they'll beg, sometimes they cry. And sometimes, once they're cornered and at a dead end, they do nothing at all. They simply stand there, resigned and waiting for my final reckoning.

I blow into town like a tumbleweed on the wind. Thin and scraggily. A woman in black, cloaked and hooded. The villagers don't see my face, not straight away, but they are not fooled.

"Eater." The whisper announces my arrival, rushing ahead of me in undertones. Along the dusty main street it goes, passing through blacksmith and tailor's shops, into the saloon. In an hour it will have reached the plains; a day later, the plateau beyond.

They know what I am. And yet, there's something in my step that makes them turn; in the 'swish-click' of my boots that mesmerises. Something in my scent that draws them in, like moths to a flame.

The first one staggers out of the saloon and finds me there in the street. There's distilled spirits on his breath and a pink flushing through dusty cheeks. He's young, pretty-like, soft brown curls grace his brow.

"I love Josie Fisher," he tells me.

The words roll over me like a sprinkling of sweet bread crumbs. I lick them up, savouring each one. Barely a snack, but I'll take it. I nod and he turns away, his shoulders relaxing, a ecstasy of relief on his face.

"I love Josie Fisher," he says again, walking away in a daze.

An innocent secret. A smile twitches my lips. They're not particularly filling, but they are sweet. A footstep crunches at my back and I turn. An older woman is there, a hessian bag of groceries abandoned in the dirt. She trembles as she approaches, her blue eyes dart to my hood, then away again, even as her mouth opens, revealing yellowed teeth.

"I stole my husband's best horse to buy milk of the poppy," she murmurs.

Ah, a secret with a little more meat. The weight of it eases into my belly, a tasty morsel. But there's more, I can smell it as sure as I smell the horse shit swept into the gutters. I peel back my hood and the woman's eyes lock with mine. She quivers like a marmot caught in the glare of a snake.

"And?" I prompt.

She hugs her arms about herself. "I told him vagabonds did it. He went out searching for them and came back with fever. It's bad this year, you know? Real bad. Young Sally it took. And the Miller's wife."

Her words are like tiny steaks on my tongue. Juicy. Succulent. I breathe them in, relishing their taste. I nod again and a gasp whistles out of her. She sinks to her knees beside her shopping and releases a sob; her burden suddenly dissolved. I step away and she blinks, awareness returning, and frowns as she finds herself slumped in the middle of the street. She picks herself up. With deft strokes, she beats the dust out of her skirts, picks up her shopping and walks off.

Perhaps now she'll have the courage to make it right. If not, well, I'll get another meal later.

I set up shop in the saloon. And soon they come, sweet and tender alike. They can't help themselves. A line forms out the door. Clearly it's been many a year since one of us has come through these parts. One by one, they sit down at my table and lean in to whisper their guilt.

"I stole a drunkard's shoes last winter." This from a girl in a woollen sweater patched over and over at the elbows.

"I put salt on Mary Cole's cake at the last town cake competition," a busty woman admits, wringing her gloves.

A sheepish grin from a grey-haired man. "I have a mistress. Every Thursday." That one barely touches the sides as it goes down. He'll come back later for sure.

"I wagered my father's fortune in cards and lost." From a gaunt young man in a fine cloak and polished shoes.

"I hate my children."

"When customers piss me off, I spit in their soup."

"I fucked a cow once." That one made me blink twice.

On and on. And bit by bit, their secrets fill me. Albeit briefly. The afternoon's shadows lengthen. At some point, Vander the barkeep lights the hearth and a slow heat creeps into the emptying saloon. The line waiting me thins and clears with the coming of night. Fear of the dark overriding their instinct to spill their burdens onto me. I curse under my breath. My mouth craves that big something I'd followed into town. Big and thick and heavy. Like wild bison roasting on a spit. It's here somewhere. I know it. Something I could sink my teeth into one hundred times over.

I scarcely notice the thin, dark haired man—boy really—when he sinks into the chair opposite until he clears his throat.

"Yes, yes," I say absently, reaching for the drink. It won't fill me the way a good secret might, but it dampens the craving. Then I get a whiff of him; of his secret. I freeze, scenting the air between us. Not quite the same *big* I'd been hunting, but there's a kinship there. Something ... important.

The boy shifts uncomfortably in the seat, straightens his second-hand vest and then fidgets with his fingers. His nails are bitten to the quick. I return my drink to the table.

"I'm listening," I say.

"I um..." His fingers twist and writhe, nimble-like, a tailor's apprentice perhaps. Or a jeweller's. They clench together as he swallows. "I saw something last night." A gulp. "Something strange."

I sip my drink, trying not to let my interest show too much. "Go on."

"I was coming home late two nights ago," the boy begins. "Closed up shop like Mr. Cole asked and cut across Roper's field—I know I shouldn't but it was late, you know, and Da was waiting at home; he gets anxious when I'm out past tea. Roper's field is just grazing for his horses, and they're all trained gentle-like, wouldn't kick a gnat if it landed on them wrong, so I figured no harm done. I've taken that way plenty of times before."

He pauses as Vander arrives and places an ale on the table before him—and lingers. "Any dinner, ma'am?"

"No, thank you."

Vander pauses again for a long moment, before slowly turning for the kitchens. I sigh. I knew his type, clever like a vulture; ready to wring every coin he can.

The boy furrows his brow at the drink, then reaches for his pocket.

"On the house," I say and wave my hand, "continue."

"Well, two nights ago, I took the short cut, like always. But half way through I heard a grinding sound," his lips purse, evidently trying to think of a way to describe it. "A pestle on mortar sound. The cracking a few steps later, like sticks breaking. I froze, thinking it was perhaps a horse having a roll in the grass, or rubbing his back on a fence post, but then I saw sparks from a flint—" He shifts back in his seat as I lean in, realises what he's done and flushes.

"And?" I ask, unperturbed.

"I rushed at it. Think even I shouted, 'Hey, what're you doing?' Or maybe I thought it. Either way, lighting a fire in a grass field was asking for it to go up like a tinder box. I wasn't raised a farmer, but even I know that." His eyes go distant, and he shivers, then takes a pull of his ale. "What I found, well. It was a fire, trapped in a stone circle, but the... *thing* next to it. I don't know what it was. But it wasn't human—I'm sure of that."

"What did it look like?"

The boy stares into his mug. "Ugly. Wrinkles all about the face." He traces a finger along his cheeks and jowls. "Snout for a nose. And small, squat. Like someone sat on it."

"And what did it say?" I ask.

The boy is silent for a long moment. "Nothing," he says at last into his ale. A deeper flush creeps up his throat and into his ears. "I screamed and ran away."

I nod, running a light finger over my empty glass. "Wise move," I muse. Which is true, though I wish he'd paid more attention to its appearance; I can name a hundred fey clans the creature might belong to. But a lead is a lead, and I yearn for something juicy. I stand.

"Show me."

#

Aben, for that is his name when I ask, rests a hand on the fence paling. "In there," he says, pointing into the dark field. And it is truly dark, the moonless night gives no light beyond our sphere of lantern light—even to my eyes. Not that my eyes are much to brag about. I'm not fae-sighted like my father. I have my mother's eyes. Mortal eyes.

And a fae's hunger.

I set the oil lamp down on the post and listen. Grass stalks chitter in the breeze. The fence creaks ever so slight. I frown.

"What is it?" Aben asks.

"No insects."

"Tucked in for the night?" he suggests, the edge of a coy smile quirking his mouth. When I don't respond, he coughs and looks down at his shoes. They're well made, shiny iron buckles polished to a gleam. A shoemaker's apprentice then. I sigh, set a foot on the bottom rung of the fence and swing a leg over the fence.

Aben swings his leg over too.

"What are you doing?"

He stares at me dumbly, as if the answer is obvious. "Coming with you of course."

I snort. "No, you're not."

His eyebrows bunch. "I can't let a lady go out there on her own."

"Do I look like I need your protection?" I quirk an eyebrow in return.

He considers me a moment there, straddled on the fence, taking in my calloused hands, the knife on my hip and the pistol holstered under my cloak. "No," he admits and shrinks into himself, looking more boyish than ever. "I want to show people I can do more than run away."

The words hit me like a sucker punch. A memory rises up: my mother dabbing a rag on my torn lip and me, ten years old, saying *"I'm not a monster."*

"I know," my mother says in that same, tired tone of a parent listening to a conversation so old it's worn holes in its sleeves.

My fists clench. *"I want to show them I'm not,"* I say.

"You will."

Atop the fence, I roll my eyes. "Stay behind me."

Aben beams and scrambles over the pilings. We creep through the field, lantern held high, dry grass scratching our legs. Halfway in, we stumble into a clearing where the grass is flattened—not trampled but carefully squashed down so that in a another day or two it might spring back. A small stone circle lies in the middle, ashes cold.

"This was it," Aben says, there's an edge to his voice as he turns in a circle and squints into the dark. He stands so close his back brushes mine. The lantern in his hand quivers and around us, the sphere of light wobbles.

"Easy," I tell him, taking the lantern and bending down to examine the ashes. "There's nothing here." I crunch a piece of charcoal in my hand and sniff. And there, underneath the smoke and soot birch, lavender and rosemary.

"Were you always a secret keeper?" Aben asks from over my shoulder. His voice is stronger now, more confident.

"Always."

I can almost hear his skin rumpling into a frown. "And you've been doing this all your life? Journeying from town to town, relieving people of their secrets." He pauses. "Why don't I feel your compulsion anymore?"

"What's to say you're not?" I dust my hands off, catch a glimpse of his face and laugh. I don't mean to, as a rule I don't pray on people's insecurities when they fess whatever is on their mind—that's a sure way to get run out of town, but his shock catches me off guard. "It doesn't work like that."

"It doesn't?"

"I can't force you to tell your secrets, deep down you've got to be willing. If you have a secret you'd never tell anyone, I can't force it out of you." Those are the ones I hunt, when they have the right scent, rich and with full copper notes. I make a show of leaning close to him and taking a whiff. "You don't have the smell, you're all leather and pomegranates since I took your secret. At most, you'll have a slight compulsion to tell the truth for a few days" —I cock a grin at him— "depending how headstrong you are. It's not foolproof. I've had lecherers fess their secrets then walk straight back into a brothel."

Aben doesn't answer, but I feel his eyes follow me as I pick my way across the clearing, pausing at two rocks nestled in the flattened grass, away from the fire pit. Both are smooth, one wide and flat, the other round and about the same size as my head. Residue cakes one side of each. I run a finger down the head-sized rock, hold it to my nose. Lavender and rosemary. "You were right about the mortar and pestle," I say, wiping my hand on my cloak.

My companion squeaks a response. Actually squeaks, like his voice has been caught on a hook and yanked out of water. I turn and find him standing rigidly still, the tip of a rusted knife under his throat. At the other end of the knife, is a squat figure wearing old children's clothes, patched and worn threadbare.

"What you want?" The creature hisses through a frog-like mouth, its perfectly round eyes are narrowed into slits. Its hair hangs limp and straggled from its brow, like its been out in the weather too long. Behind it, a mound of sticks and firewood lies scattered on the grass.

I hold out my hands for peace. "Easy, we mean no harm. What's your name friend?"

"Dalziel."

"And what are you, a boggart?"

"Broonie," the fae spits. "No boggart here."

My gaze wanders those ragged clothes again. He might have been a broonie once, but not anymore. Either way, he's old fae, from across the sea. My nose twitches, catching a lingering whiff of a copper secret. As if he senses it too, Dalziel's knife presses under Aben's jaw, all he has to do is stab up.

"What are you?" Dalziel snarls. "You look human, but you don't smell like one."

I open my palms to him and slowly crouch down so we're closer to eye level. "I am a Secret Seeker."

"Pah, lies. Seekers aren't real. Just stories."

"I assure you we're not. Not on this continent, anyway."

"Seeker," Aben's voice squeezes out his rigid jaw. He makes eyes at me, casting a meaningful look at my pistol. Dalziel's grip tightens on his knife.

"It's fine," I assure them both. "Aben, Dalziel is a harmless fae. A few pranks, nothing sinister. Dalziel, Aben is a harmless human, he's wants to be friends."

Dalziel's knife eases off Aben's jawline to hover uncertainly between its own and Aben.

"He'll trade you his shoes, in a show of good faith," I add.

"Oh, why didn't you say sooner?" It's impossible to miss the excitement in Dalziel's voice. He kicks off his worn boots, all cracked leather and flapping soles, and holds them out to Aben.

Aben shots me a glare. "I will not—

I cut him off with a glare of my own, until he sighs and reaches for his polished shoes.

"No buckles," Dalziel says.

Aben frowns a beat, then, "Oh right, iron." He loosens them off, puts them in his pocket, and at a nod from me, reluctantly holds his shoes out.

The knife drops away, sheathing back into Dalziel's belt. "My thanks, friend Aben." The boggart drops to his bottom and pulls Aben's shoes on with obvious glee. They're too big, but Dalziel's up and strutting around in them like Aben has handed him gold clogs. Then he turns on Aben, blinking his round eyes expectantly.

"Put on his shoes," I whisper to Aben, motioning to the discarded items on the grass. "It'll seal the agreement."

Aben's face twitches like he wants to object, but under Dalziel's watch he bends down and slides his feet into the old shoes. His toes poke through the holes at the tip like they're a pair of sandals.

"Wonderful! Our friendship is set." Dalziel claps his hands and admires his new feet again. "Very nice gift," he says. "A nice gift indeed. Our friendship will be grand!"

"How long do I have to wear these?" Aben murmurs to me.

"Until we leave his domain." I gesture to the field.

Aben sighs, resigned to his fate. "What about you? Don't you need to trade?"

"I'm getting to it." I raise my voice, catching Dalziel by the shoulder as he hops about. Again, that copper whiff. Very faint. But it's there. I focus my attention on him. It's harder to work my power on fae, but I can if the secret is strong enough. And with the right kind of probing. "Friend Dalziel, why are you out in this field burning lavender and rosemary?"

Dalziel's eyes turn glassy, his face relaxes. Tranced. I grimace. I've pushed too hard. I ease off the pressure, releasing my hand from his grubby coat and coax him to sit at the edge of the pit. Dalziel blinks, shakes himself and starts building a fire, building a house for the flame from his sticks and wood.

"What's with the lavender and rosemary?" I ask again, motioning to the two stones and the fresh bundles of herbs awaiting pulping.

"To ease the bones," Dalziel says simply, as if the answer is obvious.

Aben and I share a look. "Your bones?" I ask to clarify.

Dalziel snorts. "Dead bones." He thumps his chest. "Not these. These still have plenty of life left in them. The bones under here." He stomps one foot, indicating the earth below.

Copper fills my nostrils. I'm getting close. I lean in, eager. "There are bodies buried here?"

In my peripheral, Aben's face drains of colour. "Bodies?" he squeaks. And when Dalziel nods his face goes grey and he crosses himself. Funny how humans get all squeamish about these things. Dalziel busies himself with the fire, lighting it with a practised strike from a knife and flint. He's been out here a while it seems.

"How many bodies?" I ask.

Dalziel considers. "Many. Dozens. Maybe more."

Another wick up my nose. My magic prowls in, hungry. *Closer, closer.* I press him a tiny bit more. "Who puts them there?"

Dalziel stiffens, back turning rigid, his hands clamp tight around his flint stone. *He knows.* Gods and spirits sure. He knows. Dalziel's eyes find mine, bathwater grey and glistening in the firelight. "Don't make me say," he begs. The hand around the flint quivers, and what I'd mistook for tense caution reveals itself: blind fear. It's so strong I could poke out my tongue and lick it off the air.

"Please," I say. "It's important." I gesture to the field. "And don't they deserve justice?"

Dalziel stares after my finger, eyes glazing, somewhere else again. Damn, I've pressed too close again. For a fae as susceptible as this, he must have human ancestry in him, like me. Maybe not half-half like me, but it's there. Inside my chest something I thought tough and hardened squeezes. It's not easy straddling in two worlds. You never fully step into one or the other, it's always a balancing act between the two.

"My apologies," I say and I shuffle back, my stomach giving a disappointed gurgle.

Dalziel opens his mouth, tries to speak, fails, then works his lips as if trying to chew through a particularly tough bit of bread.

Aben eases down on Dalziel's other side. His face is still pale, and he looks like he's come face to face with a Reaper, but his gaze is tender. He pats the boggart's back. "We're here," he assures. "One word at a time."

"I... c-can't!" Dalziel manages, spittle flying, straining to get the words out. It looks like it takes all his willpower.

I curse under my breath. "He's been Compulsed."

Aben lifts his head, concern rippling across his face as takes my expression in. "A what?"

"Compulsed. A spell. Stops him talking to anyone about this. Nasty stuff." Before I can think, I find myself up and pacing. Nervous habit. I swear again and cast my sights nightward. I would have been perfectly happy with a simple serial killer, but no. "We're dealing with wicked magic ." I glance at Dalziel. "Nod if I'm right."

He nods.

"Shit."

There goes my easy meal.

#

"Anyone can use wicked magic," I explain to Aben. "You just need the know." Around us, leathers and needlework of his shoemaker's shop line the walls. It was the easiest place for us to confer out the way of prying eyes. Next to Aben, Dalziel looks miserable. In the lamplight, his limp hair is grey, owl eyes dim and his cheeks sallow from exhaustion. That's what a secret like this does to a person—fae or man. In this we're all the same.

223

Aben grips Dalziel's forearm and gives it a reassuring shake. "We'll find a way to remove the Compulsion, I promise."

A tick of annoyance twitches in my jaw. He is right. I'll grant him that. No one deserves to live with a copper secret eating them up from the inside. But Aben makes his promise with the conviction of one who has never dealt with wicked magic. Who thinks I can just wave a wand and everything will turn right and back to normal.

All the same, Dalziel swallows and nods. "My thanks, friend Aben."

We sink into a stony silence. "So many people," Aben murmers. We'd quizzed Dalziel on the way to the shop, taking the backstreets as best we could. The total count before Dalziel managed a nod: thirteen. Aben rubs his eyes. "How did no one notice?"

To this, at least, I have an answer. "Easy. Disguise their deaths as something else. Who in town has died recently? And what did they die of?"

Aben falls still, his fingers pinching his chin as he considers. "Sally Barton, fever. Bobby Ruthford—" his eyes dart up to mine "—fever. Frederick Sawyers," he swallows, "fever. Those were all in the last month."

My gut knots. "All unrelated? No contact? They weren't family or neighbours? Or lovers?"

Aben shakes his head. "Not that I know."

I curse. "Then it's not a normal fever." My mind darts back to the woman who'd given up her secret on the town road; who'd sold her husband's horse to buy milk of the poppy. What had she said? *He went out searching for it and came back with fever.*

Where then, had he gone? I come to my feet. "The woman with the poppy addiction, where does she live? I need to talk to her husband."

Aben scowls, his hands clenching into fists on the table. "There's more than one woman with poppy addiction here. In case you hadn't noticed." Curious. A sore point I hadn't expected. I raise an eyebrow at him and he sighs.

"My brother got mixed up in the trade. Didn't end well. Swore I'd stay the hell away from it." Dalziel places a hand on his forearm and pats it gently.

"Please friend, this is important," the boggart croaks out, skirting around the edge of his secret. I suck in a breath, scenting the air on my tongue. I'm on to something. And when Dalziel glances up at me and gives the faintest of nods, I know I'm right.

Aben sees it too. He closes his eyes, takes a moment, then releases his fists. "Describe her."

I do, and his brow wrinkles. "Sounds like Macey Gruber."

"And her husband is ill?"

Aben nods.

"Take me there."

#

We find the grave in Macey Gruber's front garden. Its earth is freshly turned and stinks of copper. The scent lies on the mound thick as a snowdrift. My hunger stirs with a faint gurgle. *Soon,* I promise it. From inside the farmer's cottage, a woman wails.

"We're too late," Aben says.

"Not necessarily."

When we knock, a bloodshot, tear-streaked face greets us. She's barely coherent enough to talk, but she opens the door and starts making tea. I sigh and take the tea pot away and sit her down at the table. Her clothes are dirty, gravel soil still stuck to them. Five miles from town and on her own, she'd had to do the deed herself. My heart twists, thinking of another grave far from here and the mother I'd buried in it. That hurt never truly left you. It faded into the background, scabbed over and scarred, but never went away, not completely.

"It's my fault," Macey Gruber says, staring at her hands. Her nails are bitten to the quick. She fidgets, anxious in her own skin.

I rest my hands on hers and flex my magic. "Where did he go, your husband, when he went looking for his horse?"

Macey Gruber stills, her pupils dilating. I don't like using my power like this, smothering people with it. I can't force people to talk, but I can make their tongues loose; fill their heads with haze until the world turns so dream-like the secret just slips out. Macey sways, her head rolls to one side.

"All the way to the plateau," Macey says. She closes her eyes and relaxes into my magic like it is a warm bath. "That feels nice."

"Up to the fae kingdom?" Aben whispers. "I knew it! They did something—ow!" This as Dalziel stamps on his foot.

"Fae don't work wicked magic," Dalziel says, indignant, and it looks like he wants to say more, but the Compulsion chokes the words in his throat. He works his jaw for a moment, a vein pops in his head, cheeks flushing with anger, then gives up with a "humph!"

"It's outlawed," I explain to Aben. "Work wicked magic and you're cast out. Magic sealed. No longer fae. Few dare risk it. Is that what we're looking for, Dalziel? An outcast?"

Dalziel shakes his head.

"Human then." At this, a copper scent curls off my words, strong and delicious. I'm closing in. I take Macey's hands again, give her a little shake.

Her eyelids flutter open. "Let me sleep," she groans. "It's all my fault. Let me sleep forever."

"Why is it your fault, Macey?"

A long pause and her red eyes, too red to be just from crying, study my face. "I sold his horse. His favourite." The smell of the old secret fills my nose like stale bread. Dry and ordinary. I've not asked the right question. "Who did you sell it to?"

"Vander."

The name drops into my belly like a bite of marinated pork. Full bodied flavour rolls over my tongue. Copper fills my nose. I breathe it in, chest swelling, my mind revelling in it. It's *here*. The trail's *here*.

"Vander, the *barkeep*?" Aben's interrupts, incredulous. "What would he want with a farm hor—" but I hold up a hand for quiet.

"Why Vander? Why did you go to him?"

Macey swallows, sensing she's on the edge of spilling it all. "Because he has the poppy," she whispers. "He runs it all."

Got you.

Copper hooks my nose, pulling my head around. A trail flares to life in my mind's eye, burning a path to my quarry like a trail of gunpowder. It points straight back to town.

Dalziel grunts. Aben and I glance over to find him twitching on the floor, nodding furiously between his spasms. Once Dalziel sees we've noticed, he slumps, utterly spent.

Aben hurries over, sits him up. "Easy, breathe," he says.

"Water," Dalziel croaks. "Please, friend Aben." Aben fetches a cup and the cold kettle from Macey's stove and Dalziel gulps it down.

"Stay here," I tell them, striding for the door. My trail beckons.

Aben's hand closes around my elbow. "I'm coming."

For a heartbeat I consider telling him no, that it's dangerous. Human my quarry might be, but he's got wicked magic at his disposal, and I can't protect him from it.

"Please."

The request tastes bitter, not quite a secret—at least not the kind I like. It mingles with the copper, defiling it with its guilt. A secret blame then. That he'd turned his back when he should have helped. Of all times to grow a conscience. My gaze roves the room as I try to find the right words to explain why coming with me is a bad idea; the worst idea actually. My eyes light on the corner of a small envelope poking out of the pocket in Macey's dress. When I bend down to pull it loose, her hand catches my sleeve.

"Stay," she begs, rousing from her dream-state. In hindsight, working my magic on a poppy addict might not have been such a wise play. "Don't go." She claws at my clothes.

I detach her fingers one by one and slip the envelop into the fire at the hearth. It goes up in a whiff of burned poppy powder. "I have to," I tell her. The trail calls. But

I don't like the idea of leaving her here alone. She needs help, more than any I can give.

Dalziel stands up with a grimace and dusts off his coat. "I will look after her."

Aben casts me a doubtful look. "I thought you said he was a prankster."

"Broonies are not pranksters," Dalziel huffs. "We help." He pauses and the flicker of a grin crosses his wide mouth. "If the trade is right."

I study the squat fae. Maybe I read him wrong, perhaps there was more of the broonie left in him than I'd thought. After all, he'd been trying to appeal the dead in Roper's field. If I gave him this chance, might he return to the fireside spirit he'd once been?

I crouch before him so we're eye level. "You would do this for me?" I ask.

Dalziel nods, then holds up one finger. "On one condition."

"Here we go," Aben mutters, attention dropping to his second-hand shoes. He'd not had a chance to change them.

"Name it."

Dalziel motions me close, "Stop the bastard." His eyes snare me with their intensity and there's something pleading in them. Something he cannot say. "*Please.*"

#

"I suppose it makes sense," Aben says through a yawn as we watch the saloon from across the street, waiting for the last of its patrons to stagger out. Our alley stinks of horse shit, cat piss and garbage, but it's the best we've got. Now that I've found the trail, the scent of copper hangs over the place, thick as soup. Coats the saloon like sticky paint. In my pockets, my fingers itch something chronic, begging for release.

"All those shipments from the coast. I thought it was just ale," Aben says. He rubs his face and slaps his cheeks a few times to stay awake. "He has them bring it right up Main Street, you know. I can't count the number of times I've seen a cart parked out front with men unloading it—all of it in broad daylight! I never thought to question. No one has."

"No one alive," I correct. If I had to guess, more than one corpse in Roper's field was there simply because they'd gotten too curious. A bit of wicked magic worked and they fell sick and died. Job done. No one the wiser.

Only it wasn't that simple. Wicked magic *always* had a cost. And my bet was the rest of the body count was Vander's way of paying it.

At last, the final patron sways out the double doors and the lamp-lit windows turn dark. I glance at the moon; three, perhaps four o'clock in the morning.

I flex my fingers, feeling the prick of claws under my nails. Time to move, before this secret has a chance to escape.

We slink out from the alleyway. The moon's out and high, casting long drifts of shadow across the street. Aben follows doggedly behind. I'd tried to talk him out of coming, but he wouldn't hear of it. And from the stubborn set of his jaw, I'd known better than to argue, else he follow and give the hunt away. No, best he see this through to its end in a place where I can keep an eye on him. With any luck, I won't give him nightmares.

Across the street and into the saloon. Aben catches the double doors so they don't swing behind us.

And there he is.

Waiting. The cold barrel of a '76 Winchester pointed our way.

"You picked the wrong night to be nosey, Eater."

Like I said. Some secrets beg. Some cry. Some do nothing at all. And some, when cornered with no way to run, turn around and bite.

Vander levels the shotgun at us.

The world sinks into fragments of time. A slick, copper-laden breath filling my lungs. Diving for Aben; pulling him to the floor. Vander's rifle cracks. One saloon door erupts, pelting us in shards of wood.

The next beat I'm up and running, leaving Aben reeling on the floor. Vander aims his gun again. Too slow. Much too slow for my fae blood all frenzied with the hunt. I dodge, vision a blur of hunger and lamp-light. A bullet whisks past my shoulder, snags a hole in the wall. Vander's growl fills my ears, anger turning desperate. He cocks the rifle again, aims... not at me.

Aben. The boy's name sounds in my head, like I'd shouted it. From the corner of my vision, I glimpse him standing in the doorway clutching his head. Before I can think, before reason or judgement sets in, my body turns.

Lunges.

Intercepts.

The bullet finds my gut. Buries deep and gnaws with a gusto that brings me to my knees. I stagger, clutching my belly.

"Ha, got you, fairy bitch," Vander snarls. He glances up to the balustrade where a small squat figure is waiting. "Another one for the field, Freda." The figure's perfectly round eyes fix on the scene below, frog mouth pinched shut. Another broonie. This one is softer than Dalziel, younger too, her hair thick and swamp green. But there are features I recognise. Dalziel's ears. Dalziel's nose. His kin through and through.

No wonder he was so insistent I end this.

She doesn't move.

"Freda!" Vander barks.

The broonie juts her jaw, squares her shoulders and stays still. Below, blood oozes from between my fingers, but I'm too far gone to feel pain. I come to my feet.

Vander curses, snatches a switch-knife from the bar and scores it down his forearm. He utters something unintelligible under his breath. Pressure washes over the room. I feel it wrap around my limbs and squeeze me still, right down to my itching fingers. *Wicked magic.* Gods and fae damn, I'd gotten sloppy. I search for Aben, but can't find him. *Double damn.*

"Freda," Vander growls. Above, the broonie's legs jerk, pulling her down the stairs.

"Why all this?" I ask. My seized jaw slurs the words together. It's not much of a question but it's all I can think of to buy time. Some secrets can't risk bragging when they're exposed. I just hope Vander is one of them.

Vander pauses, a slight curl in his lip. "What does it matter?"

"Matters... to me." I say, forcing the words through my teeth. "To the people left... behind."

Vander shrugs and nonchalantly flicks his knife open and shut. Open and shut. "Truth be I've forgotten why."

His words slide down my throat and into my belly in juicy morsels. But I want more. "Why use sickness then?"

Vander pauses, considering me. "Some couldn't pay, some wouldn't, some threatened to expose my operations. Bad business leaving them to talk." He comes closer, flicks his switch-knife out again under my jaw. "You really should have bought dinner. It would have been less painful for both of us." He indicates the gash on his forearm. It comes together in a heartbeat.

"You feed them cursed food." I swallow and fight to raise my voice. "An easy thing, I imagine, to work a spell behind a kitchen door instead of behind a bar." I still can't see Aben, but I hope he's listening.

Vander studies me, curious, as if I'm a puzzle he hasn't figured out yet. "It is."

"Why not poison?" It would be easier. And with less cost. I eye the gash on his forearm. That much blood to work a spell of binding. How much then to work a spell of killing? Thirteen people perhaps, each bled dry and buried in a field.

"Poison's traceable," Vander says. "Unless you go for the stuff on the top shelf. But it's expensive. Too expensive. No money in it." His tone is dry, matter of fact.

All about the money, eh? That's the thing with wicked magic, it can get you what you want, but it turns you cold inside. Once, he might have been an honest merchant, but the magic sunk in, twisted it all up, turned his morals inside out. It's a cost few recognise until it's too late.

Vander's switch-blade wanders along my chin and my jaw relaxes at its touch. I work my mouth open, testing the limits of my new freedom. It's not much. He flicks his wrist, and the tip of his knife burns a line across my cheek.

"Ow!"

His eyes fixate on that first red line. Then the knife quivers close again, pauses above my other cheek, then shifts to my forehead, as if he's debating where to cut next. "To think of the spells I might cast with your fae blood," he whispers. And there's excitement there. A man enthralled in the power of magic. He presses closer and the scent of his sweat and blood fills my nose. Rich and coppery. My mouth salivates. I bite down on my hunger.

"You've fucked up."

He frowns, steps back, suddenly unsure. I suppose he's used to his victims begging—at least the victims he finished like this.

"You stopped counting us," I say, and grin.

Vander's eyes search me, then dart to Freda still standing at the bottom of the staircase. Realisation dawns on him in a slackening of his face, a strickening in his eyes. He whirls—just in time to see Aben plunge a meat cleaver into a leather-bound book.

It's no light cut, Aben throws his whole body behind the blow. The blade sinks through the cover as if it's made of butter; slices through the marrow of pages beyond before it thuds into the wood of the bar underneath. It sticks there like an axe in a tree stump.

Just like we planned.

I'll distract him, you find his spell book. That had been our agreement going in. I almost thought it hadn't worked.

"NO!" Vander's shriek turns my hairs on end. He lunges for Aben, even though it's too late. Far, far too late. His spell sloughs away, releasing my limbs.

Time to feed.

My fae blood boils. Copper swims up my nose, into my lungs, driving the hunger deeper. In a heartbeat, my *chelae* extend from my fingers, long flexible claws, strong as steel, sharp as swords. They whip out; one set catches Vander in the boot, piercing through leather and sole to the floor beneath. He howls and buckles to cradle his trapped leg. My second set lock around his ribs in a cage, thumb and fingers pincering him still then drag him down in a sprawl.

I'm on him in a blur, straddling his chest.

"Don't touch me!" He snarls, just once, before I lean close and brush my lips over his. They're rough and scaled, with a hint of an old poppy on them. I kiss him. Vander relaxes in my hold, eyes rolling into his head. *Lustitia,* my mother named this. *Judgement's Kiss.* I open my mouth around his and suck out that delicious blood-tangled secret. It slips from him to me, gliding down my gullet and into my stomach heavy-like, healing and filling me in a heartbeat. Whole and deliciou*s*.

Sated at last.

My chelae retract. I release Vander; his head thunks to the floor. Limp.

"You killed him?" Aben asks into the silence.

I wipe my mouth with the back of a sleeve. "See for yourself."

Aben eases out from behind the bar, still holding the meat cleaver at the ready. His eyes don't leave me as he bends to check for a pulse. When he finds it, he blinks and his gaze breaks away as he runs a hand over the smuggler's chest, feeling the rise and fall there. "He's alive."

I snort. "Of course he is. I'm not a murderer."

Aben's cleaver drops to his side, forgotten. "What did you do?" He stares at me, searching. I smirk, it's not often I'm met with wonder. But I suppose Aben has seen enough this night to look beyond fear.

"I ate him."

"*Ate* him?"

"Him and his secret, everything that made Vander who he was." And come morning he'll wake as a blank slate. He'll never regain those memories. They're in my gut now, slowly digesting. A fresh start for a feed.

There's a humph from the stairs and a pad of feet crossing the saloon. Freda leans over Vander's sleeping form, mulling her lips. "Good as dead," she says at last. Then she lifts one foot and swings it hard into Vander's side. I catch the snap of ribs as it lands and wince. Freda straightens her tunic and turns to us. "My thanks."

#

I finger the bullet hole in the gut of my robe, frowning at the dried blood there. I'll have to get new clothes in the next town.

"You really can't stay?" Aben asks.

We're back in Roper's field. Dalziel and Freda are building a bonfire of herbs and bracken to calm the bones once and for all now that their murderer is gone. Dalziel practically dances as he does it. He is free, his daughter is returned and, if my hunch is right, they've found new hearth share at Macey's farm.

The widow for her part watches Dalziel and Freda work, holding a bundle of lavender to throw on the blaze. A faint smile plays over her lips.

"No," I tell Aben. "Secrets to find, souls to eat and all that." *More wicked magic to hunt. It's never ending.*

As if sensing my thoughts, Aben produces the two halves of the spell book and gestures it at the fire.

"Can I?" He asks. "I mean, is it safe to? I'm not going to get cursed, or jinxed for all eternity?"

A snort escapes me. "You won't." I assure. Without a wielder it's just a book. A dangerous book. As for how Vander got his hands on it. That's a secret I'd like very much to know.

We sit together, watching the pages curl into ash until the bonfire burns low and the sun breaks over the grass. Aben stands, still in his toe-holed sandals from Dalziel, and holds out a hand.

"If you must go, know that my door's always open," he says. "Don't be a stranger."

I take it. His grip is firm, yet warm, and a pang echoes through my gut. Emptiness of a different kind. Funny as it may seem, I've come to like this rag-tag crew tonight.

"You know," I say, slowly. "I might just hold you to that." A grin creeps across my lips. "You better have some good secrets to spill when I come back."

Aben grins. "Count on it."

SCORPION'S STING

Sign: Scorpio
Element: Water
Symbol: Scorpion
Dates: October 24 to November 22

The girl was dead. That much was clear as Scorpion scuttled across the hot sand. Face down, the girl's hair had spilt across the earth in dark, spider-web strands. Eagle, Ant and Coyote had already taken their fill; her eyes were hollow sockets, her rib cage cracked open to the sky.

"Died of thirst," Scorpion said, studying the body. Not a violent death as far as she could see. Her claws opened and closed on the air, tail poised high over her head. A breath of wind stirred the sand and the scorpion shifted, tilting her body into a question as she turned to the ghost huddled in the sand by the dead girl's feet.

"Why are you still here?" Scorpion asked.

The ghost girl raised her head, unwrapped her arms from her knees. Her skin was blotched and mottled in shades of blue, black and purple, just like Rattlesnake's. "You see me?" she whispered.

"I see you," Scorpion replied. "Though I should not. Why are you still here?" To Scorpion's mind, it was a pertinent question. The dead didn't stay without reason. She crawled towards the body, her eight legs picking across the sand to find cracked lips around a tongueless mouth. *Damned Coyote, taking all the best bits for himself.*

The ghost drew circles in the earth. Or tried to. Her fingers slipped through the grains as if they were made from cloud. "I died here," she said, sullenly.

"I can see that," Scorpion replied, picking her way through the dead girl's hair and up onto the head. She moved down the body, heading for the open rib cage. Perhaps there she'd be able to twist off some meat that hadn't hardened dry under the desert sun. "Most don't like to stick around to watch this."

The ghost's eyes, dark and ringed in shadow, followed Scorpion's progress, unflinching. "Where else can I go?"

Scorpion tilted her body again, tail twitching in surprise. "You don't feel it?"

"Feel what?"

"A pull..." Scorpion searched for the right words. "Onward. Away from here."

The ghost cocked her head, a faint furrow on her brow. There was a scar there too, a white ridge that cleaved one eyebrow in half. "Away to where?"

Scorpion threw her claws skyward, exasperated. "Somewhere not here." Truth be told, she didn't know. The Pull didn't apply to creatures of the Between. When their time came, they simply faded away. Scorpion had seen many fadings; thousands, or perhaps millions, over the years. Saber-tooth, Auroch, and Dodo, among others. Their bodies had turned faint enough to see the desert and grasses through them. But Scorpion had not faded yet; her children were many and strong.

The ghost, for her part, had fallen quiet, her eyes glazed as she searched inward. "I don't feel anything," she said after a long pause.

Scorpion eyed her over a splayed rib as her claws worked a chunk of exposed flesh free. "Nothing?"

The girl shook her head, hugging her knees.

Intriguing. Scorpion abandoned her meal and approached the ghost. The girl's feet were bare and transparent, but when Scorpion poked one foot, the flesh was still solid. *Curious.* She scuttled up the girl's shin. The ghost's muscles tensed underneath her eight legs. At the girl's knees, where skin gave way to a sweat-yellowed dress, Scorpion paused to look into the girl's face. "What's your name, ghost?"

A pause. The wrinkle next to her scar deepened as the silence grew. "I don't know," the ghost said at last.

This was not so surprising. Their names were often the first thing the dead forgot. Scorpion considered calling for Human and letting him deal with this, but Human was even worse than Coyote. And he stomped about something chronic, which always made Scorpion's amour ache. No, she'd manage this incursion like she'd managed the others.

"What happened to you then?" she asked, gesturing a claw at the bruises on the girl's arms.

"I was..." The ghost closed her eyes, brow furrowing as she tried to remember. "Hurting. They hurt me. A lot." Her voice grew stronger and her eyes roved beneath her eyelids. "They said I should be thankful they took me in after Ma died. But they made me work. All day. With no water. Then she'd hit me and he'd watch." Her ghostly body quivered. "I ran away."

"I can see you did," Scorpion said. "Or that you tried to."

The girl looked to her corpse and she grew still, then dragged in a ghostly breath. "I didn't mean to die." The last word came out as a sob and she buried her face in her arms.

Scorpion rested her claws on the girl's arms. "And yet here you are." If she could've sighed, she would have. But her accordion lungs weren't made for that. Instead, Scorpion tapped first one leg, then another in a melancholy rhythm on the girl's skin. *A ghost with no pull. What to do, what to do.* "I could take you back. Not permanently," she added. "A brief visit."

The ghost's eyes met Scorpion's glittering black ones. "Why?"

Scorpion shrugged her claws—she'd learned that from Human at some point over the years. "To find your pull." She had thought the answer obvious, but the girl wasn't of the Between. She wouldn't—couldn't—know these things. "You can't stay here," Scorpion said. "It's not good. For you or the Between." Her back arched at a memory of a dog who'd stayed trapped in the Between too long. At the end, it hadn't been a dog anymore. Just hunger, eating everything that moved. It devoured Coyote three times before he learned not to stick his nose there. Once was enough for Scorpion. She shuddered, recalling those monstrous teeth crunching through her carapace. She might be immortal, but she still felt pain. Since then, she'd made a point not to let any ghost stay too long. "Well?" She prompted, sting quivering. The girl didn't have a choice—not if Scorpion had any say in it. But it would be easier if the girl agreed.

The girl's tear-streaked face took in the desert sands; the scrawny grasses dotted here and there. She wiped her eyes, squared her jaw, and gave a short nod. "Yes. I'll do it."

Thank the Between. "Good," Scorpion replied. If she could have smiled, she would have. Her tail arched, venom bulb tipped and ready. "This is going to sting."

She plunged her tail into the girl's arm.

#

The girl blinked open her corpse's dead eyes. "What is this?"

"A second chance," Scorpion said, clawing her way up the corpse's dress and onto her head. "Don't waste it."

"And this?" the girl asked, pinching a lock of hair before her face. It twisted and coiled in her fingers like a worm on a hook, its end arching into a pointed sting.

"Protection," Scorpion said and left it at that.

The girl nodded, writhing locks settling on her back.

She followed her own tracks, gait measured and unhurried as she picked her way back through the desert. Her shoes were worn through and filled with the desert sand. In the glaring midday sun, her skin cracked and her bruises took on a yellow hue. The smell of sour meat grew stronger, wafting up from her open ribs. Atop the girl's head, Scorpion surveying the way before them. The passage the girl had taken before in her final hours stood out like stars in a night sky—a blaze of footprints to her Between eyes. With Scorpion's venom gluing the girl back into her shell, the ghost inside saw the way too. So Scorpion remained silent, leaving the ghost the task of plucking and pulling her skin and bones across the desert.

The tracks stretched on. And so they followed.

This world was similar to the Between. Same terrain, same clear blue sky, withered grasses and scraggily shrubs twisting out of the earth. But here, everything *moved*. Instead of still, belly-up bodies, ant trains crawled the ground and flies circled in their dozens. A pair of hawks glided overhead. There, a scrawny rabbit darted back into its

235

burrow. The world spun with life. Dizziness swirled through Scorpion's cephalthorax and she drew her senses away, turning her sight back to the Between. Her home hung there, perfectly overlaid on this World, a still and silent haze on the horizon.

Night had fallen by the time they reached the homestead. It was a tumbledown thing with one end of the porch caved in. Sand had scored the paint away years ago, except for the faintest flecks of white still remaining on the gate. The girl paused, hand on the threshold. Moonlight was kinder to her features than the harsh sun. Her bruises vanished into the shadows, as did the exposed cavity of her chest.

In the distance, Coyote's brethren yipped and howled.

"Go on," Scorpion urged, tapping a claw to the corpse's head.

The girl's hair twitched, the ends rising off her back, each lock turning stinger sharp.

With one hand on the gate, the girl hesitated. "I'm scared," she whispered.

"We're always scared," Scorpion replied. Something she had learned from her ages in the Between.

"Who?"

"Everyone."

The girl's hand tightened on the latch, steadying the shake in her fingers. She pushed open the gate and shuffled down the overgrown path, then up onto the porch, scuffing her heels on the rough boards. She paused at the door and—just when Scorpion was about to remind her that her time in this World was only temporary— lifted a hand as if to knock, then curled her fingers around the doorknob.

The door popped opened. Unlocked.

"She always forgot to lock it," the corpse murmured and Scorpion sensed the memory dart out of death's darkness like a flash of fish scales in a murky stream. With a long, low creak, the girl pushed the door wide. She listened, and Scorpion listened too. The house was still, but for a faint snore in its depths.

A boiler stove loomed in the kitchen, though the fire was out. The girl shuffled past a sitting room, worn rugs on the floor, a rocking chair in one corner, brown curtains blocking the windows. Her eyes landed on the broken shards of a whiskey glass in the hall.

Atop her head, Scorpion felt a tremor run up the girl's spine. Her broken body stiffened; hair curling into razors.

"*You*." The word hissed from the darkness of a doorway. "Come crawling back, eh?" A shadow shifted, lumbered onto its feet. A hand, viper quick, lashed out and snatched the girl's arm. A woman's face loomed out of the shadows, pale and with high cheekbones, bloodshot eyes, and lines around a mouth set in a scowl. She might have been pretty, but her expression was enough to curdle milk.

The girl flinched, shrinking into herself—submission ingrained even in death.

"Little wench." The scent of whiskey rolled off the woman's breath. A finger stabbed into the girl's collar—any lower and it would have found open flesh. "A fox got into the coop because of you! Ronk has an udder inflection because you didn't milk her—" She raised an empty whiskey bottle, threatening to bring it down on the girl's head.

Scorpion shifted, her tail arching.

The girl remained motionless but for her writhing hair.

"—my floors need sweeping. Get outside and—" The woman sniffed, her face distorting into a new, twisted variant of disgust. She covered her nose. "Ugh! You reek."

She stepped back, taking in the girl properly for the first time. Her gaze travelled down the torn flesh and broken ribs to the open abdominal cavity missing all those important organs necessary for life. The woman's face turned pale, the pinkness in her cheeks washing away. A half-gurgle rose from her throat. She staggered backwards, the whiskey bottle falling to the floor with a 'thunk'.

"God's mercy," she whispered.

"Pounce, girl," Scorpion urged. This was prey ready for the taking. But the girl didn't pounce, though the ends of her hair curled and quivered with the want. Instead, she kept her eyes focused on a second door down the hall. One step, then another, and the woman shrank through her bedroom doorway like a spider retreating down its burrow.

"Roland!"

The snore cut off mid-draw. "Huh?"

"Your gun, Roland! Get your gun. *Now.*"

Scorpion imagined the woman rousing her mate, pulling at his nightshirt, shoving the weapon into his hands and pushing him to the doorway.

"Be careful," Scorpion warned the girl. "They can't kill you, but they can break the bond holding you here. And I can't bring you back again." And if that happened, she'd become a problem for all of the Between.

The girl's hair twitched. Her gait jerked and jolted as she forced her stiff limbs to move faster. "I won't leave him." It came out nearly a growl as she pushed deeper into the hallway, past the woman's bedroom, aiming for the door beyond.

Curious. Scorpion dug her claws into the girl's hair. She was remembering more and more. A good sign. *Although...*

Footsteps thumped behind them: the woman and her mate, sounding for all the world like a pair of buffalos barreling down the hall. Their vibrations shivered up the girl's body and into Scorpion's legs. A millennia of her children's memories filled her; thousands of feet tramping outside dens, collapsing tunnels, crushing her children alive. *Humans. Always so oblivious.* Her claws opened and shut with a snap.

"Shoot her!" the woman shrieked. "The Devil's in her I tell you."

The man grappled with his shotgun, shoving rounds into it with shaky fingers. His red hair was tousled, sticking up on one side. He lifted the gun and squinted down the barrel. His face slackened, eyes drawn to the girl's exposed chest cavity. He sucked in a breath. "By God, it's—"

"I know. She's desert dead. Put a bullet in her head and be done with it."

"But, Mary—" the weapon lowered "—it's..."

"God damn it, Roland. I'll do it myself." She yanked the gun from him, swung it up, and fired.

The girl didn't evade. *Couldn't*, Scorpion guessed. *Her time is almost up.*

The bullet tore a hole through the girl's abdominal cavity.

The girl cocked her head, a little gasp of surprise echoing from her spirit. "I don't feel it," she said to Scorpion.

"Of course not. The dead don't feel pain." Scorpion tapped a leg on the girl's head. "You're wasting time. Best not dally."

The girl nodded, a movement that almost threw Scorpion from her hair, and turned for the second door.

Another bang. Another bullet tore into the wall, splintering wood.

"Just die!" Mary screamed, and levelled the gun again. She stopped as a keening, then a burbling, howling wail rose from the second room.

Ah, so that's it.

"Shit," Mary huffed.

"If she wants him, let her take him," Roland said, groping for Mary's arm and trying to pull her back.

Mary shoved him away. "He's *my* child."

"But," he floundered, "you don't even *want* him."

Mary spat at her feet. "I don't give two fucks if he dies tomorrow, but I'm sure as hell not giving *her* anything."

The girl's corpse shuddered, arms twitching as she strode for the couple. They cowered away, tripping over each other and falling to the ground.

Sprawled on the floor, the woman snatched the gun up again, ready to shoot. It emptied with a hollow click—nothing in the chamber.

The girl advanced on the couple, her hair snapping out, dark and deadly. She knocked the gun asunder from the woman's trembling arms and it clattered to the floor. The pair scrambled away.

"Have him then!" Mary cried. "Take him and get out!" She tripped over her cowering husband and they went down in a tangle of limbs. "Roland, you oaf! Get off."

Scorpion dropped to the girl's shoulder, scuttled down the blood-soaked dress and onto the floor. "Go," she said. "Find the child. Time is closing."

The girl managed a stiff nod and entered the second bedroom.

Scorpion closed in on the writhing couple. Perhaps she should have let Human deal with them, but their bickering had ground her temper raw, every oafish *thud-thudding* jarred through her body. She rubbed her jaws together, issuing a soft hiss. This had gone far enough.

She struck.

Mary jerked upright, howling and clutching at her ankle. Her mate furrowed his brow then he too yelped as Scorpion's sting found home in his thigh. Spitting curses, they rounded on Scorpion crouched in the shadows.

"Damn insect, I'll squash you flat," Mary snarled.

Scorpion twitched her arachnid laugh. "I think not."

Curled on the floor, the pair gawked. They'd heard her. Of course they had.

If Scorpion could have grinned, she would have. Instead, she snapped her claws and drummed a leg on the floor like a spider testing its web. The magic in their veins responded. Twitching, twisting and roaring to life. *Good, good.* Scorpion let the thrill ride through her. Small she might be, and old beyond belief, but even Human feared her sting—as right he should. Now it was his children's turn.

Mary gasped a breath, then folded into herself, clothes going limp.

Roland screamed, eyes bulging as Scorpion's beady eyes swung to him.

"Oh yes, you too," she said.

Roland gasped as he shrank into his bedclothes, becoming smaller, then smaller again—his bones cracking, breaking and remaking.

A moment later, two young scorpions—small and soft shelled—scuttled out of the folds of clothing. They hissed at Scorpion, arched their tails, voices chittering in her head.

"What did you do to us? Turn us back!"

Scorpion rounded on them, her claws snapping shut just short of Mary's newly-armoured head. "Don't test me," Scorpion said, opening her claws again. Next time, she wouldn't miss.

"You can't do this." Roland stomped his legs unevenly. It would take him a while to learn to use them properly, but he would learn. Or he would die. Scorpion wasn't too concerned which.

"You are my children now, I can do what I like." Scorpion clicked her jaws. "Cruelty is not befitting in my children. A life as my kindred will teach you better. Now go, before I change my mind."

Mary's tail thrashed, fisting at the air. *"We won't forget this. I'll—"*

Scorpion's claws lashed, viper quick, snagging one of Mary's forelegs and dragging the youngster close. *"Enough,"* she hissed. And with a crunch, she ripped Mary's leg clean off.

Mary screamed, her jaws clacking together. *"My leg! My leg! She fucking took my leg Roland!"*

"Mary! Oh God!" Roland scuttled about, tripping over his own feet, panic shivering up and down his one-inch stature. *"Oh God, oh God."*

"Quiet!" Scorpion silenced them both as only a mother could. Reaching out, she seized the magic in their bodies and froze them in place. *"I* am your mother now." She arched her tail. "And I've grown weary of the sight of you. Get out, before I give you a real sting to complain about."

The two youngsters retreated to the shadows, scuttling along the skirting boards, grumbling as they went. A footstep rattled the floorboards at Scorpion's back. The girl. She carried a bundle in her arms. A babe peeked out, bright eyes and a fluff of brown hair.

With a shrug of her claws—Scorpion's version of a sigh—she clambered back up the corpse's tattered dress and onto her shoulder. "You can't take him with you."

"I know," the girl replied.

"You got somewhere in mind then?"

There was a long moment before the girl forced a nod.

"Is it far?"

A stiff shake of her head.

"Good. You haven't long left."

They returned to the desert, this time forging a new path. The girl's pace had slowed, her feet dragged, and Scorpion felt her wrestling with the dwindling magic. On the horizon, a sliver of pink heralded the approaching dawn.

"Almost there," the girl whispered. "Almost there." She stumbled over a rise and there below, nestled beside on oak, lay a small cottage, a coral and barn to one side. The girl surged forward, clutching the babe to her rendered flesh. A shudder ran through her, and she stumbled and fell onto her knees.

Scorpion plopped to earth, sure this was the end. Instead, the girl crawled, dragging the bundle the final few feet and depositing it on the wooden porch as if the baby were made of glass.

"The Morrisons were always kind to me," the girl said, bowing to kiss the child's head. "He'll be safe here."

Scorpion quivered as the last traces of her magic dissolved. "Time's up," she said.

The girl sat back and looked up at the fading stars. "Anna."

"What?"

"My name." Her hollowed eyes turned on Scorpion. "I remembered. Thank you." Then her chin dropped to her chest and the corpse slumped. Empty.

As Scorpion crouched there in vigil, the girl's skin flaked away, bones shrivelling into dust until all that was left was a small mound of debris. *And then it was done.*

On the porch, the babe began to cry.

#

With a flit through the Between, Scorpion emerged again on the rise, just as candlelight flared behind the cottage window. A soft vibration on the sand made her turn. "Human," she acknowledged. The figure—long and lanky as ever—crouched down beside her. "Took your sweet time."

He winced. "Can't be everywhere, Scorpion." He sighed, long and heavy. "But you have my thanks."

Scorpion snapped a claw. "Do it yourself next time. I'm getting tired of cleaning up after everyone else's children."

Human scratched the bristles on his chin. "But you've got to admit, you are rather good at it."

"Prick."

"Grump."

Human grinned into the silence. "Come on." He offered his palm to Scorpion. "I hear Coyote's got himself into some trouble again."

Scorpion bristled. "Help him yourself, I've been up all night."

Human shrugged, gaze drifting down to the Morrisons, exclaiming over the baby below. "I guess you've earned it."

When no reply came, he turned. "Scorpion?" The space beside him was empty but for the faint imprint of her armour in the sand. Returned to the Between. He sighed again, sinking into himself.

"I owe you one," he whispered into the dawn.

NUNKI'S ARROWS

Sign: Sagittarius
Element: Fire
Symbol: Archer
Dates: November 23 to December 21

I was seven centuries old when my gift revealed itself. A mere foal by godling standards. But in that time I'd seen Chiron unlock the talents of heroes; studied how he'd drawn out Achilles' courage, Heracles' strength and Jason's cunning and released them into the world. Men and gods alike called Chiron *The Wisest, The Justest.* But I knew him by another name.

Father.

Nunki, he called me. He never said why. But then, he never said much. He hoarded words as a merchant hoards silver. Spent not a syllable more than he needed to. Besides, first names weren't important to godlings. The name bestowed when a gift revealed itself was the one that mattered. The one you were remembered for. And the day my gift came, when I should have received my new name and taken up my calling, he died.

Godlings are not immortal like the true gods. We can be wounded. We can be slain. We can be poisoned. My father was all three. A poison arrow in the end. Right through the foot.

"Don't be sorry," he'd whispered as I wept over him and at what I'd done.

My sisters and brother blamed Heracles—Father's mentee and favourite hero— who'd returned to us the night before flush with his victory over the hydra. Heracles blamed himself and his drunkenness for dropping a hydra spine onto his teacher's foot.

But that's not what happened. I remember like it was yesterday. As for my gift, well, that had surprised father and I both.

"My gift is to have no gift."

They'd stared at me aghast, like I'd not so much as grown an extra head but lost my only one. A godling without a gift. I was a perversion. A snake without its skin; a fish without gills. We were simply not made that way.

"Unthinkable," Melanippe had said, dark curls brushing her shoulders as she shook her head.

"It can't be," fair Carystus insisted. "You tried music? Father always had skill for a tune, perhaps you do too."

It had taken a butchered melody on a lyre to convince him otherwise.

Mute Ocyrhoe had rested a hand on my collar and stared mournfully into my face, her auburn hair haloed in a tangle around her head. Of all my siblings, I loved her the most. Hers was the gift of listening, she could hear across the world with it. But in the way of gifts, it was a double-edged sword; she'd not spoken a word in centuries. The secrets she learned stayed secret.

"It's okay, I'm all right with it," I'd said to her.

Her brown eyes considered me a long moment, and for a horrible heartbeat I thought she knew. That she'd been listening close to home the day Father died. But then she sighed and cupped my cheek as if to say *I'm sorry.*

So I remained Nunki, the unremarkable. The forgotten. Not banished, just left to my own devices. No pressure to breed heroes or wise men, no expectation to live up to the legacy of Chiron's blood in my veins. I withdrew to the edge of our realm and was content to fall into obscurity. A fitting punishment, I thought, for killing my own father.

Imagine my surprise when the first human sought me out in my cave at the foot of Mount Olympus. She was no hero, thin and bony like she'd slept rough for nights untold and skipped more meals than she'd eaten. From the look on her face—caught between shock and weariness—she hadn't expected to find me, of all creatures, here.

A knife flashed into her hand, the blade worn and flecked with rust. "Who are you?" she demanded.

I uncurled myself from my bed of reeds, and as I came close, her face paled.

She gripped the knife tighter. "What are you?" she amended.

That, I'd thought, was a little unfair. True, I was taller and broader than her, but that wasn't saying much. I wasn't *that* different—apart from the fur-tipped ears, the faint whorl of horsehair on my forehead and the two branches that curled from my brow. I'd always taken after my dryad mother. I was a dryad in nearly every sense but one: my gift.

"I am Nunki," I said.

The knife relaxed a little, a disbelieving look creeping over that scrawny face. "*You're* Nunki?"

I faltered. "You know of me?" Impossible. I'd not ventured into the mortals' cities, nor ever spoken to any travellers or hunters who had crossed into my woods.

"Artemis sent me." The girl put her knife away, suddenly matter-of-fact. "She said you'd train me."

Artemis. I ground the name out under my breath, cursing her in five languages. The goddess and I had crossed paths once or twice. But I'd never thought she'd ever *send* someone to me.

"Why?" I asked. "I'm no teacher."

"She said you were," the girl replied as she seated herself at my table. "Said you had a gift for killing."

I went still, the breath clogging in my lungs. *How?* How could Artemis *know?* But then Artemis is a God of the wilds, she could have heard it from a songbird, or a bug, for all I knew.

The girl grinned—a gaunt thing, all teeth and hollow cheeks. "I want you to teach me."

"*Teach* you?"

"There's a king who needs killing."

She'd been a gardener once, in a kingdom far south, she told me. From a family of gardeners. Her mother and grandmother before her. It had been hard but honest work and the royal family had been good to them. Until the birth of the prince.

"Mother said he was born with something missing," the girl explained over supper. "As a child, I'd find dead birds in the palace flowerbeds. Their heads gone; legs broken. I thought it was the royal cat until I found the cat the same way." She gave a hollow laugh. "If only that had been as far as it went."

She'd found a finger next. Skin loose and joints swollen with age. Lopped off above the knuckle.

"It was like he was teasing me, planting his bloody flowers in the garden where he knew I'd find them." Her hands squeezed into fists as she spoke. "Mother slapped me something good when I told her about the prince and what I'd found. 'Hold your tongue or you'll end us all!' she'd said."

The girl had still been young. Still thought her mother knew best. And she'd heard the fear laced in her mother's words. So, she'd obeyed. When she'd found more body parts—an ear, a thumb, a toe, all of them old and withered in the garden outside the prince's rooms—she'd cleared them away without a word.

Then she'd found a whole hand. This one young and supple. Slender fingers with calluses on their tips, those of a musician. And she recalled that one of the palace bards had gone missing two days before. Who'd last been seen entering the prince's chambers.

"We should have left then. When the old king sickened, I begged mother and father to leave," the girl said, staring into the hearth as I brewed tea. "But when the king died, we were still there. And then *he* took the throne, and it became so much worse."

Instead of parts, she found bodies. In the space of a month her family went from gardeners to grave diggers.

"I even found the queen's page boy dead under a tower window," she said. "His body was broken a hundred ways and not all of them from the fall."

She'd thought that had been the worst of it until her mother went missing. The girl stalled there, unable to finish as her face crumpled into a mess of grief. She slammed her skinny fist on my table. "We should have fled!" she repeated through her tears. "I should have made them see sense. If only we had run."

"Hindsight is a cruel knowing," I replied. How many times had I wished I'd known what I know now of my gift before I'd presented myself to my father for a naming? How excited I'd been to feel the knowledge open in my mind like a rose— of woods and metals, blades and fletching. It had not so much sprung forth from nothing, more that a particular set of learnings from my centuries under Chiron's tutelage had suddenly come together and woven themselves into a gift.

"A forger's gift. It's a sound hypothesis." Father had stroked his beard, pleased when I'd come running to him. "But you must demonstrate its validity before I give you your name."

If only I'd known then what I know now. That my hypothesis had been wrong. In all my eagerness, I'd not considered the alternatives. That my gift might not be to forge mere weapons, but death itself. And when I'd handed death to him, so lovingly and unknowingly crafted, Father's face had contorted from expectation into horror. If I close my eyes, I see him snatch his hand from the bow I'd made him. I see my poison arrow tumble through the air, end over end, and bury into his foot, laying him low.

Had I known then what I know now, Father would still be alive.

I considered the girl weeping at my table. Considered what and all she asked. This was not a job for heroes, and I couldn't make her into one. But perhaps I could turn her into something else.

"I will help you," I said at last.

I had no idea where to start. But start we did. Slowly at first. Trial and error. Me stretching out my gift's knowledge for the first time in decades, rigorously testing every skill before passing it on. Her, building up her strength, her stealth, her knowing of plants and poisons and her skill with the blade and bow.

Three years she was with me. Three years of forging her into a weapon to strike down a king. And in that forging she named herself anew: Arrow.

When she was ready, I loosed her into the heart of her enemy.

I never saw her again. But I did hear tell of the sudden death of King Tiernat in the south, brought down by an unknown foe, and I was glad. Not for a second did think I'd wake to a knocking on my cave door early one morning to find a one-armed, one-eyed man there.

"I'm told you can help me," he said, and he told me his tale. A merchant had stolen him as a teen, sailed him across the sea and sold him to a fighting ring. Twelve years he'd fought and bled, and at last he had escaped to search for the merchant who had stolen his life.

"How did you hear of me?" I asked.

The man shrugged. "I had a dream. It told me to come here and ask the help of the first person I met."

First Artemis and now Morpheus, God of Dreams. Safe to say my gift was no longer my closely held secret. The thought was not as upsetting as I thought it would be. I'd never expected to keep the secret forever. But that didn't stop the little quiver of fear ripple over my skin at the thought of Melanippe, Carystus and Ocyrhoe learning the truth.

Fletch, my second student named himself. Rough on the edges, but he'd still fly true. His body was already honed, if a bit battered. So I went to work on his mind. I filled it with plants and poisons, alchemy and traps. Five years he learned under me; his mind flexing in its new-found strength. Clever turned to cunning. Knack to knowledge. Scheming to strategy. If it weren't for his vengeance, he might have become a politician—or a warlord. Perhaps he did after. I do not know.

That is the hard thing about these stories. I never know how they end. I'm left to listen to the tales each new guest brings and guess the rest.

Not that my effort with Fletch went unreciprocated.

"You have my gratitude, Nunki," he said on his final day. "Word in the mortal cities is that your father was the finest teacher to ever walk these lands. While I was never his student, I was yours. And I'd wager you are as fine a teacher as he."

I laughed. "I'm no teacher." I looked up to the stars to where Zeus had placed Father after his death. Forever out of reach. "Father set heroes forth into the world while I..." I trailed off, not wanting to insult my student and friend on his final day. *While I set loose killers. Living weapons forged in my gift and sent across the world into the hearts of other men.*

Fletch flashed me a look through his one good eye, not fooled for a second. "Perhaps weapons are what the world needs. To strike down the evil in it. Is that not what the heroes do, in their own way?"

I frowned, thinking I'd schooled him too well in rhetoric. Yet, his reasoning stuck in my mind. "I've never thought of it like that," I admitted.

"Perhaps it's time you do," Fletch suggested. "You are not just *like* an archer, you *are* one. Your quiver is the people you teach, your range the world over." He pointed to the constellation above us. "Your father may have been the world's finest teacher, but you are its finest archer."

The weight of his last word sank in, tingling in my bones. And like that, I came to know my name.

Archer.

Which brings me to the third. She was special. I found her as a babe, all brown eyed and fawn-soft locks that melted through my fingers. Her mother was with me a single night before she succumbed to the rent in her belly. Bandits had taken a liking to my woods. And when the mother breathed her last, I closed her eyes and collected my quiver from my hearthside. I threw open my door, nocked my arrows, aimed at the stars and fired. One after another.

I trusted my gift to do the rest.

The next day I found an abandoned camp. Five bodies lay struck down in the earth—arrows in their backs and chests.

I named the babe Nock. And she grew ravenously. Despite my time with Fletch and Arrow, I'd never truly realised how fleeting mortal life is. Or how fast they grow. One day I was brewing a sleeping potion, eyes raw from sleepless nights, head in a daze; anything to get the dratted child to settle. The next, she was high as my hip and I was running after her, yelling for her to put on her Zeus-damn shoes before playing outside.

She was a wild thing. With so many brambles snagged in her hair she looked more the dryad than I. She was no good at sitting still. But she took to the blade like she'd been born with one in her hand. She loved stories, particularly ones of the heroes my father had taught.

In a mere blink she was fifteen going on sixteen. And restless.

"Have you ever thought about leaving the forest?" she asked.

"Why would we? We have everything we need here."

Nock pursed her lips, not satisfied with my answer. "But haven't you ever wondered what else is out there?"

I shrugged and continued slicing roots for a stew. "Not especially."

She flipped her knife around her knuckles—a showy movement I had never taught her—and heaved a sigh. A bit overwrought, but she was young. "Could we not go? A short trip." A quick grin. "You might find you like it out there."

"Absolutely not." We weren't adventurers, we didn't do those things. And Nock's suggestion chilled me to the bone. The thought of Arrow or Fletch's stories befalling her sent my heart pelting into my ribs. No, she was safe here. Where I was with her. Yes, I was a coward through and through.

Nock's face fell. "But why?"

I snatched the knife from her knuckles as she made to flick it again. With the blade gripped loose in my fingers, I waggled the handle under her nose. "Because I am your mother and I say so."

She blew out her cheeks and snatched the knife back.

I let her take it. "No playing—"

"—with knives at the table, I know," she finished.

That was not the end of it. All through summer she nagged and begged, debated and cajoled. Winter gave us a brief reprieve, but as soon as the first buds of spring opened, she was back at it.

"I'm going," she announced one day, as I'd feared she might. "You can't stop me."

I could, but with my gift it could turn deadly, and I didn't want that. Couldn't even bear the thought of hurting her. Or her me. She'd long ago learned everything I could teach her. But it was what I couldn't teach her that worried me.

"Be careful, promise me," I said, hugging her tight at the edge of the forest. Nock held me for a moment, then wormed out of my grip and flicked her knife again.

Who, it occurred to me to think then, *had taught her that?* Why had I not thought to ask earlier?

By that point, it was too late. My mortal child had already raced down the road, her pack bouncing on her back, knifes swinging on her belt. And there, on the rise that parted my forest from the world beyond, she paused, turned, and waved. Once. Her lips moved. I was too far to hear but I thought they shaped out, "I'll be back soon."

I hoped they did.

So I returned to my cave. Strangely quiet it was. Still beyond measure. I lit the hearth and busied myself with supper. Then onto sweeping the floors, preparing herbs, sharpening knives. The last blade of my set honed and gleaming, I held it up to the firelight and said, without thinking, "What a pretty blade, don't you think?"

The silence that answered cut deeper than any knife.

I slept poorly that night, tossing and turning on my reeds. *She's fine. She'll be fine,* I told myself over and over. Those words turned into a mantra as the days wore on, and I'd almost believed them until Ocyrhoe knocked on my door late one evening.

"Sister!" I exclaimed, delighted to see her. I showed her in, fussed about with my hearth and pot for tea. How long had it been? Decades? Centuries? But when I handed Ocyrhoe a cup of steeped herbs, her expression was all wrong. Lips tight. Brow creased. Eyes earnest. There was no joy there. But concern. Dread even.

The pot slipped from my fingers and smashed against the floor. "It's Nock, isn't it?" My voice shook.

A nod.

I swallowed. "She's in danger?"

Another nod.

"From who? The gods?" My fists clenched. If Zeus or any of his sons had laid a finger on her I'd—but Ocyrhoe shook her head. I sucked in a breath and fought down panic. "Godlings?"

My sister hesitated, then dipped her chin. Affirmative.

My heart turned over. Gooseflesh prickled up my arms. I didn't want to ask. I knew the answer as sure as the heat of the hearth burning at my back. "*Our* family?"

Another nod and she dipped one finger in her tea and attempted to scrawl a name on my table. Her gift cramped up her arm after the first letter, such was her curse: to listen and know, but never to tell. Not directly. Ocyrhoe hissed under her breath and shook out her fingers, exasperated. I stared at the wet smear on the wood. One letter but it was enough for me to put the rest together.

"Melanippe?"

I could think of only one reason why a godling, why my eldest sister would dare go after Nock. Vengeance. The truth about Father's death had finally found its way to her.

Ocyrhoe's hand caught mine and she stared into my face. *I'm sorry*, she mouthed.

My fingers squeezed hers tight. "This is not your sorrow to bear. It's mine." I should have told them. Should have owned up to what I'd done. But my gift had been young and new and terrifying. I'd been afraid of what I could do. Of what I might be made to do. And the guilt. So thick and heavy it had dragged on my limbs like chains.

So I'd slunk away. Fled from all the reminders of what I'd done. A tingle washed over me. I could not go on hiding. Not with Nock in danger.

I straightened. "Where is my daughter?"

Ocyrhoe took my hand and led me out through the trees; her hooved feet leaving little imprints on the grass. She led me to a chestnut horse tethered to a low-slung tree branch. One look and I recognised Pegasus' seed. Hard to ignore the wings sprouting from the mount's shoulders or the way those hooves barely touched the earth—like the creature was made of cloud. But when I rested a hand against his flank, he was solid and real under my fingers.

"Where did you find him?" I asked, forgetting myself.

Ocyrhoe lips curled into a faint smile. *A gift,* she mouthed. *From Carystus.*

Our brother always did have a taste for fine things. I ran a hand down the horse's neck and its baleful eyes swung to me and it whickered a greeting. Ocyrhoe pressed the reins into my hands.

"No, Ocyrhoe, I can't take him."

She waggled her finger and took my hand, miming me returning the reins to her. The message was clear. Not take. Borrow. The matter apparently settled, Ocyrhoe lifted a finger and pointed due West.

"That way, is it?" My stomach clenched at the thought of what I might find. I mounted the steed—Kallias I called him in my head. *Beautiful.*

There is very little you can do on a flying horse but watch the earth pass beneath you. But Kallias did his job, and he did it well. Carried me a day and a night to the fortress of Chyton, deep in the lands of Epirus.

Blood awaited me there. Flecked on the marble pillars in drying shades. I unsheathed my knife and I pressed through the pillars, half expecting shadows to shift to swinging blades. This was the world of humans, godlings didn't belong here. There was a reason why we trained heroes to do our work rather than do it ourselves. We can be killed, we can be slain, and we can be poisoned. And the world of humans is full of fatal possibilities. I never said I was the only coward.

And you let Nock come here without even putting up a fight. I clenched my knife and hurried on.

That's when I heard it. A soft, almost inaudible crying. The faintest sniff of a nose, a wiping of the eyes, then a ragged breath. I followed it. Around a corner, down a passage, and into... into...

Horror.

The smell hit me first. It hung in the air, thick enough to swallow, every breath a gulp of iron and dank earth. Then my eyes found the bodies. Dozens of them. Throats opened, femoral arteries slashed at the thigh, axillary arteries punctured under the arm. All of them armed, their spears and bronze swords scattered to the floor.

A knot folded in my belly. *Please no.*

Another sob. I spun.

There she was. My Nock. My arrow. Rocking back and forth, hugging a fallen figure in her arms. It was a young man, a few years older than she. Tall. Muscular. Curls for hair—and the gold wreath of a hero resting within them.

The knot in my gut wretched. A hero. There was only one place they trained those.

In a heartbeat, it all made sense. Her insistence on leaving our den to see the world. Her excitement on the day of her leaving. The knife trick I hadn't taught her.

"Oh Nock."

At the sound of my voice, my daughter straightened, peeled herself from her dead lover's body. Her eyes were wide and stricken, dried blood crusted in her hair.

"It just happened," she began. "I couldn't stop." Her eyes roved the massacre, seeing and not seeing. I recognised the look. I had once done the same with Father's death. Reliving the moment again and again, trying to figure out when it had all gone wrong.

I swept Nock into my arms and held her.

"I'm sorry, I'm sorry," she whispered over and over. Whether to me or the dead boy at her feet I couldn't say.

"Hush, it's not your fault," I said. The wrong words to say.

"But it is! All of it," Nock choked, and when I tried to steer her away from the carnage, she wouldn't budge. Her fingers gripped her lover's tunic so tight her nails cut into her palms through the fabric. For a second time I took in the body, noticing the knife embedded in his throat, expertly angled into the carotid artery. One of Nock's knives.

"I k-killed him." Nock shook in my arms. "It was *me.* I couldn't stop. Couldn't—"

I eased her grip from the hero's tunic, finger by finger. Rubbed her hands in mine. They were slick and sticky.

A tittering laugh rang from the end of the hall.

"Oh my, isn't this an endearing scene."

There was no need to turn. After seven centuries living with her, I knew her voice. "Melanippe," I acknowledged, rising. "This is your doing?"

My eldest sister strode through the bodies, the strike of her hooves on the marble hard and grating. Of all Chiron's children, she resembled our father most. Thin face, pointed chin, dark hair pulled into a warrior's braid. Like Father, her olive-smooth torso tapered into an equine body. But unlike Father, hers was all fury and pent-up energy. She was a creature born to run, to fight. Her muscles quivered as she approached, taut as a flexed bow string. A child born to all of my father's power, and none of his calm. Her gift of storms suited her well.

My fingers found the hilt of my dagger in my belt.

"All I did was give a little push," Melanippe said. "A lover to woo her here and a one hundred drachma reward to the man who claimed your daughter's head. Your dear Nock did the rest." Her eyes turned on the scene, landing on Nock still cradling the dead hero. "And what a mess it is." Her lips split open in delight. "I mean, I knew you'd forge her as you did the others, but for you to turn an innocent into such a *killer* is—" she clapped her hands together "—extraordinary."

I scowled. "Your grievance was with me, sister. Not my daughter."

Melanippe pouted her bottom lip. "All I wanted was to test my niece a little. And she was just so *fond* of my new hero." Her gaze paused on the dead boy. "A shame she killed him in her frenzy. He had some promise. Even if he ignored my instructions to leave her alone when my soldiers came. Not to worry, there will be others."

I closed my eyes, imagining his terror as Nock's instincts took over. The horror as Melanippe's trap swung shut and he realised what they'd woken.

My gaze dropped to the bodies again. I'd noted their armour when I'd entered but had not seen the shields buried among them. These were hoplites—trained soldiers—a whole phalanx of them. I lifted the edge of an upturned shield of the nearest one and glimpsed a blood-streaked crest embossed into the metal. Father's crest: the shape of his constellation emblazoned in bronze.

"You sacrificed them," I said, not quite believing it. Melanippe had always been cold, but I'd never known her to be cruel. "Sacrificed your own hero."

"Like you sacrificed Father," Melanippe spat. "You were the one who struck him dead Nunki, do not presume to lecture me!"

My hands shook as I clenched them at my side. No running from the truth anymore. "That was an accident."

Melanippe snorted, her glare turning my gut over. "Really, Nunki? You're still clinging to that lie? After all this?" She spread her arms to the dead. "A gift only works when you will it. You wanted Father dead. But what drove you to it? That he spent more time attending his precious *heroes* than you?" she sneered. "That he scolded you for not being as clever as Jason or strong as Heracles, or brave as Achilles?"

"Your words, not mine, Melanippe." I gripped Nock by the shoulders and pulled her to her feet, heedless of how her lover flopped to the floor in his own blood and excrement. "Come," I whispered to her. "Let's go home."

Nock's face remained slack, her eyes unfocused, locked in some dark dream I couldn't break.

"That's right, go back and cower in your hole, Nunki," Melanippe hissed. "Your daughter won't recover. She slew her lover, Nunki."

Her words had such venom, so much hatred, that I could only stop and stare. This was not the sister I knew. Where was the girl who'd run to the Aegean and back just to prove she could? Who'd loved with a fierce, unbridled passion, and would brush off a scolding like it was a bit of dust? Where was the wild girl I'd grown up with? My stomach twisted. Where was the woman I'd known when I'd withdrawn in my shame?

Had I caused this?

I stood frozen before Melanippe, heart and thoughts racing. Nausea crawled up my throat and I clutched Nock to hold myself steady. I could not fall apart here. Nock needed me. And yet the thoughts circled vicious in my head. *You did this. You killed him. You abandoned them.*

Why? I wanted to cry. Why didn't you come to me, Melanippe? We could have talked. Even though I'd been the one who'd left, who had shunned all contact.

But to go as far as targeting Nock. To take her vengeance on my innocent girl... My dagger jerked free with a will of its own. I could have thrown it, let it sail true into Melanippe's throat. End that sad creature in a sure blow. I wanted to. Longed to. My body shook with it. Every fibre longed to shunt my blade deep in her chest for what she'd done. One step was all it would take. One lunge and a swift cut to her unprotected neck.

I shoved my dagger back into my belt. I was not a slave to my gift. Not anymore. Enough blood had spilled today. And more than enough grief.

Hands shaking, I took Nock's wrist and led her away.

Melanippe's eyes followed us. *This is my vengeance. For what you did to Father. For what you did to me.* The words hung in the air between us as if she'd screamed them. "I'll never forgive you." She spoke low and angry, without triumph. Dead inside.

Those are the last words she said to me. They will haunt me forever.

When I glanced back, Melanippe had gone. She didn't see the tears that fell as I made my way back to Kallias and took Nock to the only place that could help her.

#

Kallias's hooves sank into the muddy bank of the River Lethe. Above, the tall arch of a limestone cavern crested—a wave of stone poised over our heads, its surface twinkling with glow worms. A faint lap of water sounded from the darkness across the cavern. Float a skiff into that black and you'd find your way to the Underworld.

Gently, I eased Nock from the saddle. She came numbly, her face still blank with the shock, and she moved hunched over and shuffling, as if she had aged overnight.

"Are you hurt anywhere?" I asked, cursing myself for not thinking it sooner.

"No," Nock whispered.

"Good." I set her down on the bank and took her hands in mine. Her fingers were stiff too, from fighting or clutching her dead hero it was hard to say. "Nock, listen to me. I want to give you a choice."

Her head lifted, watery eyes turning on me; the things she'd done mirrored in them.

A sob gathered in my chest. "This is the River Lethe." I motioned to the water. "If you want, you may drink from it. One sip. Just one. Then you will forget."

A long pause and Nock stared at the water. "All of it?" she asked.

"Everything," I said. "The pain, the blood, the killing. You won't remember any of it. Only," I hesitated, "you won't remember me either. Or anything of our time together."

My daughter studied me, a slow horror drawing her out of her numbness. "No, Nunki, I can't." A flicker of temper, just a flicker. Like a tiny flame of a candle sputtering in a storm. "How could you even suggest it?" She shook her head. "No."

Her flame wasn't snuffed out, not yet. And Gods be damned, I wasn't going to let it die. I caught Nock's chin and held it gently in my fingertips. "Think about what happened," I say. "It will be with you as long as you live. It will come to you in every quiet minute. When you close your eyes, it will follow you into your dreams. Can you learn to live with it?"

Nock quivered in my grasp. Her eyes turned distant again, reliving the horror of the gift I'd bestowed on her without her asking. Her lips trembled. Tears welled in her eyes. "I don't..." she floundered. "I can't... I... I'm sorry, Nunki." And like that she dissolved into me, holding me tight through her sobs.

I hugged her back and stroked her hair. "Don't be sorry." Father's words echoed through me, and I finally understood what he'd meant. I was the one who should be sorry, not my child. Not the girl who'd been too young to understand the power I'd taught her. I motioned to Lethe's waters.

"Drink this and you can have a life. A good life. Full of joy and laugher and love."
And you can be a woman, not a weapon, I wanted to add. That was my shame to bear.
My mistake. One on a long list.

Nock stilled in my arms. "You'll stay with me?" she asked. "Until..."

"I will," I promised. "And when you wake, you will be somewhere better.
Somewhere safe, where there's hope and happiness."

"I'd like that," Nock swallowed, and slowly—as if it pained her—she nodded. "All
right. But give me one thing."

"Anything."

"Help me choose a new name."

We chose Elpida. *Hope.* I scored it on her palm with my knife so she would see
it when she woke—and would continue to see if for years to come. Then I cupped
my hands to the River Lethe's waters and brought them to her mouth. One sip, no
more. Nock laid her head on my lap and shut her eyes, her hand tight around mine
until Lethe's sleep claimed her.

I took her to Delphi and left her in the care of the oracles there. As advisors to
kings and the great families, they knew the world of mortals better than I. Who
better to teach my daughter how to find her way in it? I never returned. Though, the
oracles assured me in their letters that she grew into a delightful woman, brash and
defiant and full of life. She lived well, they said.

She's bones in the earth now.

And so concludes my tale and brings me to yours. You've sought me out, heard
my story. You've heard that in Arrow I learned my gift, in Fletch my name, and in
Nock... in Nock I learned that my gift is not for everyone. This is a power you must
choose, and you must be willing to bear its weight. It is why I tell all my acolytes this
story. I will not see innocence destroyed like that again.

So, now it is your turn. Come, sit at my table. You have been a long time travelling.

Speak, stranger and tell me your story.

Tell me who you wish to kill.

For only then will I judge if you are fit to join my quiver.

THE SEA-FATHER'S DUE

Sign: Capricorn
Element: Earth
Symbol: Sea-goat
Dates: December 22 to January 19

I run across the sand, phone stretched at arm's length, trying to keep the video frame on Mitch. Mitch runs ahead, skipping over seaweed and the washed up driftwood brought in by last night's storm.

"You see that, Nate?" he shouts, pointing at a large clump lying on the tideline—just like we rehearsed. I zoom in with the camera, pixellating the mysterious clump, but it's enough to make out the shape. Dry scales glint orange and pink in the evening light.

"Whoa!" Mitch grabs a stick—we planted it there earlier—and pokes the corpse. I pull the zoom back and hurry over.

It's a fish tail, a marlin according to Mitch. He should know, he and his Dad go fishing every other weekend. The smell of it hits the back of my throat as he comes close. It's everything I can do not to gag—and that's just the tail. The torso and head is worse. The goat had been long dried out in the summer sun before old Hodge let me have it.

"For crab pots," I'd said. And the goat farmer had shrugged and pointed to the fly-ridden body lying in the tray of his ute. "Knock yourself out."

And crab pots had been the plan, until the marlin washed up. Then Mitch had one of his ideas.

I zoom in on our goat-fish monstrosity as Mitch pokes it.

"What the hell is it?" he asks, circling.

"You got me." I cringe as the words come out louder than intended. I pace behind Mitch, slip-sliding in the sand, careful not to let the camera land on the twine we used to sew our gruesome creation together. If I shoot it from *this* angle—I step to one side—it's almost convincing. Almost.

Who are we kidding? No one will believe this for a heartbeat.

But I keep filming. My phone is old, scratched and beat up from years of use, but it's better than Mitch's, so I'm on camera duty. Mitch is the better actor too. My best friend's face morphs through the expressions we agreed upon: open-mouthed wonder, wrinkled-nose disgust, furrowed confusion, and he grows more confident with each mask he dons.

When we're sure we've got everything we need, I flick the phone off. "Done." I put a hand over my nose. "Now get rid of it before I barf."

"No way, we might still need it," Mitch insists.

My eyes are watering. God the smell is bad, like I've stuck my head in compost. I try to breathe through my mouth, but its pungency slicks on my tongue and when I swallow, I taste rotten fish. The thought of carrying our goat-marlin corpse back up the beach makes the bile rise in my throat.

"I'm not putting that back in my car," I tell him. Once was bad enough. Never again. "Ditch it or you're walking home."

Mitch purses his lips, scrunches his nose and huffs. "All right. Help me throw it out."

Together we grab our sea-goat, one hand on hair, one on scales, and lift it between us. The marlin's tail is wet and sticky under our palms as we sling it into the surf. It bobs there a moment, the goat's hollow eyes and dry nostrils bubbling, white hairs of its pelt swirling across the surface, before a wave crashes over it, tosses it through the green room, and sucks it down.

We inspect the footage inside my sun-spotted Corolla. The video shakes something chronic, but a bit of wobble adds authenticity we reason. Besides, it means viewers can't look too closely, can't see the slap-dash way we've strung the goat-fish thing together.

"How long will you need to load it?" Mitch asks when we pull up to our rental—a two-bedroom place with peeling painted weatherboard. More of a shack, really, but it's the best we can afford.

"Give it an hour," I say.

Mitch gives me half before he's hovering over my shoulder again. He checks his own phone and our YouTube account. "Still not there."

"Really? I hadn't noticed."

Mitch gets the hint. He scowls between his locks of salt-crusted hair and leaves me to it. I connect my phone to the charger, the loading bar on the screen a quarter full, and turn on the TV.

Hours later when I check the video, it's had no hits. *What else had we expected?* And now my car smells like fish and dead goat.

I sigh and go to bed.

#

"Nate, look! We're famous!" Mitch barges into my room in nothing but his boxers, and thrusts a phone under my nose. A video plays through the cracked screen. Our video. I glance to the view count.

"260,000 views," Mitch trumpets. "Buzzfeed picked it up overnight."

I blink, forcing my sleep-addled brain to focus. This is big. This is progress. I sit up. "You're sure?"

"Yes, look." Mitch taps the screen and turns it back to me. There's a still shot from our video on display, and beneath it, a short article. The headline reads:

Boys Butcher Bodies for Hoax

My stomach folds. This is not how it was supposed to go. I snatch Mitch's phone and scroll to the comments.

Lawkli / 11 minutes ago

This is disgusting.

ObnoxiousPanda / 14 minutes ago

You sick fucks.

Nick H.

Seriously? I mean really, who do they think is going to fall for this shit? I can SEE the string.

The rest of the 243 comments are much the same. I hand Mitch back the phone, my stomach turning tight. Do police arrest people over this sort of thing? The animals were already dead, but...

"We should take it down," I say.

"No way, it's just getting traction."

"Mitch! No one believes it. They're tearing us a new one. We look like idiots."

"So what? Famous, infamous." Mitch shrugs. "A view is still a view. Once we set up video ads, the cash will trickle in."

I'm not so convinced. But Mitch persuades me to leave it up for another day. After all, what's done is done. And we got 1500 subscribers out of it. People are interested. Or perhaps just morbidly curious. At worst, YouTube will take it down. If not, well, perhaps there's a few bucks to be made.

"Ride the wave," Mitch says, "see where it takes us. Just for a little while."

I snort and get ready for work, pulling on an oil splatted uniform with *Murray's Fish and Chips* embroidered on the pocket. Just before I leave, my phone buzzes. It's Emma.

We need to talk about the video. Call me.

My mood sours. Great. A scolding is coming, and I can imagine how it will go. My girlfriend's voice will start soft, deadly even: *What the actual fuck, Nathan? What were you thinking? Did Mitch put you up to this? Another one of his get-rich-quick schemes?* Then it will grow louder as she gains momentum: *He's full of shit, Nate. Seriously, why do you put up with him? You're better than this.* And so on and so fast I won't be able to get a word in.

My phone lights up in my hand. Emma, ever impatient, has decided to call instead. I shove the phone into my bag and let it ring out.

#

It happens that evening. I head to Beacon Bay after work as usual and pull up beside

Mitch's wagon. Compared to my hatchback, it's a tank of a car and he drives like it is one too. The rims are scuffed and there's a dent in his back bumper. The fuel light is permanently on—I've never known Mitch to fill up the tank.

Mitch is out on the grass waxing his surfboard, hand running in loving circles over the fibreglass, sun-kissed face serene. Over the dune, the waves are small, churning over at knee height. Not great, but I don't care. Even if the sea was millpond smooth, I'd still go in to get the film of grease and smell of deep-fried batter off.

"Catch you down there," Mitch says, grinning as I strip down to my undies and wrestle one leg into my wetsuit. I nod and he hurries off across the dune, board tucked under an arm, stride long and eager for the water.

A minute later I'm following, tugging the zip of my wetsuit up as I go. We've got the beach to ourselves—Beacon Bay is too far from town for most locals to bother with, and certainly too far for tourists. Not that we get all that many, not out here in the middle of woop-woop.

Seaweed and debris are still scattered across the sand, waiting for another high tide to drag it back to the ocean, or pitch it higher up the beach. Mitch is already in the water, paddling through the white foam toward the breakers. If I hurry, I'll catch him before he does his first run. I'm the stronger surfer, my long arms carry me further with less effort. I splash into the shallows and the surf surges around my legs. A strong undertow urges me deeper, pulls at my ankles and behind my knees.

Odd.

Beacon Bay isn't known for its undertow. The slope of the beach is too gentle to generate much force from the backwash as the waves surge up the sand, then race back to the sea. My gut knows before I do. It curdles inside, clumping tight like spoiled milk.

A yell—more a splutter than scream—rips across the water. Mitch. He's at the breakers, bobbing up the face of an unbroken wave, kicking at the water. Fighting. He floats to the crest of the wave—and his head jerks under. His fingers scrabble on his board for purchase. Then the scene drops behind the wave and out of sight.

"Mitch!"

I should get on my board and help him. But I don't—can't—move. The water pulls at my legs.

The next wave comes. Mitch's head splits the face and he rises with it, coughing, hair webbed across his face. He scrambles onto his board, knees under him, and digs at the water, paddling as hard as he can. His mouth hangs open, bottom lip trembling as he gazes into the water. A keening reaches me. He's sobbing. No, *begging.* The wave moves under him and I see what he's trying to do. His board pitches on the crest, teetering, ready to plunge down the face of the wave and carry him away from whatever lurks beneath.

And he stalls. It's as if he's caught on the end of a rope; a fish at the end of a line. He buoys on the crest, going nowhere. His face is pale and afraid, and one hand reaches for the shore—for me. He makes no sound, but he mouths the unmistakable word: "Help!"

Standing dumb in the shallows, I see, or think I see, water trickling *up* his arms. But that's impossible. I blink and shake my head, then lose Mitch behind the wave again.

And when the wave passes, he is gone. No scream. No gurgle. Just gone.

I search the water, hunting for a shape, a sign. There's nothing but the foam and hiss of churned seaweed.

"Oh God," the words come in a croak. "Oh God."

Something grabs my leg. I feel it through my wetsuit: a cold, firm grip that wraps around my calf. I yell and leap backward, scattering spray. For a horrible heartbeat, the grip holds, tethering me in place, and its pressure washes up my legs, tightening around my thighs, my hips and groin.

Panic obliterates all my control. I scream and kick, dropping my board to the water. The grip on my legs eases and whatever it is under the waves probes the fibreglass. Water crawls over it, tendrils of wet slopping over the wax. I turn and run for the beach.

The swell nips at my heels, clawing and slipping down my legs. But I'm shallower now, more of me is out of the water than in. The grip can't hold. I hit the sand and keep running, imagining the wave following me up the beach, a great monster of salt and seaweed rising out of the blue to chase me down and pull me back in.

I collapse above the tide line. Sand sticks to my hands and legs. Soft, warm, dry. Panting, I roll onto my side and stare at the sea. The next set of waves rolls in, breaking along Beacon Bay's reef. Snatches of pink and orange glints off its peaks, catching the spray in a rainbow. Perfectly normal. Beautiful even, and for the first time, terrifying.

Bile rushes up my throat and I puke right there on the beach.

#

The media's calling it a shark attack. But I know better as I sit in the police station, waiting for them to take my statement. The coast guard was out for hours, outboards chopping the length of Beacon Bay. Divers searched the reef. No sign of Mitch. No shark at all, not one—which is unusual.

"Not even a Wobbegong hiding in the rocks," crackles the report over Constable Horgan's receiver.

"Thanks Ann," Horgan responds, clicks the receiver off and rubs a hand over his grey moustache, and I know he's trying to buy himself time to think.

"I'm sorry," he says, after a long pause. "But it's been twenty-four hours. I have to call it off."

I nod, unable to think of anything to say.

Horgan slumps behind his desk, sweat ringing the neck and armpits of his uniform. He pulls his keyboard over and dusts a stray hair off it. "Tell me again what you saw."

It's been a long day—well, night and day—since I called triple zero, half crazed, babbling about the sea. The operator thought I was off my face on weed. I told him I wasn't. He didn't believe me. I clear my throat. Perhaps I should lie, but what should I say?

Constable Horgan coughs, impatient. I'm out of time.

"The water got him," I say, then mumble, "that's what it looked like."

Horgan's eyebrows slump into a frown; his moustache bristles as his lips purse. It's the same story I told him last night. "Nothing else?" His face softens. "Look, I know you don't want to think about it, but it's important we're sure—"

"Sure of what? That he's dead?" I blurt, and my stomach shrivels because the words suddenly make it real.

Mitch is gone. Dead. Oh God. The last look on his face flashes into my mind, fear sapping his cheeks, mouthing that word to me on the beach. *Help.* My fists clench. Don't think. But my brain betrays me and it plays the moment again.

"Here." Horgan pushes a mug of hot water into my hand. I jump; I hadn't even heard him move. "Tea or coffee?" he asks, holding up a jar of instant and an English Breakfast teabag.

"Coffee."

He scoops the granules out and drops them into my mug. Water slops over the side, scalding my wrist. I don't react. Instead, I let the water sting my skin. Let it burn. In my head, Mitch vanishes behind the wave. I should've done something. Should've tried to save him.

"Now, are you sure you didn't see anything?" Horgan asks again. "We need to make sure there's no danger to the public."

My hands shake. More water slops to the floor. So that's what this is. He doesn't care about Mitch. Mitch is already dead, there's nothing he can do about that. No, Horgan's concern is for the public's safety. I understand his logic, but that doesn't stop the rage from simmering in my gut. I put the mug down on the table before I spill any more.

"It wasn't a shark." My voice is firm. "There was no blood. He wasn't eaten."

Horgan rubs his chin again and his eyes narrow, almost imperceptibly, but I notice and my gut flutters.

He doesn't think I—

On the edge of the table, my coffee cup slips and falls. With a crack and a tinkling of china, it shatters. Coffee splatters across the tiles.

Horgan swears and hauls himself up, jabbing a finger at my chair. "Stay there. I'll find a mop." He shuffles off and I hear him banging about in a cupboard down the hall. I sink into myself, staring at the black puddle pooling out from my smashed cup, but not seeing. I'm back on the beach again with the water clawing at my legs. Mitch is gazing at me, tears in his eyes, face drained of its colour. He knew then. And I'd just stood there and watched.

Coward.

A finger of luke-warm heat brushes my ankle. I blink and look down. The coffee puddle has reached my shoes, soaking the soles of my sneakers. With a 'tch' I lift my feet. They come away from the floor tacky, like I've stood in gum.

And then I see it. A string of black water slips up from the ankle of my sock. It wiggles up my leg, tickling the hairs as it inches higher—like a roach.

I yelp and brush it off—a deft flick of the hand, a move usually reserved for spiders—and scramble up on top of the chair.

The coffee puddle ripples.

One watery arm runs across the floor. It stretches towards me, like a sightless, black amoeba probing its surrounds. The arm reaches the chair leg and the rest of the puddle catches up, pooling at the base of the chair. Then the puddle begins to run *up* the chair leg.

Nope. Nope, nope, nope. The memory of that cold hand gripping my calf jolts my heart into my throat. *It can't be.*

A sliver of puddle trickles over the edge of the plastic seat, beelining for me. I ease back on the chair. *Don't let it touch you,* something inside me whispers, old and primal. The water trickles to my shoes, quicker than before. It's getting confident. *Stronger.* My skin prickles.

Fuck this.

I turn and leap, clearing the chair and the puddle with a good metre to spare. There's a flicker of pride in me as I do it, just a small one. I was a school track champion once, hurdles were my specialty. Muscle memory and all that.

My shoes hit the floor and I bolt. Out the door, down the corridor, into the foyer.

"Hey!" Horgan calls after me and takes up pursuit. "Nathan!"

Don't stop. Don't look. It's after you.

Something in the ceiling groans, the pressure of it shudders overhead, a rusted squeal, like the turn of an old tap. I sprint for the station entrance, passing a drink fountain jerking and jostling in its wall brackets. *Oh God, it's in the pipes.*

I throw myself against the door, utter a whimper of relief as it swings open, and dart into the car park. Emma is waiting in the car, scrolling through her phone. She jumps as I thump into the driver-side door and try the handle.

"Fucking unlock it!" I scream at her.

"Steady on, I'm getting to it." She leans across and pulls the tab up. I scramble in and fumble the keys out of my pocket.

"What's the rush?" Emma asks. Her eyes narrow, and they flick to the police station. "What did you do?"

"Christ, nothing, all right?!" I jam the key into the ignition and turn. My Corolla, ever reliable, hums to life and I throw it into reverse, then back into first as I pull out and zoom onto the main road.

Emma watches me the whole ride home. Her hazel eyes study me from the passenger seat, sliding from my heaving chest to sweat-slicked neck, then up to my white-knuckled grip around the steering wheel. When I pull into the driveway of our—my—rental, her expression is steely.

"What's going on, Nathan?"

"I—" I swallow— "I don't know." *Where to even start?* "I really don't." And this is true. Because it doesn't make sense. None of it makes sense. I'm going crazy. Shock, stress, PTSD, *something* is going on in my brain because water doesn't just rise up and attack people. I'm seeing things.

Emma's forehead wrinkles, and she puts a hand on my knee and squeezes. "I know we haven't had much chance to talk, but if you need—"

I swallow again, forcing saliva around a lump in my throat. "It's fine. I'm okay." I'm not. My heart jolts and jangles in my chest like I've clamped my hands around an electric fence, but what else am I supposed to say? "I'm sorry for shouting earlier."

She sighs. "You just lost your best friend, I'll give you some slack."

I nod and get out of the car. The shack is dim inside, the curtains are drawn and there's dirty dishes in the sink from two days ago. I couldn't bring myself to eat last night. Emma guides me to the couch, and I don't resist. The place still smells like Mitch. Sweat and salt.

For a while Emma sits with me, watching in silence, trying to figure out what's going through my head. Not for the first time I feel inadequate under her gaze. She's too good for me, really. We've been dating since high school, but where all I've done is get a job at a fish and chip shop and spend my weekends surfing and getting drunk, she's preparing to do honours in marine biology. Everyday she grows more distant, like a ship sailing for the horizon, leaving me behind on the shore; our worlds irrevocably sundered.

After ten minutes she gets up and goes to the kitchen. There's a clink of heavy bottles, followed by two distinct pops, and she walks back into the lounge with a beer in each hand. She passes me one.

"Thanks." The word feels thick in my mouth.

"To Mitch," she says.

We clink the bottles together and drink. The beer is cold and fizzes down my throat. Frothy, like the sea. The thought nearly makes me choke.

When she finishes her beer, Emma rises from the couch, her shape silhouetted against the TV I'm pretending to watch so I don't have to talk. "You hungry?"

I shrug. I'm not, but I should probably eat something.

"I'll call some takeout, yeah?"

I nod, and belatedly dig into my pocket for my wallet. She's already in the kitchen placing the order—pizza it sounds like—so I put it down on the coffee table for when the food comes. I sink back into the couch, staring at the paint-flaking ceiling, wondering what I'm supposed to tell her.

Hey babe, so it seems the sea has it in for me. Well, not just the sea, any form of water really.

Put it like that and it sounds even more ridiculous. She won't believe me. Hell, I'm not even sure I do. Emma's the least superstitious person I know, the kind of person who rolls her eyes in horror movies at the sheer impracticality of the plot. She and Mitch never got along, not unless I was there to bridge the gap. I'm mulling over it again when I make out a distinct slosh and clank from the kitchen. I sigh. Emma is doing the dishes.

Just bloody leave them.

And my thoughts falter. She's doing the dishes. With *water.*

I lurch to my feet. Five strides and I'm in the kitchen. Emma's back is to me, up to her elbows in it, rubber-clad gloves scrubbing at a pot.

"Emma, no!"

It probably happens in a moment. A few heartbeats at most. But time slows down for me. In the sink, the water ripples and gathers. Emma's arm jerks still, as if someone, *something* had grabbed it.

There's an intake of breath. A short sharp hush through her teeth. She stiffens; all the muscles in her shoulders tense. "What the fu—"

The water in the sink rises; a tendril emerging from the murk. It latches around Emma's arm.

She screams.

The water surges up her arms, the grimy suds pumping upward. They soak into her shirt, writhing towards her throat.

No, please no. Not Emma.

I lunge, grab her and yank her back, breaking the tendril's hold, splattering water over the floor. Emma's already thrashing. Her fingers claw at her face—at her mouth and nose—and the water keeps on coming. It condenses over her cheeks, forcing itself through her lips and up her nose. She's coughing, spluttering, eyes wide, pupils dark pinpricks before they roll back into her head.

It's in her. Whatever it is, it's in her. Drowning her.

I do the only thing I can think of. I punch her in the chest. Hard. Something pops in my fist and pain blossoms across my knuckles. Emma convulses. Water bubbles from her lips, then slips back down.

Idiot, she needs to be on her side. Recovery position, remember? A memory of a swim-safe class rises inside me. Dr ABCD. A is for airways. Clear the airways.

Cold sweat rolls off me as I turn her over and slam a hand between her shoulder blades. "Get out!" I scream and strike again. "Get out!" This last one sounds more like a plea. I open her mouth, strike a third time.

Her body jerks, coughs, and water slops out of her and onto the floor. I pull the tea towel down from the drainage board and dump it over the pool. The towel soaks it in. I hope it's enough.

B is for breathing.

And she's not breathing. I roll her onto her back, hands shaking. "Come on." I pinch her nose, put my mouth to hers and puff. Yes! Her chest rises one, two, three times. I do it twice more. Emma vomits up more water, more than I thought possible, and then, a glorious sound: a single ragged breath.

I push her onto her side again—more coughing—and she takes another breath, stronger this time, then another. She doesn't wake. But she's alive. Alive. I slump against the fridge, wipe away the sweat and tears, and dig out my phone.

And for the second time in two days, I dial triple zero.

#

"You saved her life," the paramedic says as Emma is wheeled away on a stretcher.

Slipped in the bathroom, knocked herself out on the lip of the bath and fell into it. That's the story I told. It was the best I could come up with. Horgan scowls as I recount it to him, standing there in the driveway, the blue lights of his car still flashing across the weatherboards. He doesn't believe me. But there's no evidence of foul play. No one to discredit my story. Not Mitch. Not Emma—not until she's conscious anyway, and her story will make even less sense than mine. Horgan's got nothing and he knows it.

"Don't leave town," he tells me as a paramedic asks him to move his car to let the ambulance out of the driveway.

"You can follow behind us," the paramedic says, sliding in behind the wheel of the van. Meat wagons—that's what Emma liked to call them. I used to laugh at that, but now, thinking of Emma's cold, shivering body inside, it sounds sick.

You sick fucks. The comment from the video swims up from my memory. We should never have posted it. Shouldn't even have done it. That's when it all started.

264

"You good to drive?" The paramedic asks. "Hospital's not far."

I shake my head. I can't risk it. Won't. "I need to call her Mum. Let her know what's happened."

The paramedic shrugs. "As you please."

As they pull out from the driveway, I take out Emma's phone and stare at the message again. I found it on the kitchen counter, unlocked, as if she'd been waiting to read it.

BFF Kirsty

I know it's bad timing, but you need to end it. Don't drag it out.

I should cry, scream maybe. Instead, I'm hollow. Spent. I walk back inside and call Emma's Mum.

#

The knock comes on the door three days later. I shuffle past takeaway containers and empty juice bottles to open it, cracking the door a finger-width and peering out. Two suits stand on the doorstep: one man, one woman. He's broad shouldered and bald. She's shorter, brown hair cut into a bob so straight I could hold a ruler to it.

"Mr—" the woman consults her notebook—"Holloway?"

I shift behind the door, conscious of the smell that must be emanating through the crack. I ran out of deodorant yesterday. But the suits are waiting, so I work enough spittle to wet my throat.

"Yea?" I rasp.

"We'd like to ask you a few questions about the video you posted."

The video? I stare at them, taking in their sharp suits and immaculate shoes. Detectives from the city perhaps? Though I see nothing that looks like a badge.

"It was a hoax," I say. "A fake. A prank to try and make money. The animals were already dead, I swear." *It was Mitch's idea,* I want to say, but instead I bite down on the words, swallow, eyes turning hot, despite not having enough water left in me for tears. My head is pounding."

The woman gives me a closed lipped smile—almost a grimace. "Oh, we know. We're more interested in what's happened *since* you posted it."

Her partner produces bottled water from behind his back and holds it out. It takes everything I have not to flinch. *It's in a bottle. It's contained.*

"You must be thirsty," the woman says.

I lock my knees to hide their wobble and hold onto the door handle as my stomach does a complete 360. My face must be a picture.

"It's safe," the woman assures me. Her partner waves the bottle, and I'm transfixed, quivering like a rat before a snake. "May we come in?"

They know. How do they know? And they *believe* it. Believe me. *But I haven't told anyone.* Except for Horgan, but I don't think he even deemed my statement worth noting down. *Perhaps they have answers.* I waver a second longer, then open the door. *Maybe they have a solution.* Hope flickers inside me at that.

I lead them through the rental to the lounge and they pull up two chairs while I take the couch. I perch on its edge, conscious of the house's smell—and mine. I've done my best since I turned off the water mains, ordering takeout (burning a hole in my bank account in the process), peeing on the lemon tree out back, shitting in a pit I dug by the shed. I'm managing. Sort of. But the moment it rains, I'm dead.

The man presents the water bottle. I hesitate for a heartbeat, then grab it, crack the lid and put it to my lips. Cool, sweet water trickles into my mouth, and suddenly I'm gulping, sucking it down in great mouthfuls. God it's good. I force myself to slow down, enjoy it. Sip. My headache eases.

I wipe my mouth with my sleeve. "How did you know? About the water, I mean. Have you seen it be—"

"It's our job to watch Father's enemies," the woman says.

I falter, not sure I heard right. "Come again?"

"You've offended him. Dues must be paid," the man shifts forward in his chair. It's the first time he's spoken, and his voice is deep, a baritone that shivers in my chest. The woman puts a hand on his knee.

"Easy Kaito."

Kaito's enormous hands twitch on his lap, but otherwise he doesn't move. I swallow, taking in his barrel chest and bulging arms, and shift in my seat. I don't fancy my chances if he decides to take a swing at me.

"What did you say your names were?"

"We didn't," the woman says. She places a hand on her chest. "I am Mira and he is Kaito." She indicates her colleague. "We are envoys." She pulls down her collar, and there, where her collarbone meets her neck are three dark, parallel marks. Tattoos. Each one the length of my little finger and ridged like a fresh scar. I glance at Kaito; a set of three marks pokes out the top of his collar. Are they from a gang? A chill shivers over my skin and I lurch to my feet.

"Look, I don't want any trouble."

"Trouble?" Mira's eyes flash. "You're long past trouble. Now *sit.*"

The muscles in my legs spasm. My knees buckle. I sway, fighting to stay on my feet. Mira's gaze locks with mine, her head tilts and a vein pulses in her temple. Then my knees curl, bend against my will, sinking me down, *sitting* me back on the couch.

What the fu—

Mira leans forward and grins. My stomach turns: her teeth are filed into points.

"Did you know up to sixty per cent of the human body is water? It's everywhere, even in your bones."

I freeze, horror yawning inside me, deep and cold and absolute. Yes, I have heard that before. Sometime long ago in school, probably biology class. The water in my stomach churns again and I almost feel it flushing out into my veins.

I open my mouth, start to speak, but Mira raises a finger and my jaw locks. "Hush, hush. It is easier on all of us if you go quietly." She turns to Kaito. "Did you bring it?"

The bald man nods and draws out a knife two fingers wide and as long as my palm. It is rusted and old, as if it's spent the last ten years on the sea bed. Perhaps it has.

"What are you—" I manage to get out before Mira's finger jerks up again, and the water in my stomach rises. Acid burns the back of my throat. Then water washes into my mouth and it's... salty. Like the sea. I try to scream, but it comes out a gurgle of bubbles and brine. *This can't be happening. This can't be real.* But it is. The water plunges down my throat, into my lungs, flooding them in cold.

They're drowning you.

My body jerks and twitches and I slide to the floor. My skin itches. The water inside me churns, gurgles in my throat. I'm paralysed. Unable to move, not even blink.

"Father does not forgive," Kaito rumbles.

They were already dead, I want to scream at them. *We only wanted a bit of extra cash for summer.* And are they growing larger? Or am I growing smaller?

"Father does not forget," Mira echoes. I can't feel my legs. Or my hands. White hairs swirl in my peripheral—they're coming from my face. I'm screaming at my limbs. *Move, please, just move!* My lungs burn, desperate for air.

Kaito presses the knife to my neck. *This is it, he's going to—*

With three deft strokes, he scores the parallel scratches above my collarbone. Then again on the other side. My body jerks and convulses. My vision shifts. Something wet slaps the floorboards, and I catch a sliver of orange and pink in the evening light.

"You are at the ocean's mercy now."

At once, the water's grip vanishes. I flop and stare up at them, gasping, groping for air. No not air, *water.* It's already in my lungs. I breathe it in, feel the cool rush up my airways and out the gills Kaito's scored on my neck.

"Better get you back to the sea, pup," says Mira. "Best not keep Father waiting."

The two of them grin, their honed teeth flashing.

And all I can do is bleat.

Acknowledgements

This collection has been a mammoth task in the making, mainly because it began life as a series of stories for Deadset Press' Zodiac anthology series over the course of several years. So many people have had a part to play in bringing them into the world, so bear with me as I recite a fairly long list of people.

To the Deadset Press team—Austin and Helena—you took a nobody and gave her a chance in that first Capricorn anthology. You lit a fire under me, gave me confidence I didn't have, and inspired so much from that one acceptance. The work you do for new and emerging authors is so, so powerful and gratefully welcomed, don't ever lose sight of that.

To my local North Shore Writers Group—Tim, Su, Elizabeth, Chris, Sharon, Andrew, Frances, Nicola, Bruce, Jennifer, Sarah, and Alex—your enthusiasm is legendary as is your ability to sniff out a plot problem.

To the Litopia crew—Jake, Geraldine, Rachael, Hannah, Robert, Rich, Bev, Rachel, Bloo, Robinne, Cage and so many others who critted a number of these stories over the years—your eagle eyes made these tales truly shine.

To my sensitivity readers, Kass and T—thank you so much for your time and insights.

Lastly, if I've forgotten you, rest assured it was not intentional! If you've been involved in the making of these stories along the way, you have my deepest, heartfelt thanks.

Most of all, thank you to my family who have shown unending patience and support, particularly to my husband, I couldn't do this without you XOXO.
-- Nikky Lee

ABOUT THE AUTHOR

Nikky Lee is an award-winning author who grew up as a barefoot 90s kid in Perth, Western Australia on Whadjuk Noongar Country. She now lives in Aotearoa New Zealand with a husband, a dog, and a couch potato cat. In her free time, she writes speculative fiction, often burning the candle at both ends to explore fantastic worlds, mine asteroids, and meet wizards. She's had over thirty stories published in magazines, anthologies and on the radio.

Her fantasy, sci-fi and horror fiction has won three Australian Aurealis Awards, two New Zealand Sir Julius Vogel Awards, Bronze at the Foreward INDIES Book of the Year, three Indie Ink Awards, and a Ditmar Award for Best New Talent.

ABOUT DEADSET PRESS

Deadset Press is an independent publisher of incredible speculative fiction. We provide publishing pathways for emerging writers from Australia and New Zealand, and aspire to shine the light on unique and diverse voices. You can learn more at:

www.deadsetpress.com

ALSO BY DEADSET PRESS

Radcliffe by Madeleine D'Este

A three-storey ramshackle house in North Melbourne is full of secrets.

Tamsin is lead to the building by a voice inside her head that tells her
'Death is Coming'.

With no respite from the eternal summer heat, can Tamsin find out who death is coming for
and solve the riddle of Radcliffe?

www.ingramcontent.com/pod-product-compliance
Lightning Source LLC
Chambersburg PA
CBHW010345220726
48290CB00016B/2638